F Majure Mississ
Majure, Jim.

D0893966

F
Majure
Mississ

9513690

THE

DELTA

TRIANGLE

Jim Majure

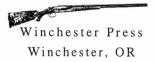

Winchester Press
Winchester, OR

MID-MISSISSIPPI REGIONAL LIBRARY SYSTEM
Attala, Holmes, Leake, Montgomery
And Winston Counties

This novel is a work of fiction. The characters, names, incidents, dialogue, and plot are the products of the author's imagination or are used ficticiously. Any resemblance to actual persons or events is purely coincidental.

Copyright © 1995, by Jim Majure.

Printed in the United States of America

No part of this work may be copied without permission of the publishe

Text design by Glenn Smith.
Jacket design by Leslie Cummins.
Cover art by Steve Parker.

ISBN: 1-886049-09-2

Published by:

Winchester Press
Box 500
Winchester, Oregon 97495

Acknowledgments:

Barry Parker, Chief of Security, Parchman Penitentiary, for his guided tour and insight into the Mississippi State Penitentiary and its inmates. Louie W. Odom, Lt. Col., U.S.A. Ret., for his first-hand Vietnam contributions then and now.

Special thanks to Gil Peterson, friend and confidante, for his aeronautical expertise and support, and to Jill Fair for her "connections" and tenacity. T. Goring Whitsett for his early editing, and Glenn Smith for his technical assistance.

Also Beth Yerger, Sarah Scruggs, Susie Brabec and Charles Allen.

Dedication:

With love to my wife, Liz, and children; Michelle, my wonderful daughter, and Matthew, my tender four-year-old inspiration, the "lights" of my life.

With loving memories to my late parents, James and Maxine, for their unwavering love; the most genuine people I have ever known.

CHAPTER 1

The flight from Los Angeles pierced the dark night's sky and made its approach into the Memphis airport, as lightning danced on the horizon. Roman Beckley watched the storm brewing from his window seat while they taxied to the gate. They were over two hours late, and night driving was not his favorite, especially with the weather he would likely encounter. He stretched his six-foot-plus frame, brushed back his thick blond hair, and breathed a sigh of relief.

The young brunette across the aisle studied his handsome face, engaging his blue eyes the second time since their descent. Roman smiled back politely and deplaned.

He retrieved three fully-packed bags from the claim area below and hustled to the Avis counter. Worldwide Safewaste Industries had reserved him a vehicle in advance, and though a black Lincoln wouldn't be his choice normally, he was glad to have the heavier car for the conditions looming outside.

He maneuvered through the maze of Memphis headlights and headed south on historic old Highway 61; the same Highway 61 that Bob Dylan wrote and sang about and the same highway that led to his destination, deep into the Mississippi Delta. Indian Bayou was over two hours away, putting him in town by midnight.

He drove for more than an hour before the deluge. The rain began to fall in sheets, making the rows of cotton fields that lined the highway barely visible. The repetitive sound of the tires flapping against the cracks of the highway segments was almost hypnotic. The blues station he had picked up out of Memphis was still coming in. B. B. King filled the airways with "The Thrill Is Gone". He strained to see any familiar surroundings from the days when he lived in Mississippi. He had not been back but a few times in the past eight years; since the days he was a walk-on quarterback who earned a scholarship at Ole Miss, and though a low round draft pick, he was fortunate to play five years with the Los Angeles Rams. Through that, he had made contact with Worldwide Safewaste Industries, and after a career ending knee injury, he had become a promising young executive, well paid and well utilized.

His mind wandered back to a year and a half ago, before the untimely death of his young, gorgeous wife, Leah. Their lives had been so enriched, so fulfilled, and there seemed to be nothing but blue skies and green lights for them, until the accident. He could not go for long without agonizing over how she could lose control of her Audi in Coldwater Canyon in broad daylight. She had handled that curve many times in the past. He blamed himself for being out of town and her being enroute to pick him up at the Los Angeles International Airport when the tragedy occurred. He remembered her upcoming birthday. They were both only twenty nine, and though it was eighteen months ago, it seemed like any eternity. He thought of the first time they met. She was a flight attendant on a New Orleans to Los Angeles flight back for the Rams after their game with the New Orleans Saints. He had finally gotten some playing time, after replacing the injured starting quarterback, and though he had a better than average afternoon passing, he managed to get intercepted on a last minute drive and lose to the Saints, who were near the bottom of the league by 21-20. His spirits were less than high, until she managed to divert his thoughts to anything but football. He never flew that he didn't think of her and their flight back that was the beginning of a wonderful, but short time together.

He shook his head abruptly and stared at the rain that was pouring down steadily, almost overtaking the wipers' frantic pace. At last, another set of headlights appeared out of the Sunday night storm. They were almost like seeing a friend. Despite the storm, he had some distance between himself and Memphis now. He was rolling deeper into the land where cotton is king, where the blues were, and are, still played and sung with deep feeling. On both sides of the winding highway the rich flat land was covered with rows of the "white gold". He caught fleeting glimpses, when the rain permitted, of picturesque barns, farm implements, and vehicles scattered throughout the plantations and small farms as well.

2

Roman squinted to see the sign for Highway 49 South, one mile. He veered right onto 49 and promptly saw the next one for Indian Bayou, 40 miles. The sign lingered in his mind for a moment, not for the Indian Bayou mileage, but below it read: 'Parchman (Mississippi State Penitentiary) 12 miles'. He thought of the gruesome tales he had heard growing up of the ominous prison that spread over 17,000 acres.

Just then, he remembered his smallest suitcase in the back seat and reached behind him as he drove. He found the handle and wrestled it over the front seat. His foot moved off the accelerator slightly, as he stared straight ahead at the sheets of rain bouncing off the pavement. His hand fumbled through some socks, on to his shaving kit, then as he reached the bottom, he felt the heavy object encased in leather. He grasped the handle and smiled slightly. He had not been relieved of the .357 Magnum. The recent TV coverage of baggage pilferage had gotten his attention. Even though the pistol had not been fired in three years, and that was at a range, it had been given to him by his late Dad and had irreplaceable value. He had decided to bring it after his phone conversation two weeks ago with his longtime friend and only person he knew in Indian Bayou, for that matter, John Sessions. John had stressed that Mississippi, in places and at times, was not the same gentle place Roman left nine years ago.

He pulled the pistol from the bag, as he drove with his left hand. He slid it under the driver's side seat, never moving his eyes off the road that was even less visible now. The only thing his eyes missed was the sign on the right-of-way, 'No Stopping for Two Miles - Except Emergency - State Penitentiary'.

Lightning flashed against the black backdrop and silhouetted the main gate to Parchman Prison. He could see the lights inside the brick building at the entrance and figures moving about inside. He slowed to less than 20 miles an hour to get a glimpse of what he could from the deserted highway. He saw no reason to not stop a half mile past the main gate. It was a public highway and he was away from the entrance. He only wanted a few seconds to see what little he could from the road. He slowly pulled the Lincoln onto the shoulder. He stayed inside with the windows up and looked through the passenger side window. With the aid of constant bursts of lightning illuminating the sky, he could barely see the outline of buildings in the distance. Parchman was more foreboding than he imagined, especially on a wretched night like this.

After no more than a minute, he pulled onto the main highway again, about to continue south the remaining 30 miles or so to Indian Bayou. Suddenly, the whirling blue lights came out of nowhere and glared through the rear-view mirror. They filled up the side mirrors as well. They were unmistakable. As they pierced through the rainy night and came closer, he could feel his pulse accelerate. Their presence filled up the once dark surroundings. He felt he had done no wrong, but remembered the .357 instantly. He tried to slide it further back with his foot.

"Get out of your vehicle with your hands up!" The deep voice rang out over the loudspeaker from the car behind. He swallowed twice quickly and wanted to say: "It's Roman Beckley. I'm only enroute to Indian Bayou. I'm down here on legitimate business." Intuition told him to get out with his hands up. He slid out slowly and tried to determine who the figure was behind the bright light that glared in his eyes. The tall man came closer before speaking.

"Put your hands on the top of your vehicle. Now!" The voice was closer now, then the hand slammed into the top of his back and pushed him. His chest and side of his face ached from landing firm against the driver's side door.

"Wait a minute." Roman reacted from impulse.

"Keep your mouth shut, mister. I do the talking, understand?"

Roman 's response was barely audible. "Yes."

"I can't hear you, mister." The hand was pushing again against the back of his neck this time.

Roman shouted back, "I said yes!"

"Don't get smart with me. Let's see your driver's license. Slowly turn and remove them." The hand slid off his back. Roman turned and faced the figure. He was at least a match in height for Roman's six feet two inches. He stared at the bony features and the prominent scar on the face in front of him. He handed the license and placed his hands by his side. This time his arms were pulled behind him, and his wrists felt the squeezing pressure of the handcuffs that were shut tight. Too tight. The lawman snatched him around into the side of the car again, causing him to stumble slightly as he struck the door.

"Look, this is not necessary. I'm here to coordinate building a hazardous waste facility in Indian Bayou. We've already paid earnest money on the site." Roman tried to keep calm, but knew this was more than an ordinary stop by a law officer. He tried to move his wrists as the circulation felt threatened. He could barely move his fingers. He breathed in deeply and stared at the imposing man who seemed indifferent to his plight, as he studied Roman's drivers license with his long metal flashlight.

"Could you loosen these handcuffs? They're cutting off the circulation." The man ignored him and walked back to the car with the blue lights anchored on top. He stayed for what seemed like an eternity and emerged with his flashlight turned off. He stood face to face with Roman. He could almost feel his breath in his face as the rainwater rolled off his wide-brimmed hat. Roman blew the water off the tip of his own nose with his bottom lip, as he turned his head away. The law officer grabbed his wrists and released the cuffs somewhat. Roman felt the blood pumping furiously through the veins in relief.

He thought again of the gun on the floorboard, when he saw the man open the door to the rental car. His mind raced: What would this forceful bastard do if he found a weapon? He wished he had left it far away in California. Then he saw the man turn and leave his back to him for another endless amount of time. He heard the spinning sound of the gun's chamber, and suddenly, as if in slow motion, it happened. The officer spun around and placed the barrel of the .357 squarely between Roman's eyes and smiled. His cold black eyes were clearly visible now. They darted with evil excitement, observing the fear when Roman swallowed. The black eyes narrowed as he slowly squeezed the trigger. *Click. Click.* Roman closed his eyes, as his heart pounded furiously. He gasped for breath. Silence. This was a nightmare.

"Carrying a weapon, huh, Mr. Beckley?" He glared and pushed the pistol sideways to Roman's ribs, then pulled it away quickly. "Couldn't you read the sign when you approached Parchman Penitentiary? The one that said 'No stopping except for emergency for next two miles'?"

"Officer, I must have missed it in the rain. I'm not a criminal, and I only stopped because I lived in Mississippi for years. Grew up here and never saw this place. I meant no harm. I was just getting a look at the prison. You can call my company president for an explanation of why I'm here, if you like. He's in Los Angeles." He knew what he was up against, and tried to sound law abiding without begging.

"I've already heard that you were coming. I'm Sheriff Zachary Stiles. Not much gets by me or my office in Wildflower County." Roman's mind raced. How did he know he was coming to Mississippi? Gardner Lowe, of Worldwide, had not told anyone about it. Not to his knowledge. He kept quiet. "I know all about when you were a football player at Ole Miss and the L.A. Rams. Well that doesn't carry much weight around here. About the gun, I'm gonna to have to keep it for a while," he said sarcastically, and smiled. Roman was dumbfounded. He could only nod. This was not a position of strength to argue from. Not now. He fought back the anger that was building. "I'm not going to take you to jail, even though I could probably think of a reason or two to do so. Now, you get this car in the road and watch your step while you're in my county. I don't care who you work for. I'm sure I'll see you later." The Sheriff pulled off his wet, wide-brimmed hat and pushed his long, black hair straight back, before replacing it. He pointed to the road. "Like I said, see you later." He screeched onto the highway, his taillights disappearing into the night.

Roman closed the door to the Lincoln and exhaled twice. He clenched his teeth and squeezed the steering wheel until his hands ached. He pulled away slowly onto the dark Delta highway and mumbled, "Later, for damn sure."

CHAPTER *2*

The alarm went off at six a.m. in room 108 of the Indian Bayou Taurus Motel, from what felt like two hours of sleep. After the welcome by the sheriff, sleep didn't come too swiftly. Roman knocked the Gideon's Bible from the small end table by mistake, cut the lamp on, and stumbled into the bathroom. He moved from there to his closet, pulled out his larger suitcase that was not unpacked, and dressed for his four mile run. He always tried to do this at least five days a week, if not six or seven. He was lacing his Nike's and he thought he was dreaming. The early morning quiet gave way to the sound of birds and one old rooster that blended in harmony from a nearby farm across the highway. The soft sounds of Mississippi were a pleasant contrast to those of L.A. He looked forward to the morning run as he stretched in the room, then stepped from the small musty space into the faint early morning light.

"Good Mornin'," the sound came from right behind him. He flinched, turning to see the old gentleman with the khaki maintenance uniform carrying a tool box toward the office.

"Good Morning to you." Roman tried to sound friendly at daybreak. "You work around here?" He asked the thin, wiry little man with snow white hair and pale complexion.

"Sure do. Been the groundskeeper or maintenance man, whatever you want to call it, for many years now. About to run?"

Roman smiled and pulled his left leg behind him to stretch. "Yes Sir, about four miles."

"Mister, nobody around here runs four miles unless somebody is after him." He stuttered and seemed to be having an unusually hard time finishing the sentence. Roman smiled, waved and started his run. Yes, this was definitely not L.A. or New York, but he watched the uncrowded beauty unfold as he ran, and he was glad it was neither. He breathed the fresh air and was impressed by the unusual bayou that weaved around the heart of Indian Bayou. It was a refreshing, momentary peace he had not known in quite a few months. A German-Shepherd puppy accompanied him most of the last mile, before getting sidetracked by an out-of-place rabbit. He felt rejuvenated after the run and looked forward to a better day than yesterday.

He showered and glanced at the white pinpoint cotton shirt he had laid out from the trip in. The wrinkles had hung out enough to put it with his paisley tie and olive cotton suit that had faired well also. He was ready for his first meeting with the Honorable Mayor Engle.

"You must be Mr. Beckley from Los Angeles. I'm Mayor Engle's secretary. He'll be right out," she announced as she sat down and rolled her chair neatly under the desk with the computer on top. She offered no name, so Roman just nodded and smiled. She pulled at her skirt and stared at the computer. Despite her long, red hair piled neatly in a tight bun, she couldn't be a day over twenty one.

The smell of the strong Roi-Tan beat the Mayor out of the door of his office. He thrust out his fat hand for Roman's, while the other one gripped the cigar tightly. The Mayor was short, completely bald, and had not missed any meals. He looked every day of his fifty-five years. He had beads of perspiration on his forehead despite the comfortable temperature inside.

"Welcome to Indian Bayou, son. You'll meet a lot of good folks around here and you might meet a few other kinds. Very few, I might add." Roman thought of last night's welcoming to the county. He could picture Stiles vividly, and remembered how he contrasted with the typical Mississippi Sheriff image. He was anything but a potbellyed, drawling, good ole boy. At over six feet, with rigid posture and longer than usual black hair, he could have passed for mid-thirties, rather than ten years older. There was the scar that ran from the corner of the left eye to the top of his jawbone. He caught only a glimpse of it last night. He quickly shut out the image and smiled at the Mayor.

"Mr. Mayor, excuse me for the interruption, but I gotta see you a minute." The voice was extremely slow and Southern. The red haired, red faced, heavy set man of medium height, motioned for the Mayor to step

8

into the smaller office by the door. He glanced at Roman with his beady eyes for a split second and looked away. Roman couldn't help but overhear some of the conversation. The Mayor was annoyed and the exchange of words lasted less than a minute. Roman shrugged this off since the Mayor of any town has to have heated words occasionally with someone.

"That Deputy can be a pain at times," the secretary thawed, chiming in to Roman.

"Deputy? I didn't notice a uniform or badge." Roman looked out the window to the main street to try for another glimpse as the man hurried out.

"Oh, he must have been off duty today. Comes in all the time pestering Mr. Engle too much."

Engle reentered the room with more of a sense of urgency than before. His frown clearly showed he was preoccupied with the deputy who'd just left. "Where were we, Mr.Beckley?" He flipped out his Ronson and lit another of the strong cigars. He blew the first cloud straight up over Roman's head. Roman's first impulse was to duck, but stood his ground on second thought.

"You had just commented on the fact that most of the people around here were fine people. That's about where we stopped." Roman still stood, waiting for an offer for a chair.

"Sit down, Mr. Beckley. Excuse my manners. My mind is slipping."

"Just call me Roman." Mayor Engle never acknowledged the suggestion.

"Roman. I'll try to make this a pleasant welcome to Indian Bayou, but at the same time there are a lot of reservations about what your company proposes to do down here. First, the advance word that we've gotten concerns me. Last thing we need is for some outfit out of California to come in here, pollute our land and atmosphere, make a lot of money, and move on a few years down the road. You understand what I'm saying?" The Mayor's voice jumped an octave. He pretended to be adamant, but his insincerity showed through. He was not making constant eye contact as he stood and paced back and forth in the small, tobacco-smelling office.

"I can tell you that will not be the case. I'll give you and all the other officials, from this office to the governor, all the specifics and what we propose. It will be a safe, environmentally clean, and top-notch operation that will come here." Roman caught Engle's eye and tried to give his most reassuring look.

9

"Roman, I'll admit, I remember you when you were quite a ball player at Ole Miss. I wasn't a fan of the school, but do remember you. Remember reading the story years ago about how you walked on there without a grant-in-aid and beat out two other scholarship boys. Didn't think I'd know that did you?" The facts were right, but it sounded rehearsed. Nevertheless, he was somewhat surprised another local official knew some history on him.

"I can't believe you remember me after ten years or so."

"I also remember that you played four or five years for San Diego after college."

"L.A., Mr. Mayor, but that's close."

"Excuse me while I make a phone call, Roman. If you'll wait out there with my secretary, I'll be out in a minute." Roman agreed, but was somewhat puzzled by the abrupt end to the conversation. He pushed the chair back and dodged the cigar butt in the direct path of his foot. The secretary blushed at his presence and offered coffee. Roman took his black and thanked her. She might be an ally, if she wasn't so shy. He knew he needed all the friends he could get around Indian Bayou. He thought of John Sessions. He had to call him by nightfall, without fail.

"Miss, that deputy looked familiar. What's his name?" He inquired with his best innocent face.

"Billy Wiggins." He's sort of overbearing to some folks, but the Mayor has the upper hand on him. Billy worships Sheriff Stiles. Follows him around like a puppy. Everybody jokes that Zach could get him to do anything." I'm sure, Roman thought. He sipped his coffee and slid back the curtains to see an elderly lady selling vegetables from the back of a parked, old pickup truck.

"Since dinner is a few minutes away, I took the liberty of getting you an invitation with me, to have some good food out at Norris Palmer, Sr.'s home. You'll enjoy seeing that place. One of the biggest plantations still producing around the whole Delta. It's only about six miles out of the city limits. Ready?"

"Ready when you are." Roman knew he was inundated with things that needed doing, but relented. He remembered it had been a long time since he'd heard lunch referred to as dinner — years ago when he lived in the northeast hills, near Tupelo.

"We can go in my Cadillac," the Mayor volunteered.

"I appreciate that, but I'd better go in my car in case you decide to stay longer. I'm just getting organized and got lots to do. I'll follow you." The

Cadillac brought a smile to Roman's lips.

"All right. Let's don't hold 'em up." It was apparent that the Mayor had not held up much when it came to eating. His huge waistline and constant shortness of breath gave witness to that.

Norris Palmer, Sr. had quite a spread indeed. It had to be four thousand or more acres Roman could see from where Palmer's signs began. Maybe more. The ranch style house was at least 6,000 square feet. There was enough new and used equipment, around the barns and sheds lining the fences, to start an implement company. The cotton was just on the verge of being picked. Though Roman knew little about the precious commodity, he had seen it for years while growing up. He knew many people in this fertile part of the state had farmed it for well over a century. The catfish industry had come on strong around these parts as well, but most people knew this land for cotton.

Norris, Sr. was well known and respected throughout the entire Delta, and in tight political circles around the State Capitol in Jackson. He was in his early seventies, a huge, sturdy man over six feet. Even with a noticeable paunch, it was evident he was tough as a chain-link fence. Roman caught a quick glimpse of a small tatoo on his left arm as they shook hands. It looked like a military squadron number with wings. He looked away, not to stare.

"Welcome back to Mississippi, son. Make yourself at home." Norris opened the rich-looking, heavy double doors and motioned him into the huge den. Roman nodded politely and made his way around the live-looking bearskin rug to the wine-colored couch. Norris was talking as he strolled down the hall with Mayor Engle, out of Roman's sight. He could only sit for a second or two. The trophies that sat in the shiny glass case and the many pictures that adorned the walls were beckoning. Not to mention several wild game heads, prominently displayed on three of the walls. His eyes fixed on the 8 x 10 of Norris, Sr., standing by the World War II B-25 bomber plane. It had a squadron number on the plane and was autographed to his family back home, "with love". There was a "Purple Heart" medal for being wounded during battle that caught his eye, framed beneath the picture, along with other medals in two more frames. He had always admired anyone who had fought to preserve freedom in this country. His own dad was an Army veteran of the Korean conflict and also decorated. Not to this extent, but nevertheless, a hero to Roman. His mind flashed back to his Dad. He missed him to this day. He had died at 56 of complications during what was thought to be routine gall-bladder surgery. His Mother had moved two years after his death from Tupelo to Chattanooga, where his only brother Peyton lived. Peyton was a successful plastic surgeon, who worked his way through college and medical school and was secure with his wife and two children. She had her condo nearby, despite the offer to live with them. She was still proud and dabbled in painting and playing her piano.

"Did you think we had left you, Roman? Food's just about ready." Norris slapped him on the back, startling Roman, but he tried hard not to show it. He saw a reflection from the mirrored trophy case move in a blur behind him. It was Norris, Jr. He was a paraplegic. He had backed out upon seeing Roman and started his wheelchair toward the hall. In his early forties, he was a younger carbon of his dad. Though the belly was prominent as it hung over his belt from forced inactivity, his arms rippled with muscles from rolling the wheelchair. A choice he had made over an automated one.

"Wait, Son. There's someone I want you to meet." Norris, Jr. kept moving. "Norris, wait up." He stopped his chair, his back turned to them. He hesitated. He inched the chair slowly, then suddenly swung around.

"Now you can meet the 'goat' of the family," Norris, Jr. quipped. "You've seen the evidence of the real hero." His eyes were strained and the hurt evident. The hurt that did not have to be explained. The handshake was powerful as Roman anticipated. His pride was camouflaged with sarcasm. Roman smiled and Norris, Jr. forced a slight one.

"That's not true, what he said." Norris, Sr. volunteered. He pointed to the other side of the trophy case to the spot on the wall. Framed also, was the "Purple Heart", awarded Norris, Jr. for being wounded in combat. "Enemy mortar fire overturned his jeep outside Saigon. Paralyzed him from the waist down." Norris, Jr. rolled out of the den immediately, slamming the heavy door behind him.

"I'm sorry. I know it's been tough on him and the family," Roman tried to change the subject. But Norris, Sr., for some reason, wanted to talk about it. Maybe the family didn't discuss it. He didn't know, but felt obliged to listen attentively. They both sat down on the couch, as the Mayor made himself comfortable in the nearby study, anxiously awaiting the call to wade through the fried chicken, turnip greens, mashed potatoes, okra, sweet potato pie, and any other morsels that he could smell cooking in the rambling kitchen.

"That boy. I shouldn't call him that. He's quite a man. He's past forty now and the last twenty years have been sheer hell for him. He had a great future ahead for him. You know, he graduated from Alabama. Good grades. Got commissioned in the Army, then this happened. He was a 1st Lieutenant in the 1st Battalion, 4th Brigade of the 6th Infantry Division. Stop me if I get carried away. Some of this may not make sense to you, but he always wanted to serve his country admirably. I guess he'd seen some of the things on the wall of mine from World War II. I wish now my wife would have left them in that damn cedar-chest." Norris's voice trailed off. "Anyway, his Battalion's mission was to conduct search and destroy operations and pacifications of Vietnamese villagers in and around Nha Be. Just south of Saigon. It was called a Revolutionary Development campaign, aimed at Viet Cong. Local Force Guerillas." Roman listened intently. Norris's tone and description had his attention. He had always wanted to hear first hand about Vietnam. He was getting the opportunity. "This was considered a battle for the hearts and minds of the people while eliminating the VC. 'Charlie', as they were known also. Saigon was still a bustling city, containing within its limits, several contiguous, smaller cities. Cholon was one of these. It was almost totally Chinese."

"Chinese?" Roman sat forward on the couch, hanging on every word.

"Right. Chinese. These operations uncovered direct evidence of their sales of uniforms. The pajama cloth. You have heard of it, I'm sure. They also sold ammunition, weapons, and rice to the 'VC'. They once captured 600 Viet Cong and their sympathizers with 50 tons of rice, weapons galore, sampons, the river boats, bolts of cloth, and 50 pounds of intelligence documents. I won't go on and on, but he and the other guys had a very valuable mission." Norris, Sr. stopped and stared off into the distance, the veins in his neck protruded, and his face grew red with anger. His voice was barely audible. He shook his head slightly.

"It must be time to eat, sir," Roman injected, as they followed the inviting aroma.

"Ella, you and the Mayor solve all the local problems?" Norris, Sr.'s voice was back to full volume. "Roman, meet my wife of too many years, Ella." Roman smiled and shook her hand. He thought he smelled the scent of bourbon. Maybe not at mid-day. Ella was a lady the years had been kind to. Her figure was full at age sixty-seven, but the eyes were still sky blue and sparkling, and her hair was the silver that had never seen dye.

"Good to meet you Roman. I've heard only what 'Big Norris' has told me about the waste plant."

"Hazardous waste facility, Ella. You make it sound like they'll be treatin' a few toilets or so. This is high tech. Big time. Lots of acres and lots of people to be employed." Norris hesitated. "That is, if it comes off without too many hitches."

"You can say that again. I hope it can. " Roman added. He shifted his weight from one foot to the other, but managed a smile.

"Where's Diana?" Ella asked to anyone who might know. Roman imagined Diana would be a great aunt who would hobble in with her "toddy" or another old friend of Ella's, joining them for lunch.

"She's down at the stable with Zach. He wants to sell her the stallion he picked up recently in Tennessee," Norris, Sr. replied, sounding almost irritated, while motioning everyone to seats at the long table covered with enough hot food for a lumberjack crew.

"Zach?" Roman frowned noticeably.

"Zach Stiles. Sheriff of Wildflower County. You met him yet?," Norris,Sr. inquired, undoing his napkin and placing it in his lap.

"You might say so." Roman looked down and brought the glass of water to his lips. His appetite suddenly waned. He wanted to stand up as hellos were being said and put his fist through Stiles's face, but he had control. He'd learned long ago as an athlete.

"Sorry I'm late. Hope I didn't delay the festivities." The soft feminine voice came from behind Roman, from the back porch just a few feet away. "Come on in Zach." Roman turned to see, and suddenly Zach seemed to be in the distance, almost nonexistent. Roman's eyes focused on Diana only. Her long chestnut hair, smooth olive skin, sea-green eyes, and full lips needed no make up to enhance her beauty. Her naturally-chiseled features were complimented by her slender, slightly muscular body. At 29, she was in virtually the same physical shape as when she was on the tennis team at Vanderbilt.

Ella did the introductions. "I think all of us know one another, except maybe Zach and Diana haven't had the pleasure of meeting Roman Beckley."

Roman was determined not to stare at her. "Diana, it's my pleasure. I wasn't aware you were part of this family." They were lost in each other's eyes briefly, then smiled together, holding hands seconds longer than necessary. "I've already met the Sheriff." He and Stiles were forced to shake hands, as every eye was on them. Roman clamped down on the hairy, dark hand and squeezed violently, smiling. The sheriff looked shocked momentarily, but managed to get a quick, short squeeze also. Their eyes locked, and the battle lines were clearly drawn. Roman smiled again at Diana as they took their seats, and she smiled back. Their eyes met more than once during the scrumptious country meal.

The afternoon was getting away. Roman finally found a small office to rent near the intersection of the two main highways in Indian Bayou. He tried to concentrate, but Diana's face was everywhere. He checked the fax and copier that he would have access to. There was the phone next door he could use until his was activated. The office was close enough to downtown, yet gave him a straight shot up the highway to the acreage Worldwide had optioned for the waste facility.

He unpacked his brief case and put away some files on various contacts in the area, as well as the state. He peered out the window at the apparent equal mix of pickups and cars rolling by on the highway of this agricultural hot spot.

He paced around the office, looking at possibilities in the space, trying to get Diana out of his mind. He felt guilty since Leah had been dead not much more than a year. The opportunities had come in his travels, but he hadn't been very interested in other ladies. There had been very few and they were superficial.

He poured a cup of the aging coffee from the hallway and straightened the only picture that was left by a former tenant; an old red barn with hay spilling out of it. He had a desk, a wastebasket, one chair, a filing cabinet, and privacy, he hoped. The privacy was essential.

He raised the one window to alleviate the stuffy smell, allowing in the unseasonably cool, refreshing, September breeze. It was time to take the insurance man up on using his phone. He would get a cellular phone later, but for now, he wanted to avoid the constant accessibility to the home office.

He dialed the number John had given during their recent conversation and after three rings, the answering machine gave the daytime number he could be reached. He dialed the seven digits. He could see "Smilin' Jack", as he was affectionately labeled in college; stocky, average height, thick and unruly red hair, and blue eyes that were as genuine as his smile.

On the first ring the lady answered formally: "Rehabilitation office. State Penitentiary." Roman hesitated, almost replying about a wrong number, then decided to at least inquire.

"Do you have John Sessions at this number?"

"Yes, we do. Shall I ring his extension?"

"Yes, please."

"John Sessions. Vocational Rehabilitation." He sounded preoccupied.

"John, you said you worked for the State of Mississippi when we spoke, but I never knew you were rehabilitating criminals." They laughed loudly.

"Roman Beckley, I'd know that smooth voice anywhere. Are you in Indian Bayou?" John asked excitedly. "Where are you now?"

"I'm setting up a little office near 49 & 82 intersection, but I'm staying at the famous Indian Bayou Taurus."

"You must be broke," John joked.

"My residence there is temporary, I hope."

"We can take care of that. Why don't I call you when I get in? It should be around six. We'll cook something at my place. At least, maybe Missy will. She's my bride-to-be."

"Say. Congratulations. It's about time some young maiden reeled you in."

"Say, Roman, like to join me for a run when I get in?"

"No thanks. I had one this morning and ate too much over at the Palmer place."

"Palmer place?"

"Right. That's an interesting family."

"Especially Diana, wouldn't you say? She is one fine looking lady."

"Since you brought her up, is she seeing anyone that you know of?" Roman crunched the piece of scrap paper and banked it into the wastebasket against the wall.

"No, I don't think so. As a matter of fact, she just came back here from Nashville. Well, I'd say about four months ago. Kind of a change I guess since her divorce was final. Her husband got caught embezzling from a bank, I understand. Married some guy from Tennessee. I can tell you for sure, that she's not that way at all. She is first class. I don't know if she's here for long or not. You'll appreciate this. She's really talented, I hear. She's had paintings hanging in art museums all over. Memphis, New Orleans, and around. Y'all might make a good pair. You still write music and sing anymore?"

"Sometimes. It's only a hobby now. I gave it a little fling in L.A. during the off season, but decided to go this route. Haven't had time to do lots that I enjoy. Like being limited as a pilot also. Haven't logged as many flying hours lately. See you shortly."

Roman hung up, his blue eyes narrowing in a trancelike stare that intensified as he slowly mumbled, "Parchman Farm." He shook his head and dialed the home office to check in with Gardner Lowe, President, who had insisted he stay in close touch. He reached the secretary, who informed him Lowe had gone to a golf tournament in Beverly Hills. Roman left a message, propped his feet up on the barren desk, and relaxed. He didn't want to talk to him anyway.

He started his itinerary for the week. There were meetings with local legislators, the EPA, landowners, and the list was endless. He glanced out the window once again.

The pale green automobile, with the blue lights on top and the official Sheriff's sticker on the door, cruised at a snail's pace, then stopped. He saw the cold black eyes once again. It left as slowly as it came.

CHAPTER **3**

R oman had no problem finding John's place. It was nestled behind a stately old two-story colonial home. The guest house that John called home was of considerable size itself. It was in need of a little paint like the main house, but both were appealing to the eye. The long driveway leading back to it was lined with numerous old bushes, two magnolia trees, and a couple of willows. Roman could smell the fish cooking as he stepped from his car. John met him at the doorway smiling. They shook hands and embraced.

"You don't waste anytime with the food." Roman joked.

"Some things don't change, as they say. Remember how I kept the old apartment at Ole Miss? Something always cooking. Of course, you had the best deal. You got to eat from the training table on campus."

"Yours was hard to beat when I had the pleasure. Only your Mom's topped that the times I went home with you. How's she, by the way?"

"Fine. You told me on the phone a couple of weeks ago that yours lived with your brother in Chattanooga. I know she likes that."

"Yeah, she's in Chattanooga, but has her own place,"

John smiled, popped another Bud Light, and handed it to Roman."You looked like you could use that."

"You're a mind reader." They hoisted two cold cans and bumped them without a word.

"Tell me about this controversial behemoth your company is going to build out in the country. Will it turn us all orange around here?"

"Now would I be with a concern that's endangering lives? You know we won't. Seriously, this will be safe for this whole area. We can discuss my livelihood later want to hear about yours." John could see Roman was the same sincere friend, as always, shifting the conversation from himself.

"Let's not talk about either for now. You may kick me, but I took the liberty of arranging for Diana to drop by." He held his hands up, as if a blow was coming.

Roman frowned slightly, moved the few feet to the cluttered den, and hesitated.

"You son of a...," Roman said, smiling. " How'd you do that?"

"Missy's folks own the radio station here. She interviewed Diana about her art. You know, it's a local interest thing."

"I guess she thinks I'm one aggressive guy now. Getting my friends to line this up. And just hours after I saw her for the first time. Oh, well, nothing ventured, nothing gained."

Missy and Diana pulled up at the same time. Roman heard the screen door squeak. It was like he was in Junior High once again, and the girls were being dropped off by their parents for a chaperoned party. Hellos and introductions were exchanged casually. Roman shook hands with Diana politely, and his eyes darted quickly to the white jeans, hugging her rear end just enough, as she turned to acknowledge John behind her. She held on to Roman's hand as she did. He was not about to let go first. Missy was an attractive, petite, strawberry blonde with blue eyes. Roman smiled, acknowledging her, but he could only concentrate on Diana.

They never got around to talking about each other's jobs much. Roman was vague, but polite, about the site when the topic arose. Instead, it was an evening of conversation about the ladies present, their interests, and lots of college stories from years that seemed too far past. The catfish, hushpuppies, and slaw vanished with a few beers for the boys and a couple of glasses of wine for Diana and Missy.

Roman volunteered to follow Diana the six miles out to the plantation, but she graciously declined. They said goodbyes at the door first, then Roman strolled out to Diana's dad's Cherokee. As she climbed into the vehicle, the soft glow of moonlight touched her face and Roman leaned in toward her. The polite good night kiss lingered, and without word they knew they would see each other again soon. Very soon.

John and Missy stared and smiled as Roman reentered the guest house. Somewhat embarrassed, he smiled back.

"I knew it! I told you that you two would hit it off," John said.

"Now wait a minute," Roman hesitated. "Well, I guess you two were pretty good fortune tellers."

"When you seeing her again?" John quizzed back.

"John!" Missy 's voice rang out.

"No problem with my old friend. He's always been nosey. Let's put it this way... she's the first one, since Leah passed away, that I've had much desire to see again."

Missy looked at Roman compassionately. John had filled her in on the tragedy before the night began.

"Say, I'd better head back to my palace on the edge of town. The Taurus is calling."

"That reminds me, John snapped his fingers. " You need to get out of there."

"No kidding."

"The big house in front has been vacant for over two months now. Since Mrs. Saucier died, it's in an estate — in limbo," Missy volunteered. " I know her daughter would be glad to have someone like you in it. We even asked about buying it since we're planning to tie the knot about ten months from now. I'll make the call if you'd like." She pointed to the phone on the end table.

Roman thought for a few seconds. "That's a lot of house for just me, but if I can swing a reasonable rent, do it."

Missy knew the daughter well and made the call, even if it was after ten. The deal was done on the phone. He could move in right away. He felt better knowing the Taurus would be history. He had intended to get a place, but not in two days.

When Missy excused herself for the bathroom, Roman seized the opportunity:

"John, tell me honestly if you think Diana has been seeing a guy named Zach. The Sheriff around here." Roman made direct eye contact, but John glanced away "Am I sensing from you, the answer is yes?"

"No. no. Not at all. I think, from what I've heard, he might like to, but it's a one way thing. He's definitely not in her class. I don't know whose class he's in. How do you know about him?" John was no longer smiling as he and Roman stacked the dishes to be washed.

"Let's just say we've met. I'll fill you in some time," Roman said, as Missy reentered the room. " Thanks for a great evening and the favor." Roman kissed her on the cheek, pushed the screen door, and walked past the porch light toward his car.

"Roman, watch that guy!" John yelled to Roman down the driveway as he opened his car door. "He's crazy as hell. He's got a lot of people around here fooled. Two personalities I think."

"What guy?" Missy asked when John came back to the kitchen.

"Nobody. Nobody." His voice trailed off as he turned on the dishwasher.

Roman spent the next two days going full speed. He had meetings with the EPA, two local landowners, and with the State Senator from the area and the Representative for the counties around there. Both Senator Ellis Fulton and Representative Crane had occupied six hours of his time in two days. So far, so good. The evenings were better. It was no problem to move into the already antique-filled, elegant, old house. He needed nothing but to buy some new bed linens. Diana even helped rearrange a few pieces of furniture, and he was home. They were engrossed, enjoying each other's company as well as John and Missy's. They were both careful not to intrude about past marriages at this point. Diana also felt obligated to be sure she was back at the Palmer's before the wee hours creeped in. She was somewhat uneasy with John and Missy that close and what they thought. Her good, old-fashioned upbringing still surfaced.

"Roman, what would you say to a trip to Memphis this Saturday?" Diana asked softly. I've got to drop off a couple of paintings at the Museum of Art."

"We'd have to leave early to make that drive and do everything and still get back at a decent hour." Roman answered.

"I didn't plan to get back the same day." Her friends had a cabin outside Memphis on a lake. She looked at Roman and blushed. Roman smiled and she did the same. The trip was on for Saturday. He made the round trip to the country to the Palmers and got ready for bed.

The phone rang at midnight. He jumped, then calmed down after hearing John's voice.

"Hey, Roman. Sorry to call this late, but I wanted to see if you'd like to go up to Parchman Penitentiary with me tomorrow morning. I know this is late notice, but you can follow in your car and come back early. I know you've got work to do. I've got some time for a change. Can show you what I do up there." John was convincing. Roman would reshuffle some things and be back after two or so. They agreed on a six-thirty departure.

The guard at the entrance got the clearance from John to let Roman come onto the grounds that cover miles in its 17,000 plus acres. He signed in and parked his car in the designated space at the administration building. He and John cruised through in John's Bronco to the first stop. Maximum Security.

"We have to get through here to the back of this building for me to show you something." The dull brick building was surrounded with high, wire fences and literally life-threatening guards, stationed high above the building in towers. Razor wire rolled throughout the top of the fence said it all.

"What something?" Roman asked, taking in the ominous surroundings.

"The gas chamber." They were admitted inside by the guards and allowed through to the death room. The lone strapped chair was stark evidence of impending finality.

A chilling sight to behold, the gray thick steel door encased the oval-looking tomb — secured by a giant iron wheel turned slowly into place — locking the inmate in for the last time. It was near the lethal injection room, now used for death more often than the gas chamber. It was cold and grim, and Roman could only try to imagine the thoughts that could run through a condemned mind.

"You know, there are inmates who have been on 'Death Row' for over ten years. There are over thirty now in there." John volunteered the facts. "I'll drive you by that unit. It's quite a ways over there. Incidentally, these units are numbered. The old maximum security building we're in is Unit 17."

They headed for the far end of the prison grounds, where the thousands of acres of cotton were farmed by the inmates. They drove and talked while Roman soaked in the vast surroundings and its inhabitants. It must have been three miles or more, flat and sprawling forever. The thousands of acres had been utilized, even more in the past, for other crops to supplement the cotton acreage. 17,000 acres. He couldn't get over it. A paved old Highway 32 even stretched through it to Shelby, another nearby small town. A sudden loud roar from above them drowned out any attempt at conversation. Roman saw the low-flying, double-wing plane dip down to no more than ten feet off the ground. It was a crop duster plane, not over 150 feet away, with a prominent white cotton boll painted on both sides of the dark green plane. He made out the words on the plane's second pass. "CB Crop Dusting" was printed in large letters.

"That's the first double wing Steerman I've seen in years," Roman exclaimed. He lowered the window and stuck his head out to watch the pilot wing away out of sight of the rows of cotton that stretched as far as he could see.

"Yeah, they're like a fixture around here. They fill the air day and sometimes night when it's a light one, since there's so much cotton in these parts. I don't have to tell you that, though. But you don't fly as much anymore, huh?"

"I try to get in some time when I can. I've never handled one of those old relics though, but they've been popular with crop dusters for a long time, I know. I didn't notice any cotton poison spraying out on the fields from that one. Wonder why?"

"Oh, that's probably Walt Peterson, himself, flying over. Just checking out the crops. He's had the contract for all the thousands of acres of cotton for years, not to mention other farms in the area. Can't miss the planes, since they've got that white cotton boll painted against that green background. Yeah, 'CB Crop Dusting will be the only planes you see around here though, coming and going." John turned down another of the long, flat, stretching roads. They were far out of sight of most of the prison buildings by now. He turned around near the end of the prison property.

"Can you believe that way down there is the end of Parchman property?" John pointed through the windshield.

Roman squinted to see as far as he could and shook his head. "What a spread!" They turned the Bronco around, and after a few minutes, came back near some of the buildings of the prison.

Roman noticed many of the inmates wore dark blue with white stripes down the legs. Others wore dingy white with dark blue stripes down the legs.

"The dark blue with white are 'trustys'. They've mostly proven they want to do their time and have earned the title. They can supposedly be 'trusted'. The white with blue stripes are 'B' custody. They are referred to as 'Gunmen'. This means you have to have an armed guard at all times when they're taken out of the unit for work details, or for any reason. The maximum security inmates wear yellow jumpsuits. 'Death Row' inmates wear red jumpsuits."

"I noticed you said the 'trustys' can supposedly be trusted. I see they can move about outside the units fairly freely. Ever worry about them escaping?"

"Most of them tow the line, but occasionally you have one or two who abuse their privilege and lose it. I know one right now that...." John stopped in mid-sentence. He looked away toward the field that was filled with vegetables; where inmates were working with armed guards walking the area.

"You started to say something about a 'trusty'. What were you saying?" Roman asked. His eyes scanned the buildings as they drove at a snail's pace.

"I'd better reserve my comments for the time being. Really it's sort of confidential." John answered quickly, changing the subject He turned at the next building. That's unit 32. One thousand inmates in maximum security. It's a newer structure than 17 where the gas chamber and lethal injection room are." Roman knew John was holding back something that hit a nerve.

"John, you've known me a long time. If something is bothering you about what I asked you...."

"It isn't!" John's voice told it all. The silence lingered. "I'm sorry. You mind-reading son-of-a-gun. Let me think about this a minute. Maybe I can shed a little light on it — if you can swear to secrecy."

Roman stared straight ahead. "If you'd rather wait, we've got time another day."

"If you happen to let this out even accidentally, it could cause problems for me, John warned. "Don't mention it to Diana, even. You've proven you can keep something confidential, so I'll just touch on it. I can't say a lot because I don't have all the evidence."

"You have my word."

John drove to near the back of the prison, where the flat land spread forever. He stopped the vehicle and pointed out the bales and bales of cotton being harvested by the inmates. Then he pointed into the distance, as far as Roman could see, toward the front of the prison. "Between here and there, something is going on that is mind-boggling. When I get the names of others, and I will, then I can tell you more. Let's just say it's extremely big and extremely illegal. What's so peculiar, is that the Chief of Security here has done an excellent job. His reputation is impeccable, and his staff, as a whole, is top notch. They run a tight ship, but you can imagine the minds here. I know that when you have over 300 guards on different shifts, there can be a dirty one or two in the lot sometimes. I'm not saying for sure, but give me time. If this is what I have reason to believe it is...." His voice dropped again. "Of course, I may have gotten some bad information. You see, in my building, where the inmates are about to be phased out to society, the jobs there are the plums. The 'trustys' work for me and other rehab officers and are allowed many privileges. Well, privileges for around here. They value these jobs around our building and have fabricated stories on other 'trustys' to try to move into their jobs. Some real convincing, sharp minds here. Also, lots of other minds. That's why I'm sure this goes beyond any gangs. This appears too shrewd. Too connected."

Roman shook his head, absorbing John's words without comment. After a trip by the canine quarters, Roman marveled at the work John told of the 35 bloodhounds. They were housed there near the horses, who were used by the guards primarily for work-detail surveillance. A black "trusty" with mirrored sunglasses galloped by on one of the favorite strawberry colored horses and waved. He was enjoying his privileged status.

"John, thanks for the tour," Roman said, slapping him on the shoulder. "I don't know the right word for it. Revealing? — I'm not sure. I guess I should say, interesting and revealing. By the way, I think Diana and I are going to Memphis early Saturday. Be back sometime Sunday night. That's for your ears only also." John winked and they shook hands, smiling.

Roman left just before noon, ahead of schedule. The trip made him appreciate his freedom. He drove to the front gate to leave, and the female guard searched his trunk. She slammed it down and motioned him on. The open highway looked a little more appealing than usual as he headed south on Highway 49 to Indian Bayou.

The coffee was hot and Roman drank his second cup by six to wake up for the trip to Memphis. The forecast was for perfect weather, cool again for September, and changing Sunday to thunderstorms, possibly severe.

The side door was unlocked and Diana let herself in. They embraced and kissed momentarily, then Roman offered a cup of coffee and slid out the plate of grits and eggs.

Over easy. Just as she liked them. She nibbled out of courtesy and slid her chair back. "What are you bringing in there?" She admired his lean muscular physique as he packed.

"You said there was a lake where we're staying at your friend's place, didn't you? I can't let this get by me without fishing a little. I'm throwing in my rod-and-reel and tackle box. Bought them yesterday afternoon. I haven't been in so long." Roman zipped his overnight bag and threw the hang-up bag on the chair. "I've got my jeans, T shirts, old sneakers, cap, and I'm ready."

He slid the old wine-leather-bag he'd bought on a trip to Mexico City several years ago into the back of Norris Sr.'s red Cherokee.

"You didn't want to go in your car, or mine for that matter?" Roman asked.

"I think that my 77' Corvette is a little cramped for us and the paintings? Besides, the Jeep seems appropriate for fishing. Don't you think so, Bill Dance?" She laughed, throwing his other bag into his arms.

" Bill Dance. Who's he?"

"He's a famous Southern fisherman. A professional who has his own TV show on fishing. I think he lives in Tennessee. He always wears a Tennessee Vols cap."

"Well, I've got my Dodgers cap. Think the fish will know the difference?" He smiled, slipping the cap on. She rolled her eyes back and laughed. "His job sounds like one I need to have. Sometimes, I am serious. A job that would be less pressure, and one where I'd be my own boss. Since I'm a decent pilot, there are lots of things I could do. I just need to make my mind up to get off the merry-go-round. Give up the money and the perks. I have my thoughts occasionally, believe me." Roman turned the radio to the country station out of Greenville and picked up a Garth Brooks song, "Shameless". "Like I've said before," he remarked, "Country music has changed so much that I'm becoming more of a fan. The lyrics aren't the same as the old raw country, even the arrangements."

"I guess lots of people are searching for more honesty and clarity in their lives," Diana commented. I admit, I'm not a fan of country music, but I enjoy the refreshing lyrics of some of the songs." She pointed to the road ahead. "I'm ready if you are."

The day was gorgeous and they put some highway behind them. He tried not to look as they passed Parchman Penitentiary, but he glanced and thought of John and their conversation. He would not mention that he had been there, under the circumstances.

They were in Memphis in two-and-a-half hours and dropped off the pictures. Roman was impressed with both paintings. He especially liked the one of the old man standing near his tired old mule, gazing at the new tractor in the field nearby. They made the stop at the world famous Peabody Hotel and, out of tradition, viewed the legendary ducks coming down to the lobby. He asked the white-haired bellman how long that had been going on, and he only knew, "for many years". They ate ribs at noon at the Rendezvous, a favorite spot of Roman's, when he was in college.

"The farmhouse is out toward Nashville," Diana announced. "Twenty miles from here. Ready to fish?" They paid the tab and headed east for the short trip to the country.

The farm at Rosemark was more than Roman expected. Two hundred and ten acres of rolling pasture land. Another sixty wooded acres of beautiful pines, wild cherry trees, and huge oaks encircled the old 16-acre lake. The huge log cabin had been made in Montana, brought to Tennessee and reassembled. The rustic structure could easily be a primary home instead of a retreat. Two bedrooms overlooked the glistening lake. Home construction business had been good to her friend's husband. Since they were in Destin at a convention, this gave them total privacy and Roman, for once, was grateful for meetings.

He changed into his fishing clothes and headed for the lake. She would be along in a few minutes to do some sketching. He caught five bass, all under three pounds, but nevertheless, fish. He noticed her more than once in total concentration of the surroundings. When she brought the brush to rest, she coyly observed him also. She decided it was time for a break. They walked, holding hands through the invigorating woods and pasture. Several sleek show horses roamed the clear land, as a few oblivious cattle grazed on the green pasture land. The setting was perfectly in tune with nature. Only the faint sound of a distant roaring jet reminded them of an outside world.

The day was winding down as they sat on the porch, watching the natural beauty unfold around them. The sounds and smells of the outdoors were everywhere. The crickets and frogs and other critters began to fill the air with their soothing late afternoon noises, in an off-beat tempo that never missed a beat, like a symphony of nature.

"Where would you like to go for dinner?" He asked. "You know all the restaurants? More than I do, I know. In the days when I came up to Memphis, I didn't have money enough to frequent many restaurants." He reached out and held her hand.

Diana whispered, "I thought you wouldn't mind if we cooked out on the grill tonight. Since the view is so good, and the freezer is full, let's enjoy it." Roman put up no resistance.

It was almost seven and the sun continued its slow, scarlet descent. Finally, the gorgeous sunset faded into an equally beautiful night, filled with stars. They skipped their no red meat regimen, and chose two choice rib-eyes. Diana had pulled them out of the freezer earlier to thaw, in anticipation of his agreement to cook and skip the restaurant scene. The potatoes were already baking.

They showered separately and made small talk, as they finished dressing in the large adjoining bedroom. His thoughts were not on the steak. He hoped hers were not either. They left the room and made it as far as the sectional couch in the huge den. Garments were strewn from the bedroom to that point. There had been no need to draw the curtains, since the only neighbors were the critters outside the cabin. Their lovemaking was better than either imagined, and once ended, nature's serenade could be heard again.

"I don't want to sound like a teenager, but I don't make a habit of this. It's been a long time since I've been, shall we say, involved," Diana softly volunteered. Roman didn't ask any particulars. He didn't want to know. He just knew for certain how much he was feeling for her in this short time. It was evident, it was a two-way street. She gently wiped the perspiration from his forehead, as he touched her hair and brushed it back from her gorgeous eyes. He admired her full lips, now stripped of even the original touch of lipstick.

"What you were saying makes no difference now. That's past and this is now."

"Roman, I didn't mean I did any sleeping around at all. On the contrary, I was talking about being out of my marriage," She propped on one elbow.

"I know that. I didn't make myself clear," he stammered. She leaned over his bare chest without saying a word and slowly touched his lips. There was no misunderstanding. It was a memorable night of being close to nature and to one another.

Diana rolled down the windows of the Cherokee, as they headed back down Highway 61, underneath threatening skies. The late afternoon turned to darkness as the storm was coming. Roman thought of the last time he drove down this route. The weather was much the same. Just a week ago and a lot had transpired. It seemed like a year.

The rain came in sheets, when they were only ten miles outside Indian Bayou. They decided to call it a relatively early evening by nine, as they both had lots to do.

"Since we're already so close to our place, why don't you take Dad's Cherokee after you drop me off, and go on to Indian Bayou," Diana volunteered, as they continued to creep along in the downpour. A crack of lightning resounded in the sky. The rainy pitch-blackness made visibility only a few feet.

They held each other longer than intended and kissed passionately at the door, then Roman turned and ran through the ankle-deep water back to the Jeep.

He leaned forward and watched the wipers work overtime, as he crept out the driveway. He was about to turn right onto the main highway, when he noticed the glare of blue lights. Not again, surely not. "Damn," he mumbled. He certainly could not make out the vehicle through the rear view mirror.

Suddenly, the blue lights pulled aside him, as the rain grew worse. He could barely make out the figure, as it leaned over to the passenger's side and rolled down the window.

Rain streamed in momentarily. Roman slipped the John Deere cap from the seat onto his head.

"Norris! Norris. We took care of the problem in town. Permanently." Sheriff Zach Stiles roared off in the downpour. 'He thought I was Norris,' Roman mumbled. His mind raced: What the hell was the sheriff talking about to Norris? Who, if anyone, was he talking about?

Roman finally pulled into the long driveway to his new abode, to see the tail lights from John's Bronco shining through the sheets of rain.

He must have just come in from Missy's. He appeared to be about to back up. Roman couldn't determine if it was John's head he could see. After waiting a few seconds, no rear back-up lights appeared. He closed his door and walked through the downpour, down the driveway and could now see the back of John's head. It was tilted to the side. Lightning resounded again. His walk became a run. He jerked open the Bronco door. John was slumped to the driver's side door. Roman caught his limp body, covered in blood — streaming down his face, down the back of his head. Roman's heart jumped into his throat.

"Oh, God! John. John." The rain washed blood away, but more came back. He felt for a pulse and couldn't tell. His hands slid around frantically for a pulse in the warm blood. There seemed to be a faint one, but he couldn't tell. Damn. He prayed out loud. Because his own heart was pounding so fast, it was hard to determine a pulse.

He leaned John down on the seat, then sprinted across the yard to the kitchen entrance. The door was locked. He took one step backwards and kicked it in. He panicked for a second. Where was the phone? He remembered where Missy had pointed to it and jerked up the receiver, jamming down the keys on 911. After what seemed forever, a voice came on.

"Sheriff's Department 911. How can I help you?" It hit him: "Hang up! John must be the one Stiles was yelling about, when he thought I was Norris Sr. That animal! That bastard!" His bloody fingers dialed 1411, and he got the local hospital number. A reassuring nurse would send the ambulance at once. She knew the address. Everyone knew everyone's address around here.

In a matter of minutes, an ambulance wheeled into the driveway, its lights looking like an angel of mercy.

"Will he make it?" He whispered frantically to the emergency medic working over John. The other medic pushed him away. There was no time for questions.

They sped out with lights flashing and siren blasting, toward the nearby Wildflower County emergency room.

Roman followed right behind, reeling in shock. He kept repeating: "Hang on, John. Hang on."

He thought about calling the law. But what law?

CHAPTER 4

The medics raced to the local hospital, rather than wasting time going to Greenville, another thirty miles west. Since time was of the essence, the two made their decision because Dr. Whitley was on duty. He had the reputation of being the sharpest young doctor in this part of the Delta. Two nurses ran alongside them from the emergency room door. Whitley arrived, barking orders, as the team began their attempt to save John.

Roman was made to stay outside in the small waiting room, just outside the emergency room.

"My God, what a wound!" exclaimed the stocky veteran nurse at the end of the operating table nearest John's head.

"I'm no weapons expert, but this looks like some caliber other than a 'Saturday Night Special', Dr. Whitley said, administering to John, with orders for injections and procedures to the nurses. "This left a bigger point of entry into the back of the skull than I've ever seen from a bullet." He'd seen many from his vantage point during his emergency room days here and at two other larger hospitals. He knew John's chances were slim. They had to get him stabilized.

"His blood pressure is 80 over 45." The youngest nurse relayed.

"Get Dr. Olson in Greenville. I know he's at his in-laws. Get my wife on the phone and find out the number. I happened to talk to him this afternoon. I need his input on this one."

The nurse followed his orders and luckily got Dr. Olson on the phone as they worked to stabilize John enough to move him to Greenville. He needed treatment that they were not equipped to handle. After a detailed conversation, the doctors agreed on interim treatment and to move him quickly by medical helicopter. Dr. Olson would do the surgery as soon as he was brought in.

Roman heard the whirling sound of the Medstar helicopter as it hovered in to pick up his friend, whom he had spent so many good times with, now fighting for his life. This happened so fast it seemed like an instant replay he had seen so many times in sports. Only this time, it was all too real. He kept seeing John's head and limp body slouched over inside the Bronco. He shut his eyes and tried to erase that horrible, indelible image, but to no avail.

Again, for what seemed like forever, instead of precious minutes, he heard the roaring sound of the helicopter lifting off with John's life hanging in the balance. Roman prayed silently while the craft moved away overhead into the darkness.

Rage began to build within him. It had to be the Sheriff! Why else would he have stopped and said what he did about "taking care of the problem, permanently". He had to control himself, gather his senses and decide who to call. He would call some law enforcement officer other than the Sheriff. Right now, he could think only of his friend who would do no harm to anyone.

"Why John? Why John?" Roman mumbled, washing the blood from his hands in the nearby rest room. He bolted from the men's room and walked as fast as he could toward the exit to the parking lot.

"No need to go on to Greenville, Sir," the veteran nurse said, slipping off the thin white surgical gloves.

"I'll be damned if that's so." Roman blurted back.

"No, I mean there's nothing you can do except perhaps pray a lot at this point. They'll be operating for a while, I'm sure. Dr. Whitley and the others will do everything they can enroute to Greenville to keep him alive."

"You really don't give him much hope, do you?"

"I'm not supposed to be giving my opinion. I've seen a few near miraculous recoveries in my time, but very few. There's always hope." Roman felt his stomach sink more. His head pounded from the tension.

"I'm going on over there. I want to be there for the moral support," Roman answered, exiting the side door toward the parking lot. Then, it hit him. He hadn't even called Missy yet. He ran back in and fumbled for a quarter. His hand shook as he punched information. He didn't even remember her last name. Did John even say her last name? Missy was all he could remember. Then he took a deep breath and remembered: Evans. Missy Evans. He got the number quickly from the operator and dialed. A sleepy, but pleasant voice responded.

"Hello."

"Missy. This is Roman." He reached for everything inside his soul not to let his voice tremble. "Missy, John's been hurt." He couldn't think of any other way to say what he needed to say. "I'm here at the Indian Bayou hospital and they're taking him to Greenville. It's serious, I'm afraid."

"Oh, God. What is it? What is it? Is he all right? Roman talk to me."

"He was shot — in the driveway — from behind. It had to be right after he arrived back at the house. I know you want to get over there. I'll be right over and pick you up. I know your address. John showed me the house. Hang on, Missy. He's tough. We'll all pull him through."

Roman wiped the tear from his eye. The lump in his throat felt bigger than it was before. It hurt to swallow. He hadn't even given Missy a chance to respond before hanging up.

He hurried through the misty night across Indian Bayou to Missy's parents' home. Even though the rain had mostly subsided for more than an hour, he splashed ankle deep in water as he trotted up to the front door. All the lights were on. He could hear Missy sobbing and trying to answer her parents. "I'll be O.K. Roman's going to take me. I'll call you as soon as I know anything." Roman saw her coming down the corridor to the front door, yelling instructions back to them. He hugged her and tried to console her as they walked quickly to the car.

The drive took only twenty minutes to the Greenville hospital, since Roman sped considerably over the limit. This highly-equipped, well-staffed hospital was in a league above what they had come from. Not that the Indian Bayou hospital staff had been inefficient, but this was clearly where he needed to be for surgery.

He smiled reassuringly at Missy as they entered the hospital and she reciprocated. They were directed to the visitors lounge as they awaited word. Word that could come at any minute or hours later.

"If I smoked, I would've gone through a pack on the way here," Roman told the baby-faced nurse at the station near the waiting room. He couldn't sit still in the cramped room for more than a few minutes. "I know you can't tell me anything yet about my friend, John Sessions. But please check and let me know the minute you can."

"I will. I know they prepped at once and should be in surgery by now." She promised to get him instant word on John. Her voice was comforting for the moment. She was compassionate and reassuring, smiling back at him as she walked away.

Roman and Missy paced and drank several cups of coffee from the vending machine. He memorized every block of highly-shined, dark-grey floor in the hallway. The nurse called his name. "The news is not exactly what you want to hear, but the surgery is going fairly well. It's been an hour-and-a-half and will probably be that much or more before finishing. It's very serious, but at least he's got the best surgeon in Mississippi, in my opinion."

"Missy, you heard that. He's hanging on. He's tough as nails." Roman put his arm around her and hugged her tightly. She laid her head on his shoulder and wiped the tears away with a tissue. They strolled back to the corner of the waiting room. Roman pulled her away from the only two other people present at this hour, a young couple awaiting the news of her father's heart attack earlier in the day.

"Missy, do you know anyone who could possibly do this to him?" Roman asked with a puzzled expression. "I just can't imagine him having enemy one."

"Not a soul. In fact, he'd be the last person, I think could have any enemies." She hesitated and choked back more tears. "Unless...," she hesitated again.

"Unless what? Who?"

"Unless its connected with his work at Parchman. But then I've even met some of the former inmates he tries to help, and they seem to genuinely appreciate him." She shook her head in disbelief.

Roman hesitated, then reached out for her hand. "Let's walk outside. I need to talk to you in private," he whispered. They walked down the long hall and exited to the front of the hospital, and found a spot near the columns of the building where they could talk without other ears around.

"Can I trust you?" Roman asked. Missy wrinkled her forehead. " I mean, I'm sure I can since I know you love John. I need you to listen to what I have to say before you comment. This all has to be just between the two of us."

"Yes. You have my word. Go on, please."

Roman cleared his throat and looked away momentarily. "What do you know about.... Wait. Let me re-phrase this. Are you close to the Sheriff, by any chance?" He hoped she wasn't a relative or friend for sure.

"No, not at all," she assured him. Roman sighed in relief to himself.

It was now just after midnight. The sheriff's office was filled with smoke behind closed blinds at the Wildflower County courthouse. Zach Stiles was clearly in charge of the meeting of the three present. The other two were Mayor Engle and Deputy Wiggins.

Zach Stiles stood from behind his desk. He walked slowly forward and stood in the center of his large, sparsely-decorated private office, staring at the lone picture on his wall. It was at least twice the size of an 8 x 10 of the Vietnam Memorial Wall. There was one lone figure in the dark distance gazing at the Wall; none other than Zach Stiles himself, wearing a fatigue jacket and posing as if to offer his own personal tribute. He turned as if in slow motion, his black eyes zeroing in on the other two.

"We took an oath when we banned together to make this operation successful. Each of us has a vital part in the master plan and must fulfill his duty to ensure success of our mission. Correct?" He spoke with military-like precision.

"That's correct, Zach," Engle said.

"Secrecy is an absolute must and only total cooperation will be tolerated. We all agreed at our first ceremony." Engle and Wiggins stared intently, as if spellbound by their leader's words. "It disturbs me that one member is not present tonight. One member who took the same oath and is not here," Stiles screamed, slamming his fist down on the middle of the desk. Mayor Engle flinched, then lit a Roi-Tan. Wiggins crossed his legs nervously and slid more upright in the chair. "We all know who that member is, and he was told personally by me earlier tonight. We know that member to be Norris Palmer, and he is not excused from a meeting, no matter what hour of the day or night — if it's deemed necessary to have a meeting."

"Maybe he misunderstood," Wiggins chimed in.

"No. I had prearranged a signal to each of you, and you know what that is. He knew when he saw me tonight that he was to be here at midnight. He knew that I would drive out, personally. This would look less suspicious to his family than a phone call late at night. Besides, I have other reasons for wanting to drive out there personally." Stiles smiled briefly.

They both knew why he liked to drive out personally, but neither smiled. They ignored the comment. "Call him now. I don't care what hour it is. Get him on the phone. I want some answers when he gets here."

After three rings, Ella fumbled for the phone on the night stand.

"Mrs. Palmer, this is Zach Stiles. Sorry to wake you, but I got one of Norris's hired hands in jail and I need him to come down. Can you get him on the phone?"

"Yes. Yes, hold on." Ella stammered.

By now Norris, Sr. was sitting up in bed and reaching for the phone.

"Norris, Zach here."

"This better be good, Zach. Hold on while I go to my study." He patted Ella, told her to go back to sleep, then moved into the study on the mobile phone.

"Oh, it's good all right. Good and bad, Norris. First, where were you tonight? I called for a meeting at the agreed time, midnight."

"What the hell are you talking about?"

"I'm talking about when you saw me during that damn flood that I drove out in. You knew the meeting was set."

"Zach, is this your idea of a joke? I didn't see you during the storm. I've been asleep for hours. What are you getting at?" Norris was clearly agitated.

"I'm getting at the fact that, if I didn't see you right out by your place in your red Jeep Cherokee in the middle of the storm, who did I see?"

"Did you say anything to this person? Somebody may have stolen my Jeep. You may have been talking to a stranger, damn it!"

"As a matter of fact, I did say 'The problem has been taken care of Norris, permanently.' I thought it was you. You know I take great pains to disguise what is said when discussing our matters."

"What problem? This can't be what I think it might be."

"I didn't say who did what or to who. But, the problem has, in fact, been taken care of."

"I'll be right down there. Give me half an hour."

Norris bolted to the window and cupped his hands around his eyes to see into the three-car garage, adjacent to the study. His pulse quickened. He threw on his favorite red, terry-cloth robe and headed down the hall to the back bedroom, where Diana was staying since coming back. He tapped lightly on her door.

"Diana, Honey, I hate to wake you, but do you know where my Cherokee is?"

Diana yawned and stretched and reached for her robe to get up.

"No need to get up, Honey. I had just gotten some milk and noticed it being gone. I know Ella doesn't know about it."

"Yes, Dad. Roman had to use it to get back to Indian Bayou. He didn't want me to drive back by myself in the storm. I picked him up in it to go to Memphis, if you remember. We'll get it back first thing tomorrow." Norris felt uneasy about Roman hearing what he did. Very uneasy.

"Oh, no problem. I just got a call from Zach Stiles and one of the hands is in jail. I'll run down in a pickup. Go on back to sleep." Norris excused himself, walked back to the bedroom and dressed.

He was at the courthouse in just over fifteen minutes. The lights from the only occupied office would arouse no suspicion. It was common knowledge that the sheriff worked late many nights. Norris knocked and Wiggins stuck his head outside as he opened the door. The Mayor extended his hand, as did Wiggins. Stiles was seated with his back turned to the door, staring out the window. He wheeled the chair around and stood suddenly, as if another military command was about to be given.

"Well Norris, did you find out who had your Jeep Cherokee?"

"Yes, I did and I still can't believe you, of all people, who prides himself in secrecy and procedure could make a mistake like that."

"Look, I told you it was pouring down, and besides that, he even had your old John Deere cap on. What are the odds of someone else being out at your place, in your Jeep, wearing your cap even? Anyway, I didn't reveal that much. What I said was a little ambiguous also. Who was it?"

"Roman Beckley," Norris shot back.

The silence lingered. Zach Stiles's eyes narrowed and he slowly eased back into his chair. "Roman Beckley. What the hell was he doing out there at that hour in your vehicle?"

"That's really none of your business, Zach. But, he'd been with Diana and took the Jeep back into Indian Bayou, so she wouldn't have to drive in the storm. Look, I'm in this operation with you and the others, but my family's personal lives are off limits. Got that?" Norris's face reddened as he took the seat across from Stiles.

"So be it. There should be no repercussion from this anyway. He has no idea what 'the problem' means."

"What does it mean exactly, Zach?" Norris asked sarcastically, staring directly into the black eyes.

"Norris, I told each of you that if anyone, or anything, interfered with our plan that it would be dealt with. The one certain individual that was causing problems is no longer around."

Norris jumped up from his seat and pointed his finger directly at Stiles. "You didn't. Surely you didn't. I am part of the operation and took the oath that we all did, but I did not know murder would be a part of it. You're cold-blooded, Zach! This is serious!" Palmer turned to the other two. "Don't you have anything to say?" They looked away, silent.

"I did not say I did anything. I will name no names. I told you that there were higher ups than me in this that were not around here. You can use your imagination. Like I said, I never said I did it. And, after all, I am the law around here." He smiled and headed for the liquor cabinet behind the closet door.

"What if this Beckley fella puts two-and-two together about this? And after talking to him a while, believe me, he'll damn sure do it." A touch of fear rang out in the Mayor's voice.

"Then he'll be dealt with also. Like I said, gentlemen, higher ups have demands."

"You just can't go around eliminating people. This is getting out of hand, Zach. I don't care who these so called 'higher ups' are, I didn't get in this, like I said, to be murdering to get ahead." Norris was evidently no calmer. He slammed his fist down on the table and walked to the window.

"Norris, we're all in this too deep to turn back," Stiles shouted back. "We all have the allegiance to the group to make it work. You said you needed the money because of your cash flow situation at that monster plantation you own. If you want out, you've waited a little too late."

Palmer hesitated. "No, I have to be in. But, let's not become total savages. Too much has been done already."

"Leave that to me and the others I mentioned," Stiles said. This is bigger than all of us." He handed the Mayor and Wiggins a glass of bourbon each. They could use the chaser of their choice from the nearby bar, concealed by the closet. Norris declined.

Missy awaited Roman's response.

"I want to be sure I know what I'm talking about when I tell you this about Sheriff Stiles." They heard the main door open at this point and turned to see Dr. Olson following close behind the surgical nurse. She looked away. Dr. Olson's eyes darted momentarily to the ground and then back to each of their eyes. His face told the story. John did not make it.

Roman held Missy tightly as she cried uncontrollably. He gritted his teeth and stared over her head in a daze. He couldn't hold back the tears that rolled slowly down his own cheeks.

"I'm so sorry," Dr. Olson whispered. "We did all we could. There was just no way.... We have to fill out a report on shootings like this. I'm sure you've called the law enforcement officials."

"No." Roman gathered himself. "You call them, Doctor. Tell them where to reach me. I don't know who to call." He put both arms around Missy and led her slowly to the car.

CHAPTER 5

Roman slept no more than two hours. He couldn't shake from his mind the picture of John's head covered with blood, his near lifeless body slumped over on the seat. He would never forget. He remembered the good times in college. How genuine John was in a world sometimes filled with less than sincere people. He thought of Missy and could only imagine her feelings, now that her hopes and dreams were dashed by the act of some coward.

It suddenly registered. During the traumatic time at both hospitals, he hadn't thought of it. If he was right, then Norris had to be involved in something with Zach Stiles. Why would Stiles say what he did to Norris, Sr.? It was too coincidental that he found John just minutes after the statement by Stiles. His head was spinning. He was tired, filled with grief, and confused. How could Norris have anything to do with Stiles? Then there was Diana. Could she possibly know? What would he do about her now if her father was connected to John's death? He fell asleep from exhaustion.

At 6:30 a.m. the pounding began on his door. "Roman Beckley. Sheriff's Department. Open the door." The deputy identified himself. Roman sat straight up in bed, rubbed his eyes, then jumped into his jeans.

"Hold on. I'm coming." He stumbled to the door to see Deputy Wiggins two feet away in full gear, scowling.

"I've been instructed by Sheriff Stiles to ask you a few questions."

"Questions about what?"

"We've been called in on the murder of John Sessions. Looks like somebody shot him last night from behind."

"Yeah, I know. I found him."

"Why didn't you call this in immediately to the law?"

Roman hesitated, trying to compose himself. "Because I was trying to save his life. I had to get him to a hospital. I had no time to call the law." The resentment was evident in Roman's voice.

"Sheriff said you could cooperate here, or I can arrest you if I need to. What's it gonna be?" Wiggins expanded his chest and flexed his muscles.

"Where's the sheriff?"

"Right here." The voice roared from a few feet behind Wiggins.

Roman glared at the evil eyes that confronted him. The scar was clearly visible in the early morning light. "Wiggins, wait outside. I'll talk to Mr. Beckley by myself. I'll call you if I need to."

"Do that Sheriff. I'll be right here," Wiggins moved away obediently.

"Beckley, why didn't you report this to the authorities at once? That is, if you really did find this man in a dying state."

Roman reached deep inside to keep from attacking Stiles. His face grew redder and his heart pounded even faster than their first encounter. He stopped short of causing himself more problems. He could see the anxious look on the face of Stiles, and knew, he too, would likely be shot if he even flinched. He would play the game — though not totally.

"I was just telling the deputy that there was no time. Some low-life coward had shot him in the back obviously." He studied Stiles's eyes for any reaction. None. "It was pouring down when I pulled in the driveway. That was about ten or so. I saw the taillights and no movement. I found him unconscious and bleeding from the wound to the back of the head. I ran in. Rather, I tried to. I had to kick the door in." He hesitated as he looked at Stiles with a stare that lasted forever. He hoped he got the message through. "Then I called the hospital. Hell, his life was more important than calling the law. Besides, you never know about the law. I mean your reaction time." He glared and stepped closer. He knew he was pushing it, but couldn't stop.

"Actually, Mr. Beckley, we noticed on our records from 911, that we had a hang up from this number late last night. That's peculiar. Wonder who placed that call? You see, we get a record of every call that comes in."

Roman never hesitated. "Yeah, I remember calling. But I hung up because I chose the ambulance over you guys. It's that simple. Same thing anyone would have done probably. Again, I hear stories about reaction time by law officers." He pushed again and no reaction.

"Let me say something to you," Stiles said, pointing into Roman's face. "I am an ounce off arresting you for murder. Let me add a very important fact. I found a .357 Magnum with your prints on it near here. I won't say where. Looks like the bullet that killed Mr. Sessions came from something like a .357. Coincidence, huh?"

Roman couldn't believe what he just heard. "You took my .357 the first night I came to Mississippi and you know that. What the hell are you trying to do?" His insides were erupting.

"What I *am* doing, is putting you on notice that I may decide to bring you in for murder at any time since this .357 is not in your possession now. In other words, it may turn up, if you get my drift." Stiles leaned into Roman's face. "What you need to do is mind your own business around here and watch your step. Don't try to be a hero. After all, I'm the law around here." Stiles stepped back slowly and smiled as he closed the door.

Roman stood frozen, but returned the smile sarcastically. He remained still as Stiles and Wiggins grinned at one another and roared out of the driveway, then looked away, doubling his fists.

The funeral was scheduled for Tuesday morning in a rural church near Natchez, Mississippi, the beautiful, historic old town on the Mississippi River in the deep, southwest part of the state, where John was raised.

Roman and Diana made the drive with Missy and her parents, winding along the southerly part of Highway 61, past Vicksburg on the mighty river, on to Natchez, another hour-and-a-half. Missy stared out the window and said very little. Her Mother tried to keep the uneasy conversation flamed at times with trivial comments about the legendary surroundings. How many battles were fought, points of interest, where General Sherman refused to burn down Port Gibson, "the town too beautiful to burn", and so on. Roman nodded occasionally, but couldn't think of the proper words to fill any silent void. Missy's Dad was no help at all. Roman wished Missy's parents had not come a couple of times, but knew the gesture was well intended. They could not have been excluded. Diana's presence made the trip better for the other four. She offered soft words of comfort to Missy at times and was moral support to Roman. He was not very attentive but she understood.

The small quaint church was filled to its 150 person capacity. The Methodist preacher offered sympathy to Missy and John's Mother, a seventy year old widow and his younger brother, but the place could have just as well been empty to Roman. He heard the words and saw the people, but his mind wasn't present. This all-too-real nightmare was consuming him. He closed his eyes and vowed from the depths of his soul that he would do anything to see his friend's life avenged. He had been raised with these kinds of values, and he would not stop until this whole situation was resolved. He was hurting, and he could only imagine Missy's feelings. There would be justice.

A soft, cool breeze blew across the old cemetery, nestled between two hills near the Misssissippi River. The sky was overcast, making the setting even more somber. Roman said his final goodbye to John, then he and Diana walked to the car to wait for Missy. Her parents followed. Missy said her goodbyes to his mother and brother. They promised to keep in touch. After a few minutes of solitude, Roman could see her black dress softly fluttering with the wind, as she walked slowly from the hill lined with tombstones of all kinds and dates. She stopped and looked over her shoulder one more time. Roman met her a few feet from the car and held his arms out.

"It's such a peaceful place." She composed herself and wiped away the tears with her linen handkerchief. "I will never forget what he meant to my life. I don't know if I can ever come to grips with this happening. He was a wonderful man, and I'll miss him more than anyone will know. I loved him so much."

"I know, Missy. He loved you very much, too. This is not the time to talk about this, but I'll make sure the one responsible for this is dealt with, trust me." She slowly nodded in agreement.

"I hope so Roman. I do. I know it won't bring him back, but I hope so."

They walked to the car. As Roman stopped to get in, he stared once more toward the hill. "They will be dealt with, John. Rest peacefully," he whispered to himself, then got under the wheel for the long trip back.

They pulled into Missy's driveway as darkness crept in. She offered coffee and snacks, but Roman and Diana politely declined. He walked to the door with Missy and they stood quietly for a few seconds. She squeezed his hand and looked directly into his eyes. "You and I never finished our conversation at the hospital. What did you want to ask me about Zach Stiles?"

"Missy, we won't talk about it now. Please do me a favor. Promise not to mention that I asked about Stiles. Trust me. I'll explain in detail later.

You must keep that to yourself. I may be able to find something out soon, if you'll just do that." Roman hugged her one more time and turned to go.

"Roman, I'll do exactly that. Be careful and let me know. I have confidence in you — that you will."

"I will. We'll be checking on you. Call if you need anything." He climbed into the Lincoln and drove away toward Diana's home.

"Roman, Honey, I know it's been a tough few days on you," Diana whispered softly. If you need some time alone, just say so. I'll understand." She leaned across the seat and rubbed the back of his head, brushing his hair downward.

"I appreciate the consideration. You're a sweet one." He tried to force a smile.

"Roman, I don't want to be intrusive at a time like this, but is something else bothering you? You seem a little distant toward me. I know this tragedy with John is enough to shake your very soul, but I don't know...."

"No, there's nothing else. Sorry I've been inattentive. Too much on my mind, I guess. If I didn't have you at a time like this, I don't know what I'd do." He kissed her on the cheek without taking his eyes off the road. She slid closer to him like they were in high school. He was trying not to let it show.

When they reached the Palmer's place, Roman accepted the offer to come in. He dreaded going back to his house, or even seeing that guest house and the driveway, for that matter. He knew Norris and Ella would be retired to their part of this huge house for the evening and very likely would not have to see Norris, Sr. On the other hand, strangely, he curiously wanted to engage him in conversation just to get a read on him. Diana and Roman were alone and talked of anything except today's funeral, or what had happened to John. The conversation seemed so meaningless, but nevertheless, helped.

"There's an abundance of good eating left in the kitchen from today, I'm sure. Always is. Let me fix us both a plate. It'll make you feel better, 'Hon'. She pulled him up from the deep sofa.

"Oh, thanks, but no thanks." Roman smiled wearily.

"I won't take no for an answer. We both can use some food at this point." They held hands as she pulled him down the long hallway.

"Don't fix me too much of whatever it is," Roman said, surveying the huge kitchen again. There were enough utensils hanging from one wall alone to furnish an average home. They were immaculate, appearing almost unused. Their household help had obviously done an outstanding job.

"How about a drink?" Diana enticed with a smile. "It might do you good. Relax you."

"I'll tell you what."

"What's that?"

"If you have one with me, I'll relent."

"What will it be? We've got bourbon, scotch, gin, beer. You name it."

"Do you have a little white wine? I'm not particular at this point."

"Let's try a little of this bottle of Paul Masson," Diana said, as she scanned the bottle while pulling it from the double refrigerator. She poured two glasses, they toasted each other, and Roman paced as he sipped. Diana pulled plate after plate of goodies from the refrigerator to warm up for them.

"Are your parents in bed this early, I wonder? Or, are they still up watching television?"

"Probably still up. You want me to get them out here?"

"No. No. Just wondered."

"Get the plates from the cabinet over there, if you will, 'Hon'." She brought out the warmed overs. They looked and smelled like they'd just been cooked. Pork chops, roast beef, mashed potatoes, green beans, turnip greens. The cornbread was even still soft enough to reheat. She sliced some tomatoes and they were in business.

Roman ate more than he intended. Probably from frustration or sheer hunger since several cups of coffee had been it for him. Diana saw the distance in his eyes as he glanced at her when he'd finished. She finished a modest amount of vegetables and pushed her plate away.

"You sure everything is all right, other than John?" She asked.

Roman hoped he disguised it well. "Sure. I'm just spent for the moment. Little time helps anything, I guess."

"Right. Maybe you can sleep a little better, since you were able to eat a good meal."

"I hope so. I could use a good night's sleep." He knew he wouldn't.

The door squeaked behind Roman, startling him. He turned to find himself almost face to face with Norris, Sr.

"Roman, I was sorry to hear about John Sessions. I didn't know him that well, but heard he was a nice young fellow." The voice sounded slightly nervous, and his eyes were a giveaway. Roman knew. He forced a handshake and stared noticeably at Norris. Diana was busy clearing the table and never noticed.

Roman couldn't resist the moment. "Yes, John was a great guy. An honest, unpretentious, damn good friend. Never hurt a person in his life. Then some coward, some sneaky, worthless excuse for a human, snuffs the life out of him from behind. It was not a pretty sight." He could feel his heart beating overtime again and his face beginning to flush. He tempered his words. "But, John's in a better place — than the one who did it is going to. Going to here- and eventually going to hereafter." Norris searched for words as he pulled open the refrigerator and poured a glass of grapefruit juice.

"I'm sure that the law will come up with something soon on his killer. Sometimes law enforcement people are slow solving these kind of things."

"It's the law that concerns me," Roman resounded. "To some degree that is. I'm not sure, since John's not really a local boy, so to speak, that they'll put forth the effort to see this through." Norris looked away, and gulped down half the glass before setting it down on the kitchen table.

"Dad, you must have been thirsty. Have you been working in the fields today?" Roman almost smiled from the uneasy sight. "No, just needed it, I guess."

"I'll bet," Roman mumbled as he turned his back to them.

"Dad, how about some food? I'll be glad to warm you up some."

"Not this late. Thanks anyway. I had plenty earlier. I'll head on in. Roman, let me know if there's anything I can do to help." Norris scratched his thin white hair, then closed the door behind him.

"You bet. See you later, Norris." Roman's voice trailed off, realizing the door had closed.

Then he turned to Diana. "How long has your dad had this place?"

"That's a good question, why?"

"No particular reason. Just wondering what the price of land must have been years ago versus now."

"I think my grandfather started the original place in the 1930s. Somewhere in there. I heard Dad say that he originally had 1,000 acres. Granddad, that is. I know Dad has several thousand acres now. I'm not exactly sure. He accumulated them in pretty good size blocks years ago. I'm sorry, I'm not much help," Diana laughed.

"I wasn't trying to be nosey, just curious." Roman wondered if the overhead had driven Norris to desperate measures of some sort. He couldn't justify it, or make sense of it at this point. Why would a man of his statue be rubbing elbows with a violent, crooked sheriff? "Have the crops been good lately? Again, I'm curious. Something to occupy my mind I guess."

"As far as I know. I really hate to admit it, but I don't keep tabs much on the business dealings of this place. I guess I should be more that way instead of being an artist. Rather, trying to be an artist, I should say." She lead Roman by the hand again back to the main den. He was glad to hear that she wasn't involved much in the financial aspects of the giant plantation.

"If you aren't an artist, I'd like to see a real one. I probably couldn't appreciate the talent, it would be so great. Seriously, I love your work. I've noticed your paintings more than you know." He pointed to the wall in front of them. "By the way, did you do that one of the stables with the lightning in the background?"

"Guilty".

"That one is exceptional."

"Thanks. You're making my head swell." She smiled and threw her arms around him, gazing into the blue eyes she loved. "I want you to go on home and try to block as much out of your mind as possible for a while. Easier said than done, but you know John was the kind of guy who would want you to carry on and live your life as fully as possible."

"I know he would. I'll just miss my friend." He stopped short of making a declaration of helping bring down the killer.

"Go home and get some rest. Call me if you can't sleep. I'm as close as the phone." They kissed tenderly. Roman lost himself momentarily in their embrace, and he could feel the passion igniting between the them as their bodies pressed against one another. But this was for a brief while, given the circumstances. They both knew there were many nights ahead for them to enjoy making love to one another. Not tonight.

He started to walk away, but reached back, and held her for a brief second, then left for his car and the ride back to Indian Bayou.

As he turned into the long driveway, he tried not to look to the spot where he had found John just two nights ago. So short a time and yet so much had happened. His eyes wandered, despite trying to look beyond the spot. It was all too vivid. He noticed one tiny light shining from the large two-story house adjacent to the driveway, approximately 75 feet away. All else was dark in the area, except for the outside light he had left on by the garage next to John's guest house. He didn't know the neighbors anywhere near him, since he had been in town such a short time. He wished, in a way, he had introduced himself earlier, but maybe he would see them soon. He saw what appeared to be a stooped, silver-haired old lady cut off the lamp. The one tiny light was now gone.

An empty feeling came over him as he opened the door to the rambling old house. He wished for a dog, or even a cat at this point. He hadn't owned a pet since his high school days in Tupelo, but one was a priority on his list whenever he finally settled down in the right place. He often dreamed of a few acres, some room to breathe, in contrast to where he had lived in the Sherman Oaks area of Los Angeles.

He was exhausted, but sleep, naturally, wouldn't come. He tried to sort out the whole situation, reasons for what had happened, what his next move would be. He thought of Diana, and if somehow, she possibly knew. He abruptly dismissed this fleeting thought. He could not figure Norris out in this. He tossed and turned, but concluded there was no doubt whatsoever about Sheriff Stiles. He knew he was right, but he had to figure out where to find some clean law officer to truly launch an investigation into John's death. He knew no one in this area would go far, if anywhere, with it. It would be closed later without solving, he was certain. Or worse, that maniacal fanatic Stiles, would implicate him falsely. He resolved to start anew tomorrow. Sleep finally came sometime after 2 a.m.

CHAPTER *6*

Roman woke at 7:00 A.M. Late! He showered and shaved, threw on a freshly pressed pair of Docker's, a long-sleeve plaid shirt and his loafers, then grabbed a cup of fresh, black coffee for the road. The foremost matter in his mind was to find that clean law enforcement officer he could explain the situation to about the Sheriff, and who would investigate him. One who would believe him. He knew it would be difficult, coming from him, someone who hadn't lived here in years and was here temporarily on a project, that itself, was controversial. He knew it had to be done, but he would move carefully and slowly, if need be. He had made his mental notes, and it was time to turn in his rented Lincoln. Too flashy. He remembered Harreld Chevrolet Co. in Canton, Mississippi the dealership that his dad had traded with for years. He knew his dad must have liked them to would drive all the way from Tupelo to Canton, some 145 miles each time he traded, for over twenty years. Roman remembered some of the shiny new Oldsmobiles he would accompany his Dad down to pick up, after the deal had been negotiated. He called information and got the number. He would lease some car or truck for the time he'd be here. This would be a refreshing change from the big black Lincoln. He wanted something that would blend in a little more with the local vehicles.

He called Harreld's and got the same salesman that his Dad always dealt with, K.W. Pace. He vaguely remembered the tall, unassuming gentlemen whose image always seemed a notch above that of most car salesmen. He'd been at Harreld's for thirty years.

"Pace. Can I help you?" The voice was deep and southern.

"Yes, sir. This is Roman Beckley. You may remember me. My dad was James Beckley from Tupelo. He traded there for years. Drove 88 Olds."

"I certainly do and I remember your quarterback days up the road. I forgot where you played pro ball. Where was it?"

"Los Angeles. That's been a while." Roman changed the subject quickly. "I may want to lease a car or truck from you. I'm not sure. You folks still do that?"

"You bet. You living in Tupelo now?"

"No, Mr. Pace, I'm down in Indian Bayou for a year or so. Can we work something out, short term, if I have to go back to Los Angeles before the lease is up? My company will be paying the lease, but you can put it in my name."

"Any son of James Beckley's can get special treatment around here. We can do whatever you like. Can you come on down and let's pick you out something that'll fit your needs? Oh, you said you were in Indian Bayou. Better watch your step there. I had a friend whose son got arrested for speeding. He talked back to the sheriff and got beat up pretty bad. I think they threatened a lawsuit but never did follow through. Anyway, watch for that sheriff."

"I'll watch for him." Roman couldn't believe a man this far away knew someone who had a bad experience with him also. "Matter of fact, I'll be down by ten or thereabouts. I've got to go to Jackson and turn in this one to the rental company. Can someone come pick me up down there since it's not but a few miles? I hate to ask that, but I don't know any other way to get there. I've already called in the billing and the rental company just needs me to turn it in."

"I'll do better than that. No need for you to drive on to Jackson. Just stop here, you pick out a vehicle you like, and we'll get the car on to the rental place."

"Great! See you in a couple of hours. I look forward to seeing you again."

Roman drove the two hours, leased a one-year-old, four-door Chevy Blazer, Navy with silver trim, and was headed northwest toward Indian Bayou by lunch. Worldwide's comptroller would be proud of him for the deal: The price was right and the vehicle was perfect for what he needed; something to haul some things in; and to carry passengers if necessary. However, this wasn't the first thing on his mind.

He drove back via Greenwood and noticed the cotton crops had mostly been picked and ginned. As he turned west on Highway 82 from Greenwood, towards Indian Bayou, his eye caught the sign posted in the other direction: Clarksdale 52 miles Highway 49 North. He knew Clarksdale was supposed to ring a bell.

He remembered. It was Lula! Lula was the very small community just north of Clarksdale where Rex McCall was from- Rex McCall who was a longtime friend of his family. They had visited the McCall home often during his childhood, and the McCalls made it to Tupelo, occasionally. McCall had been the Chief Investigator — Mississippi Highway Patrol for years. This man was known for years, throughout law enforcement circles, as one tenacious, tough cop. He had not talked to Rex since before Leah was killed, but knew he and his wife Joan had left a message twice on his answering machine to offer their sympathy. He could not remember being this glad to remember someone from the past. For the first time in days, he felt a surge of energy and rolled down the front windows of the Blazer to take in the breeze of September's end. An eighteen wheeler, loaded with chemicals, shot past him and rocked his Blazer.

He pulled into a nearby truck stop as he entered the Indian Bayou area. Garth Brooks was blasting from the jukebox inside the restaurant. He put one finger to his ear as he leaned against the wall in the hall and dialed information for Lula. He decided not to use his home phone for the call. Maybe paranoid, but better safe than sorry. A cellular phone was a priority, but he put off that constant link to the L.A. office for the time being.

"Number for Rex McCall, please," Roman asked the operator.

"What city, sir?"

"Oh, yes, excuse me. Lula. Coahoma County. I believe."

After a solid thirty seconds, she came back on. "I'm sorry sir, but that is a non-published number." Damn.

"Any other number I can help with?"

"No. Uh...." Roman placed the receiver back on its hook and stared outside. Three drivers were climbing down out of their rigs at the same time, heading for a break at the coffee shop. Two rigs were side by side rumbling enough to shake the place. The smell of cigarettes permeated the air around him. One driver sucked hard on his Winston as he walked toward the shower and special room reserved for truckers in the rear. Another short, big bellyed driver shouted into the phone in the area that was off limits to non-truckers.

MID-MISSISSIPPI REGIONAL LIBRARY SYSTEM
Attala, Holmes, Leake, Montgomery
And Winston Counties

Roman remembered Mrs. McCall, Rex's Mother. She'd have to be in her eighties by now, and possibly she still lived there. Hopefully, she was not a casualty to a nursing home like so many near that age.

He dialed long distance information once again.

"Do you have a Mrs. McCall in Lula. I'm not sure of the first name. There can't be that many. Rex McCall's number is unlisted."

"Sir, there is one more. 'L. R. McCall'." Roman got the number and knew it had to be her.

The phone rang four times. "Hello. McCall residence" The voice belonged to a younger female.

He feared the worst, but asked softly, "Is Mrs. McCall in, please?"

"No. I'm sorry, but she's gone. Who is this?" The voice was inquisitive.

"I'm Roman Beckley, an old family friend of Rex's. Just thought I'd call. I've been living in California and out of touch. I really want Rex's number. That's the reason I called."

"Can't give that out to anyone. Rex is very careful who gets his number. You understand. Maybe his mother will give you the number. She's down the road playing bridge." Roman exhaled and rolled his eyes back.

"Is there a phone where she is?"

"Certainly is. She and a couple of her lady friends have coffee every morning, and every afternoon they play bridge at a different home. They rotate. This afternoon they're over at Mrs. Talbert's. Only about a mile. I just come in each morning to help out around here. My husband leases this place to farm and I get bored. Just try to help Mrs. McCall." He just wanted the number.

"Thanks for your help."

"Yeah. You're welcome. Good luck on gettin' the line. They do some gossipin' in person and on their pipeline. Oh, I see the number here by the phone. Ruth Tolbert 899-8789. Gotta go. Hope you get that line, son. Bye."

Roman hung up and dialed Mrs. Tolbert's number. She was right. The bonk, bonk, bonk, busy sound of a rural phone system jolted his eardrum. After two more tries in succession, he got a ring. Mrs. Tolbert answered after four rings, and after several attempts to hear what Roman was asking, handed the phone anyway to Mrs. McCall.

"Mrs. McCall, this is Roman Beckley. Remember me? I used to come with my folks several years ago, fifteen or so, to visit Rex and y'all, and the grandchildren." He had forgotten the names. "I'm in Mississippi again for a while and thought I'd get in touch with your son. I haven't seen Rex in a few years and wondered how he was." Roman shifted his weight and kicked two cigarette butts away from the floor by his feet. A trucker and his wife strolled by. She cast a quick glance at Roman. He nodded to her, while straining to hear Mrs. McCall over the latest Reba McIntyre song that just came blaring through the opened restaurant door. The music subsided as the door closed slowly.

"You darlin' boy. It's so sweet of you to call an old lady." He searched for the right answer to that.

"I hope you've been well. How's Rex? How's Joan?" After listening to three minutes of Rex's whereabouts for the past four years or so, she got around to where he was presently.

"He's in West Memphis today. Some business about a trucking firm that's experiencing theft. Don't ask me what. That's all I know. He's living back here now in Lula and commuting to Memphis about three days a week. Good to have Joan around here — with all the crime going on in this world."

"I can imagine. Could you give me his phone number, please ma'am?"

"It's unlisted as always, but for you, you sweet thing, I can give it out. Hold on while I get my book out of my purse." Roman hung onto the silence, then the papers rattled. "899-9878. I know he'll want to hear from you. I do miss your mom and dad. I believe your mom's over at your brother's, the last time I heard. It's so bad your Dad passed away at such a young age. Its especially young to me at my age, you know. Well, come see us. They're calling me back to the table. Bye. Bye."

Roman shook his head and smiled warmly. Talking to Mrs. McCall reminded him so much of conversations with his own grandmother Beckley; the warm sincerity and concern ladies of that era had, and some men for that matter. There seemed to be less of that today he thought as he dialed Rex. On the first ring Rex's wife answered.

"Joan?"

"Yes"

"This is Roman. Roman Beckley."

"Sweetheart, you didn't have to tell me. I'd recognize that voice anywhere. It's been a long time. I can't believe it, because I was just talking to Rex on Saturday about you. Football talk, you know."

"Yes. I do remember. You were as big a fan as Rex. Are you both doing okay?"

"Well that rascal still lives in the road as much as he does at home. It's in his blood, you know. Guess all those years as Chief Investigator for the patrol left him restless."

"Is he still in good shape?" Though in his mid sixties, Rex was built solid, like a wrestler, with no hair, except some short silky blond around the sides. He had massive arms, and was known to wear a diamond ring as big as a quarter on his right ring finger, not to mention other jewelry. He frequented better men's shops and dressed more like a Wall Street executive than a law enforcement investigator, especially while off a case.

"To be just past sixty-five, or rather as he puts it, just past sixty, I'll have to admit he's in good shape. He still runs three miles everyday and lifts weights like he thinks he's twenty. He has a little problem with arthritis, but overall, he's still tough as nails." Roman was glad to hear this, that he was not off on some permanent fishing detail.

"Is he gone now?"

"Yes, wouldn't you know when you call, after all this time, he'd be out of town. He's flying tonight out to Las Vegas. Can you believe that? At least, he's not much of a gambler that I know of anyway. No, he has to do some investigative work out there. He'll call me tomorrow and let me know where he is staying for sure. Why don't you leave your number?"

Roman thought for a second. "Let me call him back. When do you expect him back?"

"I know he'll be back by day after tomorrow. Saturday at the latest. Be sure and call him back, Roman."

"Oh, I will. I will for sure. Good talking to you Joan. I look forward to seeing you both very soon." They both hung up smiling.

The phone rang and the clerk called for the Sheriff. The foreign-sounding voice pretended to call about work at Stiles's nearby farm to reach him. This was done since there were legitimate calls from time to time, from migrant workers who toiled in the cotton fields and other harvests, on swings they made through the Delta in search of work.

It was time to talk other than by phone. The foreign voice wanted Zach Stiles in Bogota, Columbia at once. "What's the problem, my good man? Distrustful of me?"

"No, my friend. Only it's time we meet again, face to face, rather than through channels. Get my drift." The voice was low, but firm.

"I'm not sure. I thought you were pleased with our set up. The first four shipments have gone as smooth as ice." The sheriff rared back in his chair and looked at his highly-shined, black riding boots.

"Oh, you've been counting. Just checking. I know exactly how many shipments and exactly how many pounds and ounces, Sheriff. It's a rule I have, that once I reach a certain volume with customers, I insist on another personal meeting. You have a problem with that? You know I went to painful lengths to check this out carefully before I would do business with a man of the law. Let's just say, your reputation is acceptable. I have ways of knowing. I could say, a man with his own law." The foreign voice laughed. Stiles frowned on the other end. "Sheriff, you can thank the friends you made in Vietnam every night for putting us in touch with each other."

"Yes, you never know when old connections will pay off. Well, I'll see if at least I can come down soon. I can't promise the exact date."

"You will be down here by Saturday or the deal is on hold, until I decide otherwise, my friend. There is no more discussing. You have until midnight tonight to confirm the trip."

Stiles hung up, his temperature boiling. He was not accustomed to an ultimatum, especially from a foreigner. He walked past the nearest cell where two inmates were talking incessantly about who had the best team in the NFL. Suddenly, he stopped and called a large, overweight Mexican worker to the cell door. Stiles delivered three violent blows with his hand-carved nightstick to his mid section, crumbling him to the floor, moaning. The black cellmate jumped back and fled to the corner of his cell.

"Keep the idle chatter down in my jail, you idiot," he growled to the Mexican, lying with his hands gripping his ribs. Stiles had taken his frustrations out on the nearest subject, who just happened to be Mexican. Violence was a trademark he wore proudly, but secretly. He could be upstanding and convincing to the voting public in general, but he was very careful with his dark side. He would not let anyone demand from him, not even a Columbian drug lord. However, he knew that this man was never crossed if the person wanted to live to a ripe old age. It was expected from this Columbian and came with the territory. The sheriff was another story altogether. He got great satisfaction from being a "bad ass". He learned the game well from the Viet Cong years ago, and had put that to use like no other veteran. He was intrigued by anything that was dangerous and mysterious. He stared at the picture of the Rallye aircraft he had purchased recently from an airplane trade magazine. He had it painted black for a dual purpose and kept it hidden from the local people. Yes, if the Columbian wanted to intimidate anyone, he had better look elsewhere. Still, he knew he needed the man from Bogota.

Zach Stiles made the decision in plenty of time, four hours before midnight. He used his personal telephone credit card to transact the business he didn't want to show up on the sheriff's office phone bill. He squinted to see the number from the one lamp light burning on his desk.

"Cortez?"

"Yes. This is Emil."

"I'll be there Saturday. I've got a lot of covering my bases, so I won't be obviously missed at this end, but I will be there before nightfall."

"Good. I see it is 'Cortez' now. It was 'Emil' in all our other little chats. Are you perturbed at having to come to my fine country?" The sarcasm came through loud and clear.

"I don't like being given an order, or told what to do by anyone. But to keep this operation running smoothly, I'll come. There's too much money involved. So if I must, I'll be there. End of story."

"That's all I wanted to hear." Cortez spoke slowly and deliberately." I have done some thinking since we spoke. Consider it a little test of your loyalty, or, shall we say, need to cooperate. Which is it? I guess it doesn't matter at this point. There is no need for you to come here after all. You passed the test. I will be in New Orleans Saturday and we can meet again. The last few months seem like years. We have lots to discuss about your future and mine and certain other people. I will arrive, actually, late Friday night, and see you Saturday, say, about two o'clock. I will be staying at a small insignificant hotel, The Dauphine Orleans. It's in the French Quarter. Know where it is?"

"No, but I can find it, I'm sure." Stiles was still trying to disguise the attitude he was wearing on his sleeve.

"Incidentally, come alone," Emil demanded. "I don't like crowds. Do you?"

"Never have. I'm a big boy who can take care of himself."

"Until Saturday — Sheriff." Emil faded away on the long distance line. Stiles called him a few choice names after hanging up. He didn't like Emil's attitude, but the change to New Orleans took a lot of the sting out. He would be more comfortable on his own turf, even if it was in Cajun country.

Stiles dialed Deputy Wiggins and summoned him from his bedroom to the courthouse office. He assured Stiles he'd be there in ten minutes flat.

The wastebasket in the rear of the room rattled. "What the hell are you still doing up here, lady?" Stiles barked at the slightly bent, pale, cleaning lady.

"Just finishing up, sir. My husband is finishing on the other floor. We'll be right out. She spoke slowly, barely audible. Stiles turned his back and carried on as if she were a piece of the furniture.

Then he ordered: "Don't forget to dust this desk and polish it until it shines. You're in here almost every night, so there's no excuse for missing it," he scowled, but still never turned around. Wiggins burst into the door, ten minutes flat, as promised.

"Wiggins, get the others and call a meeting for midnight at our regular place. There's no reason for anyone to miss. I've got to go to Jackson this weekend to a sheriff's meeting for the Boys' Ranch. The one sheriffs sponsor. There are matters here to be carried out while I'm gone that'll be brought up tonight. Bring the car around, not the county vehicle. Be sure to tell the others to do exactly as the last meeting. You know where to turn and where we're to meet. Make certain there are no lights once each one of you veers off Planters Road. I don't want anyone aroused at that hour. You can start the fire once you're in the field, since it's well blocked from view, that far from the road. Remember, no lights off that road. Any foul-ups and you'll be the sacrifice this time. Understand? The dress is black tonight." The door creaked as the old lady shuffled out, her rags and mop in hand.

CHAPTER 7

It was the first night Roman and Diana had been together in what seemed like a month, and they showed it. Despite the tragedy and distractions, they made love and he knew he needed her. He needed her physically and emotionally. It was mutual. The last few days had drawn them closer than they had even intended. Whenever her father entered his mind for a fleeting second, he diverted his thoughts. He would only focus on their relationship, convinced she knew nothing, and he didn't care to explore the possibility of it with her. Her family was her family, and their actions and motives were not necessarily the same as hers. He had to try to disassociate any thoughts of Norris as her father.

"I appreciate how wonderful you've been during the last few days," Roman whispered. He propped on his elbow and looked at her beautiful face glowing in the faint light of the radio on the night stand. Her sensuous green eyes slowly danced, studying his face.

"It comes naturally with you." She smiled, looking up at him, touching his chin and mouth. She gently brushed back the damp hair from his perspiring forehead. The sound of Harry Connick, Jr.'s rendition of an old Bobby Darin classic, "Beyond the Sea" was soothing the late night airways.

The ringing phone interrupted the moment. Roman jerked his head around instinctively, patted her cheek, and reached for the phone on the bedside table.

"Pardon, who?" Roman sat straight up in the bed and pointed for Diana to turn down the little volume they had on the radio. "Mrs. Hendrix? Yes.

Yes. This is Roman Beckley?" Diana watched his face as he reacted in surprise. "The Sheriff! Where did you get the idea I might be interested in him? Yes, but I'm only an employee of Worldwide Industries — down here to set up the new waste facility, not a detective." Diana watched him fiddle with the pen from the table, tapping it like a drummer getting warmed up for a concert. He was absorbing the information, but trying to be nonchalant.

Roman turned and sat on the edge of the bed and gave her a huge wink in order to curb her curiosity. "Let me tell you this. If this is some hoax or a joke, it's not very funny." There was a long silence as he listened. "I see. I didn't mean to be testy, but this comes as a surprise to me. Can I meet you somewhere to talk privately? Why not?" He listened further. "I understand. Well, we can work that out later. I don't know why you'd be doing this if you weren't truthful with me." Diana was now pacing slowly with the remainder of the glass of Chablis she hadn't finished when the lights were dimmed at 9:30. It had lost its chill at this point, but she never noticed.

"I got you. New Orleans? He said Jackson! Why did he do that? I'm still not sure why you're telling me." He pointed to his bare chest, as if the caller was present. Yet, he was convinced that the caller was legitimate. He hung up and wouldn't try to figure out why she called, just make the best of the tip.

"Honey, no need to tell you, that was a strange call," Roman said to Diana, raising his hands with palms up, his brow wrinkled.

"It must have been — by the intense look on your face. That wasn't one of your secret admirers calling you and got you in a bind, was it Darling?" Diana smiled and kissed him tenderly on the back of his neck, as he stared straight ahead. Her comment didn't get much reaction as he replayed the call in his mind.

As if awakened from a trance, Roman shook his head slightly and said, "No, you know better than that. You're all I need and can handle." She laughed and doubled her fist jokingly. "We have to talk," Roman said, seriously. "I need to talk to only the right people."

Her smile faded. "What do you mean?"

"Oh, Nothing. Just talking to myself, I guess. He stopped and chose his words carefully. "Diana, I think you know how much you mean to me. I hope the feeling is mutual."

"You know it is." Her compassionate eyes searched his face, wondering where he was going with this.

"That's wonderful. Then, we should be able to tell each other anything in confidence, if need be. Notice, I said, if need be."

"That goes without saying." She reassured him, brushing his blond hair back just above his ears, resting her other arm on his shoulder. He gave her a tender hug as their lips met.

"Now, that's what I call willful compliance." He eased back. They both smiled and looked deeply into each other's eyes.

"Diana, never tell anyone what I am about to tell you. I could possibly be wrong, but I don't think so."

"I've already given you my word. It's always been good. I was taught that years ago." Roman felt his stomach sink ever so slightly.

"I know, Honey, I never worry about your word. You are an exceptional woman."

"So, go on. Relax. It can't be that bad. Just say it."

"Diana, I have reason to believe...let me say, *strong* reason to believe that Sheriff Zach Stiles is one sinister human being. He may be involved in some, shall we say, illegal things."

"I'm not sure about that. Zach Stiles has a way of alienating people, but I think unintentionally. I mean, he has a gruff exterior, but I think he may be more bark than bite," Diana volunteered rather naively.

"Trust me on this. He's anything but pretending. The man's dangerous. That's not all." He hesitated, picked up the warm, half-filled glass of wine and downed it.

"Roman, go on," she insisted.

"I think he may know who killed John," Roman said, his voice tapering off. He frowned and set the glass down on the night table. He had stopped short of saying he *knew* Stiles killed John.

"You're serious?"

"Very."

"That's a strong accusation, Honey."

"I know it is, and I'm prepared to back it up. In time. I'm convinced there's even more to this. Again, you've got to trust me. Don't even tell your parents, or brother. Please."

"You have my word, like I said."

"The lady that called said she had some vital information about Stiles. Just out of the blue. Sounded like she was on the level. If I were a betting man, I'd say she was telling me the truth. I don't know what she would have to gain, unless its some sick prank. Or worse, she could be trying to set me up. But I don't think so. She said her name was Mrs. Hendrix. Know anyone by that name?"

"Doesn't ring a bell, but I've been away from here for quite a while."

"She told me she worked at the Sheriff's office, but not to call for her there, because it would be disastrous for her. I told her I definitely would respect her wishes. I can certainly see why she'd say that. Like I said, he's deadly. The man is possessed or something. He's one evil man. He must have two personalities to get elected around here and keep some of this behavior hidden from the public. This Mrs. Hendrix told me that Stiles is going to New Orleans early Saturday. She thinks it's a meeting about drugs with someone from far away. She couldn't be specific, but she did say Stiles told his deputy and others he's going to Jackson to a sheriff's meeting about a Boys' Ranch that the sheriffs have sponsored for years for underprivileged boys."

Roman pulled back the window curtains slowly and looked into the darkness. "Diana, I want to follow him to New Orleans to see who he's meeting down there. I'm no detective, but I'll think of something to watch him from a distance. I'll play it by ear, but I have to go. Maybe I can get a car tag number, or something, to help bring this man down. Someone has to get to the bottom of John's murder. Of course, the county sheriff's office is handling the so-called investigation. If we had lived within the city limits instead of just on the edge of town, I assume the city police would have some jurisdiction. We just fell within the county jurisdiction by a few hundred yards. I don't want to say anything further to anyone in law enforcement, because I don't know who to trust. That is, until I'm able to contact an old friend of mine, who used to be in law enforcement here. By here, I mean around Mississippi. He can steer me, if anyone can, to the right clean law man or department to get John's case solved, and the murderer prosecuted. I don't want to do anything to jeopardize that. I mean anything. I've decided that I am going down there Friday. That'll give me tomorrow to do some work here and get down there after that."

"I'm going too. Two sets of eyes see more than one anyway," Diana spoke up.

"No. Absolutely not. I won't have you taking that risk."

"There is no way I'll stay here. We'll be careful. If by some weird chance he happened to see us, we could just be in New Orleans on a lark. Besides, I have done several shows in New Orleans and have a couple of paintings exhibited there now. I'm sure even he's aware of that. It wouldn't look completely suspicious if we were seen there by him — just coincidental. Like I said, he or anyone else, is not going to see us. You can accomplish what you need better with me, as I explained." He reluctantly smiled in agreement.

"I don't mean to keep on, but it's crucial that it go no further." He pulled her long hair back, cradling her face in his hands, lost for the moment again, in those dominant green eyes. They kissed passionately and mutually made their way back to the bed. He knew he could confide in her.

Roman got Diana back to the plantation in time for a few hours sleep, before her tennis match was to begin at the local country club. It was a benefit tournament for the local chapter of the heart association. He hurried back to his place and locked the door behind him instantly. The old, stately room echoed as he walked across the thirsty hardwood floors. He had never been one to be paranoid, but pulled the curtains tightly and avoided lighted windows for a while. He undressed down to his Jockey shorts and crawled under the sheets. The radio was still on low with some tranquil, classical piece flowing from it.

What was the name of the hotel Mrs. Hendrix said Stiles would be in? He couldn't remember, but it would come to him. He couldn't call her, because he'd promised not to jeopardize her safety. She did say she would be back in touch. He remembered that much. He fell asleep after midnight.

He was up early and ran for four miles to clear his mind, besides needing the exercise to keep in shape. He was back at the house by 7:30 a.m. He showered, donned his olive cotton suit, a pale-green pinpoint cotton shirt and paisley tie, grabbed his usual cup of black coffee, and headed for town.

He passed by the nearby truck stop and decided, for a change, to eat breakfast and catch his breath. A short, squatty waitress with a pencil stuck in her hair, chewed gum non-stop while she slid the plastic menu sheet under his eyes. She automatically poured him a steaming cup of coffee, placed a container of cream before him without asking, and headed to another table. A trucker behind him was complaining about getting a scales violation near Greenville while crossing the Mississippi River from Arkansas. The waitress was back in a jiffy with pencil in hand. But she looked over Roman and flirted with the truckers nearby, before finally glancing down at him.

"I'll have pancakes and two eggs over easy. Rather, can you have them done over medium that is, because I only eat the whites?" he asked.

She faked a smile. "Why would you just eat the whites?"

"Cholesterol. Yoke has too much."

She nodded, clearly not used to this from early-morning truckers and farmers.

He grabbed a Memphis Commercial Appeal newspaper and skimmed the world news. He looked for the Mississippi section, and there was an article about the new facility proposed to be built outside Indian Bayou. It was on the second page of the second section, but nevertheless, it was there. It was fairly vague, except that Governor Dean Posey and Lt. Governor Jim Crawford managed to get some good press about their efforts to clear the way for the new project to become a reality. A couple of local legislators, were also quoted, taking their share of the credit for helping bring jobs, tax revenue and a long-term commitment for the area from Worldwide Industries' high-tech hazardous waste facility. They mentioned Gardner Lowe, President of Worldwide, and quoted him as to how thrilled he and the company were over "the marriage with the community". He specifically stressed the safety, the clean atmosphere, and dedication of the company in keeping the surrounding land intact and unharmed. Gardner Lowe was a master at diplomacy and flawless in baiting the people with figures in the millions and millions that would flow from the facility.

However, there were unfavorable quotes from a couple of outspoken landowners about the impact on the surrounding land. They definitely had their reservations. Too many people had farmed this extremely rich soil for too many years to risk even the possibility of hindering their crops from producing at full capacity. Roman's name was not mentioned, and he was glad. He had enough problems, and the job was difficult enough. He didn't want too many people knowing his name, for as long as possible. He needed as much privacy as he could get, in order to do his job, and pursue the other matter.

Roman declined the next cup of coffee, left a dollar tip and headed for the cash register. He came squarely in view of the Mayor, who ambled through the front door and slid into the only large oval booth by the cashier's station. Sort of an unwritten rule was that only the regular truckers or certain locals took this special booth. Mayor Engle's eyes darted around the room, before acknowledging Roman. He was visibly nervous, stirring madly in the coffee cup the waitress had promptly slid before him.

"I understand the boy who got shot was a friend of yours, Mr. Beckley. That was bad. I'm sorry." He instantly changed the subject, as he slurped half his coffee. "I hope you're finding Indian Bayou to your liking." Roman hesitated, the Mayor squirmed and signaled for more coffee with the raise of his index finger.

"I'm managing," Roman replied. "I'll be here to the end of the job for sure."

"Well, like I told you before, if there's anything I can do for you, or your company, all you have to do is ask. Just want to make sure that the good citizens of this town are kept abreast of anything of interest with this high-tech waste outfit."

Roman looked into his fat face, the insincere eyes, and nodded.

"Mayor, you'll be the first to know. Then you can pass it on. I wouldn't want you not to keep the people advised."

His eyes darted away, then back at Roman. "Thank you, Mr. Beckley."

"It's Roman, Mr. Mayor, just Roman." He pushed the front door open, breathed the cool morning air, then slid under the wheel of his Blazer and cruised toward his office, a quarter of a mile away.

He had written the names of the two landowners in his pocket notebook and checked the local phone book for their numbers. He dialed each and was able to make contact. He introduced himself by phone. After a chilling initial response, he was able to manage an appointment to come out for a short visit. The second did not come to the phone at all. He would wait. He searched the county records again for the other bordering property owner. It was none other than Norris Palmer, Sr. Surprise!

Roman met with the first landowner, since he did sympathize with the man's concerns. He was keen to the fact that this man was well thought of around the whole county and knew it would be a plus to win him over. He soothed a lot of the planter's frustrations about his nearby land and hopefully calmed his fears. The other nearby landowners would hear about it, he knew. A lot of battles would have to be won with the local farmers before the war was won. They didn't care what the Governor or any politician had to say about the financial impact to the community. They were concerned about their land, crops, surroundings, their livelihood. He would save his contact with Palmer for a later date.

For the rest of the day, Roman returned several phone calls, finished reports, and thought about Diana. And John. When he was about to call it a day at 6:00 p.m., he remembered the call that had to be made to Gardner Lowe. He was surprised that Lowe hadn't called Indian Bayou for him yet, so he dialed the L.A. office for his direct extension. This time he was in.

"Roman, Good to hear from you. Sorry I missed you a few days ago. I've been incredibly busy. How's Indian Bayou?" He didn't want to know.

"Not bad, Gardner. Hope I'm making some progress with the locals. There is a certain group of them with some reservations. Well-founded ones. They aren't some hillbillies, either. These are intelligent, strong-willed people. I feel like, it'll be better, given time. The site looks good. Weather's been a little rainy, but cooler than usual for this time of year, down here, at least." He'd said all he could generalize about. He didn't want Gardner Lowe to know anymore than he had to. About anything, for now.

But Gardner said, "Elton Sanders and I may come down soon, to solidify things for you. I'll give you the flight and so on. It'll be after this next week for sure."

Good, Roman thought. He could visualize these two executives coming to Indian Bayou: Lowe, in his Brooks Brothers suit, silk tie, and silver hair somewhat longer than most men in their late fifties, and with his ever-present tan, could be a mature, executive-looking model. He contrasted with Elton Sanders, "Mr. Conservative." His drab dark suits, bow ties, and wing tips blended with his very short-cropped, brown and gray hair. He could look out of place anywhere, but was never outsmarted by anyone.

"Let me know your itinerary," Roman said. I can pick you up in Jackson to the south, or in Memphis to the north. We're about half way between the two of them."

"We'll probably come into the Jackson airport. I may want to drop in to speak to the Governor, if he's in town. We've spoken once before, a few weeks ago. I've got an open invitation, if I can call a day or two in advance. May do that. Roman, I've got the meeting about to begin for the Minnesota sight. Have to run. We'll talk later. Let Elton or anyone else know of anything you need. I have confidence in you doing the job without a lot of interference at this early stage. See you later."

Roman sighed, sat at his desk for a few seconds after hanging up, then dialed Diana.

"Hello, Honey. Hope you did well in the tournament."

"I got lucky. It was just a small draw. Not too many tournament players here."

"Great. Is there anything you don't do well?"

"Roman, you're embarrassing me. Did you have a good day?"

"Uneventful, I guess. I got done what I needed. You sure you don't want to back out on going with me down there tomorrow? I still think you should stay here."

"I'm pretending I didn't hear that. Just pick me up at whatever time you want to leave."

"Is eight too early in the morning?"

"Are you kidding? I'll be up long before that."

"I'll make it at eight, anyway. That's time enough."

"Why don't you come by tonight? But, if you're tired, I'll look forward to seeing your bright little face in the morning."

"You know I want to see you, but I'd better go on and we both can get packed and so forth. Get a good night's sleep." He wanted to see her, but wanted to miss seeing Norris, Sr. at this point.

"Will you call me later tonight before you hit the sack, Honey?"

"You better believe it. Talk to you later."

He laid a suitcase on the bed and threw in two pairs of Levi's, a pair of Dockers, one long-sleeve silk red shirt, and a couple of short-sleeve knit shirts in solid and print. He unzipped his shaving kit and filled it with the usual necessities. He almost forgot an extra pair of loafers. Better too many pieces, than not enough.

Speaking of pieces, he would feel better with his .357 back under the seat. He would get another one, probably. He felt prepared after making his mental inventory. His feet rested on the coffee table in front of him as he sank into the couch. He crossed them comfortably, pushed off his soft loafers, and dimmed the lighting on the three way lamp to its lowest illumination. He picked up his old acoustical guitar, his trusty friend and solace, and began to play and sing songs he had long embraced in his memory. He had learned to play guitar from an old friend in high school, and he enjoyed the self satisfaction of making music from the strings. Singing came naturally from his early days of childhood in the church choir. He had been blessed with natural pitch and had once harbored hopes of a singing career. He kept that dream alive in from high school on through professional football, giving it up only after his pro career ended. Singing, although somewhat regretfully, was now in proper perspective as a means of expression and for his own enjoyment.

He tried to watch some television, but kept returning to the guitar, to play and sing, until nearly midnight. The feelings he released through the songs gave him momentary peace. Very momentary. Late, he called Diana. They talked anxiously, but briefly, about the trip tomorrow. With his eyes at half-mast, he hung up and fell into bed.

CHAPTER 8

It was 7:15 a.m. and the sun appeared to be out for the day. Roman threw his bag into the rear compartment behind the back seat of the Blazer, and pulled the gate up to meet the back window. He reserved space on the back seat for what he knew Diana would likely require for her bags, clothes, and other things ladies normally pack.

He ran back in the house for a quick scan of the place, before locking the door. His eyes swept across the den as he was ready to close and lock the door. His eyes darted back to the picture on the mantel of his father posing with him after a Rams and Dolphins game. Behind them on the field, a mountain of a lineman stood with his Miami Dolphin uniform in full view. That's it! Dolphin. That's the sound. Dauphine. Dauphine Orleans, the hotel where Stiles will be. That's what Mrs. Hendrix had said. What a coincidence. He smiled at the picture of them as he closed the door.

"If I don't get more work done for Worldwide soon, Gardner Lowe will be an unhappy camper," Roman told Diana, as he loaded her two large bags and a small one into the back seat area.

"I doubt that. They'd understand under the circumstances, I'm sure." She hung her olive and rust-colored cotton dress on the hook. Though fall was about here officially, it still got warm during the day, especially in New Orleans. Transition clothing was definitely the order of the day.

They pulled away from the giant plantation, and Roman had to dodge "Champ", the German shepherd, who couldn't resist escorting them to the end of the half-mile-long split-rail fence. Roman was glad Norris, Sr. was not there when they left. They waved goodbye to Norris, Jr., sitting in his wheelchair near the end of the fence. A worker sat nearby in a pickup to bring him back to the house, when he wished to return. From this spot, he watched the horses roam, cattle graze, and the few cars that passed.

"Please, don't think I'm meddling, but does he ever talk about his condition?"

"No. He never does. I know it's been tough for him. That's obvious."

"I can imagine. I can see the hurt in his eyes. It must be hard for the rest of your family too. I didn't mean to bring that up, first thing in the morning. I just wondered."

Diana seemed to take the cue. "That's quite all right. The actual wounding is never discussed. Of course, I was only eight years old, or so, when he first went to Vietnam. I do remember, believe it or not, how handsome my older brother was in his U.S. Army officer's uniform. There was quite a span between our ages, and I really idolized him. He was fourteen, I think, when I was born. You know, the late arrival in life. Then, it was unusual for a woman to have a child again in her late thirties. I used to hear as I grew up about his football days. They still remembered him around here. He was quite a star in high school. I would get embarrassed when he would have a date with some 'sweetie' and I would meet her. I was almost jealous if she took any time away from him and me. What I remember most is, that he taught me to ride horses when I was only about six, while he was in college. I know he idolized my Dad and from what Mom told me, he wanted to please Dad with all his heart. I guess that's the reason he wanted to be an Army officer in Vietnam. My Dad, you know, was a decorated pilot in World War II. Like the old saying about like father, like son. I know he really must have wanted to be. You know my brother's also quite an artist himself, but no matter how hard I try, he won't let me display any of it, anywhere. I won't give up on him doing it though. He's probably going to sketch some out there today if the mood hits him. Maybe someday...."

They were soon passing on the outskirts around Belzoni, on the way to New Orleans, via Jackson. The proud billboard read: "Belzoni, Ms., Catfish Capitol of The World". There was much evidence of that, as every few miles another group of the neatly-squared bodies of water appeared. They were man-made, well-manicured ponds filled with thousands of the whiskered, slick little fish that were money makers for the local economy.

There were several catfish-processing plants that employed many people along the way. They were a non-conflicting compliment to the king — cotton.

"How would you like to do that all day?" Roman pointed out the driver's side window to the plant they were passing, where droves of mostly black workers donned hair nets and carved and cut fish on various shifts, night and day. He had seen them coming off shifts around Indian Bayou.

"Well, it could be worse, I'm sure," she replied. If these places weren't in production, there would be a lot less jobs for them." She sipped the coffee she'd brought from the Palmer kitchen and poured Roman a black one from the thermos.

"Oh, I didn't mean anything was wrong with it. I know it's a vital industry around these parts. I'm sure everyone's glad to have the employ-ment and what it does money-wise for the Delta."

They made decent time, despite encountering an occasional piece of farm machinery creeping along the highway. Most of the farm machinery had long before made it to an appointed work place. Eight o'clock was the middle of the day for most farmers.

They noticed Yazoo City in the distance and stopped at the large inter-section of Highway 49 and 16. The coffee demanded it.

"Jackson can't be more than another hour, huh?" Roman asked, as he surveyed the hillside. They were out of the flat land of the Delta, approaching the hills.

As Diana stretched her long, tanned, shapely legs and stopped, she saw the billboard for 3-Bar-W Western World in Jackson. She pointed to the sign as they zipped past. "That's what we need! Western outfits. It said High Street exit. That's right off the interstate, right on the way to New Orleans."

"Western outfits? Are you kidding?"

"It may sound silly to you, but we shouldn't dress as we normally do, in the unlikely event we happen to get into close range of Zach Stiles. He certainly won't be expecting to see you in a cowboy hat and western clothes, especially with sunglasses. Me either, for that matter."

Roman thought for a couple of seconds and smiled. "Know what?"

"No, what?"

"It can't hurt. Why not?"

They took the High Street exit and two minutes later were shopping in the large rustic store filled with western wear, shoes, and accessories. They completed their selections in thirty minutes and were back on Interstate 55, headed south.

Roman opted for a denim jacket, jeans to match, and the standard, black-felt western hat. He crouched in the seat to see the hat in the mirror. It reached the top of the blazer on his tall frame. The Ray Ban sunglasses completed the look. Diana's boots, tight-fitting Lee jeans, and soft-beige western hat, rivaled his for a definite change of pace in wardrobe. She even threw in an embroidered, denim shirt for good measure.

Roman cocked his hat over his right eye conspicuously and laughed as he fumbled to cut the radio volume. An 18-wheeler whizzed past and rocked the Blazer as it headed out of the city. Traffic was fairly light this time of day on the heavily traveled Interstate 55.

"You know, I do dress a little like this when I ride the horses sometimes, but not quite," Diana laughed, rubbing the shoulder of her denim shirt.

"This is amazing. I almost didn't recognize myself." Roman turned to Diana for a word of approval.

"Don't get cute, 'Cowboy'." She jabbed him in the ribs, and he swerved slightly to the left.

"Let's not have a wreck before we even get there, 'Ma'am'. No, seriously, we'll need all the help we can get. I don't want that guy to even think he saw us." He gazed at the Jackson skyline disappearing through the rear view mirror.

They crossed the Louisiana line and after a few more miles were behind them, decided it was time for some lunch.

"Let's stop at Middendorf's," Diana suggested. "It's only a few more minutes down the road, and they have excellent seafood."

"I forget you probably come down here from time to time with your art," Roman said. He leaned back, stretched his long legs, and punched the accelerator inadvertently. Middendorf's came into view. They cruised into the parking lot just before noon. It was such a popular restaurant on the busy highway, that a duplicate restaurant had been built, close beside the original one. Both buildings were filling up for lunch.

"I've never been here that they were not crowded," Diana added.

"Good sign, I guess. I think I stopped here once when came down to New Orleans for Mardi Gras."

They both chose the seafood platter to enjoy the shrimp, oysters, fish of the day, french fries, and other varieties of the day.

"Roman, promise me one thing. Even though it is serious why we're going to New Orleans, can we forget the calories for a day or so and enjoy the Louisiana food?"

"I was going to suggest that before you beat me to it, Darling." He smiled, added some horseradish and cocktail sauce, and inhaled one of the dozen raw oysters they ordered as appetizers. He noticed the young waitress's Cajun accent, recognizable anywhere.

They enjoyed their meal, and though full, they were refreshed and ready to take on the task at hand in New Orleans. Roman made his obligatory phone call from the pay phone to Los Angeles. He would get a cellular later, he promised himself again. For now, he still needed the time away from constant contact. He was fortunate once again to miss Gardner Lowe, but not fortunate enough when it came to Elton Sanders. He went through a ten-minute explanation of his itinerary. What politicians were who, how many landowners surrounded the project, and numerous other questions he could have thrown at him the following week. It was not so pressing that it needed to be discussed by phone, then and there. Roman hung up, spoke a few choice words about him, then they departed. Roman knew Sanders would have lost his religion if he'd known his call came from deep in Louisiana, that Roman was on his way to New Orleans to spy on the local sheriff, who he suspects murdered his good friend. A sheriff involved in who-knows-what other mysterious goings-on. He shook his head, thinking of Elton Sanders, oblivious to his taking care of anything but Worldwide business for the next day or two.

"I can't remember when I've made this drive to New Orleans. I do remember the last time I was in the city, however. I got one of the few opportunities as a young quarterback to fill in for the regular guy. Let's just say, I'd rather forget that afternoon." A New Orleans station came in clearly as they turned east on I-10. They were not far now from "The Big Easy". "On second thought, it's a night I won't ever forget," Roman quietly mumbled.

"What's so special about that night?" Diana unbuckled her seat belt and slid across the seat, tapping him on the shoulder affectionately.

"Oh, I'd rather talk about us, Diana. Let's change the subject."

"Come on, 'Cowboy'! Don't get my curiosity aroused, then leave me hanging."

Roman forced a smile and hesitated. "Actually, it was the first night I met Leah. She was a 'stew'. I should say, flight attendant. On that long trip back. I was a little down after the loss, and my playing wasn't what I dreamed of. She made me forget the afternoon." His voice trailed off, as he looked out the window for a second.

"Forgive me for meddling."

"No, not all. You didn't know." He gave her a quick kiss as he looked away from the road. To change the tempo of the conversation, he said: "Get WNOE on the radio. They used to be one of my favorites stations."

She pressed the seek button and scanned the dial for the station. It came in loud and clear from the outlying area of the city.

They exited into the downtown area, passing the sky-scrapers mingled in with smaller, old Louisiana-style office buildings. Roman slowed down considerably, winding down the narrow, crowded streets leading to the French Quarter.

"Canal Street, at last." Roman's voice rang out like he'd reached his destination. They had almost. Dauphine Street was in the Quarter, and the Dauphine Orleans was located on it, not far from Canal. The crowded streets contained a mixture of every race, shape, and form of human being, strolling in and out of businesses, mingling like bees around honey.

"Nothing ever seems to change down here," Diana said. "They are always thick down here." They spotted three young black kids, dancing, jam box and all, passing the hat to a crowd of ten or fifteen tourists that had gathered.

"The old mystique is always here," Roman said, as he abruptly turned onto Dauphine, nearly missing it. "I just hope someone else is here.".

"You're not thinking of actually staying in that same little hotel he's suppose to be in, are you? The Dauphine Orleans is small, you remember."

"No. No. We're not going to stay there. Maybe just ride by and try to see for sure if his car is there. We'll make it quick when we do."

"We may have a little time to kill. He may not be in until late tonight, or tomorrow for all we know."

"That's what I'm about to find out."

After circling the block, he pulled down Dauphine Street again, and parked in a loading zone, taking his chances for a couple of minutes.

"Diana, I hate to do this, but stay here, if you will, for a minute or two. Lock your doors. I'll be right back. I gotta see if he's here or not."

"O.K., but be careful and hurry up." She pushed the automatic door

73

lock and left the engine running. It gave her a more secure feeling, being able to leave instantly, if necessary. She knew this was a fun city, but she knew, all too well, there were weirdos here that would rival any city in the world.

Roman sprinted across the old cobblestone street and approached a short, balding, bellman. He appeared to be in his early forties, with a slightly protruding belly. His eyes were receptive and his smile was effortless. Unusual, for a lot of men in his capacity. He stood just outside the lobby in the parking garage, slamming the trunk on a Cutlass with graffiti scrawled all over it. The young groom looked anxious and handed him a wad of bills and headed for the room. The bellman turned to Roman and smiled.

"If I made it worth your while, could you tell me if there is a certain automobile in the garage?" Roman scouted the area quickly. He wanted to move quickly and get away. "It's really a certain ex-husband, if you know what I mean." The short bellman looked him up and down in a flash, never speaking. "I don't want the guy to know I'm with his ex-old lady. Follow me?" Roman looked him straight in the eye, as he showed the edge of a twenty. Between his look of sincerity and the twenty, the little fellow was promptly at his service.

"Just ask and your wish is my command, 'Tex'. What ya' lookin' for, my man?"

"It should be easy to remember. He's probably arriving early this evening. He'll either be in an official sheriff's car with Wildflower County, Mississippi on the door, or in an unmarked personal car. Probably the personal car. I think it's a dark maroon Lincoln Continental. Also with Wildflower County, Mississippi plates."

The bell man grabbed his arm and pulled him out of the main path of the garage to a shady corner near the lobby. It was empty except for one lady inquiring about some tourist sites. "A sheriff's car? You didn't tell me he was a law man. You ain't in trouble with the boys, are you, 'Tex'?"

"The name's not 'Tex', but you can call me that if you help me out. I don't care. What's your name?"

"Clifton. Clifton P. Arceneaux."

"Clifton, I'm not in trouble now, but I will be if he sees us. He's the jealous type, you know. I think he may have heard we were coming down here and followed us. May have heard we were coming to the Dauphine." Roman pulled his wide-brim hat a little further down on his forehead, almost touching his aviator sunglasses, and shifted his weight from one foot to another. He knew Diana would be getting anxious by now.

"You not stayin' here now, for God's sake, are you?" Clifton asked. His eyes were bigger, as he frowned with concern. Roman was beginning to like him.

"No, We're going to try the Marriott. Call me there in a thirty minutes."

"How you gonna be registered, 'Tex'?"

"As Tex Cruze. Yep, that's me. Easy to remember." Roman walked a few steps, then turned around abruptly, remembering the twenty. Clifton had moved the other way to go into the lobby. He grabbed Clifton's arm. "I almost forgot the money," he said, extending the $20 bill.

"No need yet. He may not come. I don't want to take your money and have no results."

"Thanks, Cliff. It's unusual to meet a man like you."

"I trust you 'Tex'. Let's just say you got believable eyes, my man. Say, by the way, I know about these things. My wife watches me like a hawk. You know, with me being in this job, and exposed to good lookin' ladies all the time" He looked at his reflection in the window of the lobby to check himself out. He brushed back some of the few black strands he had on the side of his head and grinned, exposing a missing tooth on the upper left. "I'll be working late tonight. Gotta pull a double shift. Another bellman that works here got drunk last night and ain't gonna make it. I could kick his butt. Go on and check in at the Marriott. I'll call you in thirty minutes. If you ain't registered, I'll know you couldn't get in. Then I'll wait to hear back from you." He wrote down the number and waved them on.

Roman took off, darting down the uncrowded street toward Diana. The engine was off, and she was staring back toward him, awaiting an explanation.

"What happened? I thought for sure you were in the middle of a fight or whatever. I almost came after you." She glanced at her watch. "Six minutes. It seemed like an hour!"

"I'll explain later. Let's check in the Marriott. It's fairly close yet far enough away from this part of the 'Quarter'." He climbed in the Blazer, pulled away, and edged along the world famous area of oyster bars, restaurants, shops, and unique residences concealed in between and above them, until he was at the Marriott. The high-rise hotel sat at the corner of Canal and Chartres, on the edge of the famous Quarter.

Their checking in as Mr. and Mrs. Tex Cruze never raised an eyebrow.

After all, they were in the town that was known for the outrageous. They certainly didn't qualify for that distinction. They waited and at exactly 2:15 the phone rang. Only five minutes late. "Is this Mr. Cruze?"

"Yes it is."

"Tex Cruze?"

"Right again, Cliff."

"You can feel honored. I usually only let my four brothers call me Cliff."

"I'll call you any name that makes you feel good." Roman was quick to try to please his contact.

"You can call me Cliff. Car's not here yet. Like I said, I'll be on until late, probably after ten or so tonight. I'll check every hour or so in the parking lot. I'll probably see him drive up. Leave that up to me. I'll report back to you. Go on out a while. I'll leave a message that I called, and you can ring me back Go, enjoy the town. I bet he doesn't show up til' dark."

Roman hesitated. "Sounds good, Cliff. I really appreciate this. We'll wait for your call."

"Know what?"

"What's that?"

"You don't sound like a cowboy." Cliff laughed so loud that Roman jerked the receiver two feet from his ear.

"We'll be waiting. Don't forget about us."

"Clifton Arceneaux is a man of his word. Family trait. Count on it. Talk to you later."

Roman hung up, shook his head and smiled at her. "You won't believe the character that's a bellman at the Dauphine. The one I approached for help. He's quite a guy. Unless I'm fooled, I think he's as honest as the day is long."

"I hope so. I'm sure he must be. You seem to be perceptive and a good judge of people." Diana stretched out across the king-size bed with the picture of the old Jax Brewery hanging over the head board. She clicked the remote a couple of times and found a local station with an old Clark Gable and Marilyn Monroe movie occupying the screen. She kicked off her boots and patted the bed for Roman to join her. They tried to watch the movie, but were too distracted by Bourbon Street's proximity beckoning. So, they retrieved their hats and sunglasses and were out the door shortly.

"I guess this is increasing the chance of him seeing us, but I can't sit in that room in broad daylight, not here." Roman said, grabbing her hand as they crossed the crowded street and headed for Jackson Square. This old historic gathering place of artists, con-artists, and tourists had always intrigued him. They eased in and out of several shops. Nothing caught his eye. The last thing he was interested in was another T-shirt with anything you could imagine written on it. She found a few things of interest in some of the older, classier collections of antiques and paintings in a shop or two. He wouldn't let her tarry long. They entered the old Jax Brewery building that now housed shop after shop, and fast food restaurants, among other things, like the live candy-making place, surrounded by spectators. They killed more time, crossing street after street until five o'clock arrived. He thought he'd pushed his luck enough, in case Stiles had arrived. As big as New Orleans was, he knew the Quarter was a little exposing, and his luck had not been the best lately anyway.

"We'd better get back to the room," He told Diana. "He may have called. I've seen enough for now. Haven't you?"

"If you say so. Besides, we'll be out in this tonight, I'm sure." The boots were the first thing to go when they hit the door. Other garments followed in short order. There were no messages.

CHAPTER 9

Roman was downstairs in five minutes flat and jumped in the first cab. Clifton had rung at seven in a hurried blur, shouting over the voices in the background, since the lobby's noise level was up a few decibels. He had asked Roman to meet him in fifteen minutes at the dimly-lit spot by the garage. He had no time to talk. Diana stayed in the room for the moment against her wishes but, for Roman, she relented, flicking the TV channels back and forth.

The cabbie dropped him off a hundred feet from the Dauphine's entrance. Roman tipped him two dollars, despite the short ride. He roared away; exhaust fumes permeating the air and radio blasting, never acknowledging Roman vacating the car.

He walked down the sparsely occupied street and ducked into the little corner that Cliff had requested. Cliff met him with a handshake, a slightly urgent tone in his voice.

"Sorry to rush you down here, but we are very short handed around this little hotel, man. I'm having to do everything, except tend bar in this place. That'll be next. I couldn't talk very well. That nosey desk clerk would like to think I was doing something wrong, so he could make some points and report me to the manager. To shorten the story, I have not been able to get up there and check but once, a good while back. I've been running like crazy, but I'll tell you what might be better anyway." He lit a Camel and blew a cloud of smoke up.

"What's that?" Roman bobbed to the right, dodging the fallout.

"I can tell you where to go and you can probably spot the car much easier than I could anyway."

"Sounds fine to me." Roman slapped him on the shoulder. Cliff smiled again. He enjoyed the attention. Roman glanced over his shoulder to see if they had company.

"Does the hotel keep a log of the cars parked in the garage?"

Cliff moved in closer to Roman, like he had a deep secret to tell. "Not exactly, but we have a system of keeping up with it, if that's what you mean. It might take a while and raise a few eyebrows, if I had to snoop around asking names. Probably would not, but I knew you wanted to be careful not to alert anybody on this thing."

The Cajun might be overdoing this, Roman thought, but he was glad to get the opportunity to look personally. After all, he just wanted to see if the car was in the garage.

"Best way is for me to send you up there looking for a package you misplaced, if you know what I mean, in case anyone asks you why you're up there. Usually, no one is allowed up there but the employees. Most of the time that is the bellmen. Naturally, we ain't supposed to do this, but I kind of run the show around here." Roman nodded and humored him.

Clifton strutted to the ramp that wound up to the other floor of cars. Roman slipped him two tens this time and was off to see if Zach Stiles was indeed on the premises.

"Be careful, Cowboy. I'd hate to see you get that handsome face rearranged by the long arm of the law." Roman looked back, tipped his hat and forced a smile, acknowledging the advice.

He strolled nonchalantly from row to row, not to arouse suspicion if someone happened to appear. There were cars of all descriptions and tags from Texas, Louisiana, Alabama, even as far away as Wisconsin. But no Mississippi official seal on a green Chevrolet was there. He searched row after row. He got excited when he saw the first Mississippi tag, but it turned out to be a green Audi with another county tag, not Wildflower. He was about to leave when his eyes caught the Mississippi tag logo with Wildflower in the county space. Only this was a new black, four-wheel drive Ford pickup. He studied the vehicle quickly. How many Wildflower County people would be here, now? He checked out the windshield sticker in the right hand corner. The adrenalin pumped up a little. Yes! The Mississippi Sheriff's Association decal was prominently displayed. He left the parking garage faster than he had entered, knowing Stiles was here, and that at least he knew he hadn't been on some fool's errand. Now, to find out why Stiles was here, rather than at a sheriff's meeting in Jackson, as scheduled. Stiles had told his whole staff this story, according to the mysterious phone caller, Mrs. Hendrix. He was only to be contacted through Deputy Wiggins. No exceptions. He would know his whereabouts. He left no doubt, he did not want to be disturbed by anyone until late Sunday afternoon.

Roman quickened his pace back down Dauphine Street, hoping to hail another cab from at least a block or so away from the hotel. He was about to turn the corner when he heard her voice: "I couldn't wait any longer. I thought you might need the Blazer. I got it out of the hotel lot and drove on over here. I parked over there." Roman glanced at the Blazer at the corner, next to another loading zone. He grabbed her arm and trotted to the vehicle. She pulled away as she spoke. "Don't worry, at least I didn't come to the hotel." "I just wanted to be nearby. I was concerned, Roman."

"I know. I appreciate it. It worked out all right after all. Stiles is definitely checked into the hotel. His car is in the parking garage, and it's for guests only. He's really at a meeting for the Mississippi Boys Ranch in Jackson, isn't he?" He added sarcastically. "He came down in one of his other vehicles. I'm sure with the money he makes illegally, he can afford several of them." He kissed her cheek and they pulled out for the Marriott.

"It's still only a little after seven. I hope we can get Clifton again for a minute." Roman hesitated. "Better still, would you ask for him? Maybe the old desk clerk will think he's a stud. I get the feeling Cliff would like for the clerk to think that."

They wheeled into the parking garage at the Marriott and caught the elevator as the chime was sounding and the arrow was lighting up. They got off on seven and proceeded to room 797. Roman threw his hat on the bed and grabbed the phone from the table. He dialed the Dauphine and handed it to Diana. "Is Clifton there, please?" she asked in her softest, most alluring voice. Anything to ease the tension that was slowly mounting. The desk clerk put her on hold, abruptly.

"Clifton. May I help you?"

"Clifton, this is the other half of the western team."

After a brief silence, he responded, "Oh, yeah. Tex's lady. Where is he?"

"Right here. Hold on."

"Cliff," Roman said. He's definitely there. I saw it. He's driving a black 4 wheel drive Ford pickup." He listened and held on. He put his hand over the phone and whispered to Diana. She nodded and continued flicking through the channels with the sound muted. "Yes, that's all right. I know you're holding the fort down almost single handed. This guy is in his forties, looks a little younger. Tall, wiry, Stephen Segal-looking, dark, fairly long hair, and a scar you can't miss, from his eye to below his jaw."

He winked at Diana and put his hand over the receiver: "He thinks he knows him. Said he was rude when he asked if he needed help with his bag. Says he fits the description. He checked in only a half hour or so before I went down, according to Cliff."

He removed his hand to speak to Cliff again. " I hate to ask this, and if you can't do it, just say so. Can you call me the minute he leaves? I feel sure he'll take a cab, like almost everyone does here. Find out the destination of the cab. I know you can do that. You know the ropes more than I do in that area. I'll up the money to fifty if you can get me the place he goes to tonight. I'm merely guessing, but I'll bet, it will be before too long, probably no later than eight thirty."

"You're in luck. It's slowin' down around here. I'll stay flexible for the next hour or so. I can leave, at this point, whenever I want. I'll follow him and report to you exactly where he is. Wanna know what he orders?" They both laughed.

"No, that's okay. The address is all I want. I can't tell you how much I appreciate this. You'll be paid well. I'll leave it in an envelope at the front desk for you to pick up or whatever you want, but be sure not to lose him, even if someone picks him up. I know that lobby is small and not as congested as others down here, so I feel like you'll have a good chance to follow him." Roman stared out window, oblivious to the neons and sparkling lights of the Crescent City. "By the way, why are you willing to do this? I don't think it's just the money."

"Let's just say, I can relate to your situation, even though I don't really think he's an ex-husband. I'm pretty savvy about most people. See all kinds in and around the hotel and in this town. Like I said, you've got believable eyes. You've got an honest face, I guess."

"You're not exactly a gangster-looking guy yourself," Roman chuckled. "I'll wait right here by the phone."

Roman rolled his eyes. "Boy, have I hit a gold mine in Clifton Arceneaux. He's getting off in a few minutes and will hang around until Stiles comes down. Then he can follow and let me know. Nice to have a little good luck for a change. He'll call me when Stiles gets to wherever he's going. We won't have to hang around the Dauphine and risk getting seen any more than we already have."

At 7:55 the phone rang off the hook.

"Tex? Is this Tex?"

"Yeah." It was Cliff. "Good man. Are you sure that's where he is now? As I said, I'll leave the money in an envelope at the front desk for you. Better still, why don't you just meet me a comfortable distance from the front of the place and I'll pay you." Roman stopped. "I may even have one more thing you can do in this situation. There's another fifty in it."

"I'm game for it, as long as there's no shootin'. I draw the line there, my friend."

"No, there won't be. Look for us. We're about to head out the door now. See you in a fifteen minutes, or so. We'll get a cab and be right on." Roman unzipped his bag and grabbed the small black case. They slammed the door and rushed to the elevator as the second the ding came.

"Where did Zach go?" Diana whispered, as two older couples dressed to the hilt, hovered next to them as they began their descent from floor seven. Roman winked and she understood. They waited patiently until the elevator reached the lobby. The other four gradually shuffled out, looking carefully at their feet, where the elevator meets the floor in the lobby.

"Tujague's." He grabbed her hand, hurrying across the lobby. They looked for a bellman, but none were to be found. The concierge was obliging, however, and in three or four minutes they were piling into the black and white cab.

Roman repeated the destination to the cabby, who slapped the meter flag down and roared off in silence. They weaved through the crowded streets for the short drive. People lined both sides of the streets, laughing, gawking, generally wandering in all directions, in and out of bars and shops along the way.

"If he's meeting someone at Tujague's, they've got better taste than Stiles, I imagine," Roman said, peering out, anticipating the renowned restaurant.

"He probably never considered taste a prerequisite in choosing a restaurant."

"Stop at the corner before you get to the restaurant, please." The rotund cabby grunted and reached for his meter flag as they neared the spot.

No sooner than they put their feet down on Decatur Street, they heard the Cajun voice as he crossed to meet them. "Tex! Over here." He waved both hands.

"Cliff, let's not tell the world," Roman hissed. They moved to the privacy of a dim alley between two buildings. Their eyes darted upward from the resounding bass sound thudding from an apartment above. Someone's speakers had to be rattling from the volume.

"They have some fancy digs above some unlikely places around here, I hear." Roman volunteered to Diana.

"This is my lady friend, Mrs. Bolton," Roman said, introducing Diana. She looked puzzled for a second before smiling at Clifton.

"Glad to know you, Mrs. Bolton." Cliff sounded somewhat skeptical.

"Good to meet you, Cliff."

"Cliff, you may want to go home and forget doing what I'm going to ask." Roman patted him on the shoulder, and fanned the Camel smoke from Diana. She moved back to avoid another burst, smiling.

"I'm game for a little excitement. Excitement, mind you, but not anything illegal. I had my fill of doing the wrong thing a long time ago. I'm a good law-abiding citizen. Law-abiding, but I still like to live a little. Something out of the ordinary, I like." Cliff lifted his chest slightly and rubbed his cigarette out on the ancient sidewalk. Years of abuse had left it stained and worn, but surprisingly intact.

"This is nothing illegal, and I feel you can pull it off, if anyone can."

"What's that?"

"I've got a camera here for you to use. All you've got to do is be a roving photographer, taking pictures of customers to sell them.. You know, like they do at places like Pat O'Brien's. Only, there's one difference. You're going to pretend to take a few. Hell, take one or two for real of anybody, but take a couple of the man I described to you and anyone else at his table. I'll direct you to him."

"No problem. I know the night manager here. I can arrange it without any hassle. May have to slip him a twenty to let me do it for a while, though."

"That's fine, just do it."

"Clifton Arceneaux, at your service." Cliff was beginning to like this, and the money was better than lifting suitcases and catering to tourists. Besides, if the man recognized him as the bell man from the Dauphine, he could always be moonlighting.

"Wait here." Roman pointed to the ground. "I'll be back as soon as we're seated and I spot the guy."

"Got it. I'll be right here, waiting." Roman handed him the camera, which was small, easy to work, with a built-in flash and focus.

"Mrs. Bolton? Why did you introduce me with my ex-husband's name?" Diana had been waiting for the right moment to ask.

"I guess at this point, I didn't see any reason to use your right name." She rolled her eyes, but nodded in agreement.

He took her hand and they maneuvered across Decatur Street toward Tujague's, just as a horse and carriage squeaked past. Its driver expounded on some of the history of the Quarter to a tourist couple. Roman thought they retired those carriages at night, but the driver must have sensed a fat tip.

At least it was dark now, which made it harder for them to be recognized, especially in the western clothes.

They eased into the crowded waiting area just inside the front door. Neither removed their hats. They stood to the rear until the maitre d' reluctantly made his way to them. The tall, skinny man with the pencil-thin mustache, snubbed them for a second, until Roman palmed a rolled-up twenty into his lily-white hand. He glanced down, then smiled back at them. The 45 minute wait had suddenly become five, and they could indeed have a table near the back. He left waving menus and was back in three.

"Sir, if you and your lady will follow me, we have your table ready in a cozy spot in the back." They followed right behind him, their eyes darting quickly from one side of the front of the crowded room to the other.

After two or three steps, Roman touched Diana's sleeve to wait. He stepped up quickly and tapped the maitre d' on the shoulder. "Sorry to trouble you sir, but could I get directions to the men's room before we're seated. You know, us cowboys in the big city might get turned around and never find that table. Might stumble into somebody else's."

The maitre d' pointed the way and Roman left Diana standing near the entrance in the corner. She stayed as out of sight as much as possible. He walked briskly by the front, his hat, jacket, all coordinated, looking the complete cowboy. He stopped suddenly behind a room-divider, near the waiters' station, and scouted the diners seating. There he was. His profile was not easily missed. A quick glance across the table brought a dark-complexioned man with a tightly pulled, jet-black, pony tail into focus. He appeared to be in his late thirties, his dark eyes rivaling those of Zach Stiles, himself. The few seconds were all Roman could risk. He did a quick about-face and returned to Diana in a flash.

They hailed down the maitre d' again, who was on the verge of losing patience. They asked to be seated to the right in another little section, so they would be out of sight from Stiles and his villainous-looking dining partner. So far so good. He ordered a Bud and she chose a glass of Chablis. The waiter stared and tapped the pen on his pad, to get their order rolling. Eating was the last thing on their mind, but it was necessary to accomplish the task at hand.

"Excuse me, Honey. Let me check if Cliff is out there with camera in hand and ready." Roman slid his chair back, walked casually out of their section, checking over his shoulder, as he went out the door. He walked to the building next door and scanned the area. No Clifton. "Damn. Guess he cut out and left me," Roman mumbled to himself. He searched across the street, straining his eyes to see in the dark places. Not a sign. He decided to wait one more minute. He should have known Cliff was too good to be true. He was headed back to the front door, when he heard a hiss. It was Clifton, crouched behind a Jeep illegally parked three spaces from the front door, smoking the ever-present Camel.

"I had to run over a block and get some smokes. I would have never gotten them in there with that crowd." Roman let out a deep breath.

"I'm glad you didn't let me down."

"Clifton never breaks his promise. My family instilled that in me as a kid. Besides this is sort of like a made-for-TV-movie to me. I'm enjoying the change of pace."

"I can imagine," Roman said, the urgency showing. His usual handsome, relaxed face looked anxious.

"I'm ready when you are, Tex."

"Count to twenty five, then come inside and look to your right, next to the aquarium. We'll be there. I'll get up a few seconds later and walk to where you can see this guy. You know him by now — from the hotel and my description.. He's with a dark guy with a black pony-tail sitting across the table. Foreign-looking. He's wearing one of those loose fitting, double-breasted, Italian suits. Pale green, with a black shirt underneath. Oh, yeah, for your information, the lawman has on civilian clothes. Red shirt and beige pants. Get their pictures after you have asked and made a few more for people around them. Got it? Don't foul up. If he recognizes you from the hotel, just say you're moonlighting. You seem to know how to improvise. Play it by ear. Then get out of here and call me at the Marriott."

"Gotcha. Relax. You're in good hands with Clifton Arceneaux." Cliff cupped his hands like the insurance company he was imitating and grinned. Roman opened the door to a mild roar of voices and waiters banging and hustling around, and made his way to Diana. He smiled, more confidently now, hoping that they had time before Stiles and his guest were done with dinner.

The waiter gave an impatient look, displayed his pencil and menu order pad and shifted his weight from one foot to the other.

"Give us just a few more seconds," Roman urged. "We may be slow where I come from, but we pay well." The waiter's impatience cooled, changing frown to smile. He was now at their service, smelling a good tip from the cowboy and his lady.

"I don't know what I would have done without my helper outside," He told Diana, instantly catching a glimpse of Cliff out of the corner of his eye.

"Excuse me." He nodded to the waiter, turning to Diana. "Order me the blackened redfish and whatever you want." He slid his chair back again. The waiter frowned slightly and pointed behind him, "I guess you're leaving again."

"Yep, that Bud went right through me. The lady will order for us. We do things opposite in Texas." He smiled and winked at the skinny waiter. He knew this defied etiquette he'd been taught, but time dictated another route. As he walked past him, he nudged Cliff, who followed closely with camera in hand.

"Got the camera ready?" Roman asked.

"Like the Boy Scouts, I'm prepared."

"You're full of little sayings tonight aren't you?" Roman flashed a quick smile.

"Humor keeps the world loose, my man."

Roman anticipated the "my man". It was an endearing term by now. "There he is," Roman warned. He stepped behind Cliff, partially behind the divider. The busy waiters were oblivious to their presence.

"Yep, Tex, I can't forget that face. He's a mean looking dude. Matter of fact, the other one ain't exactly got choir boy looks either."

"Hurry up." Roman was getting more anxious to get the pictures and get out. "Take the couple next to them and then get their's. Got me?"

"I keep getting the feeling, you ain't no average cowboy checking out some woman's ex-ole man." Cliff smirked as he started toward the tables.

The voice boomed out of nowhere. "We don't allow just anyone to take pictures of our guests." The maitre d' came from behind the partition, feeling his authority. Cliff already had camera in hand, focused on a young couple a few feet away, who were posing graciously.

"Sir. Sir." Roman flagged down the maitre d' again.

"It's you. You're everywhere tonight, aren't you?"

Roman peeled off another twenty and greased the pale man's palm. "Only be a few seconds. Merely a hobby for my friend. He's in it for therapy. Problems, you know." Roman pointed to his head to signify mental problems for Cliff. The maitre d' rubbed his thin mustache, pivoted around and vanished. No one had heard him but Roman.

So much for Cliff knowing the night manager and getting that little detail taken care of. This was getting expensive, but well worth it. He moved quickly through the place and back to the table where Diana waited. They ate very little, picking at the delicious seafood and keeping an eye out for Stiles. Finally, he hailed down the impatient waiter and asked for the check. He would be right back with it.

Cliff made his way to the young couple in the section to his left. He snapped one and told them he would be back with their little treasure that captured the moment forever. Then, he strolled directly across from Sheriff Stiles and friend and snapped away at the large woman with two small boys who were throwing crayons and parts of a coloring book she had given them. The scene was set. He stepped back and framed the two of them and clicked twice in succession. He moved the camera away from his face and smiled. His eyes met the cold dark stare of Zach Stiles.

"Come here." Cliff pretended not to hear and clicked another one of them.

"Would you two like a picture? You're not obligated."

"He's talking to you 'Air Head'." The deep slow voice was deliberate and hostile. Clifton turned his back, pretending to focus on another couple close by, but a hand grabbed his shoulder and spun him around. It was Stiles. Cliff knew it was trouble. He was lucky Stiles didn't appear to recognize him from the Dauphine.

"This is a private meeting. We prefer no pictures. Let's put it another way. We demand no pictures." The Sheriff backed down, after a second. "You'll have to excuse us. We're undercover officers and..., well, you understand. I also need those negatives."

"No problem." Cliff turned his back momentarily and popped open the camera and handed him a roll of Kodak film.

"I appreciate that, 'little man'. The sobriquet ticked off Cliff. He didn't like being called that by anyone. He didn't like being reminded that he was only five-four, especially by that bastard.

He managed a smile and moved toward the front of the crowded, old eating establishment. He thought the scene had faded and blended into sounds of glasses tinkling and waiters rushing around with plates of delicacies, headed for hungry patrons in all parts of the building. His eyes darted nervously, hoping to see no one who'd blow his cover.

No one seemed to pay attention the near confrontation. However, as the sinister-looking pair ordered a round of drinks, they leaned forward at the table. "Emil, have you ever seen that little guy before?" Stiles motioned where Cliff had been.

"No. Have you?" He looked away, then shrugged his shoulders.

Cliff nodded to Roman as he stopped near his table. Go on, go on, Roman wanted to say. Instead, his eyes got the message across. He motioned his head towards the door. Cliff took the hint and headed into the night. They watched for the emergence of the two as the waiter finally brought the check. Roman left the amount in cash, plus a generous tip. He decided against American Express, because he wanted no record, just to be safe. He shook his head. The personnel at Tujague's should love him. His roll of bills had diminished considerably.

Roman and Diana looked back one more time briefly and had pushed their luck enough for the time being. They stepped back onto the 1400 block of Decatur and positioned themselves out of sight between two nearby buildings, with their eyes glued on the entrance. They would be out soon, for sure. Then, Roman heard the same sound as before. The hissing. Cliff was behind them practically, not ten feet away. Roman turned to voice his displeasure, but one look at that face changed his mind. He was eager to please. Roman hustled him into the nearby alley.

"Tex, he got red in the face and took my film."

"Damn. I told you to be careful and casual about it. Not to raise any suspicions. I might have known that was asking too much."

"Hold on, before you get your blood pressure up. I pulled the old switcheroo and gave him a blank roll of film."

"Good. I hope he just throws it away and doesn't look for anything in the film frames. If he sees you gave him a blank one, he may get a little suspicious about why."

"You're readin' into this too much. Don't get paranoid about him. He's not that smart." Roman thought, if you only knew. "Pretty smart move, huh? Like I told my brother-in-law, I could track down his old lady and save him a detective fee. She's been having a thing with this car sales-man while he's cuttin' meat down at the grocery." He stood as tall as he could, threw out his chest, and lit another Camel.

When Roman didn't comment, Cliff said, "Well, the question is, do you want me to hang around and help you out on following this dude or not?"

Roman thought for a second, then looked toward the door of Tujague's at a young couple leaving hand-in-hand. Another group of loud college kids exited. "Yeah. But you've got to keep out of sight and remember this guy can get out of hand." Cliff gave his best savvy nod.

At last, the ominous looking duo came into view, stopping less than fifty feet down the street from the restaurant's front door. Pony-tail lit a big cigar and blew the smoke out slowly. He raised his right hand, and a long, black limousine zoomed to the curb, three feet from where they were standing. A lone figure sat in the back seat, near the tinted passenger-side window. The door swung open. Pony Tail extended his hand to the figure who remained seated. They shook hands and exchanged brief greetings. Zach Stiles followed suit and they eased into the back seat. The car rolled away. Roman's eyes were fixed on the figure on the outside that never got out. Just as they passed, despite the darkness and tinted glass, the fleeting profile looked familiar. Maybe not. He couldn't be sure.

He scrambled to get the tag number as the car sped down Decatur Street. They picked up speed after they turned the corner. He strained to try to see the license plate.

"I can't believe I couldn't make it out. I think there was a 1A1 and that's all I could see. There must have been five other letters." He turned to Diana who had trotted up to join him. He exhaled and rolled his eyes back. "I thought I'd seen that guy in the back. I just didn't have time. Oh, well. So much for that." He reached for her hand, starting back toward the res-taurant. "What happened to Cliff?

"I guess he headed in for the night after all. He disappeared. I lost sight of him when they came out, and the limo came on the scene," Diana said, excitedly.

"Looking for me?" The voice came from behind them again.

"You're getting good at that disappearing act, aren't you Cliff?" Roman asked, pointing off into the distance.

"I went to the other end, behind the limo, and chased it . I was too busy gettin' the tag number." He smiled and held up a piece of paper. Louisiana plates. 1A109873.

CHAPTER *10*

Seven a.m. couldn't come fast enough this morning. He and Diana had discussed the previous night's events at length, and he was anxious to get the film developed. He knew he wouldn't have the slightest idea who the pony-tailed man was, but was eager to examine the film. Any doubts Diana might have had, for whatever reason, about Zach Stiles, were waning. Roman paced slowly, sipping the cup of complimentary coffee the hotel delivered to the door with the continental breakfast. They didn't touch the pastries. The "Times Picayune", left also as part of the pampering, lay untouched in the chair by the door. He could barely wait for Cliff's word about the tag. His friend at work had another friend at the tax collector's office with access to automobile license tag registrations. Roman wanted the name of the limousine owner, who must be a player in whatever the sheriff was up to. The registration office opened at 8:00 a.m.

At 8:30 there was no word. He worried about Clifton coming through. Where else could he go to get tag registration information if Cliff's sources couldn't get it? It might take time. As he tried to think of other ways to obtain the information, there was a knock at the door. Roman froze, put his finger to his lips, and motioned to Diana for silence. He looked through the magnified glass of the security peek hole and saw the distant face of his new-found friend. Cliff had decided to deliver the word in person. Diana sprinted for the bathroom in her sheer gown so Roman could let him in.

"How about breakfast at Brennan's?" Cliff beamed, holding his hand out to shake. Roman gripped the offered hand, eased him inside, and closed the door.

"That might be a little public, if you know what I mean," Roman said, but then thought about it. Cliff wanted to start the day off right. After all, he had some information. "Well, why not?" he relented. "I guess the chances of running in to that twosome or threesome aren't very likely. Have a seat by the television. I'll be right back." He conferred with Diana in the bathroom, Yes, they would have breakfast at Brennans.

"Cliff, what do you have for me? That's more important than breakfast. Did you find out about the tag, and who owns the limo?"

"Yeah. I did. Are you ready for this? Looks like it's registered to New Vanguard Services."

"And who is that?"

"Supposed to be some limo company, but they're not listed in bold print in the business pages of the directory. Must be small."

"Just because they're not in bold print, doesn't mean they're small," Roman argued.

"That, along with the fact that I never heard of them does. I've seen a few limo services around this town, but never that one."

"I'll call them and see what they say. I'll play it by ear again."

"No need. I already did," Cliff smiled, looking up for a reciprocal smile. He got it.

"You are something. You should've really been a detective. Missed your calling."

"My man, 'Tex', Cliff stopped, staring out the window toward the "Quarter". "I think you should leave this one alone. That's all I need to say. Believe me."

"Cliff, don't stop short of telling me what you know." Roman stared directly at Cliff, as the little man retrieved a cigarette from his shirt pocket and tapped it nervously, waiting to light it away from the room.

He paced across the room and wheeled around. "Okay. A good source tells me that this so-called limo service is owned by one Peter Ardovino, better known as 'Big Pete'. He's three hundred pounds if he's an ounce, and connected to 'you know who'."

"No, who?"

"Tex, do I have to draw you a map on this? He's supposed to be part of the Mafioso. If not that, he's definitely a big time hood here in New Orleans. Whatever he's into, it ain't no good. I don't know how big time he is, but I think he handles some things for other people when they need favors in New Orleans. Sort of the local connection."

Roman shook his head. "Cliff, you couldn't know all this on your own. Where'd you get this information?"

"This could get someone in trouble."

"It won't go any further than this room. I think you can tell that."

"All right. Not a word of where this came from. I got another brother-in-law who is a city detective here. He enlightened me, I guess I could say. Doesn't matter. He said — not to be crossing this guy. Not if you're not a law officer. No one should risk that unnecessarily, according to him. He knows. He's been around a long time."

Roman hesitated and sipped the last of the courtesy coffee. "In other words, you really didn't have anyone at the tax collector's office. The detective got the tag information also. Doesn't matter. We got it. Go on to Brennan's and get a table. We'll see you there in twenty minutes or so. Lady needs to freshen up. You know?" He winked, Cliff smiled and was out the door.

Diana and Roman got a cab in no time from the parking garage. The bell man hustled and swung open the door. He could smell a tip and reacted accordingly. They were at the famous 417 Royal Street address in a matter of minutes. Cliff had arranged for a table at the rear, slightly secluded by some large ferns that blocked much of the view of the restaurant. He was on his second cup of coffee, talking with an older, heavy-set waitress and a large-breasted lady in a tight black dress, who appeared to be the manager. This made Roman a little nervous as they approached the table.

"I can't believe we've gone to such precautions and slipped around, then come to one of the most famous places in New Orleans for breakfast. Makes a lot of sense, doesn't it," Roman said sarcastically, as he surveyed the tables nearby. No one looked familiar. They were busy. He would forget about it. They wouldn't be here.

"Tex, this guy I mentioned..."

Roman winked at Cliff and shook his head quickly, as Diana observed the flowers on the next table. Cliff, for once, took the hint. He would wait for a sign from Roman.

"I assume there is one of those one hour, or instant-photo places around here where we can get this film developed when we finish eating." The heavy-set waitress with dyed black hair slid the menus in front of the three. "Coffee?" She stared at Diana and Roman, without smiling. Years of waiting on too many tourists had done that to her. They accepted the coffee, followed Cliff's advice, and ordered Eggs Benedict.

"Cliff, if I had champagne, I would propose a toast to you, but this will have to do. If I'd hired a private detective here, I couldn't have done better. In fact, probably not as well." Cliff could not subdue the huge grin that spread across his chubby little face.

Diana excused herself for the ladies room. They could talk a little more.

"I stopped you because I don't want her knowing too awful much. She already knows plenty, but some of the details I want to keep to myself. You can understand."

"No, not exactly. I know you're not some hayseed cowboy trying to track his lady friend's ex-husband. I know it's deeper than that. I ain't a rocket scientist, but I didn't fall off the back of a turnip truck yesterday, either."

"You said this guy Ardovino is supposed to weigh three hundred or more pounds. Is he very tall or just very heavy?"

"Very heavy. Not very tall, I think. Why?"

"Because the guy I saw on the side next to me, the passenger side window, was not fat. But I only got a glimpse and with that tinted glass and at night. For a split second, I thought I had seen that profile before. Maybe not." Roman's eyes darted around the tables in sight again. A quick check, just to be sure.

"Well, you've got the tag information and very shortly, we'll have the pictures to see if you can tell anything. Now, tell me your real names, Tex." Cliff whirled his spoon around in his coffee at top speed, unconsciously. "I've had a feeling about this from the start. About the names and what you're doing." Cliff leaned forward on one elbow, placed a Camel firmly between his lips, and fired it up. Smoke boiled out over the ferns. Roman fanned at it, grateful they were at least in a smoking area. He could tolerate it for all the help Cliff had been, above and beyond the call of duty.

Roman sipped water from the ice cold glass that had made a ring on the table where it sat, just outside the linen. He stared at the glass, held it upright on the edge, and slid it back and forth. He stopped suddenly and engaged Cliff with a fixed stare.

"Its' a fairly long story and you and I don't have the luxury of taking the time for it. I will tell you this. We're not the criminals in this. I think you can read between the lines a little and know who is. Maybe some day soon I can fill you in more. For right now, I hope you understand." Roman leaned across the table and slapped him on the shoulder. Cliff winked and nodded his head three times in quick succession.

The waiter and Diana arrived back at the table at the same instant.

"I'm ready if you two are," Diana smiled, admiring the plates brought over from the waiter's folding stand set up next to them.

"He's asked for our real names," Roman revealed. Diana studied his face for the right reaction. Roman's eyes gave the hint as he looked away and back. "I'm Roman Beckley and this is Diana Palmer. Same folks exactly, but now you know our real names."

"Roman Beckley. That name sounds familiar. I'll remember, sooner or later."

They finished their plates of Eggs Benedict and an assortment of fruit, and paid the bill, which would rival most dinners in average restaurants. They then headed down Royal Street to a little, fast-photo developing place Cliff knew. He volunteered to get the work done here so Roman and Diana could take in a shop or two nearby. Diana needed at least a few minutes in this city to browse.

But Roman could stand it no longer than fifteen minutes.

"Wait inside here. I'll be right back. Checking on him." She stayed in the small shop; one cramped and filled to capacity with antiques of all shapes. There was only one older couple with a distinct New England accent, dressed in polyester matching bermudas of bright blue and T shirts, identically emblazoned "Bourbon Street" in bright yellow against a light blue ground. All they lacked was the word "tourist" scrawled across their back. Diana smiled at them and checked the ancient ice box for sale near the rear. The shop owner eagerly offered assistance, but Diana politely declined and continued to browse.

Roman walked briskly back toward Royal where they had wandered from across the street. He had taken no more than a few steps when he saw the little guy headed straight toward him. When they were but ten feet apart, Cliff gave an obvious nod to the right and walked directly across the sparsely occupied street. Roman got the message and ducked into the only open shop at this early hour. It was filled with T shirts with decent and suggestive writings on them. There were hundreds of logos to choose from that could be pressed on to shirts of all colors while customers wait. He peered across the mound of cotton shirts and saw Cliff, motioning that the coast was clear. From what though?

"You won't believe this, Tex. I mean Roman. I damn near walked right into that limo when I made it to the corner of Royal. I mean, what are the odds of that happening?"

"Gotta be a long shot, huh?"

"Are you kidding me?"

"Would I kid about that?"

"No. I hope not. This is no joking matter. Did you get the film developed?" Cliff gave a yes and handed him the little white envelope. "Meet us back at the Marriott in fifteen minutes, if you will," Roman said. Cliff headed for the corner for a cab. Roman glanced at the pictures for a second of two, shook his head, then stared at the two again. "I don't know you, but I know him. Someone will find out what you're up to. This is a start....for you, John," Roman whispered. He put the pictures in the pocket of his cotton shirt then hurried back to the antique shop for Diana.

"It's time to get on out of here and head for Indian Bayou."

"Just like that?"

"It's time. I've got that feeling." Roman gave her a bear hug around the waist and they caught the first cab back to the Marriott. Cliff was strolling and smoking in the hallway despite the sign. They packed and headed for the lobby. After the attendant retrieved the Blazer, they threw the bags in and were ready for the five-hour journey back to the Delta. They had made a friend. Even though they had crossed paths for a short time, he seemed more like an old family friend. His personable demeanor made him someone not likely to be forgotten soon. It was evident he was searching for the camaraderie.

"I may call you sometime soon, if you'll give me your phone number." Roman said, slipping him his last two big bills, a fifty and a twenty. He stuffed the crumbled piece of paper into the watch pocket of his Levi's.

"Thanks for your help, Cliff. Take care." Diana smiled warmly, as Roman pulled away from the corner of Chartes and Canal streets. She looked back at Cliff.

"Wait, Honey, he's waving at us to stop." Roman pulled slowly to the curb about a hundred feet away. Cliff ran to the driver's side window. He gripped Roman's forearm.

"Better watch your rear end, or I could be going to a funeral. Got me?" Roman smiled and started to pull away again. Cliff crossed around the car quickly to Diana's side and leaned into the front. "You forgot something."

Roman reached for his billfold again.

"No! No. It's your phone number. I need your number too. You forgot to give it to me when I gave mine in a hurry." Roman handed him his card. They were touched.

Roman leaned across the seat toward him. "I know you're definitely not in this just for the money. Something still you want to tell me ?"

Cliff scanned the sky and then looked back down at both of them. He hesitated for once. "It's my wife. She and her Mom always act like, without saying much, that I'm a failure. Sort of a nobody. Tough on me with two teenagers. For a while, with you two, I was somebody." His eyes watered, as he looked away and back. "You see, I know a lot about criminals. That's why I keep telling you to watch your step. I was once in the 'Big House' myself. I worked at the airport in the parking lot. To shorten this story, I was young and stupid. I only wanted to impress my young wife. I borrowed, so to speak, a Mercedes once, while the owner had it parked. Took my wife for a ride and told her I was thinking about buying it. Got a raise. You know. This led to another lie and another car for her to try. I got caught when I wrecked a Cadillac not five blocks from the lot. I got sent up and did two years. I am trying to be accomplish something to show my wife and her Mother and my kids, that I am responsible, that I *will* be somebody. I want to be more than a bellman. I want them all to admire me so bad. Does that make sense?"

"Sure does, and you are definitely somebody. Keep on plugging. Your wife is proud of you, I would bet on it, no matter what you do for a living. We will stay in touch for sure." Roman reassured him. Diana gave Cliff a peck on the cheek and Roman took his hand in both his and shook it firmly. They waved goodbye and rolled in behind a station wagon, headed out of the Crescent City.

CHAPTER 11

The trip back was uneventful, but seemed to pass in no time. They talked about anything but what they had just seen and done. Roman could not get John from his thoughts. Was he doing enough to help find his killer? He would get the picture and the Ardovino name to the right persons through Rex and put something in motion. Surely, someone might know the dark man with the pony tail and expensive tastes, but who was the lone figure that had his profile exposed for a split second to him? He decided he had probably not seen the man in the car. Just a close resemblance somewhere.

"I can't believe we made such good time. Your hometown is about to come in view." Roman smiled at Diana. She stretched and leaned across the seat for a quick kiss. He caught a glimpse of the muscle in her calf. Her long legs had the best shape he had ever seen.

"Why don't you come back with me to the house after we get in?" She asked. "No need to hurry to your place. Besides, it's not even dark."

"I'll go check on things, phone calls and whatever, and call you. Is that o.k.?"

"You know it is. If you've got too much to do, we'll make it later." Diana was considerate as usual.

They pulled down the long drive from the main road as late afternoon approached. Roman dreaded going back to his place near town. It had been especially depressing when he first would enter the rented old house, even though it was beautiful in its own way. He did not look forward to it, but he looked forward even less to engaging Norris, Sr. in conversation at this point.

He unloaded her bags and personal gear, then kissed her goodbye at the gate to the neatly manicured yard that surrounded the sprawling home. The slight smell of hay, for the horses out back, only enhanced the natural beauty of the place to him. He longed for a home of his own and stability again. He hoped it would come someday. For now, he must stay focused on other pressing matters.

He pulled into the long driveway and parked near the front door. He wanted to avoid the garage for today. John's Bronco was still parked there. His Mom and brother had not come for it and he wished they had.

He pulled down the tail gate to his Blazer and noticed the separated curtains fall back together in the old two story home next to him. He caught a glimpse of a figure move slowly away from it. The silhouette appeared to be the old lady again...guess curiosity got the best of her. Not to mention the fear, since John's murder. It was too late now, but he would introduce himself at the first early opportunity.

He threw his bag on the bed and slipped into some running shorts, T shirt and his Nike's. He yearned to run to clear his mind. Good decision. For four miles he pushed himself faster than he had been accustomed. His mind flew as his pace accelerated. He didn't feel the pain he normally would at this pace. It was as if his mind was outside his body and no pain existed. He eased off his pace as he returned within sight of the house.

He'd taken on a couple of admirers: Two boys, no more than ten, followed him on their bikes. He feigned a race with them for the last quarter mile. He waved as he slowed to a walk at the end of his driveway. They grinned from ear-to-ear, thrusting their arms up in victory signs, as they pedalled without touching the handlebars. He smiled, and watched them disappear down the long, flat road. It was almost dark, and he knew someone would be waiting for them for supper. He thought fondly of his own boyhood for a few seconds as he walked toward the empty house.

He showered, donned a pair of jeans and an old Ram's blue and gold jersey. It was time to make the call to Rex. He had put it off; maybe for fear of not being successful in getting help, or not knowing exactly what to say to him. But, he thought of what happened a few feet from him and started to dial Rex. Then he thought about while he was gone. What if his phones were now bugged? A little paranoia crept in. He grabbed his keys and pulled out the driveway for the nearby truck stop, where he had stopped before. He was there in less than five minutes, leaning against the wall, decorated with phone numbers and fingerprint smudges, not to mention a few grease stains. A picture of a missing girl was stapled to a bulletin board three feet away. A burly trucker, with his gut hanging over his too tight Levi's, was talking to someone on the other end of the line about his lack of desire to drive an eighteen-wheeler anywhere near New York City or its turnpikes.

He dialed and after three rings came an answer. "Hello". Joan was her usual pleasant self. Roman instinctively felt Rex was not there, but hoped otherwise.

"Joan, Roman again. Hope I didn't get you away from anything."

"Heavens no. Just doing a little cooking for tonight. I know you want Rex, not me. Hold on. By the way, I'll be looking for you to get up here to see us." She laid the phone down. Roman breathed a sigh and smiled.

"Sooner than you think," Roman said, but she'd gone for Rex and didn't hear him.

The deep, strong, southern voice on the other end of the line had not changed anymore than the man himself had. "Hello, Roman. Boy, it's good to know you're back in 'God's Country'. Roman held the receiver back to offset the booming volume.

"Rex, I can't tell you how good it is to hear your voice."

"Joan told me you called the other night. Still in L.A.?"

"Yeah, but I'm back here on a project the company I work for is developing."

"What kind of project and company?"

"Hazardous waste. They're a pretty good size operation. Got facilities in several parts of the country. L.A. is the headquarters. Anyway, they're got me in Indian Bayou to get the thing constructed and up and running."

"How's it going so far?"

Roman looked away for a second. "Fine, oh, fine. Lots of work, but it'll come around." He had forced the words. His heart wasn't in the project for the time being.

He changed the subject. "Are you still a tough, old law man?"

"Watch how you say old, you young rascal. You know how vain I am. I don't like gettin' old one bit." Rex laughed.

"Anyway, it's good to hear your voice again," Roman laughed with him. "I know I haven't stayed in touch lately, but you know that's not like me either."

"I know you've got to be a good man. You come from good stock. Any son of James Beckley can't help but be. Your Mom's a wonderful lady herself."

Roman shifted his weight from one foot to the other and smiled. He could see Rex and his father together fishing. "I appreciate that. You know the older I get the more I miss both of them, Rex." He couldn't hide the emotion in his voice.

"You got problems, Son?" If you do, you know you got a friend in ole Rex. I know you didn't call twice for no reason at all. Not that we're not friends, but something tells me there's some kind of trouble in the air."

Roman almost thought he was talking to a fortune teller. It was uncanny that Rex knew. He did have problems. Where to begin was one of them. "Say, Rex. You still like to fish?"

"When I can find the time."

"Can you make the time for an old friend's son, who wants to catch a bass at your lake in the big hamlet of Lula? Is tomorrow too soon?"

"I wouldn't do this for just anyone, but for you, I'll take the time. Besides, if I recall, and that was years ago, you showed up the old master. Only, if you're going with me, we have to get out there early. That city life may have you used to sleeping late." If Rex only knew how little sleep he had lately, Roman thought.

"You name the time. I do have to drive from Indian Bayou, so allow for that."

"I'll allow for that. Was gonna ask you to be here at five, but under the circumstances, I'll up that to six or six thirty."

Roman knew what a stickler Rex was about time and promptness, like practically all the men of his generation were. He was determined not to let on — that it was pushing things a bit. "Make it five thirty. I never lost that Mississippi upbringing about getting up with the chickens. I'll be there ready to catch double what you do." Laughter filled the line before they hung up.

He decided to dial Diana while he was still at the trusty truck stop. She insisted he come for dinner. There would be no one around since the folks would be over at the country club for their once-in-a-blue moon night out. He couldn't say no. Besides, he was becoming so attached to her that he wanted to see her more and more. The feeling was mutual. She sensed his needs and understood what he was going through, especially being new in town and scarcely knowing anyone. She was enjoying a new-found happiness she had not known in years. Like Roman, she had not been looking for anyone. That made their finding each other even more meaningful. She closed the oven that housed the roast- duck and began preparing the rest of the meal for the two of them.

"It's me," Roman knocked and announced, as he strolled into the den. The grandfather clock by the study door rang eight times. He was thirty minutes late. Diana rounded the corner from the kitchen wearing a short, navy cotton skirt that clung appealingly to her shapely frame. Her teal-green blouse matched her sensuous green eyes. She wore beige loafers with no socks, showing her tanned lovely legs. The thought crossed his mind; he was underdressed in his khaki shorts and black T shirt. He dismissed it instantly when their eyes met.

She took his arm and gently pulled him out the back door to the patio. "Wait here — be right back." She emerged with two glasses of Dom Perignon, compliments of the Palmer wine cellar.

"You look more beautiful every time I see you. Even if it's only a few hours between." Roman brushed back her long hair, a motion helped by the gently-blowing, early-fall breeze. He marveled at her eyes and full pink lips, as he pulled her to him. Their kiss was long and tender and exciting. The scent of her soft perfume next to her smooth, flawless skin, swept away any thoughts of the outside world. He was lost in her presence.

"Wow! We'd better go and check the food," Diana said, as they eased apart.

"What food? Who's hungry?" Roman reached for her hand, pulled her close and kissed her again. She readjusted her soft, clingy skirt and they headed for the kitchen.

"You can take a seat any minute. Want a drink?"

"No thanks. I'm a little tired. If I have another I may be here for the night."

She smiled, raising her eyebrow, as she pulled a large pan from the oven and set it on the stove top. "I could think of worse places to be."

"You can say that again. Anywhere with you would be enjoyable."

"You know the right things to say." Roman wondered, as he was about to say some he had said before.

He cleared his throat lightly. Diana handed him a small piece of duck to sample. He chewed it briefly, smiled, and signed approval with his index finger touching his thumb in a circle.

Then his smile faded. "You know what we discussed before the trip? I don't want to be redundant, but you must keep this to yourself. I meant to mention it when we got back earlier, but got sidetracked. No need to worry your Dad, or Mom, or Norris, Jr., for that matter. Trust me, it's better for now."

She stopped and held both his hands. "Roman, when I told you I will keep this in confidence, I meant it! Including my family. Don't worry." She smiled reassuringly and brought out the salad and casserole to compliment the roast duck.

They ate and limited the conversation to themselves. Light and breezy. Nothing of John's death, or the sheriff, or anyone else. The meal was delicious, but Roman felt fatigue creeping in after he finished his plate and a second glass of expensive spirits.

He stirred himself, however. "You said your parents were gone to the club. But, what about Norris, Jr.? I wanted to speak to him. At least say hello."

"He's in his room. He seems especially despondent this evening. He's probably reading. I appreciate the gesture, but we'd better leave him alone. Sometimes, it's best that way."

"I understand. Speaking of rooms, I guess I'd better get to mine. I have to be in Clarksdale at the crack of dawn in the morning. Got an appointment with a couple of people. It may be late when I get back, but if it's okay with you, at least I'll call." He didn't know why it didn't sound right to tell her about Rex and involve her further for the time being. He was going to Clarksdale, a little past it, but nevertheless, to it. He did have a meeting, an early one at that. She gave an understanding look and started to clear the table. He grabbed an apron off a nearby rack and began rinsing dishes for the dishwasher.

Roman could easily have stayed much longer, after kissing her goodnight for the third time. But, somehow, he had the good sense to try to get a few hours of sleep, at least. Four a.m. would come extremely early. He would not be late for Rex, or the bass that would be lurking in the lake. The thought of bass fishing was not as alluring as usual. But he had to indulge Rex. That was the least he could do for what he was about to ask.

CHAPTER *12*

The alarm clock pierced the silence of the early morning. He sat straight up in bed and slapped the button down, yawning and stretching for a few seconds. He thought of Rex and headed for the coffee machine. He cranked it up to do two cups and hit the shower. He threw on a pair of old jeans, a sweatshirt, his worst running shoes, and was out the door with a cup of Maxwell House in hand. His headlights hit the street at exactly 4:25 a.m. He would make it to Rex's by 5:30. Traffic was almost non existent, except for an occasional pickup and a giant mechanical cotton picker or two, rolling along.

Finding a decent radio station at this dark hour seemed futile, until he tuned in the powerful Jackson country station, airing the "Art & Scott Show", two humorous local DJ's whose company he welcomed. There was not much music he didn't like, from country to blues, to jazz, and classical when the mood was right. But, he had begun to like country music more because of its sincerity and the lyrics relating to everyday life.

He tried to get lost in the lyrics of a song coming in by Clint Black, but try was all he could do. His mind wandered back and forth. What was the connection of Norris, Sr. with Zach Stiles? Who was Mrs. Hendrix, and why did she call to tell him about Stiles's trip to New Orleans? Who was the man with the pony tail? Who was the person in the back of the limo that met Stiles and him? Most of all, why did John have to die? He shook his head and tried to concentrate on the music.

It was still the not quite daylight when he noticed the road sign for Parchman Penitentiary. The memory of that first night scene, when he first met Stiles, shot through his mind and left a bitter aftertaste. As he approached the sprawling grounds, he could feel the anxiety surface. Was it something going on in there that got John killed ?

As he approached the grounds, which were slowly becoming visible from the highway, he turned the volume off and lowered both of his front windows. Nothing was audible but the eerie sound of crickets, as if they were in a symphony with other creatures by the roadside, blending with the humming of the engine. He shivered, turned the radio on again, and hit the up-window button. He put his foot to the accelerator, taking his chances on seventy instead of fifty five for as long as he could. The long, flat Delta highway presented that opportunity more than most roads.

As daylight crept onto the horizon, he could see rows and rows of cotton lining each side of the highway. Huge cotton-picking machines sat conspicuously by the roadside every mile or so, it seemed. They looked like giant mechanical cages with wheels, filled with tons of the white filament bound eventually for the marketplace, to be turned into money for some hard-working farmer. This year's crop looked better than some he had seen growing up in Mississippi.

Rex's two-story ranch-style home was framed by a split-rail fence that rambled across the front and around both sides, and must have covered at least two-and-a half acres within its boundaries. There were hundreds of other acres that were theirs, but they were scattered and separated in all directions from the main house. He came from a long line of successful planters. He had broken the tradition by going into law enforcement. But the legacy and money that were left him, afforded him some luxuries that a law officer's check would not. Still, he managed to remain unpretentious and accessible to his close friends. He was known as tough, but fair, depending on the person you talked to and what side of the law they were on. He was well known throughout Mississippi and much of the South in law enforcement circles. He was labeled tough, tenacious, even controversial, on more than one occasion.

Rex stood by the front swing, appearing to study the dark soil just off the end of the porch. He looked up just as Roman approached the steps, rod-and-reel in hand. They shook hands vigorously, then embraced and slapped each other's back.

"You know, we can dig some damn good worms from that black dirt down there," Rex hinted, "They might do better than those plastic worms you probably brought."

"You gotta be kidding, Rex. I don't want to waste the time and effort to dig worms, when I got a selection you won't believe in my plug box." Roman smiled and swatted a mosquito circling his head, thankful he'd bought artificial bait.

"Okay, now that we got that settled, how in the world are you?" Rex smiled and looked Roman up and down quickly.

"I'm better now that I've seen your smiling face."

"Flattery will get you some hot coffee and a couple of ham and biscuits. Joan's still asleep, but she fixed em' a few hours ago. All I've got to do is pop them in the microwave for a few seconds. I've already eaten mine."

"I won't turn you down on that deal. The ole stomach says its time to eat before I catch all the bass up at the lake." Rex shook his head and grabbed his gear. Roman swallowed his breakfast, and they hit the door like there was an emergency.

He observed Rex as he strode out to the shed where the boat was housed, impressed that he had stayed in good shape at his age. Excellent shape. It was a good feeling to be going fishing with an old friend of his Dad's, especially an old friend he hoped would have some answers.

The family lake was about a mile and half deep into the woods that encircled a giant cotton field, naturally. The scarlet sun creeped over the horizon as they pushed away from the bank. The weeds had grown up two feet high, a good inducement for some rather large snakes and other varmints to make themselves at home around the lake side. Roman was relieved to see none this morning, so far. The 21-acre body of water was so still this early morning, that one could hear, almost feel, the slightest trickle of water caress the side of the 16-ft. Starcraft as they left shore.

Rex used a small trolling motor instead of the big motor to cut down on the noise. They also had plenty of time and didn't need the power or speed of the big one. They silently eased up on two huge old tree trunks that jutted out of the water about fifty feet or so from shore. Rex eased the anchor down several feet to the cold depths of the lake's bottom. The depth finder read six feet. They each cast in different directions. Not a word had been uttered, and Roman tried to look engrossed in fishing. He would try. He wanted to speak, but waited for Rex to break the silence. After all, Rex must know there was something pressing on his mind for him to drive up here in the first place. He would wait a few more minutes.

The intensity lasted ten minutes when Roman spoke the first sentence.

He almost whispered, in order to not disturb the fish or throw off the concentration Rex had mounted by now. "Rex, you've known me for a long time. You knew my Dad even longer and better. You know I didn't come just to fish. Don't get me wrong. I enjoy it, but...."

Rex quietly interrupted, which was a feat considering his deep baritone. "You never have to make excuses to me, son. You're with family now. Well, practically. Tell me what's on your mind. I could tell by the phone call, it was important." He nodded to Roman. "Go on, son, the fish don't care if we talk." Rex leaned back and cast to the bank's edge with perfect precision, not missing a beat.

Roman held his spinning rod out of the water momentarily. "You may think I've gone wacko or something when I finish telling you all that's transpired lately. I won't bore you with all of it, just the highlights. Or, in this case, low lights."

Rex reeled in his line, but stared and listened intently. "Go on. I may cast a few, but I hear every word and I'm taking it in, believe me."

"I'll get some of the shocking part out of the way, first." Roman stopped again, looking toward the lake's edge. He shook his head slowly. "This will sound hard to believe, but hear me through. I'm almost certain that the Wildflower County Sheriff is into something highly illegal, and I don't mean some small time nickel-and-dime deal. I mean big! I know almost for certain he killed, or had someone kill one of my best friends. Happened in Indian Bayou. In fact, John was the only person I knew when I came there recently."

Rex put his fishing rod down in the boat. "Go on. I'm listening."

Roman exhaled slowly. "Do you know this guy? Zach Stiles is his name. Macho-type to the bone. Ex-Vietnam veteran, enlisted man. Tall, about in his early forties...."

"You don't have to go on any further describing him. I know him. Not well. I met him once on a stakeout a few years ago. I think he's been re-elected at least once there."

"Yeah. He's got somebody fooled."

"Anyway, on the stakeout I got the impression that he thought the world of himself. I remember he was a cocky sonofabitch, for sure. Didn't talk to him much. Didn't want to, so I shouldn't be quick with my opinion of him. He did leave me with a bad taste about him. That much you're right about him."

"Let me put it this way, Rex. If I can convince you that what I told you is true, or has a damn good chance of being true, will you help me get to the bottom of this?"

"Son, you know I will, but why are you so interested? You could get in over your head. After all, you're not a lawman. It may be some small time operation, anyway. Some illegal gambling or any number of things like that. A sheriff like that is not going to take many chances on something that'll get him in trouble. Got me? I mean, you shouldn't get too involved."

"I don't know if I can explain why I'm taking this so personally. It's gone so far that I am willing to do anything it takes to bring this cruel bastard down." Rex zeroed in intently on every word Roman spoke. "I know an innocent man that I cared a lot about lost his life. Murdered in cold blood. I know Zach Stiles is up to something dark and wrong."

"I did hear about the shooting."

"How'd you hear? Paper?"

"It was in there, but I heard through some other guys around."

Rex leaned back and cast smoothly to the bank again. Roman kept his rig in the bottom of the boat and looked at the spot where the lure landed. Rex gave a lightning-like tug on the rod. He set the hook on a bass. The reeling began, water rolled and splashed near the lure.

"Let him have a little line," Roman said, simulating the motion. "Sorry about the advice. I forgot you know what you're doing."

"You're right though." He released the line to let the fish play. He reeled his line tight and let it go again. He repeated this until he could feel the big bass was tiring. "Get the net." Roman reached out the long aluminum pole and submerged it below the bass, but the fish swerved one last time just underwater, then leaped three feet into the air, fighting, flopping all the way down. Roman caught him as he splashed back into the water and emptied him gently into the boat.

"He'll go five pounds at least, Rex."

"Close to it. This makes getting up before daylight worth it, huh?" Rex unhooked and placed him in the container filled with water. Under a pound went back into the lake. This one was a keeper.

"Now, back to the business at hand," Rex said, as he rinsed his hands by leaning over the side of the boat. "Where were we?"

Roman smiled. He was eager to resume. "I know you'll think I'm crazy for what I'm about to tell you, but I've already done it. I followed the man to New Orleans." Roman cast his line out once again and let the lure sit. "I got a call tipping me off that the sheriff was going down there to meet someone. Don't ask me why, but it turned out to be true. Stiles told his staff that he'd be in Jackson for the weekend, at a Boys' Ranch meeting. But, he didn't slow up in Jackson. I saw him at dinner, with a shady-looking foreign guy, pony tail and all. They got in a limo after dinner at Tugajue's with another guy and wheeled off. I think I might have seen the other guy before. I'm not sure. It was dark, and the limo had tinted windows. It was all like a flash, almost. I won't go into details, but I have pictures of Stiles and the foreign guy. Also, the big fat guy they were with is named Ardovino. Local hood, I hear. Believe it or not, I made friends with this bellman from the Dauphine Orleans, whose brother-in-law is a cop. He got the information on the limo and passenger, Ardovino. I'll give you the Louisiana tag number."

Rex reeled his artificial plug slowly, without a sound. "Who called you with this tip, and why would they?"

"Again, this sounds strange, but this lady called me just a few nights ago, just before Stiles left for New Orleans. She said she worked in his office and her name was Mrs. Hendrix, but I had to promise her I would not call her or cause her any problems. It was like she knew of the problems I'd had with Stiles. I'll fill you in on that later. Anyhow, all I know is that she sounded like a sincere lady. I was afraid, at first, it might be a set up, but it obviously wasn't. Still, I can't figure out why she did it. She said she'd be in touch, for me not to call for her. Like I said, there's quite a bit more to this thing that I'll explain. One thing that I keep thinking about is something John — my friend who got murdered, told me. He was a vocational rehabilitation officer at Parchman and took me on an informal tour of the place just a day or so before he was killed. He said he was 'on to something big'. I believe, that's the way he put it. The way he talked, it sounded like whatever it was had to be going on right there in the penitentiary. I didn't quiz him enough, because he was obviously reluctant, to tell me anything. He just said he'd tell me later, when he could get some more names and facts. I never thought I wouldn't get to discuss it with him again. I've tried to remember just exactly what he told me. He did indicate that it had to do with the prison, I'm certain. At least, *he thought* it had something to do with the prison. I know that." Roman jerked the line and missed his only strike thus far.

Rex never noticed. "Anything else that you think is pertinent? Might as well discuss it now, out here." He maneuvered the boat another thirty feet, near a large stump.

"Well, yes. The first night I came in from Los Angeles. I was driving a rental car and stopped during a storm outside the prison for a just a few seconds to look. Next thing I knew, that demon had me thrown up against the car. Took my .357 and handcuffed me. The whole bit. He overdid it. He was anything but cordial. Told me to watch myself. I tried to tell him up front what I was going to be doing down here. He even said — yes, I remember, he said, 'I know who you are. I'm the law around here and not much gets by me'. Said he knew all about when I played ball for Ole Miss and the Rams. I had almost forgotten he said that until now. It was a little spooky. One more important thing. I've been seeing this young lady whose dad owns this big spread. The same night that John was killed, I was using her dad's Jeep Cherokee to go home during a hell of a rainstorm. He pulled me over, thinking I was her dad and yelled, 'We took care of the problem. Permanently.' Then he roared off in the storm. Only a few minutes later, I found my friend shot in the back of the head, in the driveway. He was renting the guest house behind the house I'm renting. In fact, his girl friend helped me get the place. They were supposed to get married soon. It's sad, to say the least."

"Let's finish fishing, and you need to stay overnight with us. I got some good ribeyes and Joan can fix up the rest. I need to get more facts, if possible, no matter how insignificant you think they are."

Roman breathed a little easier. He knew he had an ally at last, that he could get moving on this. He thought of the red meat he didn't need, but if Rex wanted him to spend the night, he would.

The official sheriff's car was parked off a side road that bordered Norris Palmer's catfish ponds. There were eight of them, perfectly squared off, in the middle of nowhere, surrounded by cotton fields on all sides. The farm-to-market road ran parallel to the ponds, and this road was even less traveled. The sun was slowly setting, as the two men met near the front of the pickup truck. There were no observers except the wild critters that roamed the fields and woods around this part, especially after dark.

"Zach, what's on your mind?"

"You, Norris. Just you. You know how I like to meet in person. Want to make sure you're dedicated to seeing this thing through. You seemed a little hesitant at the courthouse and at our midnight meeting." Stiles picked up a piece of straw, put it between his teeth, and chewed slowly.

"Zach, we've had a conversation or two about this. I don't like being questioned. Damn it, I mean it! I told you I was in, and that's final. I need the quick money. I've told you about the cash-flow problem I've got. It's a squeeze on me with all this land, and the way crops have been the last couple of years. You know my overhead is tremendous. There's no getting out for me at this point."

"That's good, Norris, because I've been talking to my source and he's beginning to get very pushy. He is demanding more and more, and can damn well get it somewhere else, if we don't come through. I've got others to answer to, and I have to have assurance that my people are committed."

"That's another thing, Zach. Who are these 'other people'? I believe you referred to them once as 'higher ups'. I don't exactly like the idea of doing something of this magnitude without knowing who is really runnin' the show up the line."

"Well, Norris, you'll just have to live with it for now. I can't divulge that information. In due time maybe you'll meet them. I can't promise. Just do your part now, and you'll be rewarded even more later. If you don't do your part, bad things could happen. Even to you!"

"Are you threatening me?"

"No. Making you aware of where we all stand in this. You are in too deep to turn around without serious repercussions, if you get my drift."

"No need to be redundant. I'm in and ready. By the way, what is whoever doing to become pushy with you? You getting threatened or is someone else in danger?"

"Not exactly. I just feel that he will put more demands on soon, to test our loyalty and dedication. He doesn't need us as much as we need him."

"Well, I'm heading home. You know how to reach me whenever it's absolutely necessary." Norris slid into the pickup and started the engine. Stiles placed his hand on Norris' elbow, which was resting on the door with the window down.

"Norris, between you and me, I'd watch that Roman Beckley. He's trouble, looking for a place to happen. He may find it soon. Real soon." Norris and Stiles each roared off in separate directions, as the sun slowly sank into the western horizon.

"How would you like your ribeye?" Rex shouted from the patio to Roman, who was locked into Joan's shopping tale of Memphis, and what was, or was not, on sale.

"Oh, about medium, thanks." Roman's vow to cut his red meat consumption to a minimum would have to wait. Besides, it sounded damn good. He was in Lula and he would do as Lulans do.

He accepted Joan's offer of a cold beer after a day in the sun. "Joan, Rex showed me the horses. I'd forgotten you both were into that. I know you're proud of them. They're beautiful. Diana would love them." He stopped. "Oh, I forgot to tell you about Diana. I've been seeing her lately. It seems like for a long time, but actually it hasn't been. She's quite a lady, and she's beautiful on top of it all."

"I'm glad to know you're seeing someone. We haven't been in touch much lately, but that doesn't mean we haven't been thinking of you after Leah's death. I can only imagine how that's been on you. We did call a couple of times and left a message on your machine in L.A."

"I know, and I appreciate that. I was in such a fog for so long. Still am somewhat. I don't know if I'll ever come to grips fully with what happened, or how it happened. Broad daylight. A curve she had made so many times. She was a good driver. I guess I'll never know why." He looked away briefly.

Joan changed the subject quickly. "Let's check on the chef and see if he knows what he's doing to our steaks." She grabbed his arm and eased him out the door to the patio, which was nestled next to several pecan trees in a back yard that went on forever. Crickets and fireflies made their presence known in the background. The aroma of the steaks sizzling on the grill appealed to the senses. He was hungry and ready. Who said there was anything wrong with eating red meat? Especially, tonight.

Joan ran back to the kitchen to check on her fixings, affording an opportunity for Roman and Rex to talk openly. Roman strolled around the patio, absorbing as much of the pastoral calm as possible. He hadn't known much lately and was enjoying the peace. The Bud he was sipping was so cold he felt the condensation slowly rolling down the aluminum can onto his fingers. He tried to start the conversation lightly. "Rex, I guess you won the battle of the fish today. That doesn't mean the war is won though. I'll be back for a rematch."

"Anytime." Rex yelled over his shoulder, over the sound of the ribeyes sizzling on the gas grill. Smoke boiled out, the smell tempting the most fanatical, dedicated vegetarian.

"Getting back to our conversation about the sheriff and others, I do have good reason to believe that, on top of everything else, Diana's Dad is involved with him."

"Is that based on what he yelled from his car the night of the murder? You know you may have misunderstood him, Roman. He may have been talking about anyone or anything. It was raining, after all. Pouring, I believe you said. Something to think about." Rex flipped a steak over and looked at Roman briefly. "Like I said, something to think about. You want to be sure. Especially, when you start suspecting sheriffs of murder and asking people to investigate them."

Roman's relaxed expression changed for the moment. "Rex, I am not going off half cocked about this. I know what I heard. I also know what I saw. Stiles was not in Jackson, but New Orleans. I have also been threatened by him. I guess I'd call it that. He took my .357, as I told you. He came to my house the day after John's funeral and hinted very strongly that my pistol could turn up — that I could be a suspect. That made me furious, but he had me for the time being and he enjoyed it. I reminded him that he had my pistol and he gloated, saying it might turn up if I got out of hand. He left no doubt, it's in his possession. It was my dad's and I want it back for sentimental reasons and other reasons that are obvious."

"Come with me for a minute," Rex motioned, as he moved the steaks off to the side. They entered the sliding glass door into a tremendous den. Rex walked to a mahogany gun cabinet and pulled down rifle after rifle. Weapons of all sizes, calibers, and range were housed there. He reached to the top shelf, slid the leather holster down, and handed it to Roman. It was a heavy, blue-steel .357 Magnum, similar to the one Roman's dad had given him. "Take this with you and you'll have a little company. I call it six more men, to be exact. If this pistol could talk, you might enjoy some of the stories."

Roman admired the pistol and studied it, holding it away from Rex and pointing it upward. "I hate to take your pistol, but I can't say I wouldn't mind the company."

The stories connected to it were probably true, he thought. He didn't want to know.

"Here's some extra ammo. I keep enough around here not to run low." Rex grinned and closed the gun case. "Better check on those steaks. They ought to be ready by now."

The steaks were ready, and so was Roman by now. They decided to eat on the breezy patio underneath the stars. The meal was better than he even expected. Maybe it was the company of old friends. Whatever it was made his day. It was also later than he realized, and he needed to call Diana. After a few minutes of clearing plates, he excused himself to the privacy of the study and dialed the Palmer home, using his credit card.

Diana answered, to his surprise and delight. "Hello."

"Hi, Honey. I'm sorry, it's after nine, and I just got chance to call. I've been strung out most of the day. I'm so tired, I think I'll stay here tonight and come on in first thing in the morning. Besides, I need to make a stop by a landowner's place on the way back to Indian Bayou."

She couldn't hide the disappointment in her voice, so she changed the subject.

"When you get in and do all your things around the office tomorrow, come by the Club. Maybe we can have a late lunch. I'm teaching a little art class that meets once a week there. May get in a game of tennis afterwards, if I can find someone to play."

"I'll do my best to be there. You can persuade me to do most anything, you know."

They laughed together briefly. His voice trailed off softly. "I can't tell you how much I think of you when I'm away from you." He stopped short of saying anything else for the moment.

"The feeling is mutual. See you tomorrow."

He did miss her, and thought of her much more than he ever intended. He felt that it was indeed mutual. He eased back to the patio where Rex was signalling him to the big wrought-iron chaise lounge. Roman took a seat in it and Rex slid the matching chair up beside him. Joan was busy hauling dishes in to the house.

"Roman, when I asked you those questions about Stiles and I said you might be wrong, with the rain and all, and the way I sounded doubting, it was a test. I guess that's what you'd call it. I wanted to see, for sure, if you had true conviction about this guy and whatever's going on. I think you're convinced. That doesn't mean you're a hundred per-cent correct, but you show some definite conviction." Roman's blue eyes were fixed on Rex. "This Parchman Prison thing could warrant the FBI getting involved. I'm sort of close to an agent in Memphis. I've known him for years. He's got lots of experience and isn't on some ego trip to make a name for himself. Hell, he's proved himself already. Name's Lynch. Harold Lynch. Through the years, when I was chief investigator with the Highway Patrol, I had my differences in tactics with them, but he's different in a good way. He's a pro, flexible and reasonable. He's a bird dog too. He's tenacious as hell.

Never lets up when he's on the trail of something big. He'll listen and take action accordingly. He's not one of those know-it-all types. We've worked together on a couple of cases through the years."

Roman hung on every line. Couple of cases? Rex could always avoid being specific. He was cunning and vaguely informative. Just his nature, Roman thought. He had always been evasive. He had also been very successful in his career.

"Let me sleep on this. You be thinking of any slight, however insignificant details you might have forgotten, or haven't realized yet. I'll get hold of Lloyd and get with you soon. Son, I've been around a lot of dangerous situations in my life and let me say this, you are in one. You must watch your back and front. Try to carry on your job you were sent there to do as normally as possible. Of course, don't mention this to a soul, not even your lady friend. No one must think you are doing anything but setting up that waste deal. As hard as it may be, bite your lip and don't lose your temper if you're around that sheriff. If you're anything like your Dad, and you are, it takes a lot to set you off. Then if it does, it's curtains. I knew him well."

Rex stared for a few seconds into the gorgeous night's sky, then back at Roman. "Don't call me, I'll call you. Your phone is very likely, tapped. Home and office. If we call, it will be a code that you can't miss. Remember, don't call us until we call you. Be sure to go to a pay phone, or one you can count on being untouched by the bugs. I know Harold Lloyd will want to meet with you soon, somewhere away from Indian Bayou. We'll all agree on a town far enough away from there. Remember, and I know you should realize it by now, your life is in danger. Live accordingly."

They called it an evening just after ten, but sleep was elusive once again. Roman tossed and turned until after midnight. When his eyes finally became heavy, he drifted off, knowing that it was a start. He would not let up until it was finished, no matter what that involved.

CHAPTER *13*

R oman arrived back home early enough to shower, shave, change clothes and be at the office by 8:30 a.m. He had renewed vigor after enlisting Rex's help. He grabbed three fax messages and five off his answering machine. There was the dreaded sound of Gardner Lowe asking a return of his phone call of 5:00 p.m. central standard time the day before. He seemed to like to do that since it was only 3:00 p.m. west coast time. Two legislators had called and a representative from the Environmental Protection Agency left a message. The day was cut out for him.

He punched in the number of the LA office. Gardner Lowe was once again out of the office. The congenial secretary said, "Mr. Beckley, Mr. Lowe asked me to tell you that he would be flying to Mississippi on Thursday. This Thursday. I am following that up in a few minutes with a confirmation by fax. You just missed him. He said no need to pick him up. He'll get a rental car and be in the office by 8:00 a.m. Just to meet him on Friday morning at the office. He said he would get directions to the office from someone in the town."

"Oh?" Roman hurled a wad of paper into the wastebasket. "Is he coming alone? Is he coming commercial or using the company jet. And where is he coming in ?"

"I almost forgot. Mr. Elton Sanders will be with him. They're using the company jet. He only said Mississippi, not the specific city, so I'm not sure."

"And, how long to they propose to stay?" He managed to suppress the

116

irritation in his voice so that Lowe's secretary wouldn't notice. He was having to extract information as if he were an unknown at Worldwide.

"He is booked to leave there late Friday night, I believe. I don't know if they're going anywhere from there, but he's got the company pilot on duty all week end." Why all week end, Roman wondered, if they were going back to LA Friday night? That's all he needed, the two of them down here right now. Oh, well, they sign the checks. It's business as usual. They could not have come at a worse time, but at least they're only staying the one night, he thought. He hung up, placed a pencil partly off the desk's edge and tapped it into the wastebasket as well.

He waded through the other calls and faxes and made it out by high noon. He wanted to see Diana, if but for a few minutes. There were two more appointments after two, but he would have some time if he hustled on to the Wildflower Country Club.

There was no mistaking her body and the way she moved, even from 100 feet away. Her tan legs were striding gracefully, as she retrieved and sent the tennis ball back with topspin and speed that was surprising. Her opponent, a somewhat heavy-set teenage girl, had to huff and strain to stay competitive. He only needed to watch another two points being played out to see what the outcome of this match would be. After serving an ace for the final point of the match, Diana was a graceful winner as she patted the red-faced young girl on the back. She promised to give the younger one some pointers on the game, as they parted at the net with a friendly wave.

"Wow, you were something else out there," Roman whispered, as he walked up behind her while she packed away her racket in a leather bag.

"Hi, Honey," Diana responded, as she toweled off. "Don't give me too much credit. That girl has promise; she just needs a little more work. She'll probably pound me a year or so down the road." She smiled and touched his cheek. He threw both arms around her waist and slipped in a quick kiss.

"I'm a little too wet with perspiration for that, but I'll take it anyway."

"Hey, the sweat doesn't bother me. I missed you, even if it was just one night."

"You're not the only one. It seemed longer. Did you get much accomplished?

"I think so." He felt a little guilty for not divulging everything, even if it was better for now, that she not know everything.

"Go on to the clubhouse and I'll be in the dining room shortly. I have to shower. Be out in a jiffy." She pointed toward the clubhouse and trotted toward the showers near the poolhouse.

The Country Club was buzzing with activity, even though it was week day at noon. The sound of tennis balls being hit back and forth on the hot surface blended with the voices of the golfers nearby, teeing off at the first green. Children were scarce, since school was in session. There were, however, toddlers being attended to by two older black ladies in neatly-starched white dresses, strolling around inside the clubhouse in search of another few minutes of diversion for the youngsters. It was definitely the place the affluent of Wildflower county and thereabouts frequented. For the most part, Roman had found these fortunate ones to be friendly and cordial to a stranger such as himself. Especially, a stranger helping a California company come down here to set up a hazardous waste facility. But, still there was no doubt there was a social barrier not easily meshed into by just anyone. It took a while to be accepted into the inner circles, he observed. Not that he wanted to, for certain.

Roman made his way to the dining room, filled with men in golfing attire, and women whose tennis outfits had been more than casually chosen. The small frys had been delegated to a room nearby. He thought about the several phone calls still hanging in the balance and headed for the pay phone area. Two spotless phones were mounted on the rich mahogany walls, unlike the truck stop phones he had grown accustomed to. He could see the parking lot and part of the first green. He had just finished his call with the E.P.A. representative, who nearly gave him a numb ear, when he spotted the car. He thought he might be mistaken, then leaned forward enough, stretching the phone cord to see more of the parking lot. It was that same, damn, green Chevrolet with the lights and star on the door. It seemed to be everywhere. He noticed the driver park at the back of the lot in the shade of a huge oak tree. He could not tell if it was a deputy or Stiles, until the driver pulled off his official hat and brushed back his long black hair. Roman's eyes widened. It was Stiles, no mistake. The Sheriff sat staring straight ahead, through dark aviator sunglasses. He must be waiting on him again. Then, out of nowhere, the red Jeep Cherokee rounded the aisle where he was parked and slowed to a crawl. Stiles waved and pulled up beside Norris Palmer. Roman swallowed, his mouth suddenly dry, his stomach feeling a bit queasy. "Damn it. I knew it," he whispered, mumbling to himself, watching.

"I thought you were going to be discreet about our meeting with one another, Zach," Palmer said. "What happened to that?"

"Oh, there's no problem with the sheriff chatting with an upstanding citizen like yourself, Norris. This couldn't look suspicious to anyone. Besides, this will only take a minute. I doubt if anyone will see us to begin with."

"What do you want?"

"I don't want to interrupt your social time or golf game, but I hope you took my advice about Diana not getting too thick with Beckley."

" First, I don't have much social time and I don't play golf. I came to see Diana play tennis for the first time in years. Just a change of pace. As far as Diana's private life, I told you how I feel about that. She's a grown woman."

"Well, I have a little plan that will eliminate him from her life."

"Zach, damn it! I said no more violence. I'm in this other mess up to my eyeballs, but I won't hear of any more. Besides, I certainly don't want my daughter's safety jeopardized. Do I make myself clear?"

"Don't get me wrong. There won't be any bloodshed or violence of any kind. Let's just say, he won't look to good in her eyes anymore."

"Just remember what I said, Zach."

"No problem. You wealthy plantation owners got too much time on your hands to worry about insignificant things. Or, should I say, a wealthy plantation owner that's in debt to the hilt. Remember who's your ticket out of that debt, Norris. Remember. I'll be in touch about the next meeting. Same time. Same place."

As Stiles and Norris, Sr. roared away in opposite directions, Roman rattled the receiver into the phone cradle without looking and headed back to the dining room. His appetite was gone.

Across the room, by the large picture window, sat Diana. She motioned to Roman with her sunglasses. Her hair was still wet and brushed straight back. She was smiling and he tried to do the same.

"Something wrong?" she asked. "You look a little distant."

"Oh, uh, no. Nothing at all." He slid back the chair, squeezed her outstretched hand, and sat down. "You picked a good table." The view was of a meticulously manicured course, stretching into seventy-five-foot oaks wrapped around a serene kidney-shaped lake some 150 yards away.

"How was your trip to Clarksdale?"

"It was good." He tried to smile and changed the subject. "Do you play golf out here, as well as tennis?"

"I try sometimes. Let's say I'm more of a tennis player." She smiled as the lady approached their table, menus in hand.

Roman ordered the tuna sandwich with iced tea, and Diana chose the chicken plate. Lunch was quiet until she was paged to the phone. Soon after she had excused herself, he decided a trip to the men's room was in order. He rounded the corner to the bathroom, which was adjacent to the house phone and pay phones. He was suprised to see Diana, her back to him, engaged in a conversation on the house phone nearest the ladies' room. He didn't want to eavesdrop, but heard only an apparent answer from Diana: "Yes, Dad, I know we discussed it, and I *will* tell him. I'll do it soon."

She sounded slightly irritated, which was unlike her, but she also sounded disappointed. Before she could see him, he stepped away from the phones and eased into the men's room. He could not imagine what the answer implied. He anticipated the worst, but brushed it off. She could be talking about her brother, or anyone, but himself.

As he returned to his seat, they smiled uneasily at each another. He commented on the view again, searching for words. Just then, a rotund, older man teed off and laughed wildly with two friends, obviously joking about golfing skills. Their food arrived shortly, but Diana picked at her chicken salad, rearranging the lettuce noticeably.

"Roman, there is something I want to discuss with you," She said, suddenly becoming serious. His stomach dropped, but he smiled broadly to disguise his anxiety.

"I'm all ears." He had no clue what was coming as he stared into her soft green eyes.

"I was going to wait until tonight, but decided the sooner, the better." He really felt his stomach churn now. He set the tuna sandwich down and pushed it a few inches away from him. He prepared himself to face the music. After all, he had done no wrong, to his knowledge. "Dad has asked me to go to Europe with Mom for a few weeks." He hated it, but was determined not to show any disappointment. "This is sort of sudden, but I feel I owe it to them."

"I understand." He didn't.

"That's not all, I guess. You know I've been back here for a few months and really living off them, more or less. Mom will be coming back in three weeks, but there is this art school I've been wanting to go to for quite a while. I have been accepted and I guess I'll be there for several months, studying. I don't know though...."

He sipped his tea and showed no emotion outwardly. "Where in Europe? Sounds exciting."

"Paris. It sounds that way, but leaving you gives it a different light." She reached across the table and held his hand with both hers.

He withdrew slightly and leaned back in the chair. "Hey, you do what you've got to do. I understand." He didn't totally. By this point, the sandwich was abandoned.

"I haven't decided for sure. I do feel some obligation to go with Mom. Her life is in need of ..., let's say, some uplifting. I do feel I owe it to both of them. She has been drinking more than she needs to, so the change will be good, I think. Like I said, it's sudden, I know, but Dad pleaded with me just last night. It's like he wants my Mom to enjoy the time away and the trip, but he can't get away to take her himself."

It was becoming clearer what was going on and who really wanted the trip to Europe and art school, and it wasn't Diana. He slid his chair back and leaned forward slightly, staring into her eyes. "Sounds like you two can get re-acquainted and have a great time doing it. Sometimes, I wish it was me doing something like that. In fact, I've never been to Europe. Plan to one day, though."

"The reason I wanted to talk about it now, instead of tonight, is that we are leaving soon."

"Oh, how soon?" He tried to sound casual.

"Friday. Seems Dad got my ticket and made all the arrangements a while back without telling me. I'm not sure why he waited only two or three days before we leave to ask me. Anyway, guess I should enjoy it, huh?" She looked lovingly into his eyes and leaned forward toward him. "I know I can't stay in Europe for that school. I think we both know that. I can't be away from you that long. Even three weeks seems like an eternity. I may have to cut the trip shorter than we are booked for. Strange, I should be looking forward to it, and normally would, but since I met you there is a different light on things."

Roman was relieved to hear her true feelings, but couldn't begrudge her the opportunity for the school if she wanted to stay. "If that's what you want to do, then by all means, do it. I'd be lying if I didn't say I'll miss you, but I've got lots of work to do and so on." He smiled and grasped her hand. "Hey, let's change the subject for now. You decide about the school and do what's best for you." He gathered his thoughts and decided to leave some doubt himself. "Besides, I do have a lot to do. Need to go back to LA and see some friends, not to mention my home office."

"Will you come out tonight and pick me up? I feel like we need to be together, away from my house. Know what I mean?" She smiled and winked, showing her dimples prominently. He returned the wink, agreeing totally.

He finished the rest of the day in a busy fog, and nighttime came sooner than he realized. After a meal at the local Chinese restaurant, they were finally alone at his place. Only a few words were spoken as they entered and very few that were audible until half an hour later. He brushed back her soft hair and leaned on one elbow. She gently wiped the perspiration from his brow and touched his face tenderly. The stream of dim light hit her face just right, revealing her radiance to him, even in the darkness. He knew it would be painful for them to be apart. She knew the same. They kept the conversation as light as possible until time to take her home, just after midnight. He saw a tear in her eye as he kissed her again at the Palmer's porch. He pulled a handkerchief from his back pocket and gently touched it to her face. They held each other tightly and kissed goodnight three times. Finally, they eased apart. As he walked toward his car, he turned slowly and saw her silhouetted against the moonlight. One night apart would be a long time, much less three weeks.

Roman pulled out his guitar, strummed some old familiar tunes, and tried to get his mind away from her. With his eyes half-closed, television didn't interest him at all. Finally, he fell asleep, reading a book of poetry Leah had given him when they first met.

Less than two hours later, the sound of knuckles rapping on his front door jarred him from sound sleep. He scrambled for his jeans. No time for a shirt. He grabbed the .357 Rex had loaned him and checked for ammunition as he stumbled and rubbed his eyes. Stunned by the intrusion, he gripped the revolver, extended it with both hands, and walked toward the front of the house.

He stopped four feet from the door. He saw a figure, but he couldn't make out who it was through the stained-glass upper half of the old solid-core door. He immediately thought of the local law, but he noticed the figure was smaller. Roman yelled out with authority:

"Who is it?" He glanced around for the grandfather's clock in the adjoining living room. 2:05a.m. "I said, who in the hell is it?"

A sultry voice came through the door. "It's Patricia. I've had some car trouble. May I use your telephone?"

"Who?"

"Patricia Wells. My car quit on me about 100 yards from here. I'm stranded. I won't be but a minute." The voice was strained.

Roman hesitated, then cracked the door, keeping the safety chain still intact. She was a shapely lady in her 30's, who seemed legitimate. Her bleached blond hair glowed as she passed by the one light near the front door. "What happened to your car?" Roman yawned, rubbing his eyes. He had slipped the .357 into the back pocket of his Levis. He looked out into the darkness as she pressed the buttons on the phone.

"Can you come pick me up? I just had my car quit, out near the intersection of 82 and 49 highways. You can't miss it. It's near a big two-story white house with a guest house in the back. I think it's the one where the man got killed the other night. Thanks, I'll see you in five minutes or less." She hung up the phone and smiled at Roman, glancing quickly at his lean, muscular physique. Her eyes rested for a split second on his bare chest. She glanced away. "Thanks for your help. Didn't someone get murdered here? The other night?"

"Yes. he did." Roman confirmed without explanation. She didn't ask for one. "You can wait here until he arrives if you like. I heard you say five minutes." He pointed to the sofa and offered a seat.

"No. No thanks, he'll be here in less, the way he drives. I'll just go on and wait in the car." She glanced at him seductively. He noticed this time, but moved his eyes away from hers, momentarily.

"Well, suit yourself. I'm glad you've got help coming," he said, as they walked toward the dimly-lit foyer. He opened the front door for her, and as if in slow motion, she turned, threw both arms around his neck, and planted a long, passionate kiss, full on his lips. He was flattered, but his mind was on but one lady. Besides, this sudden display of affection shocked him. She held the kiss until he placed his hands on her waist to move away. In the darkness of the yard, the camera clicked twice silently. The photographer knew how to use the infra-red light from his Vietnam days. The dim light from the hall just enhanced what he needed.

CHAPTER *14*

T he envelope was placed before daylight on the wrought iron bars holding the Palmer mailbox at the end of their long drive-way. It was addressed to Diana Palmer and marked "Personal and Confidential" and "Photos. Do Not Bend."

Coffee was brewing and cigarette smoke billowed from the Wildflower County Sheriff's office. It was 7:15 a.m. and a few of the regular day time shift were arriving for various duties. The man himself was seated behind closed doors with Deputy Wiggins. No one dared enter without a knock and good cause. This morning no one did.

"Sheriff, those pictures were as clear as a bell, to be taken at night. How'd you do that?" Wiggins grinned and wrinkled his brow.

"Something I picked up quite a few years ago in a far off country, Wiggins. It comes in handy at times. It did this time. Looked real natural, him standing there with just his jeans on and his hair messed up, with a blond in his arms in the black of night. Couldn't have asked for a better shot if I'd asked them to pose. I even had my blond friend follow it up with a phone call to the Palmer girl, bright and early, about their little night together. That should do it."

"You bet. One other thing, where'd the girl come from? She's quite a looker. I know I've seen her around here a time or two, but missed her name."

"The name's not important, deputy. Let's just say that she owed me a favor for something I got her out of a year or so ago. Know what I mean?"

"She did a number on Beckley. Looked like she'd just left from a little rendezvous at his place, didn't it?"

"Precisely. Knowing what I do about Diana Palmer, I imagine she has seen the last of her handsome friend. With her class, she probably won't even tell him why. One way or the other, that picture would take some tall explaining. Impossible, I would say."

"Hell, yes. He's history with her." Wiggins exclaimed, grinning to gain points.

"He will probably be history in more ways than with her. Permanently, I predict." They laughed and Stiles whirled the well-oiled chamber of his huge pistol around, admiring the deadly, clicking sound. Wiggins's black cowboy boots thudded against the floor as he headed out, adjusting his wide-brimmed hat. Zach Stiles donned his aviator sunglasses and stared out the window. He crossed his legs, and his size 11 eel skin boots came to rest on the edge of his desk.

He yelled out without turning around. "Wiggins. I want you to watch Mr. Roman Beckley. Don't be too obvious, but don't let him stray far without us knowing. Got it?"

"Right, Sheriff. You can count on me." The door slammed and a sinister smile crossed the Sheriff's lips. He twitched his finger on the trigger—then kissed the barrel.

Diana came down early, as usual, for breakfast; not as early as many farmers and farm hands that stirred in black darkness to start the day, but earlier than she had to. 7:30 a.m. and the smell of hot biscuits and ham saturated the air. She picked up a cup of coffee and searched for the morning paper in the kitchen, where Norris, Sr. usually left it at the crack of daylight.

"No paper in here, Diana," Norris Jr. volunteered. "But you do have a package addressed to you. An envelope, that is. Looks like someone must have left it at the mailbox during the night." Norris, Jr. manually rolled his automatic wheelchair up to her with the eggshell colored envelope in his hand. He turned away and made his way down the hall, as if to give her privacy. She laid it on the kitchen table, then sweetened her coffee and added a splash of cream. Her eyes were drawn to the prominently scrawled words. Her curiosity aroused, she picked it up and headed for the den, and sat near the light at the end of the sofa. She eased open the envelope, reached inside, and grasped the edge of the glossy 8x10. She flinched, holding it with both hands. She felt a wave of anxiety and disbelief. She closed her eyes in denial and reopened them. It was still there and no this was no dream. She studied the figures again, then quickly slid it back into the envelope. She felt the tears welling up inside and shook her head, searching for composure. She put the envelope inside the drawer of her dad's rarely-used, small table next to his desk. She walked from the room, wiping a tear from each eye, hoping to appear nonchalant if she should see Norris, Jr. She was glad he was out of the house on the back porch. She rushed down the hall towards her quarters.

"Honey, aren't you going to eat anything?" her Mom called from the kitchen. She had seen her pass the door.

"No, Mom. I've got some painting to do. I don't seem to have much appetite this morning. Thanks anyway. See you a little later on."

Roman spent the rest of the day returning phone calls, answering mail, and responding to fax messages. It would be easy to justify, asking Gardner Lowe for a secretary when he arrived tomorrow. He was too busy to do his own typing, along with thousands of other things to do, and he needed to be out of the office much of the time.

He paced the floor after signing a couple of requisitions for some office supplies and faxing them to LA. Diana's impending European trip was looming in the forefront of his mind. He had nothing more important to do until time for his meeting with the major contractor at the site, outside Indian Bayou.

Later, he drove to the huge site and spent most of the afternoon going over various plans with the general contractor. He arranged for a small trailer to be located at the site for the convenience and coordination of the project. He also drove to Greenville to purchase a mobile telephone for his Blazer. He decided not to inform Gardner Lowe of the number until later, avoiding constant accessibility for a few days.

He drove back to the office and checked his messages. So far, so good. No call from the home office. Lowe and Sanders were probably airborne by now from LA to Mississippi. Surely, he would get a call tonight, rather than them merely showing up as the secretary had said. He was surprised that there were no messages from Diana. He would call her from home in a few minutes. He locked the door and headed to his home on the outskirts of town.

He stared at the guest house and John's Bronco. The family still had not come for it. He thought about going in, to see if there were any clues left after the so-called investigation the Sheriff's staff had conducted He would do that later tonight.

After entering the house, he pulled the refrigerator handle and stared at the lone Bud Lite on the top shelf. He decided against it and filled one of his glasses with some two-day-old ice tea. Beer made him slightly groggy, and with his lack of sleep lately, he needed any advantage to stay awake and alert.

His fingers touched the phone for the third time before he gave in and dialed Diana's number. It rang four times. He started to hang up when her Mom drawled out a hello.

"Mrs. Palmer, is Diana in?"

"Let me check. She was painting. Then she went to the stables to ride. I'm not sure." Roman sat down on the couch and pulled back and forth on the long extension cord as he waited. He flipped on NBC's six o'clock news with the remote and propped his feet on the coffee table.

Mrs. Palmer finally responded. "Son, she must be riding again. I don't see her around her quarters. Can I have her call you?"

He hesitated. "Oh, yes, if you will. She has my number at home. Thanks." He hung up, wondering again why she hadn't called, then brushed off the thought.

Seven-thirty arrived and still no call. He became concerned. Maybe her Mom didn't give her the message. He reluctantly dialed back.

"Hello." Her voice was soft and unmistakable.

"Everything OK over there? I called for you earlier and got your Mom." His voice trailed off. He was surprised that she answered and had not called him back.

The silence lingered. She quietly cleared her throat and spoke barely over a whisper. "I've been doing some packing and a few things. Time sort of got away from me." He sensed immediately that something was wrong. Her usual warm response was not there.

"Is anything wrong? You don't sound the same as usual." He was determined not to push. After all, she was the one leaving town for Europe, not him. He let the silence stand. She would have to speak first.

She did, finally. "Roman, we need to talk for a few minutes."

"That's fine." He felt the chill; the cool distant tone of her voice was easily detected. "Want to come over to my place?" He picked up the tempo, trying to remain calm, considerate, and upbeat.

"No. Why don't you come out here? In, say, an hour?" She continued to speak very quietly.

"I'll be there, then. See you after a while." He hung up and sat in a daze. What could be the problem? He tried to think if he had done anything wrong. He couldn't recall. He showered in a daze, then changed into some old Levis and a red sweatshirt he had bought in Yellowstone Park several years before. He killed a little more time, even though he was anxious to find out what this was about. He told himself it couldn't be anything pertaining to them.

He pulled into the Palmer driveway at 8:35 p.m. and walked to the front door. Again, he was glad the rest of the family appeared to be gone, for now anyway. She answered the door, dressed in black cotton Bermudas and a white placket-front shirt, with a tennis racket displayed on the collar, and tennis shoes. She looked gorgeous, as usual, but her smile was obviously strained. He leaned forward to kiss her, but she pretended to hear a noise behind her and turned her head, leaving him feeling stranded in the doorway.

"I thought I heard the cat or somebody behind me," she said with cold politeness. "Come on in." The dreaded anticipation made him more than uncomfortable.

She led him to the same room he and Norris, Sr. had met, the first time and discussed his son and Vietnam. He observed the same room filled with trophies, war medals, pictures, momentos and hunting trophies. But, it didn't look the same to him, somehow, this time. She avoided eye contact until they were seated, facing each other. She was in the upright chair and he had sunk into the leather couch.

She spoke a little louder than on the phone, but she took forever, and chose her words carefully. " Roman, I can only say that maybe we rushed this. Whatever is between us, I mean."

He swallowed. "I thought you knew what was between us. I'd like to think I do. I don't understand. Only a few hours ago we were both in a different frame of mind and heart too, I guess. Now, something is wrong. Tell me what's on your mind. I really don't know." He was genuinely confused.

She glanced away and then back at him. "You don't?"

"No, I seriously do not!"

She stood, walked toward the fireplace, then turned and smiled half-heartedly at him. "It's just too much, too soon. Let's leave it at that. I thought we had more than we did." She stopped again.

"I am at a loss for words. I really don't understand. Let's don't play games like we're some junior high school kids. I'm not being sarcastic, but let's get it out in the open." He had no clue what had cast this black cloud over their relationship. Or did they have a relationship left now?

She looked deeply into his eyes for the first time of the evening. "Maybe we met at a time when we were both not completely ready for commitment again. Total commitment, I mean. I would rather leave it at that, if you don't mind."

He could barely hear her last sentence. He could see she was obviously deflated by something he must have done or was supposed to have done. He wanted to respect her plea, though he had no idea what had come over her.

"I will say this, Roman, I'm going to stay in Europe and enroll in the art school, and maybe do a little teaching, or whatever. That's the plan. I hope you can read between the lines. I don't want this to drag on. It's too painful for both of us. Maybe one day soon, you can make some sense of it. If you can think of anything you have done that would have come between us, please let me know. Try, and if you do, maybe there will be reason for us to talk. Maybe." She looked down at the floor, then raised her head and her eyes met his.

"I can try," He said, shaking his head in bewilderment. I guess I will never know what brought this on, but if you're that determined, I'll leave and stay out of your life." His voice was a little shaky, but he managed to hide most of his feelings. He stood and started to walk away, but turned and kissed her on the cheek, and held her for a brief moment. "Be careful. If you ever decide to tell me what went on, please do. I am in the dark." She smiled, as they eased apart, and turned her head to wipe away a tear.

He drove away in silence, no radio this time, just the sound of his Blazer's engine, whining down the long, winding driveway. He was too stunned to shed a tear. He couldn't believe this was happening and more than that, why? As he turned onto the main road, he glanced over his shoulder and saw her silhouette in the large window of the living room, watching him drive away. He looked once more through the rear view mirror, seeing her image grow smaller as the darkness separated them.

CHAPTER *15*

Roman woke at 6:00 a.m., suprised to still be on his sofa. His guitar was nearby, as were one empty and one half-full Bud Lite. He had never been a beer drinker, but it did induce sleep that he needed. His first thought was of Diana. He shook his head and headed for the shower. Afterwards, he donned his running gear, burst out the door and ran four miles. The second shower felt like paradise. He dressed with more care than usual, as Gardner Lowe and Elton Sanders should make their presence known today. He looked like a top male model in his Navy pin-stripe double-breasted suit and red tie dotted dark blue. He needed the lift. He psyched himself up for Lowe's visit, for whatever might happen with Diana, and in his quest for justice for John's death. He felt ready as he hit the door at 7:30 a.m. and backed out the long driveway using the rear view mirror, never veering from the straight concrete. He had forgotten to look in John's cottage as he had planned last night. To-night he would, or as soon as Lowe left town, for sure. He hit the main road and stopped for coffee and a cinnamon roll to go at his favorite truck stop.

At 8:15 he heard the knock on the front door of his office. Before he could react, the door opened and in walked Gardner Lowe and Elton Sanders. Lowe was dressed to the hilt in an olive-drab worsted suit that hung nicely on his tall, trim frame. His paisley tie blended perfectly. His thick salt-and-pepper hair was combed perfectly straight back, complimenting his piercing dark-brown eyes. Sanders wore his usual conservative black suit and trademark bow tie. He was Lowe's complete opposite, his bald head shining more than his suit. At five-feet-three, he contrasted even more. The attaché cases hit the floor and handshakes were exchanged in seconds.

They both opted for coffee with sugar only, no cream. Roman obliged and directed them into his private little office. They seemed pleased he had gotten so much for so little. It was definitely an act for Lowe and Roman knew it. Sanders was impressed though with his frugality. The dollars were no problem in this company, but nevertheless, this type simple arrangement seemed more like a dedicated company man. Roman had never been a fanatical corporate type, but he knew they had gotten more than their money's worth, especially down here. If they only knew how much — down here. He smiled and played the game, as they dove into the business at hand.

"How was your flight down here, Gardner?"

"Smooth as could be. Weather cooperated, and we had a little tail wind. Our pilot earns his pay most of the time, but I think he'll enjoy this trip. Rental car even ran well over here from Greenville." He chuckled to make his point.

"You all planning to stay over the week end?" He shuttered at the thought, particularly now.

"No. We're going on back to L.A. Too much to do to stay here long. That is, unless you've got some fair maiden that needs some company." Lowe eased out a laugh to disguise the truth. His trifling reputation was practically unparalleled for his age.

"I'm afraid I can't accomodate you in that category." Roman tried to smile.

"I was only kidding. I'm getting past that point." Roman remembered the old saying that a lot of truth is flung in jest.

"And, how have you been Elton?" Roman inquired politely. "You keeping the money flowing in the right places for the company?"

"I'm trying to do that, Roman. Still trying to run a tight ship." This could be the gist of Elton's conversational contributions for the rest of the time here.

"Where did you all stay last night? I sort of expected a phone call from you as to where you were staying or something." Roman added, as if he had felt neglected.

"We landed at Greenville. It was past eight, but even after nine by the time we got to the room. I didn't want to disturb you. I know you have been awful busy, and all. By the way, we had dinner with Lt. Governor Miles Crawford. In case we were seen by someone around here, I didn't want you to hear it second hand."

"I'm impressed." He wasn't, but played the game. In fact, he was a little miffed at being shunned.

"He is coming to the luncheon today, as you know. He called and decided to come up last night and meet us in Greenville. There really wasn't any reason for you to be there on such late notice. Like I said, I know you've got so much going on. No need to push you any further by having you meet us over there." It wasn't like Lowe to give such explanation for his actions. "You already met him when you first arrived anyway, I believe." Lowe was, as always, the diplomat. Again, it crossed Roman's mind that this interest by the Lt. Governor was unusual, but he kept his suspicions inside. Gardner Lowe was always on a power trip. The Lt. Governor meeting him was another notch in his ego, Roman supposed.

He changed the subject quickly. "I've got a trailer located at the site, and I'm meeting the contractor again tomorrow morning. Oh yeah, you'll be out of here by then. Maybe he'll be out there today. I know you both want to see what's being cleared and all that's going on out there."

"You bet," Lowe said. "I need to use your other phone for a quick phone call back to L.A." Roman picked up on the signal for privacy. He pointed to the other room and escorted Sanders to the front, near the coffee pot for a refill. Sanders grabbed another cup and smiled in his usual uncomfortable way without a word. Roman picked up the USA-Today paper and flipped through it as they sat on opposite sides of the room. Lowe reentered smiling and clapped his hands together, like a coach cheering his team on.

"Let's head out to the site. I can't wait to see how the development of this money-making facility is progressing. His remark again struck Roman somewhat off key. He had been going through hell, to say the least, and the timing was wrong. Lowe was the boss, however, so he would humor him for the few hours.

They piled into Roman's Blazer and rolled from the parking lot, out Highway 82 East toward the turn-off-road for the land.

"Where did you get this vehicle? It's not a regular rental one, is it?" Lowe asked, looking over his shoulder to the back of the Blazer.

"No. I got a good deal for a flexible lease, I guess you would say, for the time I'll be here. Wouldn't you say so, Elton?" He looked back at

Sanders for an answer, since the lease copy was forwarded to his office for approval.

"Oh, definitely." Other comments were kept primarily to the local scenery and small talk, until they turned onto the narrow, bumpy road that lead to the sprawling site. Roman dodged through a mine-field of holes, pretending to be oblivious to them.

Lowe spoke up. "We need this road widened, and some of these pot holes patched, or better, resurfaced out here. With the multitude of big trucks and heavy equipment coming in, this thing won't be too functional." He had begun his so-called constructive criticism.

Roman repressed his impulse somewhat, but managed to retort: "If this was totally resurfaced now, that would do two things that would not be practical. First, it would be a delay. You can't just knock this out in a few days, the resurfacing, I mean. Secondly, it would be torn to hell and back in no time again with all the weight of this machinery pounding on it. I've already discussed this with the State Representative from this county and the board of supervisors for the county. They are willing to do what's necessary to accomodate, but what is 'necessary', not streamline things to make it a luxury to ride on. I can see their point." He looked to the front passenger's side to Lowe. "Can't you?"

Lowe stared straight ahead for a moment and looked back at him. "I guess that makes sense. Still, try to get it resurfaced. As soon as possible!" He looked even more adamant, leaning back. He was bound to get in the last word to assert his authority.

Roman kept his eyes fixed on the flat, straight, old road. "That's already been agreed to, naturally. These people are aware of what the pluses are, but they're not going to totally give away the ship. They are, for the most part, good businessmen. You know they are willing to give those tax breaks we discussed, and the work force is plentiful and reasonable. Believe me, though, there is still a good deal of resentment about us coming to this area. That's not unusual in our business, but particularly so here."

"Why is it more here?" Lowe shot back.

Roman never missed a beat. "Because most of these people are natives of this part of the state. They have a lot of tradition here. The land is rich and has provided a lot of them with livings for generations. Their land is very special to them. It's almost sacred. I'm talking both large and small land owners. They compete in some ways, but they stick together. They don't want anything that might damage the environment around here for the future. They are skeptical by nature, especially when it comes to anything near their land. I knew that before I came back here to start this."

"Well that's where you come in," Lowe argued. "I'm sure you've reassured them about our safety record and how fail-safe this operation is. I know you've told them that we won out over many other companies that were dying to come in here with lesser resources than we have. That other companies might not take the same painstaking efforts we will — to ensure their safety and the continuous good environment precautions." He was on a roll. Roman was glad to see the beginning of the site appear a few hundred yards away.

He grinned slightly, looking straight ahead as the road got even rougher.

"That's what I'm constantly trying to do, Gardner. Reassure them. Before too much time has passed, I hope you will come and spend a couple of days. Maybe speak to some of the local clubs, the Rotary, Lions, and so forth." Lowe nodded. "Oh, and before I forget, I need a secretary. I've been trying to handle it all, but I need some help."

"It will be my pleasure to come back, and it'll my pleasure to approve a secretary for you. Get one today if you can, or as soon as possible. You choose the salary. Money is not tight." Not unusual for Worldwide where money was plentiful. Lowe straightened up in the seat more and loosened his tie, as he glanced at himself in the rear view mirror mounted on the door.

Three yellow bulldozers buzzed and puffed around in all directions, moving dirt back and forth, loosening stumps and debris, making huge piles to be burned. The fertile, black dirt gave off a fresh, earthy smell. Dust was non-existent due to the recent rains. Gardner Lowe smiled at the obvious progress. He could imagine much of the 1,000-plus acres filled with giant structures, as people and vehicles milled around with tons of hazardous waste being disposed of, and money pouring in from all directions as a result. It would be at least another year, maybe longer, before it was operational, but the dirt work was being done, and that was a start.

They stayed until lunch time, then departed to meet the Lt. Governor, Mayor Engle and a local state representative for lunch; the best he could do on short notice. The Mayor would alert the newspapers. Roman knew Engle wouldn't miss a opportunity.

Again, Roman would be a guest at the Wildflower Country Club. Only this time, he would be minus Diana. He thought of that, as they pulled into the parking lot. It was filled with Cadillacs, Mercedes, and fully loaded stretch pickups of all kinds, Chevrolets and Fords primarily, but even a few Toyotas. Every other person seemed to drive a pick-up with a long aerial of some sort, especially the men. It was the trademark of a successful farmer, even not-so successful farmers.

Lunch was uneventful, except that the Jackson newspaper did send a reporter to do an article on the facility and the progress to date, along with the Lt. Governor's presence. Thoughts of being snubbed at last night's dinner flashed though Roman's mind, making the luncheon's arrangements less of a priority. They did have a private room separated by an expandable divider from the rest of the lunch crowd. Gardner Lowe and Lt. Gov. Crawford did most of the talking with the reporter, as expected. This suited Roman fine. He was not in a particularly festive mood. More important matters occupied his mind. Lowe did a masterful job on the Mayor, Representative, and the reporter. The Lt. Governor already seemed spellbound. Through Gardner Lowe, Worldwide Industries made promises of jobs, high paying ones at that, with security and benefits, and offered assurances of Worldwide's dedication to preserving the natural resources of all the surrounding area. The Mississippians came away smiling. Roman knew that many others would not be so convinced as were the politicians. But he kept smiling and added what he could, when he was able to inject a few words. Sanders said even less and even managed a smile or two. Roman smiled, again, as the conversations looked as though they were coming to an end.

Then Mayor Engle slid his chair back, stood, and motioned for Lowe to do the same. "I understand you arrived last night and will only be here through today. Where'd you stay last night?"

"The Ramada Inn at Greenville." Lowe answered, hesitating, almost like he was embarrassed. Lowe quickly changed the subject, as the Mayor was not invited to dinner. What he didn't know wouldn't hurt him, Lowe thought. "Mr. Mayor, the State of Mississippi, your town and surrounding counties will benefit from this facility for many years to come. Call on me for anything I can do at any time. Of course, Roman Beckley is here at your service in any way also." He put his arm around the rotund politician and patted him soundly on the back. The Mayor grinned and wiped beads of perspiration from his forehead with his handkerchief, then reached for a big cigar in his coat pocket.

Roman expected a long afternoon of questions by Lowe; maybe even some financial ones by Sanders. He was prepared with progress notes and a file full of names and addresses that opposed the project to-date. It never happened. Gardner Lowe checked his watch as Elton Sanders crawled into the Blazer. Lowe took the Lt. Governor by the arm, and they stepped a few feet away, huddling quietly. They each smiled. He slapped Crawford on the back, then turned toward the Blazer.

Roman had thought about it all day. Lowe and Crawford are two of a kind. Tall, striking, dapper-dressers and hell, they even favor. It was their eyes that look so similar. Roman was impatient to get the show going. Finally, the two shook hands, then Crawford loaded into his chauffeur-driven, black continental and headed south for Jackson.

"I going to give you a break, Roman," Lowe roared, as he strutted toward him. "It looks like you have the situation well in hand at this point." He lowered his voice. "When we really need to come back is when we are further down the road. When hiring is going on and building has begun, that's when we need to." Sanders nodded agreement and looked out the window at a stray dog standing outside the kitchen, hoping for more scraps from lunch. Roman started the engine and looked at Lowe, somewhat puzzled.

"You mean you're leaving this early? All the way down here, and not stay until I've introduced you two to some more people. I know some landowners whose property borders the project that would love to see you." He couldn't resist the temptation to add that.

"You can count on us coming back, but we have to get on out of here late this afternoon. Incidentally, you're probably due back in L.A. for a couple of days in the near future. There are some technical matters you need to be brought up to date on by some of the inside people. It can be at your choosing, more or less, but it needs to be done in the next week or two, probably. I'm sure the West Coast may look good to you after you've been here a while longer."

"Probably so." Roman masked his indifference to coming back. He could take or leave L.A. at this time.

They spent most of the afternoon discussing the project and going over budgets, construction time-tables, contracts and sub-contracts. Shortly after 4:30, Gardner Lowe reached for the phone. He dialed his pilot at the Greenville airport. He instructed him to get the Lear ready to enter the sky. They would be ready to board in thirty minutes, more or less. They said their farewells. Promises were made about Roman coming to L.A., and Lowe and Sanders coming back to Mississippi. Roman still could not understand the short visit. Lowe was the boss, however, and today was a good day to cut short. They roared away from the office, west toward Greenville and the awaiting company Lear jet.

Roman closed the office and headed toward his place on the edge of town. The bayou that weaved its way around Indian Bayou reflected the golden sun edging its way down in the West. There was a definite touch of fall in the early October air. He thought of Diana, and the day seemed suddenly dreary compared to recent ones. She would not be there for him this time.

He pulled into his driveway, observing the sun's slightly further descent even since he'd left the office. He noticed how much shorter the days were this time of year. Maybe it just seemed darker this day. He got out of his Blazer, loosened his tie, and cast a lingering look toward John's cottage. He would definitely check it out thoroughly, after going into his own place, showering, and changing from his suit.

As he started to close the door on the driver's side, he noticed the trim, black attaché case resting on the back seat. Elton Sanders had left his prized possession. He picked it up and noticed it locked for sure. He was glad. He knew it was none of his business in there and didn't want the slightest temptation to peek at any company secrets. He took the case inside and dialed information for the Greenville airport.

"Hello. Control Tower?"

"Yes. This is the Tower."

"This is Roman Beckley. I'm an employee of Worldwide Industries, of Los Angeles. They have had a Lear Jet there all day with their pilot awaiting two of the executives to go back to L.A. Have they left yet?"

"They've been airborne for two minutes."

"I have an article they left. Oh well, I'll ship it back to him. Oh by the way, did they file a flight pattern to Los Angeles?"

"No Sir. They filed a flight pattern for Gatlinburg, Tennessee."

"*Gatlinburg*?" Roman hesitated, unable to think what to say.

"Sir, did you hear me?" The control tower employee asked.

"Yes. Yes, I did. Thank you so much for the information." He stared out the window and rattled the receiver around to hang it up, while looking straight ahead. He walked to the refrigerator and popped the top on a beer. It tasted a little better than usual. He sat down, wondering why they wanted him to believe they were flying to L.A., instead of Gatlinburg, Tennessee.

He shook his head and decided it was their business. Hell, Gardner

Lowe might even have a little meeting with some young blonde. He had heard tales about his past, but thought he had mellowed. He knew damn well that Elton Sanders didn't have a rendezvous set up, though.

Regardless, Gatlinburg is a resort town with any number of attractions around it. It could be any number of reasons, and Lowe was the company President. They didn't really have to answer to anyone since the President and Controller of the company were calling the shots for the plane's destination. He had other things more important to be concerned about. It was really none of his business, and he was glad they were gone. He hit the shower and rejuvenated himself. He slipped on some comfortable black Lee's, a white sweatshirt and loafers, then slid a beef Stroganoff instant-dinner into the small microwave. Roman loved the old place and its decor, but he also appreciated the only modern appliance in this stately turn-of-the-century home.

His heart beat a little faster as he used the key John had given him for convenience, if he ever had to check on anything there. He never thought he would have to use it. Not like this, anyway. The light from the back porch of the main house was not quite enough to illuminate the cottage's front door. He fumbled with the lock, then finally went to his Blazer to get his flashlight. He heard a bark behind him and jumped instinctively. It was the elderly lady's Collie he had only heard but never seen, except from a distance. Roman whistled at a low pitch and held his hand out slowly. She wagged her tail and sat down beside him. He exhaled and rolled his head around to release the tension, glad for the company. He went back inside, got the rest of the TV dinner, plus a roll, and offered them to the Collie. She gobbled it up, then sat obediently. He had made a friend for sure. He went back to the lock and jiggled it until the door cracked open.

"I hope you're not breaking in there, young man." The elderly voice rang out from behind the shrubs. It was the lady from next door.

"Oh, no, Ma'am. I live in the front house. My name's Roman Beckley. I've been meaning to introduce myself to you. But I've been so busy with the tragedy and all...."

"I know. We haven't been able to sleep too well since that happened. John was such a fine boy. I don't know what this world is coming to. I can't believe anyone on earth would have a reason to harm him. Must have been robbery. I heard the sheriff say he thought it was just a random robbery. We're glad to know you're still staying here. Oh, by the way, I'm

Lucille Barnes. My husband is pretty well bed-ridden with a bad stroke. Has been for years. His name is Willis. You said your name was Roman?"

"That's right. Roman Beckley. It's a pleasure to meet you, Mrs. Barnes."

"Same here, Mr. Beckley."

"Just Roman, please."

"Call me Lucille. I feel old enough without all that 'Mrs.' stuff."

"Whatever you want, Lucille. Excuse me, if you will, I've got to pack some things for John's folks to come up and get. See you later." Roman entered the door and reached for the light switch on the right side by the door. He could still hear her talking as she disappeared back through the hedges toward her rambling old two-story house, with thick vines growing from the ground to the top of the chimney. It was in much more need of repair than his place, but he could tell it had been a lovely home years ago.

He found the light switch and the darkness came to life at once. It seemed like he should be able to call John's name, and he would come out of the small kitchen with a beer in hand, and that smile on his face. His heart sunk slightly, realizing the finality.

It smelled a little musty already. He raised the window in the combination den and living room. A gust of fresh evening air filled the room. A soft beige curtain swayed back-and-forth as the wind pushed through it. There was an eerie silence. Every footstep echoed as Roman gradually made his way from the window to the kitchen.

He swallowed, listening to his footsteps on the old hardwood floor. He didn't know what he was looking for, but there had to be something to shed some light. Some little shred that the sheriff had not picked up, had to be here.

He made his way to the bedroom. The sight of John's clothes, still hanging in the old cedar chest, almost got to him, especially. He saw the old blue Ole Miss jersey he used to lounge around in. Number 14. He could see John in it, vividly. He searched the pockets of his pants, hanging in the closet. He opened every drawer. He had to fight the sense of urgency to leave the cottage. This had to be done. He went from room to room, but could see nothing. Maybe John's office at Parchman would divulge something. Roman knew he needed to get in there some way, without too much suspicion. He would think of a way, if he didn't find something here. He picked up the phone that was still activated, and a dial tone buzzed in the silence. He saw the blank message pad that John had magnetically affixed to a metal lamp base next to the phone. He thumbed through it, but all the pages were blank. He reached underneath the lamp to position it to be drawn again to the base of the lamp. He started to turn away but stopped, straining his eyes to focus again on the pad. He sat down instantly on the sofa, took the message pad off again, held it under the light and scrutinized it.

He strained, then held the pad at another angle. He could see the outline of the word. An indention was definitely there where it had imprinted through from another page that John had written on.

At the top of the page was the word COTTON B; near the bottom, he make out another word or two as he squinted — PANTHER. — then the number 17 with a circle around it. That was all that was on it.

What did this mean, if anything? Cotton, followed by the letter B, Panther, and number 17 circled.

Maybe it meant nothing, but his gut feeling was there was something to this. It just had to be! John wasn't interested in cotton. He certainly wasn't a cotton farmer, nor did he hunt panthers.

Number 17 was another story. It could mean anything. But at least this was something to go on. He would ask Missy, John's folks, and if he could, some cohorts at Parchman, discreetly. He cut the lights and left the blackened cottage, for what he hoped would be the last time, for certain at night.

CHAPTER 16

It should have been a good Saturday morning, but Roman felt an emptiness deep inside when he awoke at 6:30. It was an Indian Summer for sure. The temperature had climbed back from the cool mornings of the past week. In fact, maybe too much. It was evident that this day would be back to the high 80's. Today, he took his morning run in a different direction, away from the city limits of Indian Bayou. He ran alongside the highway for two miles east, then returned. He hoped any change would help his frame of mind. He knew any minute now, she would be leaving for the airport. He hadn't even asked if they were flying out of Jackson or Memphis en route to New York, then Europe. He tried not to think of her. He would not call. After all, she abruptly halted the relationship, not him. Despite missing her desperately, he had his pride.

After a shower, he changed to his khaki shorts, T-shirt, and deck shoes and headed to the truck stop to get a decent breakfast. He wanted to call Rex. He couldn't understand why he had not heard from him, though it had only been a couple of days. The words and number he uncovered at John's place, maybe had some significance. Hopefully, he had something to go on, and he was ready to pass this on to Rex. He was also ready for a progress report on the investigation of John's death. He convinced himself that Rex would come through, that he must temper his impatience. He was also ready to meet FBI agent Harold Lloyd, but he had no choice other than to wait until Rex gave the word. Surely, it would be soon.

Roman decided to throw himself into his work full bore, particularly for the next few days, weekend and all. He had lost valuable time and wanted the project to be right on time. He didn't want Gardner Lowe or others from Worldwide on his case constantly. The timing couldn't have been worse for Diana to break the news to him, but he was a fighter. He learned perseverance early in life and maintained that attitude in sports and everyday life. As sensitive as he was, he had never let his guard down totally. He was not a quitter. He thought back on his professional career. If he hadn't always been extremely competitive and tenacious, other athletes might have prevailed, those with a little more speed or some other slight edge. He had been an 11th round draft pick, after all, and it took fierce determination and zeal to keep a spot on the Rams roster. He'd done that, and he would do the same now.

He pulled into the truck stop and dodged the 18 wheeler that approached from his immediate right. The crowd was slimmer than usual. The elderly, heavy-set lady, who owned the restaurant, smiled and placed a menu on his table near the rear. He awaited the regular waitress, who came immediately with coffee pot steaming. He smelled her strong perfume before she was three feet away. They exchanged smiles, and he decided to get a ham-and-biscuit to go. He needed to get to the office and catch up on some reports and other duties. He also wanted to get away from the house, under the circumstances.

He entered the small office building, the only one present at this early hour. Maybe all day, since it was Saturday. He was reaching for his keys when he heard the phone through the door. He wrestled with the ring of keys and by the time he was in his office, the fourth ring was beginning. He thought for a second it might be Diana, that maybe she'd had a change of heart and plans. He was hesitant to answer for fear it would be someone else. Another voice not so soft and alluring. He was right.

"Hello."

He recognized the voice as Rex's, sounding slightly restrained.

"This is your ole fishin' buddy. Got some information on those lures you asked about that were made in Arkansas." Roman realized this was the code call Rex spoke about. He had almost blurted out after 'fishin' buddy', but caught himself in time.

"Hey. I appreciate it, but can you just drop it in the mail. I hate to be in a hurry, but I've got to go back to a restaurant. I think I left my wallet. I'll call you sometime." He hoped he didn't sound too rehearsed.

"That's no problem. I'll put it in the mail to you, brochures, prices, and all." Rex was doing a good job. It almost amused Roman.

He remembered Rex's warning of "bugged" phones and decided against office, home, even mobile, which he doubted. But, better safe than sorry. He hustled back to the truck stop and ordered another coffee to go. While the waitress was busy pouring and putting the lid on, he headed for the familiar pay phone. Just as he was about to punch in the numbers, he thought he saw someone in his peripheral vision, staring at him. He kept the receiver in his hand, gradually turning his head, until his eyes fixed on Deputy Wiggins, no more than five feet from him, between him and the hallway door leading back into the restaurant. Roman pretended not to notice Wiggins and quickly faked a conversation.

"Stan, don't forget: if Ole Miss happens to upset Alabama, I definitely will hold you to that dinner at the Peabody in Memphis. I know the odds are against it." He hesitated and laughed. "No, we weren't lucky enough when I played. This is now. Oh, I'm fine down here. The people are very nice, and everything's going well. O.K., call me after the game. Yes. I'll be at home. Talk to you later." He turned around to reenter the restaurant and saw the deputy pivot and make tracks back to his car, wasting no more time around the restaurant. Roman exhaled slowly, shook his head, and grinned as he opened the restaurant door. He would go somewhere else though, just to be sure.

He left the truck stop, headed east in search of another pay phone in a private, inside location. He knew of none, since he'd been here such a short time. He hadn't particularly made that a priority, looking for secluded pay phones. He drove past the Wal Mart, but the parking lot was too busy. Anyway, he wasn't fond of the condition the phones usually were in around those places. He was growing impatient by the time he spotted the sign indicating Shaw was only a few miles away up Highway 448 North. This farm-to-market road shouldn't take long, and it would provide some privacy for sure. He was in Shaw, a sleepy little town of 1500, in a matter of minutes. He scanned his rear-view mirror for the fiftieth time to make sure no one was following. All was clear.

He zeroed in on a phone booth next to a convenience store on the main drag. It was enclosed except where the bottom panel had been knocked out. But this was a blessing, because as he unfolded the door, the foul smelling aroma of urine mixed with spilled beer, met him head on. The old glassed-in booth was a victim of too many Saturday nights, or any other night for that matter. Too many calls by too many drinkers. The smell made it impossible to breathe or concentrate, without hanging halfway out the door.

He stretched the cord as far as it would go for fresh air. He would have looked further, for another phone, but time was important and other ones in town would probably rival it for filth. He punched in the credit card number, but the second it was about to ring Rex's number, he slammed the phone down. It was his company credit card. He envisioned Elton Sanders scouring over his bill and checking out every number called. Again, he was determined to take no chances, so he used his personal telephone card that would be billed to his Los Angeles number code. No one would get that bill but him, since all his bills were being forwarded by the young medical student leasing his place in Sherman Oaks.

Rex answered his home phone, "Great Fisherman's One Stop". His humor was intended to relax Roman. "You didn't waste much time getting back to me. I'll give you credit for that."

"It's been a long couple of days." There was a silence like Rex was waiting for him to ask questions. Roman gave in. "Well, I didn't call to hear you breathe. Tell me if anything has transpired. Oh, I do have something for you. I went through John's house and the so-called law had already been through. I don't know what they got, but I did uncover this scratch pad with the top sheet gone. There was still an imprint of the words COTTON B and PANTHER with the number 17 circled. I have no idea what it means. Maybe nothing. However, I know John knew no more about cotton than I do, and he was not a hunter, as in panther. I feel that the words are connected to his murder. Maybe he was doodling when he talked on the phone. It was right by it. I've seen him do that before. Don't forget this. Maybe the FBI man can link it to something. Now, do you have anything to tell me?"

"We've started some preliminary things. Let's say there are a few things in the works. It's early yet, but give me time and there'll be more, if it's out there to be found."

"I don't doubt that for one minute." Roman replied, feeding Rex's ego. "Tell me I wasn't wrong now about all the things I told you about Zach Stiles and so on."

"Wait a minute. Let's don't get too far ahead of ourselves. One thing at a time. I might have a little something, not the whole case wrapped up and everybody in it." Rex was a master at being vague and cunning.

"Like what?" Since Roman had pen, but no paper, he decided he could remember anything Rex revealed.

"First, I met with Harold Lloyd. He is anxious to talk with you and like I said, under the circumstances, a little distance away from Indian Bayou. He wouldn't elaborate, even to me, but you particularly got his interest with what you told me. I related it to him as you had told me, fairly well. I also got some information on your, shall we say, nemesis. Seems this renegade did more than get a 'Purple Heart' over there. There's a lot to tell you, so we'll get to that when we meet with Harold Lloyd. One thing for damn sure, Stiles is no choir boy. Even I am shocked."

"That's exactly what I figured you would find out." Roman pounded on the metal ledge just below the phone. "Yes! Yes! I knew I was right about that devil."

"Oh yeah, another thing... your phone has more bugs than a windshield around here on a summer night. I'm sure. Well, just one is all it takes."

"How'd you find that out? That really burns me up! Some bastard can check out my private life at his will? I'll get my turn with him. Wait and see!" Roman strained his voice and slapped the wall of the booth with his left hand. He leaned out, took a deep breath, and exhaled. "I'll go get the bag phone activated and have, what I call, a phone umbilical cord, after all. I don't know which is worse, constant phone contact with my boss, or my phones bugged by Stiles and his cronies."

"First, I got ways to find out if phones are bugged. It's irrelevant how I know. I also understand you being teed off about it, but we may be able to use this to your advantage down the road. Follow me? You may be able to give some erroneous information on purpose. I'm not sure you'll need to, but it's nice to have the opportunity if you need it." Roman relaxed some as he thought about it. Rex was shrewd as always. "I wouldn't get too passionate with your lady friend on there if I were you, if you don't want them picking up on it." Rex laughed briefly to lessen the intensity.

"I don't have to worry about that happening." Roman's voice trailed off softly. "Probably not for a long time. Not to say we ever carried on some illicit phone affair, Rex." Roman managed a slight smile.

"If you're having women problems, don't let them get you down. My grandmother used to say that there was one gettin' off of every bus." Rex made another stab at being humorous.

"That's another story. If it's meant to be, it'll happen. You know I haven't let it consume me yet." Roman hid the truth nicely.

"How's your Monday? If you can get away for several hours, I can arrange this meeting with Lloyd to get his input."

"Where do y'all want to meet? I'm flexible enough. You name the town. I can stay as long as necessary for this. I'll probably get fired anyway." He laughed.

"How about your old alma mater?"

"Ole Miss?"

"Well, yeah, Oxford. Harold has to be at the Federal District Court there on a case set for 8 a.m.. He would come to Indian Bayou, or wherever, because he's interested in this thing you're onto; but I thought I could swing over there if you can. Only a couple of hours or so for you, huh?"

"That's no problem. I haven't been back there since I graduated. More years than I want to remember."

"Hell, Roman it hasn't been that long. What has it been, seven or eight years? Wait until you're my age. Time flies then. You'll see, if you live that long." Silence. "I didn't mean it literally."

"Yeah, I know. If I live that long." Roman managed a weak laugh, nevertheless.

"Look, go on back to your home or office and get this off your mind as much as you can, son. After all, you're not a law enforcement officer. You're in a dangerous position, as I told you, though. I'm more convinced now it could be more serious than I realized when we first talked. Just watch your back. He, and whoever's with him, are obviously playing for keeps, and I don't want to down play that. I know your Dad would have wanted me to tell it like it is to you, the danger of it all. I don't want to sound redundant, but don't deviate much from your regular routine."

"It hasn't been too routine lately."

"You know what I mean. Try not to let on to anyone that you're interested in anything but that nuclear deal, whatever it's called."

"I'll handle it. At least, I'll give it my best shot. By the way, where in Oxford?"

"Harold said he should be out of Federal court about 11:00, or thereabouts. We can have some lunch around 11:30. Hell, there's no reason to meet in some motel room since we're that far away from Indian Bayou. How about the Gin? I'm sure you remember it. That time of day we'll get in for a good table before all the students come up on the Square for lunch."

"You're right, it's not very private, but it should be fine. You're the expert on that. I'll see you Monday about 11:30 at the Gin." Roman hesitated then practically pleaded: "Anything else you can tell me? You know my curiosity about this. Curiosity is not the right word. Obsessed, or consumed, may be the word." Roman leaned outside the booth.

His eyes darted back and forth, and he still seemed in the clear.

"Like I said, there's too much to get into on the phone. Really, I can fill in the blanks when we meet. You're not missing that much. Trust me, Roman. Don't call me unless it's an emergency. You don't need to be running to phone booths too often. Get my drift?"

"O.K. I'll see you both on Monday. Thanks, Rex." Roman slid the glass door together and filled his lungs with fresh air as he stepped from the booth. He glanced around one more time before getting back into his Blazer. There were no watching eyes, that he could see. At least a half dozen empty beer cans were scattered around the convenience store parking lot. He eased the Blazer away, dodging three or four huge potholes that dotted the perimeter of the store. Two black teenagers leaned against the dirty wall, covered with graffiti. They peered through the plate glass window at the obese black man playing the old pinball machine, bumping and shaking it for more points.

The Memphis airport was crowded for a Saturday. Diana tipped the sky cap $10 to handle and check the six bags, fully packed for the lengthy stay. Her Mom was close behind. She was wide-eyed with excitement about the European trip. Diana smiled back at her when they made eye contact near the counter. The 11:15 a.m. flight to New York was scheduled to depart on time.

"Honey, you packed an awful lot for the trip. I only have the two bags and they're loaded with easy pack things. Lots of permanent-press dark cottons, you know."

"I know. Good idea. But you know me, always overdo the packing." She handed the agent their tickets and they moved to the gate for departure.

The flight to New York was jammed. This was one time that flying first class was appreciated. "You know, when your Dad and I used to fly a good bit to wherever, I used to tell him not to waste money on first class. However, on a trip this long, at my age, it's worth it. I wish he could have come. I know he's busy with the place this time of year, with the cotton just being brought in and all, but I'll miss him."

"I know Mom. I'm sure he'll miss you." She stopped short of saying Norris, Sr. told her he would miss her mom.

The big jet lifted off; Diana stared down at Memphis becoming smaller below. She thought of Roman and wondered if he was all right. She could not get over the fact that he never once offered any explanation or confessed to anything. She wondered if there were any possible explanation, and, for the first time, it hit her: Who took the photographs? Why would they do that, and why did they put them for her to find? Her eyes moistening, she turned away from Ella and gazed out at the clouds the big jet was now parting. She touched the corners quickly with a tissue. As she slowly turned back, Ella appeared preoccupied, staring ahead. After they leveled off, the flight attendant brought their lunch of roast beef, new potatoes, salad, green beans and dessert. Diana barely touched hers, merely rearranging the tray. Ella ate salad only, then turned to Diana.

"Honey, you know I don't want to pry, but something is wrong, isn't it? You can't fool me." She spoke again before Diana could answer. "I've known you a little too long, young lady." She patted Diana's leg and winked. Diana noticed the hand shake visibly as she moved it away from her leg and back to the arm rest.

She squeezed her Mom's hand as it came to rest on the seat divider.

"Mom, I am so happy to be with you on this trip. How could anything be wrong? We're going to Europe, we'll do lots of sight-seeing, eat good food, shop. What could be wrong?" They stacked the trays together for the attendant, who promptly grabbed them out of their way.

"Roman Beckley. That's who. I'm no genius, but I don't have to be to notice that last night the two of you were not together. I'm not sure, but I don't believe he even called. Something is wrong between you two. Again, I couldn't help but notice how happy and contented you've been in the short time you've known him. I don't know if I've ever seen you react that way totally, with any man. That even goes back to college and high school when you had a few mad crushes. I won't keep on, but if you want to talk while we're on this trip, I love you and am right here." She squeezed Diana's hand and Diana reciprocated. "One more thing. Why did you pack so much? Don't give me that old deal about always over packing. You have never done that. You have always been organized and never overdo it."

Diana felt like she was truly back in high school. Her Mom was more perceptive than she remembered. She hesitated and almost blushed. "Mom, you're still as sharp as ever. How can you always tell, no matter how hard I try to hide it, when something's going on? You never cease to amaze me." They both turned and looked at one another and laughed, as if on cue.

Then, Diana's smile turned somber.

"I've decided to stay in Paris and go to that art school for several months. It's the one I mentioned to you and Dad a few months ago. I called at the last minute and they seem to think I can get in without much problem." She stopped and looked out the small window at the white rolls of clouds and the cracks of blue sky that appeared every second or two. She spoke softly and slowly. "Yes, Mom there is something going on. I will tell you about it in time. Right now, let's enjoy the flight."

Her Mom looked on with compassion and patted Diana's hand softly. "Sure, Honey, sure."

"There is one thing that is concerning me that you might can answer. If you don't want to of course....

"You know I will. What's that?"

"Is Dad in any kind of financial trouble, or is anything bothering him more than usual? He seems to be extremely intense lately."

"You know he quit telling me about the finances years ago. I assume nothing's wrong. He has been a little restless lately, now that you mention it."

"Restless? Like not sleeping or what?"

"Yes, not sleeping. But then, that might be because of some of late night phone calls he's gotten from time to time. You know me. I don't meddle in your father's business, and I trust him explicitly, but I know he's lost some sleep."

"You have no idea who's calling, Mom?"

Ella looked away for a second or two and lost eye contact with Diana. Then she said, "Well, yes, I do. Some of the calls." Her voice jumped a notch as she began talking a little faster. "He would have a fit if he thought I paid any attention to the calls or when he up and leaves at such late hours. He thinks I sleep like a log, but I'm aware of more than he thinks, even after a few drinks."

Diana leaned forward and frowned slightly as she looked intently at her Mom.

"I know you're a patient and understanding wife, Mom, but who is calling there at late hours?"

"I may be wrong, maybe just coincidence, but it's happened several times in the last few months.

"Mom, who is it?"

"Zach Stiles! He's the one. Maybe it is coincidental, but they've never been close. I hope none of the workers are in trouble with the law."

Diana suddenly remembered the night her Dad woke her when the late call came in, asking about his Cherokee. That was so unlike him at that hour. It was also the same night of John Sessions's murder.

Ella glanced around again, looking deeply concerned, just as they hit some turbulence and the big jet vibrated. The overhead bin rattled. "You don't think one of the workers has done something and Dad is not telling us, do you?"

Diana hesitated, managing to smile. "No, Mom, I don't think one of the workers has done anything at all." She stared into the distance, watching the clouds zip by. Her expression was unchanged for her Mother's sake, but her insides churned and she searched for answers.

CHAPTER *17*

The weekend dragged, though he had plunged into piles of work in a futile attempt to get Diana off his mind. Monday was finally here. He wished he could have met Rex and Lloyd even on Sunday, but it wasn't up to him. He was ready at 5:45 a.m. while darkness still shrouded the early hour, hoping this would lessen the chance of anyone seeing him leaving town. He wondered if he was being extra cautious. Maybe so. Maybe not. He took only taking one change of clothes, in case he had to stay overnight .

He filled his trusty coffee cup and headed out the driveway. He would skip breakfast this morning. He wouldn't chance stopping in Indian Bayou. As he headed out the driveway, he glanced at the window next door with the lone light on. Lucille Barnes leaned toward the window next to a chair where her husband reclined. So much for getting up and away without anyone seeing him! No hour appeared to be too early for some people here. He knew they must be on edge after the murder. Maybe their nerves had awakened them. He wouldn't do it, but wanted to tell her there was probably nothing for them to be afraid of, except the law itself. He headed east toward Greenwood, then out of the flat Delta toward the hills of Northeast Mississippi and Oxford.

Twenty miles had rolled past when he noticed his gas tank at one fourth. He hadn't wanted to gas up in Indian Bayou to avoid calling attention to himself at the early hour. He suddenly thought he might be carrying this too far. After all, he'd have had to gas up if he was only going downtown. The very early time was his justification. He didn't want to be tarry-ing around filling stations at the crack of dawn, increasing his chances of seeing Stiles or Wiggins, possibly.

He searched for the nearest Exxon as he entered the city limits of Greenwood. This was the credit card chosen by Worldwide, so Exxon it would be. Then as he pulled off the highway onto the service station drive-way, he decided against that. He again visualized Elton Sanders and his accounting bunch, scouring his expense report and finding Greenwood on Monday, checking it out on the map, then reporting that their boy was out of range of business for the day. He could cover this fairly easily by having any number of reasons for being there or passing through. They probably would never notice or say anything, but he was keeping it simple. He had enough concern, without Sanders questioning him about expenses. He never had, but there was a first time for everything. So, instead, he pulled down the road a half mile into a BP station and squeezed out an even $15.00 of unleaded. He helped himself to the "squeegie" resting on the wall by the pumps. He slid it over and over his windshield, until it squeaked twice, signalling the end to the ever-present Delta bugs that had ended up on the glass.

He bought another cup of awful coffee and started out the driveway. An old farmer in a dirty grey pickup screeched up behind him and nar-rowly missed making an accordion out of the Blazer. He jumped, grateful for a coffee lid. The old man waved an apologetic gesture and shook his head. Roman nodded, smiled sheepishly, and drove on.

After thirty minutes of driving, he could see the out skirts of Winona, Mississippi, the beginning of the hills, with the flat lands of the Delta behind. The contrast in the terrain was never more evident than now to him. After spending the time he had in the flat land, these hills gave the illusion of mountains in comparison.

He spotted a familiar old motel and coffee shop, just off on busy Inter-state 55, a main artery from New Orleans, through Mississippi to Chicago. He recognized the old, huge, neon wagon-wheel mounted on the front of the cafe. He and his parents had stopped here occasionally, when traveling south to Jackson and other points. The sign was a local landmark; its flo-rescent spokes contrasted with either light of day or dark of night as a backdrop. Today it was dark. Closed permanently.

By now, the urge to eat breakfast had subsided altogether. He would head on north toward Oxford. For a change, he had some time to spare. He wanted to call Gardner Lowe from his car phone and ask about Gatlinburg,

Tennessee. Catch him by surprise. He could not figure why the secrecy and deception about the trip. Hell, Lowe could have told him the truth; the truth that he was hustling young women again; that money was no object and distance was not a deterrent in his quest. Roman could care less what he did with his private life, if that was in fact what he was doing.

He set the cruise on 65 and enjoyed the scenery for the moment. Eighteen wheelers passed him like he was doing 40. A knight of the road passed him in a huge, shiny, black rig with the words Rocky Peak Ranch, Sheridan, Wyoming emblazoned on the door and in the middle of its long trailer. It was clear he was doing 15 to 20 miles over the limit, but who wouldn't speed to get back to the gorgeous, serene Rockies.

Just over an hour later he was approaching the out skirts of Oxford. The hills were more prominent here. The beautiful, old, historic town brought back many memories of his days at the University of Mississippi, better known as Ole Miss to most. It was also home to a string of nationally known authors, past and present. Among them the late William Faulkner, whose home, Rowan Oak, is now an historical landmark. John Grisham, Willie Morris, and others had resided in this literary mecca.

Since time was on his side, he drove leisurely down Fraternity Row. More outlandish parties had been thrown within a square mile, than anywhere else in this part of the country, perhaps. He noticed fraternity boys filing by in their starched shirts, khaki pants and loafers, streaming to and from classes. He had neither the money nor time to belong to a fraternity when he was a student athlete.

He eased along, away from the frat houses, toward the stadium at the end of the same street. He smiled, and slowed the Blazer to a crawl by the stadium that had been host to its share of tough Southeastern Conference gladiators, who battled on Fall Saturdays each year since the late 1890s. He had some fond, and not so fond memories of the old playing field, so rich in tradition. His fondest memory was of his first start as a sophomore against Georgia, when the first team quarterback injured an ankle. Despite an average day passing and running, he and the team held together enough for the win. He was also grateful to the school that awarded him, a walk-on try out, a full athletic scholarship. He appreciated the opportunity more this way, rather than signing a Grant-In-Aid full scholarship right out of high school. It was sweeter to him to earn it the hard way. He drove past the famous 'Grove', where giant tail-gate parties were thrown by alums and fans of all ages, before the games.

He was happy to have dusted off some fond memories and revived them for the moment, but now it was time to take care of business. He drove on to the Gin, the popular eatery for students, faculty, and general public. He heard the deep voice almost as soon as he entered. Rex was in the waiting area up front, leaning against the cigarette machine.

"Roman, over here."

"Where's Mr. FBI?" Roman asked, shaking Rex's hand.

Rex slapped his back solidly and said, "In the rest room. Even they gotta go." Just then, the rest room door opened and Harold Lloyd emerged, straightening his tie. "Roman, meet Harold Lloyd."

"My pleasure, Roman." His handshake was like a set of steel pliers, his eyes never moved from Roman's.

"Pleased to meet you, Mr. Lloyd."

"Call me Harold, if you will."

Roman barely smiled and thought about how personable he appeared to be. Disarming would be more like it. Despite Lloyd's fifty years or so, it was apparent that under that Navy poplin suit, was a man in top condition. His posture was as straight as his grip was strong. He exuded confidence, but spoke in a voice softer than expected for a man of his build. His dark brown hair, sprinkled with grey around the temples, was combed straight back. Looking into his deep brown eyes, you got the impression he was the real thing, not some GQ look. He definitely was not fashion conscious. His striped tie was effective enough, but lacked the zing to make a statement. All in all, he looked the part of a seasoned FBI agent.

"Rex, you're looking spiffy," Roman added. Rex grinned, not at all embarrassed to be wearing the bright blue jacket, green cotton pants, yellow shirt and tie, featuring a huge parrot in the middle of it.

What's with him and the exotic birds? Roman wondered. This reinforced the fact that he had chosen the right dress for the day: conservative Navy blazer, khaki cotton pants and paisley tie, appropriate attire to meet a career FBI agent. He wanted to seem credible when telling his story to an FBI agent, especially of a highly suspicious lawman.

"Let's get our table and get down to business, gentlemen," Rex suggested, pointing toward the awaiting hostess with menus in hand. They walked past the bar to the back of the large dining room, which was already filling up at this hour with students. Later, a crowd of lawyers, businessmen, and a professor or two from the University, would likely file in.

Rex got right to the matter at hand. "Roman, Harold and I have had a couple of long conversations, in person and on the phone. I have filled him in, as best I can, from a second hand position. Take it from the top if you will, and don't leave anything at all out. Anything, whether it seems insignificant or not. He'll decide what's important, and take it from there. Right, Harold?"

"You said it perfectly," Harold replied, as he sipped his water casually. "Feel free to divulge anything you want, no matter what you think. Don't be embarrassed to tell anything."

Roman wondered where he got the embarrassed bit. He was glad to tell what he could to help this investigation. "Harold, I'm certainly not a trained lawman, but neither am I stupid. At least not most of the time." Lloyd nodded and smiled, making Roman feel more relaxed. "Seriously, there is something going on around Indian Bayou and others places that is highly illegal. And it's big. I'm not talking some small-town operation with a little dope dealt around." Roman loosened his tie and sipped some water. "I'm no psychic either, but I do get these feelings when things are not right. These eerie feelings. Call it what you want, but I can sense it. You know?"

Harold nodded again and leaned forward, listening intently.

"The first night I drove down here from Memphis, I had this strange feeling about Parchman. Something told me that I would be involved some way with the place. I don't mean as an inmate for sure. I'm a law abiding person. Anyway, that night I was stopped right outside the prison by sheriff Zach Stiles of Wildflower County. Ever heard of him?"

"Rex has filled me in some on the man."

"The instant I saw him that rainy night, there were bad vibes between him and me. No mistaking the feeling. He dislikes me. It was like he was laying for me that night outside the prison. Uncanny." Roman took a deep breath and slowed down somewhat. "It's like he fears I'll foul up something for him. Believe me, the feeling is mutual, and I'll do all I can to see this man brought down." Roman thumped his fist on the table and slid forward, as if to shut out any eavesdroppers. There were none. The nearest table contained four attractive sorority sisters too busy getting the scoop on who was dating whom for the upcoming Saturday gridiron contest.

"I'm listening," Lloyd assured him, but Roman felt uneasy.

"You doubt me already, don't you?" Roman stared at Lloyd and frowned slightly.

"No, it's that I don't make any determination until I have all the facts.

I can't go off half-cocked about this sheriff. I have to give him the benefit of the doubt, until I see some evidence." Rex slipped Roman a wink, so Roman kept calm and continued his story.

They spent the rest of lunch going over the same facts he had touched on earlier at Rex's home. That first night scene at Parchman; Stiles taking Roman's gun; the night of John's murder when Stiles mistook Roman for Norris, Sr.; and the anonymous call from the lady for whatever reason, tipping him off about the Stiles rerouted trip to New Orleans. He told Lloyd everything he observed while following Stiles and Pony Tail, their rotund associate, and the mysterious man in the back of the limousine. Clifton was detailed and how he helped in New Orleans. He answered Lloyd's questions about Norris, Sr., his son, and even Diana. He didn't like it, but he did. They covered John's job at the penitentiary and how it might possibly be connected to his murder. They discussed the words Cotton, Panther and 17 that had printed through on the scratch pad, and how John had seemed vague and apprehensive about what he might have stumbled onto, when he took Roman on the tour of Parchman.

They talked on through the meal, dessert, and two rounds of coffee. Lloyd busily filled up several pages in his black notebook, writing down every fact. Rex remained uncharacteristically quiet, only to explain Roman when he seemed ambiguous about facts. That was very little, however, as Roman delivered a convincing load for Lloyd to digest.

"Harold," Roman confided, "What I can't get over is, when Stiles was so damn sure he was yelling at Norris that night in the storm, when it was me instead. Then a few minutes later, I find John dying, the back of his head blown half away. That's just too coincidental. But that was just the beginning. Everything that's followed, just compounds that beginning."

Harold Lloyd leaned forward and tapped Roman's shoulder, trying to offer more assurance. "Roman, we will move forward with what you've told me. If you think of any other information, like I said, no matter how insignificant it seems, let me know."

Roman stared into the Lloyd's poker face and felt a rush to his own face. He slid his chair back a few inches, anticipating the end of lunch and the conversation. "I sense that you're not totally convinced. I hope you are but, if not, then I will do whatever I can to bring this guy down, with or without the FBI."

"Roman, don't worry. Everything will be done to get to the bottom of this. I never said I was not convinced. But, as I said before, I have to look carefully at the facts and investigate this fully. I can't tell you point blank that Stiles is guilty. I can't just go out and arrest him to stop whatever it is he's involved with, until I have justification. Trust me though."

"I trust Rex to get results. He put me in touch with you, so I'll have to trust that you'll do what you say."

"I will. I also need for you to get what you can about Norris Palmer, Sr. Be extremely careful. I know Rex has been over and over that, but I wouldn't want you to become another casualty, while we're working on this. Don't put yourself in danger. Carry on as normally as possible with your project. Don't ask the wrong person the wrong question, if you know what I mean. Leave that to us." Roman listened, but absorbed what he wanted to hear. The rest went out the other ear.

The three were about to slide their chairs back, when Roman added one last comment: "I'll find what I can about Norris. But one thing bothers me — Diana and her Mom suddenly left the country for Europe. Diana and I seemed to have a great relationship going, then she cuts it off like a faucet. She not only goes with her Mom for a few weeks, but decides to stay on in Paris to attend an art school. I feel her Dad wants her away from me. If for nothing else, for her safety. He and Stiles, maybe others, know that I know something. It was so unlike her to do this about face with me. It was as if I'd done something terrible. I can't figure it out, but someone must have gotten to her with something about me. I can't imagine." Roman frowned and stared away from Rex and Lloyd. They pushed their chairs under the table. Two of the sorority girls blushed when Roman glanced their way. They checked him out, sighed, and went back to their huddle.

"The FBI will pay for this one," Lloyd spoke up, grabbing the check.

As they headed for the cashier's station up front, Rex tapped Roman on the shoulder and pulled him aside. "Don't try to figure out females. You know how temperamental most of them are, so don't get your feelings hurt from what I'm about to say." Rex's eyes narrowed, maintaining a stare at Roman. "You may not agree just now, but don't discount that young lady being involved. Stranger things have happened. She seems to take Dad's requests to heart. She could have turned down the European trip."

Roman felt a silence in spite of the noise around the cashier and buzzing from throughout the restaurant. Rex's observation was painful to explore. He felt she could not be involved, but for the first time, he opened his mind to the possibility.

Lloyd returned, offering mints to the two of them. Rex and Lloyd walked with Roman into the parking lot full of vehicles. They side-stepped a group of six or seven male students rushing toward the restaurant, then stopped next to his Blazer.

"Sometimes, it's easier to be objective from the outside, like myself. I'm suspicious by nature. Always have been. It's paid off more than not for me. It's hard to look at things from the same perspective when you're romantically connected with the person. Know what I mean?" Rex said, giving Roman a slap on the back and a firm hand shake.

"I guess you're right. I'll keep that in mind." His voice was not as adamant or defensive. Lloyd raised his eyebrow and wrinkled his forehead, as if he agreed with Rex. Roman had the message.

Harold leaned inside the Blazer as Roman buckled his seat belt. "Remember, no calls on any of the phones you normally use, home, office and so on, for now. I have a plan I'm tossing around in my mind. Let me do some more work. I'll be able to finalize it in the next day or so. I'll have to get some approval on it, but it'll be a huge step forward. I'll call you. Might even get you to meet me somewhere near, but outside Indian Bayou, like Greenwood. I'll call you in a day or two. Be careful."

Roman nodded and received a wave from Lloyd and Rex as he pulled away onto the Oxford square to head back to Indian Bayou.

As they watched his Blazer disappear down the uncrowded street, Lloyd turned to Rex. "You said he was determined about this. More like obsessed. He is one intense young man."

"Yep. He meant what he said to you. Just like his Dad. You can bet, he meant what he said."

"That's what bothers me."

CHAPTER **18**

The midnight fire was built so far back into the large field, that it could not be seen from the main road, especially since a clump of trees stood between the black robed participants and the road. Two hooded figures lifted the small calf high into the air, then lowered it to the wooden platform that had been transported to the field. The towering figure made his way to the table, and with one fell swoop of the large, razor-sharp blade, laid open the throat of the helpless animal, killing it swiftly. The sacrifice had been made, and its blood was used in the ceremony that continued. The calf's executioner talked of brotherhood, unity of purpose, and riches to come. He emphasized their bond of secrecy and the need for perseverance through any obstacles that lay ahead. The leader then ranted and raved about an outsider who could end their mission and cause their demise. He demanded a vote that anyone standing in their way be eliminated.

A name was put to the vote. Three of the four present voted in favor of death, and one was targeted by the group. It was a matter of time before the sentence be completed. The right time and the right place and it would be done. The group could no longer take any chances with what he might know, or get to know. They were assured by the leader that he, and he alone, would be the executioner. He would pick the time, place, and means of death.

The fire was barely smouldering as the meeting ended. One conspirator roared away in a large pickup with the calf's carcass in the truck bed. It was to be buried at a predestined spot nearby. The towering leader left in a separate direction in his automobile. The two that were left stood by the remains of the flickering fire.

" I want to talk to you, now that he is gone."

"Go ahead. Are you sure he's long gone? I don't want to take any chances by hanging around too long. He's so suspicious minded he might read it the wrong way."

"That's part of what I want to talk to you about. You act like you're scared to death of him."

"I am, by God. Go on, let's not take forever." He was visibly nervous as he disrobed and threw it in the trunk of his luxury automobile. The other man had already shed his symbolic garment.

"I am in this thing for one reason, and that is to make some quick money. This other business that we are doing makes me sick. Speaking of sick, he is for sure. Where did he get indoctrinated to this? I never knew things would get so out of hand. You know I need the cash, or I wouldn't be in this. I'll continue this facade, but only to make sure the operation goes smoothly. I'm afraid of what that demon might do to any of us if we don't go along."

"You can say that again. He's scary. This is no act to him or his cohort. They are deadly serious about the devil, but I don't mind that, if he leaves my hide intact and the money comes regularly. He is convinced, in that mind of his, that if we are bonded by all these ceremonial rituals we'll keep silent and stay dedicated to the cause. I'll play my part and rake in the money. Yes, I will."

The two drove away in opposite directions, headed back to their respective homes and unknowing families.

The next two days were unusually long for Roman. Despite meetings, reports, and even a speaking engagement at the local Lions Club, time seemed to stand still as he waited for word from Lloyd or Rex.

Finally, the code call came at 7:15 p.m. to his home. This time it was about the suit he had "ordered" from a clothing company in Memphis. Lloyd's soft voice was convincing as a tailor. Roman threw down the local paper he had been trying to kill time with, and jumped into his Blazer. He reached for the cellular phone, but remembered he hadn't asked Lloyd and Rex if it might be bugged too. Again, he would take no chances.

He headed back to the same nasty phone booth in Shaw. He passed his favorite little restaurant that he had frequented so much. At least five big rigs were pulling in an out around the perimeter. The place looked moderately busy for a week night.

He looked through the rear view mirror for the tenth time since he had left the house only minutes ago. He saw no one that might be suspicious, so he drove on past the truck stop restaurant about a block, then hit the right-turn signal indicator. He hooked a quick right at the next street and drove only a hundred feet or so, then suddenly turned around and headed back toward the truck stop. He would make this damn call from there.

There was no need in such precautions, he chided himself. He could easily be using the phone for any reason. After all, it was a decent hour, and besides he hadn't eaten since a carry out ham-and-biscuit this morning. He would order food then use the phone.

He was in luck. The truckers had vacated the hallway where the phone was mounted, and he could see perfectly if anyone like the sheriff's bunch showed up. No one did. He got hold of Lloyd, still in his office in Memphis.

"Harold. You called?"

"Yes. Can you meet me tomorrow for lunch in Greenwood? I think we'll be fine there. Just make sure no one follows you over. I said I would call you on the plan I have. I'll fill you in when you get there." His voice did not have the same reassuring ring that it did in Oxford the other day. "You ever hear of the Crystal Cafe?"

"Believe it or not, I have. That's kind of public, isn't it?"

"Possibly. We can make it Grenada, 30 miles or so to the east."

"You don't have to worry about directions around here to me. You forget, I was raised in this state. I know exactly how far. About 55 miles roughly. I would feel a little better there, since a lot of people from here go to Greenwood every day."

"O.K., there's a unique little restaurant right next door to the Holiday Inn, near Interstate 55. I can't remember the name right off, but you can't miss it. It's the first one east of the motel. We'll make it right in the middle of the lunch crowd. That's even better. Is high noon suitable to you?"

"You bet. I'll be there tomorrow."

The restaurant was packed with tourists off I-55 and locals from Grenada. It followed the same decor as a T.G.I. Friday's or Bennigan's and other similarly-decorated southern chain-restaurants. Roman stopped at the door, where several couples and singles congregated to be seated. He scanned the bar area and recognized the profile. Lloyd was sitting squarely in the middle of the bar on one of the stools, taking in the local news. Roman tapped him on the shoulder, signalling him to walk toward a table near the bar.

"Back this way," Lloyd beckoned towards a booth, instead. "I already have us one waiting right behind me." He pointed to the booth the bus boy was cleaning. Harold avoided eye contact for a few seconds, unlike the Oxford meeting. The petite, blond waitress dropped menus and water down and hurried toward the kitchen. Roman pushed them aside and leaned back against the high-back booth. He looked around the crowded restaurant, then stared for a second at the stained-glass light fixture that hung from the ceiling, three feet above their table.

"What is it Harold?" Roman asked, raising his eyebrows.

"You are perceptive, aren't you? Well, it's nothing that can't be worked around."

"What do you mean? I knew something would be wrong. I knew it."

"Now wait until I finish." Lloyd stopped as the waitress approached with pencil and order pad ready. They both quickly chose the lunch special. It didn't seem to matter what it was. She raked in the menus and headed for the kitchen. "I had a plan that had to be approved by people above me. There has been a slight snag."

"What kind of 'snag'?" Roman's sarcasm rang through on the word snag.

"I have given this much thought and with all the information pointing the way it does, I need to get someone *inside* Parchman. I wanted to plant an informant, but they didn't like the idea of using one of our own men."

"I guess I can see that. They wouldn't be very believable. Some Harvard-looking preppie agent wouldn't fit the mold."

"It's not just the young ones. My boss doesn't feel very comfortable risking one of our own. It never seems to work right. Too much danger. Besides, they are not sold that there is enough evidence to pursue this matter without further investigation, and that could take some time."

Harold Lloyd looked genuinely disappointed, so Roman hesitated, tempering his reply.

"I told you I get these feelings. I could tell by the tone of your voice last night that you were having second thoughts."

"I wouldn't say that at all This is a temporary setback. There are ways around it.

Roman sipped his ice tea and stared straight ahead past him. Then he suddenly set the heavy glass down and leaned toward Lloyd. The waitress appeared again with the meat loaf and vegetables. He leaned in again until she hustled off. Neither man paid any attention to the food in front of them.

Now that the waitress was gone for sure, Roman said, "Listen carefully. I have a plan of my own. First of all, I would gladly volunteer to go under cover there myself, but I know that wouldn't work. Stiles is obviously there at times, and he might see me. Plus, I strolled around there for hours with John before he got killed. I got the grand tour and I'm sure some of them would recognize me, but I swear I would love to go inside if possible." Roman hesitated. "I'm not sure he would consent to it, or that it can be worked out with the right officials, but I may have the perfect prospect...I think."

He had Lloyd's attention. "Let me interrupt. First, if you have another inmate in mind, whether he is a 'Trusty' or not, forget it. Another inmate will tip off other inmates before we get started. They can't be totally trusted. Pardon the pun, but you can imagine. They may act a charade, but they will not usually squeal on the 'heavyweights'. They are too afraid of retaliation from most anyone in there. Some will squeal, granted, but it's rare, and they have been screened before any questions are asked by the law. They've been promised something in return for their information. Can you imagine asking some of these characters to be your eyes and ears in there and risk their lives possibly, without something in return? So if you think we will use another inmate, we won't. Not on something like this. Hell, we're not sure what we're looking for."

Lloyd was adamant, but sounded somewhat disappointed too. It was like he might have gone for the idea, but other officials would not. It was like he had over rehearsed his reason for not using another inmate, maybe to convince himself it wouldn't work, after hearing it from his bosses. But it didn't matter to Roman anyway, because he had a different proposal for Lloyd.

"What would you say if I could get you someone, if they are willing, who is very capable and knows the ropes, that you could trust?" Lloyd sensed the enthusiasm in Roman's voice. His eyes were dancing with excitement and fixed on Lloyd's.

Lloyd jumped in. "I've been in law enforcement a long time and have never heard of using someone other than an inmate or another lawman. An outsider, I don't think so. You can't use just any person for this. I don't have to tell you that it's dangerous. Deadly would be more appropriate."

"Would you at least listen to who I have in mind and a little about him, before you close your mind?"

Lloyd nodded slowly, pointing for Roman to take the cue. "I'm listening."

Roman smiled, moved up in his chair, and leaned forward toward Lloyd. "Harold, I already told you a little about the guy. He's the fireball bellman I mentioned who was so helpful when I was in New Orleans checking out Zach Stiles and his partners in crime." Harold leaned forward himself to speak, but Roman held up his hand. "Wait, hear me out, then I'll answer any questions. This little guy is a native wherever he lands. He can smooze with the best of them. He is so savvy, and, trust me, he's street smart."

"Is that all? Do you know him well, other than that night? What about his background? Hell, he could be a criminal for all you know."

"That's just it." A cunning smile crossed Roman's lips.

"Just what?"

Roman still smiled and stared at Lloyd. "He was one."

"One what?"

"A criminal. He was. Note I said he *was* one."

Harold Lloyd shook his head. "Wait. hear me out. You would have to have met this little fellow. He's small of statue, but big in heart. I'm not wrong. You know what I told you about my intuitions. Anyway, when he was very young, he worked at the airport in New Orleans and lifted a car or two. Temporarily, mind you."

"Temporarily?"

"Yes. He wanted to impress his very young bride. Told her that he got a raise and wanted her to pick out the one they would buy. That sort of thing. Like I said, if you only had met him. He's genuine. I know I only knew him a couple of days, but I connected with him and vice versa. It was one of those things, and I'm not one to take to just anybody instantly. He wanted to help me because it was intriguing. It gave him a break from being an everyday bellman. The man yearns for the respect of his family. He must have spent years trying to live down that early mistake in their eyes. It's a feeling I've got, but I think if the details could be worked out, he would do it. Do it and do it well. He also wants self esteem. He was so excited when he helped me find the registration of the limo that Stiles and the others were in. He could be the man. I hope I'm not wrong. He might turn it down. It's not exactly a vacation he would be asked to take. Never know until you try. Let me approach him and see if he's receptive."

"Roman, this is more than highly irregular. I don't even know if I can get it cleared. We would have to have him come into prison as a convicted felon. I would have to work that out discreetly with the State. Paper work and records authenticated, every little detail taken care of, so no suspicion is aroused." Lloyd stared at his glass of iced tea and spun it around slowly. "I don't think they'll go for it, but maybe I can try. I must be losing my mind. Oh yeah, If by some chance this is cleared and given the go ahead, I would naturally have to personally interview and brief him and so on."

"Of course, I understand." Yes. Yes! Roman thought to himself. A ray of hope to get Cliff inside, to start getting information. Find some clue as to what was going on in that chilling world of razor wire, locks, fences, towers, inmates and armed guards. A world where every kind of sinister and even ingenious criminal mind existed that one could imagine. He was convinced that there was a definite link between the penitentiary and John's death. Now, would Clifton really be willing to take such a chance if he was given certain assurances? No way to know without asking and he would ask. Nothing ventured, nothing gained.

"Although I have not had time to investigate Clifton Arceneaux fully," Lloyd said, promisingly, "I am willing to try to get this approved by my superiors. I guess you've convinced me. You seem so sold that he can do the job, it's intriguing to consider the possibility. If he is as good as you say, it could just work. He'd better be very street wise and a hell of an actor." Lloyd rubbed his temples softly, took his last bite from the blue plate special, then mumbled, still chewing, "Personally, I have my doubts that he will actually go undercover up there."

"Not to worry. Leave that to me. Since everything about this is highly irregular, as you said, why don't I call Clifton to feel him out? After all, it's a lot to ask a man to go back to prison. Especially to go back when you've done nothing wrong." Roman's voice faded softer, almost inaudible. "The more I think about it, I may be speaking out of school. I may be volunteering him for something he doesn't want to do at all. After all, who am I to assume he would agree?"

"Now you've convinced me, you start to doubt yourself. Let's either do it or not."

Roman was glad to see Lloyd's willingness to chance it, renewing his confidence. "Well, I think he'll seize the opportunity to prove himself, to put himself in the face of real danger and prevail." The check arrived just then, and Roman grabbed this one.

"We really need to talk to him first, but I guess under the circumstances, that you can call and test the water with him. Let me know immediately. And you know...."

"Yes, I know. No calls from my home or office. That's second nature now. I've got to get a cellular phone. I keep intending go to Greenville and get one. However, Rex said I might use the bugged phone to my advantage, if I feed them some erroneous information. I may or may not, but it's good to have the option. By the way, why don't you have a cellular?"

"I've been accused of being archaic by some. And sometimes, like you, I don't want a constant link to my whereabouts." Harold Lloyd looked surprisingly sheepish.

"Why don't I try him from the lobby of the Holiday Inn next door? Roman suggested. "I might get him when he can talk. If not, I'll try him back when he can."

"That's fine with me. Let's get over there." Harold pulled down the frontage road in his grey Chevy Biscayne with its black wall tires. It was fitting that his car be equally as conservative as he was. Roman was right behind.

The lobby was as abandoned, as was the parking lot. Most of last night's travelers had checked out and incoming guests were yet to arrive at this early afternoon hour.

"Roman, one more matter before you call him. Make certain he does not breathe a word to anyone, family, friends, not anyone. Do whatever you have to do to make him aware of this, whether he decides to come in as informant or not."

"I will, Harold. I'll make sure he knows it's a must he keep quiet." Roman thought about Cliff's gift of gab and how he could talk incessantly. He had to be secretive or not go undercover at the prison at all. Cliff would be quiet, he told himself.

A young, heavy-set girl with a beautiful face, glanced at Roman more than once, as he and Lloyd passed the lobby desk where she worked. He never noticed her until Lloyd brought it to his attention as they stopped at the phone in the hallway.

"I think she likes you, Roman." Harold grinned and slapped him on the shoulder. Roman turned and looked her way, smiling politely. "I think it's you she likes, Harold. The older, strong silent type." Lloyd's face turned slightly red.

Clifton's phone rang for the fourth time and Roman got an uneasy feeling. This could be a wrong number. What if the little guy gave him the wrong number by mistake? He figured Cliff would not be at work for the night shift yet. It was still not even 1:45 p.m. He hung up and dialed right back. The second ring produced a weary voice on the other end of the line. He could barely be heard.

"Clifton? Is this the Arceneaux residence?" Roman spoke louder, pressing his finger to his other ear to shut out the distant whining of the vacuum cleaner down the hall, operated by the cleaning lady. Harold Lloyd leaned against the wall next to him and studied Roman's expression.

"Answer is yes to both of 'em. And who is calling?" The Cajun voice sounded strained, but came through at last.

"Cliff, this is your old buddy, the Cowboy. Roman Beckley, remember? You haven't forgotten me already, have you?"

"You know better than that, my man. It's just that I was asleep. I know it's after lunch, but I had a rough night. To tell the truth, I didn't get much sleep. See, my wife left me again two nights ago. Went back to her Mother's. It's been hard to sleep. Too much booze don't help much either. It makes me wake up all during the night. I can numb myself and fall off to sleep, but I wake up in the wee hours. That's why I was asleep at this hour."

"I apologize for waking you."

"No problem. I gotta get shakin' soon and down to the hotel in a couple of hours."

"I'm sorry about your wife. I'm sure this is temporary. She'll be back soon. She take the children too?"

"Yep. My boy 13 and my girl 15. Her Mother is half the problem. Like I told you before, always fillin' my wife's head about how big a failure I am. Guess she's right. I try, but I know I don't make a lot of dough. I don't give her or the kids much to be proud of."

"Don't be so hard on yourself and cut back on the drinking. It'll only compound the problem and make you look worse in her eyes. Make you feel worse too. You haven't got to be told that, huh?" Roman's sincerity came through. Harold Lloyd noticed and nodded in agreement.

"This ain't the first time she's left, but it looks bad. I keep trying to look good and keep fouling up. I thought I could win some pretty big bucks in a poker game the night before she left. Lost my butt. She wanted some new clothes for the kids and some curtains. I let 'em down. Anyway,

I'll keep pluggin' away. Maybe she'll have a change of heart and cool down and come back."

"She will, Cliff. Go easy. She will."

"Thanks. I appreciate comforting words." Cliff's cleared his throat and his voice picked up. "That's enough of that. Let's talk about why you called. I hope some good news about the lawman, huh? Can you hold on while I pour me a hot cup of black coffee?"

"You bet."

"Now, where were we?"

Roman hesitated and smiled as he looked out the window to the pool area.

"Cliff, if I told you that while we've been talking, I could visualize you as a hero of sorts, what would you think?"

"I'd say, you're easy to please in your taste for heroes," Cliff laughed.

"No, this is a distinct possibility. Furthermore, you'd be working with some top law enforcement officers."

The laughter on the other end escalated. Cliff clearly took it as a joke. Maybe a cruel joke. "Cowboy, you know I can't become a cop. I've been in prison, not put others in, remember? Please don't play games with me. I took a liking to you, but my ego is a little fragile right now. There's no need for it to be abused further. My wife has done a good job of deflating me. Her and that Mother of hers. I don't need people I like doing the same."

Roman's voice was reassuring. "No, seriously. You could be valuable to law enforcement officials in uncovering an illegal operation. It looks big. Very big."

"Yeah?" Cliff's became excited immediately. "Tell me more."

"I can't tell you everything by phone, but some other law enforcement officials can. It will need to be in person. A long interview, but you've got to swear to secrecy."

"I will, but what about?"

"No one, but no one, must know we even had this conversation. Not even your wife."

"My wife wouldn't listen, anyway. You have my word. One thing I can do is keep my big mouth shut if I give someone my word. If your word ain't good, you don't have much to offer the world. My Dad didn't have much to give us six kids, but he taught us that."

"Good, I knew you were an honorable fellow, or I wouldn't be calling you with something this important. Think you can work closely with the FBI?" Silence.

"Did you say FBI?" What is goin' on, and why in hell would they need me?" The excitement peaked in his voice.

"This will be gone over in detail with you. I can only touch on it now to see if you'd be interested. It might, rather, it would be, dangerous."

Cliff interrupted, "I don't care. I don't care. At this point, I need something different. I want a challenge. I want to make a difference and be somebody."

"You'd better not answer so quickly until you hear me out. You would be put in the Mississippi State Penitentiary in an undercover role. You'd have to pose as a convict and gather certain information about some illegal goings on that are suspected there."

Cliff took forever to answer. The silence made Roman nervous. He shifted his weight from one foot to the other, shrugged his shoulders, and turned his palms upward to Lloyd.

Cliff spoke a little softer and slower. "I don't like the sound of that last sentence. You seriously want me to put in time at the 'Big House' in Mississippi? You don't know how I hated every minute of every day I was behind bars. I swore I'd never go near one again or give anyone any reason to put me back. Now someone wants me to volunteer? That's almost bizarre."

"I understand fully, Cliff. I really do. It was a thought only. I apologize for asking. The FBI insists that you never mention this to a soul. Forget this conversation took place. I know you will. I'll be in touch sometime when I'm down that way. I hope you get straight with your wife. Give her some time and keep yourself busy. It'll work out."

Roman was about to put the receiver back when Cliff spoke again.

"Now hold on! Will I get my name in the papers if I work out well. Know what I mean? At least, will I get some sort of recognition?"

"I can't promise the papers, but you will be recognized by the authorities, I'm sure." Roman turned to Lloyd wanting an assuring nod. Lloyd responded positively.

"I'm game. Hell, I didn't pose as a convict in Louisiana. I was one. I got lots of experience. I can do it if anyone can. I said I never wanted to go near a prison again, but I also didn't know I'd be this stagnant at this time in my life. All I want is a promise that I can get out when I want to. That is, if the heat gets too bad."

169

"I know you can do that. You'll be briefed on all that by the FBI."

Lloyd tapped Roman on the shoulder and asked, "Has he got a beard, or mustache, or longish hair?"

Roman looked a little puzzled, but asked Cliff, "You still got the mustache? How about the hair in the back? Is it still long and curled up on the ends?"

"What is this, a beauty contest I'm entering?"

Roman looked to Lloyd for an answer about the hair and mustache. Lloyd leaned toward him and whispered, "Tell him to shave the mustache and cut his hair very short. It will help if, by some remote chance, somebody there could recognize him. Some of these guys have made the rounds from prison to prison in neighboring states. There shouldn't be anybody, but do it anyway for an extra precaution, especially if he had long hair and mustache in the Louisiana prison."

"Did you have your hair about the same and the mustache when you were in before?"

"My hair was a little thicker in those days and long in the back. I've also had this mustache for more years than I can remember.

"They want you to look fresh shaven with short hair. You don't mind, do you?"

"No, I don't. That'll be another change for the better. I need all I can get, I guess."

"Remember, not a word. I know you keep your word. It's a matter of life an death on this one. Well, I shouldn't say that but...."

"Say no more, I understand."

"Mr. Harold Lloyd will be in touch with you right away to interview and brief you in person. Should be in two or three days, or maybe before. Go on about your business as usual. He'll do the getting in touch. I know the man and he can be trusted. He won't ask you to do anything that will unnecessarily put you in danger. They will be monitoring you closely. I told him you were one sharp Cajun who knows his way around. I explained why you were sent up before. You can fill him in on any other facts. I know you'll cooperate. I think they're very glad to have you on their side. I appreciate this too. I know you can get the information needed if anyone can. Be careful. I'll make sure they take good care of you and I'll check on you as much as possible."

Roman hesitated. "Oh, and one more thing. Don't call me at home or the office, those numbers I gave you on my card. They're bugged. In fact,

I won't be able to communicate with you once you go in. You never heard of me while you're there. It's for your own good. Some people mixed up in this, I strongly suspect, are watching me very closely. If they put the two of us together, it would be a dead give-away. Sorry to use the word dead," Roman's laughed faintly. "I'll keep up with you through the FBI, and I'll be waiting for us to celebrate when you're through with this assignment. That sounds good, huh, assignment?"

"Wow. I'd be lying if I didn't say I was a little scared," Cliff responded. "Scared, but ready. So long." Roman hung up after Cliff and took a deep breath. Cliff was in. He drove away with Harold Lloyd's word that Cliff would be monitored closely and not be put in harm's way more than absolutely necessary. That in all likelihood, he would not be exposed to a life-threatening situation. Roman hoped with all his soul, that he was right.

CHAPTER *19*

S heriff, three farmers are waiting outside to talk to you," The red-haired secretary announced from his doorway. "Sounds important. They don't seem like they're in a very good mood."

She started to withdraw, but he barked at her: "Wait! Come back here for a minute. Don't ever give me some vague information and expect me to handle some irate farmer. Get back out there and find out what it is they are here for, so I can be prepared. Tell them I'm on a conference call or something. Find out." Stiles's glaring dark eyes made the skinny young lady nervous. She fumbled for the door and made her way to the farmers, each of whom owned large spreads, who stood anxiously waiting to see Stiles.

"Gentlemen, Sheriff Stiles is on a conference call with someone in Jackson at the moment. He said he looks forward to seeing you all in a few minutes. Can I get y'all some coffee?" She lingered as they stared, none of them knowing exactly what to say. It was a toss-up as to who was the most uncomfortable. She broke the ice. "Have y'all had a break-in or someone steal some machinery?"

One of the men, in his thirties, well educated and sporting a Rolex, hesitated, then answered coolly, "No, but we've had something unusual happening around our place." She searched for the words. The men looked at her, then turned away and began to mumble among themselves.

She finally managed another question. "Are any of you catfish farmers?" No one was. "I'll bet someone is rustling your cattle," she ventured.

The oldest one, who had a sizeable paunch, fielded the last comment, scowling, "Worse, young lady. Someone is mutilating them. Cuttin' out parts. Some type of ritual, I guess. You don't want to hear anymore details." Her face turned redder than her shocking red hair. She could muster no response. She felt all eyes on her as she turned and bolted for the Sheriff's office.

He was sitting in his favorite position, leaning back in his huge leather chair with his boots of the day propped firmly on the corner of his desk. She opened his door and pointed toward the room where they were waiting. Her voice was shaky and more high pitched than usual.

"They are out there because they said someone, or something, has been mutilating their cattle. Seems like at more than one place. I don't know how many. That's the best I could do. You'll have to take it from there, sir." She waited for his response, shifting her weight from one foot to the other and rolling her ring around on her left ring finger with her thumb, over and over.

He sat in silence and stared at the picture of the Vietnam Memorial Wall that hung nearby. He never moved a muscle or showed any sign of concern. A sly grin moved across his lips as he lowered his feet and placed them under his desk. He sat straight and transformed himself into the ready-to-serve Sheriff of Wildflower County.

"Come on in, gentlemen," he boomed, and the three filed into his office. "Sorry I was on the phone, trying to help solve a case in conjunction with the Highway Patrol's chief investigator. Another rash of break-ins. This one looks like it'll be history by tomorrow. We'll have them in custody in a few more hours. I can't believe the ignorant idiots that think they can commit a crime around here and not get caught eventually. But, you didn't come to hear all that. What can I do to be of service to you three fellows? Just name it."

The young one took the lead. "Zach, to put it bluntly, we've had some cattle mutilated. It has gone on more than once. One time with something like this, you can maybe dismiss it as some kids' prank, but there have been several cases over the last month or so. At least, that's all we've found. There may have been more."

"What have you found with the cattle? I mean exactly what's been done."

The older gentleman spoke. "They've been disemboweled. Their throats were cut too, like a deer hunter would do to a buck. One even had the figure 9 on it in three places or could have been seen as a 6, I guess. Looks like the numbers were branded on. That was one of my cattle and I don't brand at all. Never thought it was necessary around here. We're damn well concerned and want this bunch of weirdos caught." He slammed his fist down on Stiles's desk. Stiles glanced at his fist only a split second.

The young man chimed in again. "You know I've seen television shows about devil worship. It could be some sick souls are using our cattle as some sacrifice or for some sign. Hell, the three 9's could be, instead, 666, the sign of the *Devil*. I don't know, but it doesn't set well with me." Stiles's left eye twitched three or four times in succession. He sat frozen, almost trance-like. Then, suddenly, he jumped up and slapped his hand, palm down, on the table next to his desk.

"It is probably those damn juveniles I've had to run off before from around here. I think they're from Greenville. Just a bunch of kids that are smart asses wanting to shock somebody. One of them's daddy is divorced, and they all come over here stay with him up the road. I'll check it out." He put his arm around the older gentleman and escorted them out the door. He turned to the young farmer and smiled strangely, as his eyes narrowed.

"You know, devil worship is not some figment of the imagination anymore. There are actually people who practice it, and believe in its powers, totally." He blinked his eyes for a second. "I'm sure it's those juveniles, but I'll check out the possibility that it could be an occult thing. I'll handle it and get to the bottom of it. No need to worry. I wouldn't say anything to anybody. You know? No need to spread any unnecessary panic." They agreed and were content for the moment that Zach Stiles would handle the situation.

When they were gone, he swung his office door to and punched down the intercom: "Where is Wiggins? I want him in this office immediately."

A county dispatcher answered: "He's off today for a family funeral. It was cleared by you, sir."

"Get him anyway, and tell him to report to me by 1500 hours. That's three o'clock to people like you who have never served any duty in the military. Now get him and tell him to be here on time or before!"

"Yes, sir." The dispatcher hung up and mumbled under his breath.

At 2:30 p.m., Wiggins rounded the curve outside town with siren blasting, doing at least 20 m.p.h. over the 55 limit. He drove 55 within the city limits and was at the county courthouse in another four minutes. The dispatcher and a female deputy peered out the window as he made his screeching, blaring arrival. "They said you wanted me here, and that it was important, Sheriff." Wiggins wiped his brow with his bandana and automatically took a seat.

Stiles stared at him and never spoke. The deputy shuffled his feet and crossed his legs for the second time. His face was strained, though he tried to relax. Stiles's right hand was hidden from view, underneath the desk. He slid it into his holster and grasped the .357 Magnum tightly. Like lightning, he jerked the gun out, its cold steel barrel aimed right between Wiggins's eyes. Wiggins blinked his bulging eyes and alternated between a smile and sheer horror.

Stiles had him locked in his sights. As he stared, his right index finger twitched on the trigger three or four times in succession. Finally, he spoke, in a slow and deliberate tone. "You idiot. First, you are not Barney Fife.... Then, maybe you are. The more I think about it, you act a lot like him. I am tempted to blow your brains against that wall and swear you attacked me."

Wiggins squirmed and exhaled loudly, his voice trembling as he spoke: "Sir, what's this all about?"

"It's about you and your incompetence. I had a group of farmers in here earlier who were upset over the fact that some of their cattle had been mutilated. In other words, they found them. Yes, they found them. There is no excuse for your negligence. You were ordered to bury those animals and told where to do it. Why in the hell didn't you do what I told you to do?"

"I didn't think they'd be found where I put them. I thought the buzzards would pick their bones clean. I really thought no one would come near that field, as far back as I dumped them." Stiles lowered the weapon, but stared intently. Wiggins wiped his upper lip and tried to smile.

"Wipe that smile off your face, Wiggins. So you dumped them. Dumped them! I specifically ordered you to bury them, not dump them. As far as coming near that field, it borders two of the farmers' properties. You should know these guys run all over their land and all around it. They've got eyes like hawks when it comes to something changed around their land. They can spot anything. Now I've got to cover this up and calm them because of your lack of intelligence." He spun his chair around and looked out the window, into the street. His fingers strummed the desk top. Without turning around, he spoke very deliberately, "Get out of my sight for the rest of this day. Maybe the rest of your days, if I change my mind. If I didn't have you so deep in the project, I would either kill you or run your dumb ass out of town. Now get out of here, Wiggins. I'll decide later what to do."

"I'm sorry, Sir. It...."

"I don't want to hear your apologies or excuses. Now go."

Wiggins tipped out and eased the door to, very gingerly.

Stiles sat motionless, his eyes fixed on the Vietnam Memorial. His favorite picture. He was lost once again in it. Finally, he shook his head slightly and mumbled to himself, then walked to the corner of the room and opened his closet. He slid garments from left to right until a long black robe appeared. He touched the garment near the top, closed his eyes momentarily, then smiled and walked away.

CHAPTER *20*

For the next two days, Roman put in long hours at work and tried to occupy his mind with the business he was sent down for. He created work when there was not enough. He answered every piece of mail, and even read the company employee manual, which he had previously been unable to digest past the first three pages. He arrived before daylight, and left in darkness. He even ordered his food delivered to the office.

No matter what he did though, his mind was preoccupied with images and thoughts of Diana. The harder he tried not to, the more his thoughts ran to her. It seemed like a month, rather than the few days since he had seen her. Now she was far away. Was she thinking of him? He hoped. He vividly recalled the touch of her thick, lustrous hair, how she smelled, so fresh and alluring, the way she moved, and, most of all, those green eyes that seemed to see into his soul. He longed to call her, but would not relent. She made the decision to leave, and he would not fold to his emotions. Somehow, he felt she would be contact him, but every passing hour chipped away his hopes that she ever would.

It was almost 8 p.m. Darkness had long set in, as had fatigue. He closed his filing cabinet, not consciously hearing the grating noise it made as it slid shut. The sound of his fax machine jarred him back to reality. He watched the slick white paper slide to its destination at the top of the machine. It had to be from Elton, or some clerk at Worldwide, wanting a correction on his expense report or something trivial. He was surprised to see there was not the usual Worldwide heading.

It came from Memphis: Attn.: Mr. Beckley: To confirm our conversation of last week about our telecommunication assistance program for your company's hazardous waste project. I need you to call me at your earliest convenience. You have my card and my request that you call collect or on our 800 number. Sincerely, H. Lloyd." Roman glanced at the message. Harold was more clever than he thought and definitely not taking chances with his messages.

Roman left immediately through the rear entrance of the building into the dimly-lit alley behind his office. He cranked his Blazer, turned on the lights, and eased out of the small parking lot. As he rounded the corner of the building onto the main road, his headlights illuminated the reflective sign on the side of the pale green car. The shape of the star was hard to miss, along with the blue lights on top and that profile under the wheel. He glared defiantly as he passed within ten feet of the car, then proceeded to the main highway. The headlights fell in behind him after he had gone no more than two hundred feet. He kept his speed within the limit and headed toward his home. But he was damn sick and tired of this. He suddenly turned right and swung into his old home-away-from-home, the Taurus Motel. The official car shot by without slowing down.

Roman walked to the pay phone in the tiny lobby and started his call. There would no more hiding from the bastards. If they came in, he could always hang up or fake it. At least, he got a certain amount of satisfaction out of this maneuver.

He dialed Harold's office and got the usual answer in a ring or two.

"I am about ready to rip the bug out of my office and home phones, if I can find out how. Just kidding. I know, I may use them to my advantage. But this is demeaning, to have to run to a phone to have any privacy."

"No smart, not demeaning. Roman, do I have to resort to reminding you about what we said, and who you are dealing with?"

"No. You're right. Patience. It better pay off."

"It will. I'm sure. I wanted to update you on Clifton Arceneaux."

"Good. I've been anxious to see if you've talked with him. I knew he was in for sure.

"I've done better than that. I met with him yesterday in New Orleans, and it looks like we may be able to put him inside."

Roman rattled the change in his pockets and paced back and forth, the extent the wire phone cord would stretch. A wave of anxiety came over him again about Cliff. How could they guarantee his safety? They could not, and he knew it. Harold Lloyd knew it too. Certainly not under prison conditions. Especially, if he has to mingle and gather information.

"Roman, you still with me?"

"I can't help but think, now that it is about to become a reality, about the little guy sticking his neck out. Sticking it out for someone he doesn't even know that well. I hope he watches his back. Do you think he can hold his own in there, behind those walls?"

"I hope I'm a good judge of people. I've been in this work for many years. If anyone can pull it off and blend in, it'll be Cliff. He's savvy and very street wise. You were right there. I've briefed him, and we'll have ways of keeping our eyes on him. You will not believe the amount of work and phone calls and coordination it has taken to put this into motion."

"I want to hear what's being done as far as he goes. How does he get in?"

"I've worked that out with the right people. Officially, he'll be in for felony check forgery from Harrison County on the Gulf Coast. He will bypass the Rankin County processing center near Jackson and be brought directly up to Parchman. Trust me, the details have been worked out. He will be given 'trusty' status in Parchman so he can move about freely to all parts of the prison. In case he is asked, he has been briefed to say that the county jailer recommended him for 'trusty', since he had been model prisoner for the five months he had been there, waiting to be sent to the penitentiary. Also, the felony check forgery is not a severe enough offense to prevent him from getting that privilege. More severe charges would have raised some suspicion as to how he could come straight from county jail to Parchman as a 'trusty'. We've arranged for a deputy to carry him, along with a county prisoner from the processing center, up to Parchman tomorrow."

"Tomorrow? You don't waste any time. You also said a deputy would bring him up. What if he's not familiar with what's going on and says something out of the way to arouse suspicion about Cliff?"

"Like what?"

"I don't know. It seems like someone special could have made the transport."

"Someone special will. He's one of our men. That's my job. Relax on that part." Roman sensed a touch of irritation in Lloyd's voice.

"Hope you understand. I feel responsible for him going up there in the first place."

"Go on about your business as usual. I promised I would keep you posted on the progress in the prison. If you need me, you've got the number. We will get this underway. Oh, and by the way, Cliff said he would look to see you in New Orleans after this is solved. He said you'd know what he was talking about." Roman smiled and hung up. He scanned the parking lot for the county car, but saw no trace. He took a deep breath of the cool fall air and pulled out for home again. Many of the houses along the way showed little light, as their inhabitants had retired to get ready for tomorrow's early morning rising. He would try the same.

Even though they covered approximately 300 miles from the Mississippi Gulf Coast to Parchman penitentiary in the northwestern part of the state, the day was passing too quickly for Clifton. Maybe because he was about to have his freedom stifled, despite the circumstances. He became a little more apprehensive than he had anticipated, as his mind jumped ahead to the sound of steel doors slamming and locking behind him for the next few weeks. He hadn't forgotten that sound and the desperate feeling. Still, he was unwavering in his dedication and mumbled to psyche himself up for the role of his life. He would not fail and would follow the orders given him. This was his long-awaited chance to perform an honorable service for law and order.

He would do his part and do it well. His children and wife would be proud. He would make sure of it. It was all systems go for him. The St. Christopher's Cross his Mom had given him as a teenager, hung around his thick short neck. It contrasted with his dark hairy chest, which had begun to sag from too much age and too little exercise. He reached for the cross as he stared at the sprawling grounds unfolding ahead. Rubbing the cross, he strained for a better look ahead through the wire cage that separated him from the deputy. He looked to the side out the window, then straight ahead through the cage and windshield. He mumbled, and the chosen deputy glanced at him and gave a thumbs up, just as they came into view of the three armed guards awaiting their stop.

The agent, posing as a deputy, said: "Clifton, you know once we get out of this car, it'll be strictly business. No one should suspect any collusion." They pulled up to the main gate and stopped. A tall black guard motioned for them to pull ahead another few feet. He looked even more somber and threatening than those he remembered from his stint in the Louisiana prison, years ago.

Cliff inadvertently made eye contact with the guard. He did not get a warm glance in return. The huge man locked onto Cliff's arm and gave him a helpful shove straight ahead. The handcuffs had not been uncomfortable yet, since the posing deputy had been wise enough to stop a few miles back, before clamping them on.

He was led to the prison processing building. The photograph of the bloodhound displayed on the wall, caught his eye. It was framed, engraved and dedicated to Lil' Red 1976-83. He smiled slightly. He had always been a dog lover, but the picture was a stark reminder of where he was now. After a couple of hours of paper work, photographs, and more fingerprinting, he unceremoniously became Mississippi State Penitentiary inmate 9856773. He was then escorted by another smaller, stockier guard across the street to the prison infirmary for a physical. He was given the usual examination, from head to toe, by a very young doctor who looked fresh out of medical school.

"Your pulse is elevated considerably. 125 is quite rapid. Your blood pressure is not very normal either. "

"What is it?"

"165/96," The baby faced doctor said, as he rolled his stool away from the examining table.

"With all due respect for your expertise in medicine, Doc, yours would probably be rapid as hell too, if you'd just been admitted to this place as an inmate." Cliff sat up and buttoned his new issue prison blues. His new look would be a blue shirt and dark blue pants with a three-inch white stripe running down the legs. This would be seven days a week. This denoted his category "A" status of "trusty". He was glad to be wearing this color designation rather than the more restricted white with blue stripe, category B, and especially glad not to have to wear the severely restricted C group's yellow jumpsuits. At least he could move about most of the prison without an armed guard at every step. Although he had restrictions, which Lloyd had familiarized him with, he knew the ropes. They were similar to Louisiana's. Not the same, but he knew the overall picture would not be drastically different.

The guard slammed the gate to his iron cage. The sudden, clanging finality of it made him jump slightly. A wave of nausea came over him. Even though he knew better, it seemed for a split second that the bars would never be opened again. He remembered how he hated that helpless, trapped feeling. His mind was running in high gear. It didn't matter where it was, being locked up again, under any circumstances, brought back painful memories. It was like they had been in some corner of his mind, waiting to be resurrected.

He was housed in a unit with many other "trustys". Some had been there for a number of years; others had many more to serve. He put down his gear and looked around. The room was dismal and gray. Drab steel bunks and old footlockers lined the bleak walls, and two old ceiling fans barely turned above. Despite the relatively mild weather outside, it was stuffy in the unit. Cliff wiped the perspiration off his top lip with his hand. The musty smell was almost stifling. The high, small windows were tightly covered with foreboding wire and steel supports. Only one other inmate was around; a large, black man sitting near his bunk, applying some sort of wax to his hair, who pretended not to notice Cliff. The other inmates were about their duties somewhere on the grounds that spread over the 17,000 acres and miles of flat prison grounds. Some of the units were relatively close to others, but some were spread many acres away. The isolated units were for inmates in the witness protection program, who were kept away from the rest of the prison population to prevent retaliation from other prisoners they had testified against in court. The maximum security units were also away from most of the general population and were much more heavily guarded. The medium security units were closer together. Cliff, as a "trusty", would have some freedom of movement near most of these buildings, since they were not as restricted to their unit area as the other prisoners. It had taken years for most "trustys" to earn this privilege.

A picture of Jesus was prominently displayed above the iron single bed next to Cliff's. This was comforting for the moment. Maybe someone here is a notch above most of the population, he thought.

"You never saw a picture of Jesus, huh?" A deep rumbling voice came from behind him. It was Alonzo Waters, a huge, muscular black man with a bandana tied around his shiny head. He was serving 10 years for drug trafficking.

Cliff turned and gave a firm, but friendly response. "Yeah. I sure have. I'm glad my Mom took the time to teach me about the Bible."

"Right, 'Big Man'. You'll get plenty of time to catch up on readin' in this joint. Probably need the Bible before you get out, if you do. Don't mean to sound hard, but you never know." Cliff stared for a second and walked away. What was he trying to do? If it was to scare him, it worked.

Not for long though. He brushed it aside and unpacked his gear. This wasn't the kind of housewarming he expected, but he could handle it. After all, this was temporary. Cliff glanced back and watched Alonzo amble over to his bottom bunk and prop his size 12 feet on the end of the bed rail.

The rest of the 25 inmates began to file into the unit from their various duties of the day. It was noisy, the bunks were close to each other, and privacy was nonexistent. But, at least, they were not under the same constant surveillance as the rest of the population. Nevertheless, they all displayed that certain look of a man without his freedom. Few smiles were showing, except for a couple of blacks grinning and tussling around for a few seconds, before the guard yelled at them.

Cliff heard a soft whistling sound from the bunk next to his. It was his other neighboring cell mate, Elicio Fernandez, who was either shy or had no desire to be friendly at this point. He ignored Cliff's extended hand and turned away. He was thin and wiry in stark contrast to his black neighbor. Elicio has already served four of his ten year sentence for attempted assault with a deadly weapon and kidnapping his ex-wife. He had taken her against her will on a long journey, after losing his job with a group of wandering farm workers who had landed in Mississippi.

Cliff was no stranger to all types of prison personalities. He had learned that you could never determine by the first meeting or so, truly what kind of criminal you might be engaging in conversation, or what they were really like. Back in the Louisiana prison, a young man befriended him during his first week on the grounds. This young man was appropriately nicknamed "Baby" because of his youthful innocent looks. He was 21 years old, but could have easily passed for sixteen. Cliff didn't ask what he was in for. He later found it was for the double murder of his parents in Baton Rouge. It seemed they had denied him the privilege of living on campus at LSU, since they had a residence in Baton Rouge. He also stood to inherit their estate, valued at over 2.2 million.

Yes, he knew not to judge a book by its cover, that criminals came in all guises. He wouldn't form a quick opinion on these two near his bunk, especially not a favorable one. He could not let his guard down. He could feel Elicio's quick eyes following him, sizing him up, as he finished unpacking his bare necessities. Every time Cliff tried to make eye contact with him, Elicio's eyes darted away like lightning. Gone with a flick. Gone, but he could still feel the eyes when he turned his back. For now, Cliff decided he would turn his back as little as possible around Elicio. For the first time since he left the Louisiana prison, he was grateful for having been there. His instincts had been sharpened there and that would give him an edge here. He definitely had the advantage, he kept telling himself.

The temptation to ask a few questions could wait until after the night meal. When the feeling came on, he could visualize Harold Lloyd and his words of stern caution. "Don't ask anyone any questions the first day or two. No matter whether you think you have a friend or not, don't do it. That might send up a red flag, asking questions. Remember, Cliff, red flag!" He thought of the red flag several times in the first hour alone. He would play it cool and pick his time and inmates.

When it was time to file out for the night meal, he fell in with the group and tried to avoid making eye contact with anyone. He looked at the floor, the walls, the ceiling, anything but another inmate, hoping to avoid a conversation this first day. He wanted to watch them and size them up individually. He would have plenty of time to talk after this first night.

The mess hall was noisy and hot, and again, he tried to not to talk to anyone. He even nodded for his food as he went down the line, as if he had much of a choice. The meal was as bland as he had remembered from his Louisiana prison days. Still it was filling, since the anticipation boiling inside him had made him hungry enough to eat most anything.

As they were herded back to their respective lock-ups, his eyes missed nothing along the way. He watched the cooks, the guards, other inmates, and made mental notes of everything he could absorb. For the next few days, particularly, he would pay particular attention to the other "trustys," those who appeared to be leaders, and those who seemed followers. He would also try to infiltrate the other category B units, and even try to finagle some kind of duty around the maximum security units. He felt confident about what was wanted. He knew that, with enough time, he would pick up enough information to uncover what they were looking for. He knew that if something big enough was going on down on the sprawling grounds, not everyone could keep quiet about it.

The night was winding down. He knew all eyes were, at one time or another, on him. He was the new guy. A big-bellyed man with greasy hair and several teeth missing, appeared and propped his foot on the end of Cliff's bunk. His face was red and pocked in places, his eyes wild-looking, yearning for trouble.

"Hey! What you in here for, 'Shorty'?" He grinned and looked around, as if inviting the other inmates to join in. Cliff looked away and said nothing.

"I'm talking to you, 'Shorty'. He leaned down, breathing inches from Cliff's neck.

"You must be hard of hearing! Are you?" He was yelling by now.

Cliff turned slowly and faced him. "I may be short, but I don't need some 'redneck' to tell me about it."

The big man leaned back in semi-shock. He grabbed Cliff by the back of the neck and pushed him into the bunk, face down. Cliff turned his head, twisted loose from his grip, spun around behind the big guy and hit him on the back of his head with all his strength. The big guy stumbled, but didn't go down. He swung hard, but Cliff ducked. A crowd gathered. Someone yelled to hurry because of the guard. Cliff landed a punch to the man's stomach and drew back again to swing. His adrenalin was flowing, pumping to a peak, and he even heard a cheer or two for him. Suddenly, he stumbled on the foot locker and big boy was on him, grabbing his head, drawing back to crush his face. Then, out of nowhere, the big guy was flying into the bunks, tangled with an even-bigger giant. Alonzo Waters was pounding him.

The fight between these two was over before it began. The big man retreated to his area at the far end of the building. Cliff pretended to shrug it off, putting up a good front. He straightened up his bunk area. Finally, the guard appeared, inquired about a fight, and got no response. He shrugged his shoulders, pivoted, and returned to the front of the building. Lights went out.

"Alonzo. Thanks." Cliff whispered.

Alonzo mumbled, "Okay, but don't think I'll make no habit of it." Cliff smiled.

CHAPTER *21*

Two days past and Roman heard nothing from either Harold Lloyd or Rex. No news should be good news, he assumed. At least he would have heard had something disastrous happened, he consoled himself. If there were ever a time in his life he could use some moral support, it was now. Still, he persevered and spent hour-after-hour paving the way for the planned controversial waste facility to become a reality. He read in the morning paper where a competitor in the waste business was fined $550,000 to settle an EPA enforcement action against an Iowa landfill it owned. He had met one of the officials of that competitive company, not over four or five months ago in Los Angeles. He was a former aide to a U.S. Senator. This was a very lucrative business and many of the competitors spent money, hand over fist, to secure big contracts. Often, lobbyists and former politicians worked certain areas trying to secure these waste contracts for companies they represented. Well-connected law firms also reaped the benefits of being on retainers, and some members of firms even landed on the board of directors of these companies. Money flowed freely, and influence was peddled night and day, for the contracts to be finalized.

So far, Roman had encountered irate landowners with property surrounding the site, local politicians wanting to exploit the fears about the site, constant scrutiny by the EPA, and some heat from the locals, about its effects on the environment. He was holding his own with them all, but had to answer their questions hourly. As far as he knew, Worldwide won this contract over other similar waste companies with less competition than they usually encountered at other state sites they owned. He remembered the battle between Worldwide and other companies for the Minnesota site, before Worldwide prevailed. He knew his company was rich, and this was comforting when dealing with all factions. Their resources and technology were second to none. Besides, he was convinced that once its high-tech methods were in place, it would be safe for the environment. It would be lucrative for the county and surrounding area as well. Their operation would accept Mississippi hazardous waste initially, then possibly other states and even other countries. The scope of the operation showed endless promise.

It was 10:35 and Jay Leno had just finished his monologue. Roman turned off the television; it was only noise to him, just some company. He couldn't remember feeling so alone, except right after Leah's death in LA. There were so many people surrounding him in those first grief-stricken days, that he hardly had time to experience the truly alone, desperate feeling. That came later and lingered for what seemed like two lifetimes.

He had to get out of the house. He grabbed the keys to his Blazer and stopped by the refrigerator on the way to the garage. He needed a cold Bud. He tore three loose from the plastic ring-holder and started to open the back door. Leave two and take just one, he decided. All he needed was to be stopped by the friendly law and have enough alcohol in him to get a DUI. One beer would do fine. He placed the remaining two back in the cooler. As he slid behind the wheel, he wondered if he forgot to turn anything off. He remembered to turn on the answering machine and also activated the Caller I.D. service that identifies the incoming calls by area code and number. He'd had this identification service added to his phone after getting a series of hang-ups and strange-sounding wrong numbers, as they said. He hoped that Diana's voice might be waiting soon on the recorder. Maybe she'd had a change of heart. He had to remain optimistic about them.

He cranked up his Blazer, slipped in an old Steppenwulf tape, and backed out the driveway. The dashboard clock showed 11:05. Steppenwulf was too loud and "Magic Carpet Ride" was not the mood he was in. He chose the radio, punching the digital buttons, searching for the right music. He landed on Aaron Neville doing an old George Jones song, "Grand Tour". He was amazed at the velvet, R&B voice, and what a great job he was doing as a crossover artist, singing a true country tear-jerker. He felt much better moving down the road, with the radio as his friend, than sitting inside his house. He lowered his windows and let the cool fall breeze blow through his hair. It was therapeutic to be on the move, to see the stars and feel the wind rushing through, as he headed east toward Greenwood. The moonlit night and virtually empty road made his driving even more relaxing and he could think clearer without the interruption of phones, fax machines, and visitors.

As he passed the combination convenience-store-bait shop about three miles from the city limits, he did a double-take. A shiny, green pickup pulled under the lights of the store, and Deputy Wiggins, in civilian clothes, was getting out of the passenger's side. He went inside, while the driver remained in the truck. Wiggins's back was to Roman so he was sure he didn't see him. He shook his head and kept moving east at the 55 mph speed limit. No lights followed, and he was glad. He steeled himself not to flinch every time he saw him or Stiles and fear an arrest or worse.

His habit of changing radio stations kicked in. He punched the scan button and let it run across the dial, stopping momentarily at each station until he settled for the jazz station airing a laid-back, relaxing, tenor saxophone number.

As the 1100-acre site turn-off road was coming into view, he glanced in his rear-view mirror and saw headlights at least a half mile behind him. He drove past the turn off road to the site, as he was spending enough time there, off and on, during the day. He wanted to clear his mind, not be reminded of business. He paid no attention to the headlights far behind him, as they didn't appear to be gaining on him. But seconds later, glancing back, he saw the lights swing left. They had turned off onto the old beaten up road and were headed toward the site.

His foot eased off the accelerator slightly, but he kept going straight on Highway 82 East. It seemed odd that a car would be turning down that practically abandoned road at this hour. No one lived down it now, and there was only some farm property along the way to the site. It could be a farmer checking on something. He drove another hundred yards or so and stopped. Since he saw no one approaching ahead or behind him, he did a quick U turn and headed back toward the turn off, about two miles back.

As he eased onto the access road, he reached under his seat and fumbled until he felt the pistol in his grip. He raised it to the seat and placed it beside him. It seemed darker along this narrow road, because the few trees were lined right next to the road, blocking out the moonlight. There were a few other trees off in the distance, but tonight, even they seemed to help block any light on the road. He drove until he knew he was getting close to the site. No car or truck was to be found yet. As he bumped along the road, he looked for familiar gates and openings in the property, to signal the immediate approach to the site. Finally, he saw the reflection of the shiny new gate that bordered the property to his left. He turned off his lights and radio and slowed to a snail's pace. The moonlight was just enough to illuminate his way through gaps in the trees. The moon looked twice its size and was now almost totally visible. It had never seemed so useful to him until this very moment. Barely moving at five miles per hour, his windows down, the sound of his tires crunching and grinding on pieces of gravel and broken asphalt seemed louder than he could stand. Then he saw it! The gate to the site was closed, as it should be. He could see no one around. He checked the gate. The lock was positioned to look like it was locked, but was merely pushed together. Someone with a key had just entered, he thought. But then he couldn't be sure. He knew he hadn't given out a key.

He thought he'd told the man who delivered the blocks for the trailer to lock up after he left. But had he? Nevertheless, he felt there was someone out there, somewhere on that huge piece of land. He pulled onto the site, jumped out and closed the gate back exactly as it was. With his lights still off, he eased the Blazer over the land. His eyes darted back and forth furiously, scanning from left to right, and ahead and behind him. He drove for what must have been a mile, then, in the distance, a pair of headlights beamed towards another object that looked another fifty feet away. He rolled slowly toward the lights then stopped approximately 100 yards behind them. Straining to see, he made out an airplane in the other vehicle's lights. An airplane with double wings, one a few feet above the other. He waited. His heart pounded and he tightened his grip on the .357. His palms were sweaty, his mouth dry. He swallowed and waited. A figure emerged from around the front of the plane near the propeller. The other vehicle switched off its lights. A light appeared from the plane searching the ground in front of it. It was strong and appeared to be hand held. Roman saw the figure step onto the wing and climb into the cockpit. This was another of the double-wing Steerman planes like he saw with John during his tour of Parchman prison. Then he noticed the back cockpit was already manned by another figure. Obviously, this was the figure that held the light from the plane. He could not determine any features; he only saw the silhouettes of their heads.

The plane's engine reverberated over the huge field as the pilot revved it to life, preparing for take off. He slowly turned the plane to the left, as if to head straight towards Roman. He jerked his vehicle into reverse and shot backwards, turning in the opposite direction, well out of sight from the hand-held light. The unusual looking plane roared and taxied down the level field, its engine deafening. Roman had positioned himself a hundred feet off to the side. He began looking frantically, as it neared, for any kind of letters or numbers for identification. As the plane was exactly even with him, he could clearly see its profile. There was no mistaking the large, white cotton boll painted on its dark side. As the fuselage flashed by, he caught the letters CB and another long word. That was it! "CB Crop Dusters". It was the plane he saw at Parchman with John that day, or another exactly like it. What was the man's name? Patterson. No Peterson. The man who had the penitentiary's vast cotton acreage spraying contract. Yes. Yes. It was definitely his plane. Being a pilot, Roman froze and watched the one light go out as the old plane climbed higher without it, thanks to the moonlight. Then, as he saw the plane bank and turn due west toward Greenville, the regular lights came on. In a matter of seconds, the red light above the tail slowly faded from sight.

Roman kept his lights off for the time being and drove up to the vehicle parked in the distance. He cut his lights on for a second and focused his eyes on the green pick up that Wiggins and the other man were in. The truck sat near the very edge of the site, barely over what he felt was the property line. He copied down the Wildflower County tag number. Then, turning on his headlights, he slowly drove away. A giant, camouflaged tarpaulin lay out of sight on the other side of the big oak trees that grew on the property line.

Roman arrived home after midnight. The night's events replayed in his mind, as he lay awake.

The Steerman landed at an abandoned airstrip near the Mississippi River, just outside Greenville. It was truly secluded, a narrow strip nestled very close to the mighty river's bank. A mixture of oaks and sweet gum trees, along with thick, uncut underbrush bordered the other side, away from the river. There was no hangar, only a dilapidated old shed, overrun with tall weeds. However, the strip itself had been cleared and graded just enough to land without problems. Wiggins and his pilot deplaned and walked outside the plane, scouting the skies. The pilot lit a cigarette and paced back-and-forth. Soon, they heard an engine approaching, and similar to their Steerman flight, the incoming plane had no lights.

Suddenly, the sky at the far end of the strip lit up and the other plane descended quickly, touched down and taxied to rest within twenty feet of the Steerman. It was a Rallye, a single engine plane also, that could take off and land in a very short distance. Shorter than most other aircraft. Oddly, it was painted black and had no letters or identifying markings on it whatsoever.

The pilot emerged from the cockpit, stepped onto the wing, and jumped to the ground, flamboyantly. "Don't just stand there, men! Get this cargo unloaded and transferred to the Steerman. You know who is waiting. Wiggins, you wait here. I'll make this leg with Peterson."

"Yes Sir. How was your trip up?"

"No time for idle chatter, but talk while you load. No problem. Just like last time. Flew her no more than ten feet over the river. Nothing but water beneath me for over 200 miles, all the way up from New Orleans. Extra precaution. I don't really have to do that since I have a radar interceptor in it now, but I take no chances. Too much at stake."

The loading was complete, and the Steerman was revving up for take-off.

"Remember to wait here and keep your eyes open. You know what to do if...."

"I know, Sheriff."

CHAPTER 22

The USA Today paper arrived at the office at 6:45 a.m. and Roman was there to greet the delivery man. He highlighted the paper, sipped his coffee, and waited. He was dying to call Harold Lloyd, and if he hadn't heard from him by mid-morning, he would do just that. Last night's airplane discovery was too much to let lie. True, he could see nothing illegal except maybe trespassing, but he knew there was much more to it than that. Surely this would be of interest to Lloyd.

His eyes caught the article on hazardous waste and all the complex issues surrounding the industry. This article eluded to the fact that Mississippi had been offered a guarantee from the world's largest handler of waste produced from certain manufacturing processes, and that the state's industries would have access to a national network of 32 treatment and disposal facilities for the next twenty years. This got his attention. They might be the world's largest, but Worldwide was the world's safest, best equipped, and possessor of the latest edge in technology. He had never taken a back seat to anyone in representing his company. This article, among other matters, prompted him to pick up the phone and call Gardner Lowe. What if the largest company in the world pulled it off, and the state accepted this guarantee of access to this national network? Where would this leave them in the future, after all the time and money invested here? This would be disastrous for Worldwide. This, plus the fact that the U.S. Environmental Protection Agency's hazardous waste planning process would focus on how many facilities were available nationally, instead of by state, could possibly affect Mississippi's decision. Despite some cooperation from local legislators and leaders, Roman didn't have an overabundance of support to avert something of this magnitude.

What was next, he wondered? But the article was still minor compared to what was really on his mind, and getting more complex daily. Still, he had an obligation to his company and had to protect their interests. He would call Lowe when the time moved to 9:30 a.m., or 7:30 West Coast time, knowing he was usually in by then.

He waded through all the work around him, and returned as many calls as possible. As soon as 9:30 arrived, he dialed Lowe's direct line in L.A. He picked up after two rings. "Gardner Lowe." His answer was quick and businesslike. Exactly like the man himself. Always direct, decisive and confident.

"Gardner, I hope you've got a minute." Roman fumbled with the felt tipped pen, sliding the top off and on as he spoke.

"For you, I'm never too busy. You know that. Besides, You've been a little remiss in calling, I believe." The elephant memory came into play again. He never forgot anything. Especially, if it he was right. He took immense pride in knowing everything he could about all his employees habits, good or bad.

Roman didn't appreciate the subtle dig about the phone calls. " I talk to you more than anyone I know, Gardner." He tempered his irritation some, not wanting to get caught up in Lowe's little mind games. He moved the phone to his other ear and waited for a response. He was determined not to be too defensive. After all, this was his boss.

Lowe laughed aloud and leaned back in his plush, black-leather chair that was backed up to a window, with a view of downtown Beverly Hills. He had found it necessary several years ago, as President, to move his company's executive offices from the industrial area of Los Angeles, several miles away, to a more prestigious area. No one had ever second-guessed him since the bottom line had always shown a heavy profit. Millions and millions. In fact, just the day before, a national trade magazine featured him on the front of the month's issue, and carried a long flattering article. He worked and lived lavishly.

"Sounds like you may need a few days off, Roman. I detect a little testiness. You've been working too hard. Take what you need. Get rested and ready to go."

"There's no problem, Gardner. Sinus trouble affected my sleep last night, that's all. Nothing major."

"Good. What can I do for you?"

"I called is to keep you abreast of what the other companies are trying to do to get into Mississippi. I know you mentioned we'd have another one in later, somewhere within the state, after we are up and running here. I didn't imagine that, did I?"

"No. It's a possibility, but we have that one pretty well sewn up and we have the contacts to bring in all the business we can handle."

Roman proceeded to relay the USA Today's contents and the EPA update. He explained the local Environmental Protection Council, another factor, and its public meeting recently. He recited all the potential roadblocks for Worldwide's growth. Lowe remained silent. He slid his swivel chair forward, leaned on his elbows on the highly shined mahogany desk, and smiled confidently. Almost a sneer. One that Roman would just as well not see at this point.

"Three words," Gardner finally said. "Three words and they are, 'Not to worry'. Trust me. All is well that ends well, and this project will be completed. We have contracts in hand and contacts in the plan." A low laugh emerged again. Roman kept quiet. "Not only will this be completed, but it will extremely profitable for years and years to come. Trust me."

"Well, I'm glad you have a handle on everything." Roman almost slipped back into a sarcastic mode, but managed to lift his voice at the end of the statement.

Another silence. Roman wondered how this man could be so pompous and self assured about this project, with the sudden surge of competition circling around like sharks smelling fresh blood. Roman hadn't been too concerned about the competition, until he read the article. Maybe Gardner is out of touch with what is going on, or does he know something he's not divulging? Thoughts raced through his head like runaway comets in the night.

"I don't mean to interrupt," Lowe said, "but it's probably time you come back out to the coast for a day or so. You know, some briefing and to do some yourself. Pick your time and come on. If you can get the discount fare, fine. If not, come when you can arrange your schedule. Let me know, of course, so I can make myself available. If you will, bring me that report on the landowners whose properties border the site. Hope you've had a chance to do that." Lowe was making an attempt to sound congenial.

"I've gotten as much as possible. It should suffice. The clerk at the county office wasn't that accommodating. In fact, down right evasive." He wadded up three pages of scratch paper he had doodled on and hurled the round mass across the room and off the wall into the wastebasket. It was his favorite telephone pastime.

"You even sound a little preoccupied, Roman." Roman rolled his eyes back and stared at the ceiling. How could Lowe be that perceptive? He knew he didn't miss a beat. Nothing got past that intuitive mind. It was like he had a mirror into his soul, or at least thought he did. Roman fidgeted with the phone cord, re-crossed his legs, and positioned them on his desk top. He visualized Lowe as he listened. He might be perceptive and cunning, but he was also pompous and self-indulgent. He was so wrapped up in himself, that he was guilty of making mistakes that he would not acknowledge. It was always a game of wits with him, but Roman felt he too, could play this one upmanship when necessary. Roman knew no one more tenacious and determined than himself. He would not be outsmarted, outmaneuvered, or let a couple of decades of experience intimidate him. He never had and never would. He also knew if he didn't stand his ground with Lowe, the man would not respect him.

After a few seconds of total silence, Roman eased his feet off the desk, stood up, and stared out the side window at the light, slow moving traffic outside Indian Bayou. "L.A. sounds fine, Gardner, but it may be another week or more. Maybe sooner, if possible. I'll let you know the schedule. Talk to you later." He was nonchalant, just enough.

After the call, Roman thought of the new caller identification device he had installed with the telephone. He had gotten more than his share of hang ups at home at night, as if someone wanted to speak but had second thoughts, and he needed to find this Mrs. Hendrix. He knew she did not work for the Sheriff, but why she called him about Stiles's trip was mystifying. She could be so valuable in solving this if she would just come forward.

He checked the device that he had forgotten to check when he first came in. He had been told these were fairly new with the local bell service, especially in tracking the origin of harassing or lewd calls or a hang up. It could not always be depended on to pick up on long distance calls. Sometimes it would or wouldn't. So far, he was batting zero on seeing unfamiliar numbers. If anyone had been hanging up, it had to be long distance, he felt. His average went up with this one. This one had to have come in late last night after he left, or very early this morning. It was from Greater Los Angeles, area code 310. He did not recognize the other seven-digit phone number. He studied the number for several seconds and tried to think of who it could be. He dialed the number and a middle-aged female voice responded, "Executive offices." He stayed on the line, but didn't speak. "Executive offices," she repeated. He had heard the voice before, he thought. His mind poured over the possibilities, as he replaced the receiver without speaking. It would come to him before the day was over. He went over and over the voice in his head. He knew he had heard it before. Maybe whoever it was had dialed a wrong number, that was just coincidentally from LA. Were there that many people calling from L.A. to a wrong number in Indian Bayou? Not hardly. He copied down the number and slipped it into his desk drawer.

Roman had still not heard from Harold Lloyd by noon. He had decided to give him until then, before initiating contact himself. The usual phone trip to the truck stop was changed to the car phone. He thought now that they could not get to it, or any cellular phone. He regretted not using a cellular phone before now, as it would have made his life easier than running to pay phones to call. Lloyd's assistant answered but would give no trace of his whereabouts. Roman left his name and a message that it was fairly urgent. He still received no encouragement except that the information would be passed on, possibly within the hour. Roman hung up, hoping like hell that he was right about no one could bug his car phone.

After an hour, the code call came in concerning a shipment for the site. It was Lloyd's voice. Roman jumped into his Blazer and started driving. He thought again about the phone. The next move was to get another phone or some other type he could carry on his person. That would be one of tomorrow's many things to complete. He dialed Lloyd. "I'm sorry I was out, but I called as soon as possible," Lloyd offered apologetically, "The assistant said it sounded important."

"It is." Roman filled him in on every detail about the Steerman, its crew of two, the pickup, and its tag number. He told him about the lack of lights, and how they turned them on as they lifted away from the field, heading due west toward Greenville. He described the CB Crop Dusters logo and sign on the craft. Roman was excited, thinking some headway was being made.

But Lloyd cut him short. "Roman, don't get me wrong when I say this...."

Roman interrupted: "If this is another speech about how they're innocent until proven guilty, or whatever, save it for someone else."

"I'm not saying that. It does sound strange to me, but again, I can't go arrest someone now."

"I don't expect that, and you know it. Not now, anyway, until the investigation has turned up enough evidence. I just want you to have all the pieces I can give you to the puzzle. I hope you're getting some too. You are, aren't you?"

"You can bet we are working hard on it. You know it really could be some crop duster pilot showing the plane to the deputy. Was he on or off duty?"

Roman answered slowly. "Off duty."

"Did you see any cargo, or weapons, or anything you can identify?"

"Hell no. It was almost midnight. He sure picked a hell of a time to demonstrate a plane though. Don't you agree?"

"I agree, and I'm taking it all in. Do you know who was in the pickup with the deputy?"

"I'm almost sure it was that Peterson guy who owns CB Crop Dusting. This is the key to why I called. He owns the crop dusting service and has had the cotton poison spraying contract with Parchman penitentiary for years. My friend John told me that the day we went all over the place. He said Peterson comes and goes without anyone paying attention, since he's been all over there with his planes for years." Harold Lloyd was silent. "You still with me, Harold?"

"Yes, I was listening to every word. I'll get on this, and I also should have you a report tomorrow, at the latest, on Clifton Arceneaux."

"God, I hope he is making it all right up there. Don't forget about him for one second, please." Roman was now on Highway 49, headed south near a large catfish processing plant. Droves of black workers and some whites, with nets on their heads, were making their way back from the lunch break. He turned around in the driveway next to the plant and headed back toward his office.

"I'll call you tomorrow, before the end of the day." Lloyd promised.

"Which reminds me, I'm glad to stop running to truck stops.

"I'm sorry about that inconvenience, but that seems very minor now, doesn't it?" Lloyd laughed and Roman managed a broad smile as he spotted his office coming into view. He hung up, feeling a little better about Lloyd. Still, if the FBI didn't produce again, he would go on to plan B. He would not let up, no matter what the cost.

The end of the day found Roman busily interviewing ladies of all ages and descriptions to fill the secretarial position. He had gone through seven so far and had a couple of promising prospects. Most all of them were congenial and eager to work, but one in particular fit the bill he wanted. She was older than the rest, though still attractive, and could type 100 words a minute. She seemed quick to grasp the duties he explained. In addition to being a mother of four and highly qualified, she needed the job. So he hired Martha to come in tomorrow morning, first thing.

After what seemed like a rare few minutes with his guitar, Roman fell asleep on the couch. At 12:30 a.m. he stumbled to his bed. He needed sleep badly. He slipped off his jeans, flipped his T shirt to the floor, stripped to his shorts, and slid in between the cool clean sheets. After no more than thirty minutes of sound sleep, the jarring sound of the telephone for the third time, shook him awake. He sat straight up in the bed, rubbed his eyes, and grabbed the receiver from the night stand. There was a silence for two or three seconds, then: "Mr. Beckley?" It was the voice of the older lady that first called him about Stiles.

He shot back . "Can I call you right back, *please*?" His stomach dropped when he heard the sound of the receiver rattling, as she hung up.

"Damn! How could she? All I wanted to do was call her back so we could talk — confidentially." He mumbled.

He made some coffee and returned to the bedroom. He knew there was no way he could sleep any time soon. Then it hit him! The new phone device may have gotten the number. He scrambled round the bed to his "Caller ID" box, looked at the little window where the digital number would be and Bingo! He couldn't believe it. He rubbed his eyes, leaned down, squinting to be sure. The call came from the Los Angeles area. Now why would Mrs. Hendrix be in the LA area? The box showed the area code as 213. There was a problem, however. The seven digit number that followed the area code did not register. He knew this was for local calls primarily, but hoped he would get lucky with the number. The only problem now he feared, was that she would not call back again after his plea to call her back.

The upside was that he knew two calls came for him. One possibly a coincidence, from area code 310 around Greater Los Angeles, and the other definitely called his name and came from 213, another L.A. area code. Two calls from L.A. in one day at the office and home. Too much coincidence.

He shook his head and turned out the light. He would pursue it in the morning to find out who this Mrs. Hendrix was, or if her name was Hendrix at all.

Burning the midnight oil was a familiar sight at the sheriff's office. Only the florescent desk light illuminated Deputy Wiggins, who sat across the desk, anxiously awaiting the next word by his boss. His eyes were fixed on Stiles, casually polishing an AK47 assault rifle on his desk, the latest addition to his collection that would outdo most arsenals. Stiles stared at the rifle almost hypnotically, as he gripped the trigger and tightened his grip. With one swift jerk, he pointed the deadly weapon at Wiggins and pulled the trigger, simulating an automatic rifle sound himself. Wiggins jumped, blinking wildly, then managed an uncomfortable smile.

"You know who I would like to use this on?" Stiles inched the rifle down.

"I can guess and bet I get it. Beckley, right?"

"You're a mind reader," Stiles replied sarcastically. "But you know I can't do that, since his friend met an untimely death very recently. There aren't any clues either. Like we said, must have been a random drive-by shooting, or who knows who his enemies were. Could have been a former Parchman inmate. Lots of possibilities when you're the law and can make all the deductions, yourself." Wiggins roared. His red face glowed in the light of the small lamp. He stopped abruptly when he noticed the somber look on Stiles face.

"No I can't use it so soon after the mysterious death of Sessions, but Roman Beckley could be the victim of an unfortunate accident. The time is near." Wiggins sat still, waiting on Stiles's change of expression, to clue him as to how he should react. And when a sinister grin moved across Stiles's face, Wiggins eagerly joined in from ear to ear.

CHAPTER *23*

E ven the magnificent beauty of the Swiss Alps couldn't keep Diana's mind from wandering back to Roman. She had tried night and day, but with very little success. She adored her Mother, but she was beginning to wear on her nerves more than she imagined. She was making every effort to be a devoted daughter, traveling companion and confidante. She was even filling in for Ella's bridge club friends when they could find another pair to play. She knew her impatience was because of her preoccupation with Roman. She would try harder to concentrate on the moment and her Mom.

Every couple she saw made her feel out of place without him. Then, Norris Sr.'s words of caution about Roman rang in her mind. She wondered why he became this way after she had been around Roman for a while. Why the about-face? He seemed to like him instantly, she thought.

Then she pictured that incriminating photograph of Roman with the blonde woman. She would try to convince herself that her dad was right. If it were all true, it was a dead-end relationship. Nevertheless, she felt an emptiness that only Roman could fill. She wanted to believe there was an explanation for the picture, because she thought he loved her as much as she did him. But what could it be? She was having too much time to think in Europe. She tried painting, but it was futile. She had lost her inspiration, especially the last few days.

She was sure he had to feel the same way. He couldn't just abruptly turn to another woman, when they were so obviously falling completely in love with one another. After all, theirs was not an empty marriage, kept together by superficial reasons, a marriage weary from years of going through the motions and becoming insensitive to one another's needs. Their relationship was fresh, beautiful, and intense. There had to be a way she could see him again and receive a logical explanation. Then, feel the tenderness and sincerity she had become accustomed to with him, and with few words, he would make everything like it was before. She shook herself back to reality, brushing it from her mind for the moment, as Mom tried on the fifth dress at Geneva's most ritzy boutique.

That night at the hotel she checked their itinerary. Germany was next on the hastily planned trip. Her Mom had three more weeks to go before her leg of the trip was over. Diana thought about the art school. Her heart was not in it. Time was her ally and had helped soothe her feelings from the break up. She thought about three more weeks like this, and it might as well be three years. She was forcing herself to enjoy Europe. But the quaint surroundings and picturesque landscapes only awakened a longing to share the beauty with him.

Her Mom wasn't getting any younger and she needed this. She had been taken for granted for so long. Even the drinking had stopped during the trip. The old gleam of excitement was in her mother's eyes for the first time in years. Diana could not let her own feelings interfere with her Mom's newly awakened happiness. She suggested a good restaurant and complimented Ella's latest choice of dresses. Ella nodded excitedly, they made their way to the lobby, then took a bus to the restaurant near the base of the mountain.

A waiter approached their uncrowded dining area and asked if they preferred wine with the meal. Diana pretended not to notice Ella's glance, seeking approval. They each ordered one glass of a white wine, suggested by the waiter. Ella seized the moment.

"You know, you said you would elaborate on what was wrong back home. I don't mean to pry, darling. But, do you want to talk about it? I've noticed that Europe, in all its splendor, has not made it go away." Her eyes were soft and compassionate as she squeezed Diana's hand. Diana looked away, then smiled instinctively.

Diana's smile lasted a split second only. She rolled the wine around in the glass and stared into it. She slowly looked upward, her eyes meeting Ella's. They both smiled. She was relaxed and ready to divulge what had been bothering her. She could see that her Mother's instinct was right on target as usual. Ella knew, but had not pushed it. Diana knew that she had never been able to tell even a tiny fib as a child, without her seeing through it. Somehow, now, she was glad, and needed to confide in her, for the first time in years.

"Mom, I have tried to hide the pain to spare you that. I wanted to make your trip more enjoyable...."

"And, you have. You have been delightful. I simply know when you are hurting. You are now. Go on, Honey."

"Roman and I had such a wonderful relationship. I thought we loved each other intensely. He made me feel like no other man has ever made me feel. That included my marriage. Then, you remember Dad sort of urged me to beware of him. Like something was wrong with him. That part I'm not sure of. It was like he was afraid I would get hurt by him, or I was in danger by being around him." She thought of the New Orleans trip to spy on Stiles and what they saw. She would keep her promise not to tell anyone. That still stood. Her dad's possible entanglement with Stiles raced through her mind. She stared down again at the glass without speaking.

"Diana, are you all right?" Ella leaned forward and patted her on the back.

She shook her head slowly. "Fine, Mom. I'm sorry. Thinking. I do too much of that."

"Go on. I'm listening." The waiter arrived and offered more spirits. Diana declined and Ella followed suit by placing her hand over her glass as well. They ordered and the waiter raced off to the kitchen.

"Do you remember seeing that large envelope addressed to me. Someone had brought it inside and... well, I don't remember who, maybe Junior. I guess the shock of it is all I remember. Anyway, that's not important. There was an 8 x 10 picture of some woman wrapped in Roman's arms, late at night, at the front of his house. He was only wearing jeans. No shirt or shoes. It doesn't take a genius to figure that one out." She lowered her eyes again and stared aimlessly at the table.

"Did you say the picture was in that big envelope marked to you?"

"Yes. Why?"

"That's funny. If I remember right, Norris, Jr. brought that in from way out front. Said it was propped up on the mailbox, I believe. I thought that was strange, but forgot about it. Wait a minute." Ella's eyes widened as she leaned forward and stared at Diana. "I remember, he made the comment that he was out by the horses at 3:30 or so in the morning. You know how he gets up all hours of the night — how restless he is."

"Yes. I feel for him so much — about everything that happened to him in Vietnam. I know he has trouble sleeping."

"Well, he said he out there sitting by the fence. His favorite place. That he was almost positive he saw Zach Stiles drive up in his sheriff's car, get out and put the envelope on the mailbox supports."

"What? Zach Stiles left that?"

"Norris, Jr. said he didn't think much about it. Thought it was something for your Dad, since they've been keeping some strange hours lately together. He doesn't think I hear, I guess, or pay attention. You know, the man has called our house at midnight for Norris. To be honest, I'm getting a little tired of it."

"Mom, are you sure about this?"

"Norris, Jr. said after he saw your name on it, he thought maybe Zach was making a play for your affection. He didn't want to pry and ask questions."

A smile came across Diana's face and her eyes danced with excitement.

"Mom, do you realize this might shed a completely different light on things. You don't know Zach Stiles like I do. He's capable of lots of things. He may have even arranged this, or something. I don't know, but now I can ask Roman. I would call him, but this has to be done in person when we return. Thank you for telling me." She leaned across the table and kissed Ella on the cheek.

"I didn't do anything."

"Yes, you did."

"I don't mind either."

"Don't mind what, Mom?"

"If we cut the trip a little short. A few more days and we're homeward bound. That is, if you're not going to the art school in Paris."

Diana rolled her eyes back in amazement. "You are unbelievable. You are a mind reader."

"No honey, just a Mother." They embraced and their smiles said it all.

CHAPTER 24

The birds outside his window awakened Roman at the crack of dawn. After hurrying his usual routine to get ready for the day, at 6:30 he realized it was only 4:30 on the West Coast. He decided to take his time and make the call as soon as the eight o'clock hour arrived in Los Angeles.

He spent time familiarizing his new secretary with the office and her duties over the next few months. She seemed to grasp it well and he knew the choice was a good one. She was given boundaries to work within and what not to discuss outside the office. He didn't dwell on it, but asked for her consideration. She said she was happy to oblige. He excused himself to run down to the convenience store for a paper. This was a charade for her benefit, or he would have simply sat parked in the car to place the call. He would definitely be happier if the telephone calls could be made openly.

It was straight up ten o'clock when he made the call to the 310 area code. The same soft voice responded. "Executive offices."

He had rehearsed his quick inquiry. "When will the boss return?" He tried to give the old familiar routine.

"Within the hour. He hasn't arrived yet. May I ask who's calling?" He strained to hear each word. The voice was close, very close to the Mrs. Hendrix voice, he thought.

"Oh, Mr. Beckley."

"Roman Beckley? Is that you?" She warmed up to his reply.

He was stunned. He leaned forward on the seat and swallowed. "Yes. Who is this?"

"Marilyn Chandler."

"Marilyn Chandler. Are you not at Worldwide anymore?"

She laughed. "Sure. You reached my direct number. It's different now since I moved down the hall from Mr. Lowe. I'm handling the coordination with our insurers now." Her voice trailed off like she was unhappy. "We've gotten so many new numbers and changes around here, you probably didn't recognize the numbers. New phone system too." She never missed a beat.

He was silent for a second. Now it dawned on him that the 310 area code included Beverly Hills. He knew that! The disappointment was hard to hide in his voice.

"Well, excuse me, Marilyn. Someone gave me the wrong number. It was good to talk to you anyway. Talk to you later." He slammed the phone down hard in disgust. It echoed in the car.

He drove immediately back to the office, grabbed a cup of black coffee, and paced back and forth in his office. Why didn't she say, I called you yesterday or the night before at the office? There should have been a mention. The number was right. He had been careful to get the 310 area code and all seven digits. Could someone else have called him from Marilyn Chandler's office? Still, Marilyn's voice sounded like "Mrs. Hendrix". Was she afraid to mention it from the office? He could wait no longer to find the caller.

He purposely dialed from the office, reaching the frequent flyer 800 number, and booked an 8:20 a.m. flight direct out of Jackson, via Dallas to L.A., arriving at 10:15 a.m. their time. He reserved a bulkhead seat to stretch his long legs in.

"Martha, hold the fort down. I'll be back shortly. Take any numbers." He jumped into his Blazer and drove down the highway. Using the car phone, he changed his reservations to a flight from Memphis instead. Indian Bayou was almost half way between Jackson and Memphis. The new flight left from Memphis at 11:20 a.m. and arrived in LA at 1:25 p.m. He hoped this time they listened to the call from the office, and it would throw them off. He never knew who might follow him from Indian Bayou. He had a stop to make in Memphis anyway at the FBI office. This would allow some freedom from the prying eyes and maybe have some fun doing it. He hoped they would drive to Jackson and fly out on the wrong plane, with him miles away headed from a different route and time. The thought brought a huge grin. In fact, to authenticate the reservation, he would call back later from the office, reconfirm the flight out of Jackson, its departure and arrival. If they needed convincing, he'd enjoy it for a change.

The day that seemed to be one giant haze, so Roman decided to call it quits around seven and went directly home. Again, for some reason, the house he was leasing seemed like a protective solace from the maddening circle he was caught up in. This same house where his close friend was murdered only a few feet from, where he was slept every night. He could not drive down the driveway without looking at the cottage and thinking of John and promising him silently, that he would get his killer. Either he would help the law, the right law, or if they couldn't bring someone to justice, then he would take other action. Time would tell.

He tried to do some house cleaning, but stopped after the dishes. He was not in the mood for the chores of keeping a spic and span house. Not now. Instead, he played his guitar and sang for a hour or so. He thought of Diana and how she enjoyed his playing and singing, or, at least, pretended to. It worked, whatever she did. He put the guitar down and turned on the late movie, only to doze off half way through it. The .357 rested under the pillow next to the one he slept on.

The early morning dew glistened, as the sunlight danced off the grass alongside his driveway. Two squirrels chased each other up a tree by his Blazer as he approached it. He felt rested. The beauty of the early morning motivated him to lower his windows and breathe some of the fresh, early fall air, as he rolled out his driveway just after daybreak. The cool, crisp breeze was invigorating, and, as always, he began searching for some musical company on the radio.

As he approached the intersection where he would either turn North to Memphis or South to Jackson, he slowed, then stopped. He checked his rear view mirror and glanced around in all directions. It looked clear. He headed south toward Jackson. After driving about three miles, he did a sudden u-turn and headed back north. No one seemed to be following him. He slipped through the big intersection again. And again, he seemed to be in the clear. He let the hammer down to get some highway between him and Indian Bayou. He was not in the mood for company. The hope that they would drive to Jackson, again brought a smile. Whether they did or not, he had laid the groundwork.

It was barely daylight and a fitting grey haze hung low over the miles of grounds as he approached Parchman Penitentiary, enroute to Memphis. On his left, he saw the thousands of acres encircled by the low lying fog. Somehow, it looked fitting.

Somewhere inside those grounds was Clifton. He had a sudden urge to stop and ask to see him. Maybe no one would even notice or care. He knew he couldn't stop. That was insane. Besides, it could cause Cliff problems, or worse, get him killed.

The motor responded as he stepped down on the accelerator. He wanted to get away from the place, under the circumstances. Memphis was not much more than an hour and a half away. He had time and didn't need to get to the FBI office in the federal building until at least 8:30. He would give Lloyd time to open his mail and have coffee.

He wanted to relax his mind and stay loose, to arrive L.A. fresh and ready to get some answers from whoever is "Mrs. Hendrix." He purposely daydreamed to divert his thoughts to trivial observations such as the vehicles everyone drove in this part of the country. He noticed the ratio of larger automobiles to small ones down here compared to L.A. People here tended to drive the larger automobiles and larger trucks, even the used ones. In California, there were many more medium and small cars to maneuver the crowded freeways. Not down here. There had to be even more pickups than cars. The standard pickups were equipped with the ever-present gun rack in the rear window, the long waving aerial, four wheel drives in many, and most were loaded with tape players and other luxuries. To be one of the poorest states, you could not tell it in the Delta. Not to say there weren't enough older, dilapidated, smoking old dinosaurs that had seen their best miles years ago.

His father had helped him learn this kind of mind manipulation to stay relaxed, years ago in junior high school, before football games. He used it often in college and even the pros. He found that by removing his conscious mind as much as possible a few hours before the task ahead and up until a couple of hours before game time, his intensity was quickly magnified when he got into the heat of battle. He knew how to peak.

He recalled his Dad's first lesson concerning handling the stress of an upcoming game. It was his first start as a junior high quarterback. He couldn't sleep beginning Tuesday before the Thursday night game. His Dad took him to his uncle's farm about ten miles outside Tupelo. It was unplanned, and his dad was ad-libbing as they strolled over the pasture right before dusk, when they saw a single light on in the old red barn. The same barn he had played in for years in the hay and helped brush his share of horses. Despite its aged exterior, the barn was neatly swept and the hay smelled as fresh as morning dew. They quietly entered the barn to find his Uncle Pete with his back to them. He turned and acknowledged them with a grin, then turned back around immediately. It was then that they could see that he was staring down on a beautiful bronze mare giving birth to a colt. The moving experience had begun.

After a few more seconds that hung like minutes, they could see more of the bleary-eyed, matted colt, wiggling and struggling to emerge into this new world. At that instant, Roman didn't know there was a football game in the world, much less that he was starting his first game in two days. When that shaky-legged little guy wobbled and pulled, and finally balanced himself to a momentary stand, Roman felt chills down his spine. Even if the little fellow crumbled after a second or two, he had arrived. This left an indelible impression with Roman. He knew everything had to be put into proper perspective. Seeing that colt's birth and triumphant entry into his new surrounding and being nestled with his mother was a lesson in perspective. He knew he had priorities, but somehow they would come, fall in place, and football was not all there was in this world.

There was the sensation under his feet as the elevator surged upward. He punched 10 and watched as three men in conservative black suits hustled off on seven. An intelligent-looking, young blonde with her hair pulled straight back, dressed in a conservative suit and heels, got off with him.

He looked for the sign. His eyes fixed on it immediately. "Federal Bureau of Investigation". The door was straight ahead. The blonde entered before him and turned right inside the door. The receptionist, a thin older lady with a heavy southern accent, stopped him.

"Yes sir. May I help you?" She inquired with a quick smile that was gone in a flash.

"I'm looking for Agent Harold Lloyd. I'm Roman Beckley."

"Is he expecting you, Mr. Beckley?"

"No, as a matter of fact, he is not."

"Let me ring his office."

"Lloyd speaking."

"You have a visitor here. Mr. Roman Beckley."

Roman strolled around the reception area, taking in the photographs on the wall of the President and Director of the Bureau, and a few other decorative paintings. In a matter of seconds, the double door opened and Harold Lloyd came out in full stride. They shook hands and he led Roman to his crowded office down the hall. Roman glanced at the agents lining the way and wondered if any of the three wearing shoulder holsters knew anything about this case. Lloyd offered him a chair and coffee and motioned to a baby-faced young man, who was back in a second with black coffee for them. He wondered if he was an agent. Surely not. He had to be a clerical helper, Roman thought, as the young man left.

"Well, this is unexpected." Lloyd said, looking genuinely surprised, as he leaned back in his chair. Roman viewed the plaques and numerous framed pictures of Lloyd with several dignitaries, even the President himself.

"Oh, excuse me." Roman's attention returned. I was taking in your pictures and awards. That's a nice collection."

"Thank you. Sometimes there is some gratification in those. This can be sort of a thankless job at times." He told the young clerical worker to take his phone calls at his desk, that he wasn't to be disturbed. "Sometimes it rings incessantly. What's brings you to Memphis, unannounced? Not that you have to have an invitation...." Lloyd's laugh was strained.

"I have to go to Los Angeles in a little while on company business." He thought about telling Lloyd about going primarily to find the caller who pretended to be a Mrs. Hendrix, but decided against it for now. He didn't want anyone prying around on this before he got the chance first hand to see if it was Marilyn Chandler or whoever. "I'm sure you know why I came by here first."

"I can guess that one." He toyed with a pencil he retrieved from his desk, then stopped and locked into a stare with Roman. "I hate to be vague with you, but Cliff is making some progress. Not enough time has passed for him to get into the swing of things. You know, to gain a fellow inmate's confidence. I can't tell you who, but I do have someone checking on his progress daily."

"Can't tell me?" Roman set down his coffee. "All right, I can buy that, but is daily enough? I mean, what if he gets in danger? Harold, as I've told you, I really feel responsible for this little guy."

Lloyd spoke very deliberately. "I will answer the first question. Daily, yes. We can't be in constant touch, every minute. It might jeopardize the undercover work for Cliff. Also, if he gets in danger, we won't be far away."

"Who is we? Can't you give me a hint?"

"Let me put it this way. You will know in time, like when this is over. You'll feel better then, after the fact. For now, let's say it is not another undercover inmate. We're doing better than that. I told you were are in control of the situation." There was a sign of irritation in his voice, but he smiled to cover it .

Roman tried to temper his impatience. "I hear what you're saying, but can you can tell me if you're checking further into Sheriff Zach Stiles and the guys he was with in New Orleans?"

"Yes. Again, I would rather not get too involved in details. Let's say you were right that he was in some sinister company. I will fill you in when I am able to." Lloyd was obviously trying to end the conversation.

Roman pushed back his chair and stood, his eyes fixed on Lloyd. "I know you have your reasons, and I'm not a law officer and all, but I hope I am hearing the truth. Let me put it this way. I hope a lot of information is not being withheld from me for fear I'll blow it. You've got to remember, it was my friend he killed and I've been toe-to-toe with Stiles. I am a big boy, Harold. I'm not going to lose it, and go out and run my mouth and do something crazy. I do want to be informed, and not fed what you want to feed me."

"I know you are very responsible or I wouldn't have told you as much as I have. Try to understand that. There are reasons. We are making progress, and I will tell you all I can, as soon as I can. By the way, as we discussed, the main thing I need from you is anything you can lend about Norris Palmer, Sr. Also, we have been checking into this so-called Mrs. Hendrix who doesn't work for the sheriff. Has she called back?" There was a slight urgency in his voice.

"No. Haven't heard anything yet."

Roman stopped in the lobby long enough to use the phone before heading to the airport. He called his home in Sherman Oaks and left Gil, his renter, a message that he was arriving today, but warned him not to divulge the time to anyone. He amended the message to not telling anyone he was arriving, period. He would explain when he arrived.

The dispatcher took the call for Zach Stiles and immediately buzzed his office.

"Deputy Wiggins is on line two, Sheriff."

"Well. I've been wondering where in the hell you've been. You'd bet-

210

ter have some news that I want to hear." Stiles stared at his shiny armadillo boots propped on his desk and puffed a foul-smelling cigar.

The silence lingered. "Afraid not, Sir."

"What do you mean?"

"He never came this way. I've been down here since before day-light. Must have gotten here before five on the county line, like you wanted, but he never came this way."

"Did the other deputy radio you when he left up here?"

"He didn't see him leave either. He waited below town about five miles so he'd have a good chance to spot him. Away from town, you know. I came on down further another ten miles, like you said. I was right by that bad curve and ready. We both tried. We both watched. Him at that end and me down here, but he wasn't in his vehicle. I mean we checked em' out, every vehicle, lookin' for that Blazer."

"You idiots know he had to come that way to go to Jackson for that flight. I give you an easy situation to handle and you botch it. It would have been so simple to make it look like an accident, like we planned. I even gave you a back up plan, but no, you lose him on the only normal way he would have come. You'd better hope he wasn't on that plane out of Jackson. I mean it." Stiles hung up, his eyes trance-like as he stared at his lone tribute to Vietnam on the wall. "He's on to us, for sure." He slammed his fist down on the desk and mumbled. "If you want a job done right, do it yourself. When the time is right, I won't fail."

CHAPTER *25*

A merican Flight 1133 lifted off only ten minutes behind schedule and the skyline of Memphis disappeared. After word from the captain, Roman pushed the release button and laid his seat back. He never boarded an airplane that Leah did not come to mind. This time the air space was his haven, his place that no one could be a threat to him. Knowing he didn't have to watch his back side for a few hours, he settled into seat 10C and fell asleep instantly.

He was awakened from the restful sleep by a gentle nudge of his shoulder and a soft voice. "Sir, please return your seat to the upright position and get ready for landing."

"Sure." Roman rubbed his eyes and brushed back his hair. It was longer than usual; He'd not had enough hours in the day lately for a haircut. He stretched his long legs, glad to have booked the bulkhead seat behind first class to get that extra leg room. The company was free with their money, but frowned on traveling first class. That was reserved for people like Gardner Lowe. Roman only flew first-class the short-lived times he and Leah flew free, one of her airline attendant privileges.

A short, fat, little man in a tight business suit bumped his elbow for the third or fourth time, trying to get the edge on the arm rest. He was squirming in his middle seat and breathing heavily from the effort. Roman leaned down to better see the sprawling configuration of cities connected below. Miles of freeways entangled with one another, and the tiny cars from this viewpoint went on forever.

The landing was smoother than usual. Though he was not jet qualified, he could appreciate the pilot bringing the big jet down with very little
bumping.

He walked past the hordes of nameless faces to the baggage claim area
and grabbed his bag off the revolving ramp. The contrast in the laid-back
attire of southern Californians, with the slightly more fashion-conscious
South, was never more obvious.

He made his way to the rental car booth and was out the door in minutes with the keys to a teal-blue Chevy Cavalier. He meshed into the sunny
afternoon traffic flow on the San Diego Freeway North and headed for his
home in Sherman Oaks. The office was on the way in Beverly Hills, but he
would pass it by for the moment. He wanted to get to the house first, then
go back. He needed to see if the young intern, who was leasing the place,
had taken care of it as promised. Actually, he would have paid the intern to
stay there and house sit, but luckily the young doctor needed a place as
badly as he needed an overseer. There was another reason he wanted to see
the intern as well, if he could spare a little time tonight.

He pulled into his driveway on Allott Street in Sherman Oaks. It still
looked in order from the outside, at least. Gil swung the door open. He
was bare-chested, wearing long shorts, and had a Coors in hand. He was
over six feet, with a flashing smile and shaggy dark blond hair. He was in
his late twenties, but looked even younger.

"Hello. It's good to see you again, Roman." They shook hands firmly.
"Believe it or not, Marie just left. She just finished a good job cleaning the
place. She can't stand to see her fiance' living in a place that's a big mess!
Glad you caught it when the place is clean." He pointed proudly as he
turned back into the house.

"Good to see you too, Gil." Roman smiled, carrying in the bag he had
retrieved from the trunk. As he entered the house, one glance confirmed
that Marie had done a good job indeed.

"I got your message," Gil shouted from the kitchen. "Sounds like you
don't want the ole corporate boys to know you're in town."

"No. It's not that. Let's say I don't want them to know what time I
came in. Got my reasons, you know." Roman threw his bag on the wine
leather chair in the den.

"I sure do. I know you need to unwind first, but I'll give you all the
messages, mail that wasn't forwarded, and so on, in a few minutes. You
might be able to wade through it by the end of the day." Gil laughed and

tossed the empty Coors can from 10 feet away into the yellow trash can resting in the kitchen corner. "Say, want a Coors?"

Roman, passing the kitchen, shook his head and replied, "It's a little early for me. Maybe later. I'll take a shower for now and get with you in a few minutes."

The shower was refreshing, like a cool shot of energy. He slipped on some old Levis, and pulled on a black cotton T shirt with "Vail" written across the front in light green. It was a souvenir from one of his skiing trips four years back with Leah. It was a favorite of his, along with the high-mileage jeans. White deck shoes rounded out his comfortable gear.

He joined Gil by the kidney-shaped pool. The four o'clock sun showcased the dancing, crystal-clear water, as the pressure from the jets inside its walls kept it churning. He was relieved that Gil had kept his promise here also. The pool had been vacuumed and chlorine added. The relaxation lasted only a short time before Roman dropped the small talk.

"Gil, what are you doing later on tonight.? Say about eight or nine?"

"You're in luck, landlord. I've got the next 36 hours free for the first time in forever. That hospital was about to put me over the edge. Ever get that way?"

"If you only knew. I'm kidding." Roman thought how close Gil had hit with his humor. Now the humor was about to stop.

"You're still in good shape, Roman. That Mississippi cooking hasn't disagreed with your waistline. I wish I had that natural body that never gains weight and women love."

Roman stared at the pool and shook his head abruptly, as if waking up. He had barely heard what Gil said.

"Guess I've been lucky, being tall and all, but I have to work out and watch it like everyone else to some degree." He hoped this made Gil feel better since his slightly protruding stomach was hanging three inches, or so, over his belt. He caught him from the corner of his eye, sucking in his belly while glancing at his profile in the reflection from the sliding-glass patio door. "Back to what I was saying. If you can go tonight, I need your help." Roman turned to face Gil who had taken a seat in the chaise lounge next to him. Gil was all ears. "If you're worried about your stomach a little, I know a flight of stairs that go on and on for about ten floors that need to be climbed." Gil laughed. Roman's smile lasted just a split second. "I'm not kidding, but this is not primarily for exercise."

"This sounds like something clandestine." Gil was barely smiling now. He jumped up and took a slug from another beer he had just opened. "If it is, count me in. As long as it's not illegal or something. I'm ready for a little something different. Anything to get that hospital grind off my mind." Roman smiled and thought of Cliff's readiness to do the same. A little different reason, but he too, welcomed a change. He was batting a thousand so far in that category.

"Look Gil. You seem to be a sincere and honest sort of guy. If you weren't, I wouldn't have leased my place to you. This is not some game I'm playing. I'm not a criminal, but let's say that I'll be bending the law a little. There's some information I need to look for in my home office. I can't go up the regular elevator tonight. I need your eyes for a few minutes to keep watch for me. Maybe divert somebody's attention. My boss has a pretty elaborate security system with guards and all. I'll show you what to do. You won't be in danger, but I need you in order to pull this off with no problems." Roman stared convincingly into Gil's eyes.

"Wow," Gil nodded affirmatively.

Roman smiled and slapped him on the back. "We'll leave at eight."

Clifton lay in the top bunk staring at the drab grey ceiling. The sound of steel slamming shut echoed throughout the unit where they were housed. Alonzo lay below reading the only letter he had received in over two weeks, one from his mother. Cliff glanced down at the letter and thought of his wife and children. They thought he was in Alaska working on some government project. They would get the truth soon. He hoped they would be pleased. He wanted to think this would not go on too much longer. So far the progress had been slow. He had to feel his way around to gain some inmates' confidence and not make too many waves too quick, or he could be coming home soon all right, in a pine box.

Cliff hung his head over from the top bunk. "Alonzo, can I ask you a question? Just between us?" Elicio was asleep on the bottom bunk next to them.

Alonzo laid the letter on top of his chest and exhaled deeply. "What's on your mind? It better be important, cause I don't like to be interrupted when I'm readin' my letter."

"It can wait until you're through." Clifton was learning how to work him.

"Go on now, 'Short Stuff'. You broke my concentration. Might as well go on."

"I was wondering if a man could make some money around here." He waited and no response. "You see, Alonzo, my man, I am having problems, besides being in the joint. My wife and kids are in a bind. It's too long to explain, but I need some 'bread' quick, and I don't care what I gotta do to get it. Follow me?"

"You better take my advice and do the time and get on outta here. You don't want to tack a few more years on that time, you idiot. That is, if I read you right, you're willin' to break the law from in here like some other morons do. Am I right?"

"If I can get some money, you're damn right. I don't think I got a chance at becoming a banker or a lawyer in here, or getting a good paying regular job in here. If you can tell me how to do it legally, be my guest. I know you know your way around with a lot of the inmates and you get the word. I value your opinion — so is there any action to be had?"

Elicio raised his head to their surprise and sat up on one elbow. " Tell him who you know, Alonzo."

"Who asked for your opinion? Were we talkin' to you Elicio?"

Cliff's ears perked up. "Come on guys. Tell me. I won't breathe a word about it. I've got to have some money. My old lady is about to quit me for good and take my kids if I don't send some dough for the bills. She's been sick and needs it now. I got nobody else to turn to." Cliff was convincing and practically cried.

"I ain't talkin' to nobody about nothin' goin' down for money," Alonzo said, lowering his voice. Now I'm gonna get some sleep. You do the same, Elicio and quit volunteering information that might get your butt done in." With that, Alonzo and Elicio feigned sleep. Cliff rolled over also, since the lights had been dimmed.

The profanity and horsing around had subsided. Clifton heard one inmate praying aloud a few feet away. No one bothered him. Cliff was trying to sleep and beginning to nod off, when he felt a tap on his shoulder. It was Alonzo, standing from his bottom bunk, with his face was no more than six inches from Cliff's face. He could feel the heat of his breath on his face as he whispered.

"I hate for any man to be desperate. I done spent much of my life that way, and I am about to see the light at the end of the tunnel. I don't want to take no chances..., but if you do...."

The silence was killing Clifton. "I do, big man. I do. What were you going to say?"

"There is an inmate across the way. A 'trusty', matter of fact, that if he thinks you're cool, then you might be able to get in on makin' some money. He's one mean bastard, so don't let the 'trusty' part fool you. He's got some people up here fooled." Alonzo stopped and stared at Clifton . "No. I can't do it. You might run your big mouth and get me in trouble, then I might have to make you wish you hadn't."

Cliff began to feel like what little friendship he had cultivated was slipping away. He gave his most convincing look at Alonzo. "You know I would not put the finger on you. I wouldn't gain by it. I'm a lot of things, but not that. I wouldn't want to cause you any trouble if I got caught. Besides, it would be your word against mine, since there are no witnesses that you told me about this guy, or guys, or whatever they're doing. Can you give me a name?"

Alonzo shook his head. "No, not now." he rolled back under the double bunk and fell into the bed. The springs squeaked and the bed shook as his huge frame settled in for the night.

Cliff leaned down in the darkness, "Thanks, my man, for considering me. I appreciate it." He thought he heard Alonzo whisper. He waited until he knew he did. "You talking to me, big man?"

Alonzo's whisper was barely loud enough to hear as he never turned over. Cliff hung further over the side, as close as he could to the bottom bunk, without falling out.

"What's the scariest black animal in the woods?"

"Uh, I'm not sure." Cliff whispered back.

"Panther, man. Panther. That's his name. Not a word, and you know I mean it. I'll fill you in on what I know tomorrow. It's time to sleep."

Cliff's could see the animal as he stared at the dark ceiling and whispered to himself, "Panther. Panther."

CHAPTER *26*

R oman and Gil left Allott Street in Gil's Toyota, rather than the rental car, and headed south through Coldwater Canyon toward Beverly Hills. A little precaution in case the rental was seen parked nearby tonight, and Roman was seen parking it there tomorrow. The office would be long closed by now. Even the most ambitious young executives would no longer be laboring in their offices or roaming the halls at Worldwide.

Roman knew Gardner Lowe and Elton Sanders kept their offices and their files, not to mention their attache' cases, locked up tight. He wondered about Marilyn Chandler's office. Maybe not. He also knew the security guards watched the monitor in the highly-shined marble lobby like hawks. Lowe and Sanders expected him to arrive today, but it wouldn't be unusual if he didn't show his face in the office until tomorrow morning by 8 a.m. He needed this uninterrupted time to be able to move about behind the areas of the cameras. He knew where they were located and how someone could get at the right angle and not be taped. Someone with knowledge of the layout of the 25,000 sq. feet of offices on the three floors.

They rolled onto Wilshire Boulevard. Roman leaned forward, pointing through the windshield. "Only about two more lights. It'll be on the right, near the corner. I'll tell you when."

Gil turned down the radio that had been blaring since they left the house, and slowed the car. "Don't let me get on it too quick. These eyes are not that old, but reading too many anatomy books has taken a toll."

"That's it." Roman pointed. "The big white building with the waterfall in front. Go past it to the end of the block. We'll park on the main drag, if we can." They circled the block twice and spotted a silver Rolls easing away, back onto Wilshire. They slipped the Toyota straight into the slot.

"Bet that Rolls couldn't park like that. No maneuvering," Gil joked. This is the first time I remember seeing this building, but I don't frequent Beverly Hills that much. What's a company in that business doing in a swank part of town anyway?"

Roman slammed his door as Gil closed and locked the car. "Well, the biggest part of the company is at the City of Commerce. You know where that is — in the industrial area. There are a couple of VIPs who chose these quarters and I'll leave it up to your imagination as to what their reasons were. I'm not sure I even do. They've got plenty of money, I know. Anyway, that's the place." Roman nodded straight ahead at the well-lighted exterior of the art deco, six-story building, which denoted prestige and wealthy tenants inside its walls. Two giant palm trees swayed gently in the cool fall breeze, framing the spotlighted front entry.

They walked slowly toward the building. Roman looked around for anyone familiar that might be lingering at 8:20 p.m. Traffic was light at this time of night on this main drag, but the ones that were out were expensive; Mercedes, BMW's, and numerous sports cars. Roman motioned toward the front entrance, then grabbed Gil by the arm and stopped. "I want you to go to the front door and tap on it." He looked Gil up and down quickly. He was sporting starched khakis, a white cotton button down with a soft printed tie and penny loafers. "That's why I had you get out of that beach-bum looking outfit." Roman had stayed in his jeans, T-shirt. The deck shoes were not for comfort, but because the soft soled rubber was quieter when walking.

"Tap on it until the guard comes to the front door," Roman said. "His name is Lonnie. I feel sure he's on duty, as usual at night. He always hangs around the front. Makes him feel more important than the other guard. Detain him long enough for me to use my key to the side glass door. I've used it at times when Lonnie was napping. He gave it to me when I first started at Worldwide. He was a big Rams fan and remembered me from there. The key was his way of making me feel special. Anyone else, he puts through more red tape to get in. I don't want anyone seeing me going in at this hour, especially if I don't show up on the surveillance film later. I prefer this way, to not give any record of me being here. No camera seeing me or Lonnie. He's not exactly Sherlock Holmes, either. Tell him that you're a free-lance writer or something, and that you're doing research for a story you'll be writing for a publication in a month or so. That you want the inside scoop on the job description and so on, in security. Make him feel important. God bless his soul, that won't be hard to do. That'll give me time to get in and up the stairs unnoticed."

Gil nodded and gave a thumbs up. "Let's do it." Gil turned to walk to the front door.

"Hold on. Not so fast. There's another guard that works nights along with Lonnie. Huge, rotund, guy, but not quite as slow or receptive as Lonnie. He takes his night meal at 8:30 for an hour. Lonnie told me something once at a company Christmas party when his tongue was loose. He said the other regular guard, the big one, eats in his pickup and has some waitress join him for some quiet time in the truck. Seems she gets a break from her restaurant duty around the block then. Lonnie said it was like clockwork, an every night thing. I hope it's still going through tonight."

"You're kidding." Gil rolled his eyes and grinned.

"Not kidding. Get your mind back on what I'm telling you. Once you gain his confidence about the story, ask him about Worldwide. Ask about other companies listed on the directory in the lobby. There are several more throughout the other three floors. Be particularly interested in Worldwide. Got me?"

"Yeah."

"Ask him if he could show you around the sixth floor. Convince him somehow. My hunch is that he'll be reluctant at first. Tell him you'll mention him in the article. That ought to work. If worse comes to worse, tell him you heard about the big guy's rendezvous. He'll show you for sure then. Don't do that unless all else fails. Once you're on the sixth floor, look around the office and as you are about to leave, look for a switch about one foot to the right of the main door. It will be behind the door when it's swung open, about six inches off the floor. Somehow, push the button down with your foot. You may have to wait until Lonnie's pulling the door closed to do it, so position yourself. Be sure and look for it on the way in, so you can be ready when you leave to push it down. That will deactivate the alarm system. Otherwise, when I unlock the door without it being off, clang, the alarm goes. Also when the switch is down, the surveillance system will focus on other areas than this for a while. He won't see that on the screen downstairs. My boss had this rigged up so he could go undetected when he was having an affair and didn't want this part of the offices to be filmed. They'll never pay any attention downstairs when he gets back. Trust me. Besides, they'll think it's engaged and working in the lobby." He slapped Gil on the back, gave him a nudge toward the front, and hustled away toward the side entrance. Roman called back to Gil, now twenty feet away. "Got it?"

"Got it!" He waved and continued toward the brightly illuminated door.

Gil's pulse picked up. A bead of perspiration popped out on his upper lip, even though it was cool for L.A., at 50 degrees, in October. He positioned a pen behind his ear and fetched a small black notebook from his back pocket. No wonder Roman asked him to bring them along, he thought. What reporter would interview anyone without a notebook and pen to write down the details?

He tapped on the front entrance with his pen four times in succession. "Hello? Hello! Lonnie?" Gil cupped his hands around his eyes as he searched the shiny, but dimly-lit lobby. He saw a shadow appear around the corner, preceding the person behind it. At six-feet-three, Lonnie was difficult not to see, even though he was pencil thin. His handle-bar mustache curled perfectly at the ends as though it had been starched. His boots thundered on the marble floor as he hurried to the door. He looked to be the ghost of Ichabod Crane appearing out of almost darkness. He stood back with his right hand near his holster, prepared for any eventuality, squinting at Gil, who was well exposed to the light.

"What is it you want?" Lonnie yelled in a high-pitched voice through the thick glass door.

"Hi. I'm Gil Chamblee, associate editor of "Men and Women of Law Enforcement Magazine". He didn't know how that came out, but it sounded good.

"Sir, let's see some identification. We don't take too kindly to people stirring around here after dark." Lonnie's voice bounced off the walls of the lobby.

Gil retrieved his billfold from his back pocket in a flash and flapped it open like lightning, pressing it against the glass, then taking it down as swiftly. A quick flash and maybe Lonnie would not read the fine print. It worked. The hospital card he possessed from the City of Angels Hospital was embossed with an official seal, lots of typing, and a huge official looking signature at the bottom. It was laminated, and shiny and hard to read, but did the job. Gil didn't hesitate after the display and withdrawal of the card. "How about letting a guy in, who might put your picture on the front of our next big monthly issue?" Gil smiled broadly.

Lonnie showed no reaction for a couple of seconds. "You really gonna do an article on somebody around here for your magazine?" Lonnie tried to look in command, but the curiosity was killing him. Gil looked beyond Lonnie and saw Roman move swiftly past the few exposed feet of glass to the side door.

"Won't take much of your time officer." Lonnie brought himself to a more rigid stance after being called that. It pleased him, and it was a rarity he relished. Gil sensed his eagerness to cooperate.

The lobby directory read like a "Who's Who" of the financial world. There were several big time tax attorneys, financial planners, mutual companies and a prestigious real estate firm housed in the building, along with Worldwide. It was a relatively small building compared to others in the nearby Los Angeles area, but loaded with monied tenants. Much of the building was decorative space to impress wealthy clients or aspiring clients living the facade of wealth and struggling to accumulate it. This was, after all, Beverly Hills, not your average town.

Lonnie's black military dress shoes squeaked as he walked to the ringing phone on a desk near the corner. The desk was home to only a phone, log book, pen and flashlight. Lonnie patted his pistol that hung in its holster below his waistline and walked back toward Gil. The phone call had been short, but obviously not sweet.

"You married, Mr. Chamblee?"

"I'm about to be soon."

"Well, I was gonna say that if you're not, then don't get that way. That woman runs me ragged." Lonnie hook his head and smiled. "But, I couldn't live without her."

Gil nodded and grabbed his pen and notebook, displaying them prominently to move Lonnie along.

"Lonnie. It is all right if I call you Lonnie, isn't it?"

"Yeah. How'd you know my name to begin with?"

Gil scrambled, never missing a beat. "My company does a little research before they send me out on a story like this. You must do an excellent job around here. Your reputation precedes you."

Lonnie stood even straighter, his chest expanding ever so slightly. "I try."

Gil stared at the impressive directory. The names were lettered in bright gold with a black background. "Take this Worldwide Industries for instance. Let's take them since I see they're on the sixth floor. Can we go up there? I always like to start at the top in anything I do. Know what I mean?" Gil quipped. Lonnie smiled, showing a gold tooth in front. "Why don't we go up there, just stroll around and you show me what you look for when you secure an office and so on. Of course, if you'd rather not, we can pick another one."

"No. No. Even though Mr. Lowe is the most particular tenant in this building, I have the free run of any zone I decide to go in."

Gil breathed a little easier.

The elevator doors came together almost silently and Lonnie nonchalantly pushed the six button with the night stick he had just undone from his belt. Gil felt the adrenalin pumping as they ascended each floor, watching the numbers flash by. They felt the hesitation, the bumpy uplift, and the doors parted onto the sixth floor. Double white doors displayed the large gold sign, "Worldwide Industries". The inside decor was expensive, yet not too pretentious. A rich paneled hallway led to the front door. Lonnie opened it like he lived there. The reception area was lined with thick black leather chairs, resting on jeweled-tone oriental rugs. Even the plants, strategically placed in the greeting area and the hall, were professionally manicured. They strolled through the hall and Gil noticed the offices on each side were shut tight. At the end of the long hall, the name of the President, Gardner Lowe, was displayed so no one could mistake the pecking order here.

"I would never guess he was the president of this company," Gil chuckled.

"Yeah. Mr. Lowe's got expensive tastes as you can see. There are stories that go around all the time about how he spends money. I hear he has a big yacht down at Marina Del Ray. Understand he's quite a ladies' man. A young ladies' man. He's a stepper — to be married." Lonnie stopped abruptly, sensing he had let his mouth get out of hand for the moment. Gil thought of Roman again and checked his watch.

He pretended to take notes. "Oh, go on. You can tell me what you want, off the record. I won't use it." But Roman might find these tidbits useful, he knew.

"By the way, did you say that story was gonna be out next month?"

"That's the plan. November issue. Probably two or three pages at least." Gil was getting carried away and enjoying it, pouring it on, and interacting with the perfect one. His watch and his better senses told him that Roman would be getting edgy, since it was now 8:33 and he knew much more time would bring the big guy back from his parked love nest. "Say, Lonnie, I know that you've got lots to do, securing other places and all. Let's go back to your station in the lobby so we can both kick back and finish for tonight. I'll get my information written down there. I can't get comfortable in strange offices. Especially plush, expensive ones." Lonnie nodded in agreement.

They turned down the hall to the main entrance. Gil began straining forty feet before they reached the front door to see the switch. What if he couldn't find it? What if ole Lonnie was watching too closely? Then he heard the jangling of Lonnie's keys that hung from his waist. Gil's eyes darted frantically back and forth, up and down for the switch. Lonnie grabbed the edge of the heavy door and began to slowly pull it away from the wall, toward him to close. Just as the door left from against the wall, he saw the oval-shaped, beige switch that almost blended in with the wall. It was no more than two inches long protruding from the baseboard.

"What was that?" Gil pointed in the opposite direction toward the other offices. Lonnie turned instinctively. With one fluid motion, Gil's size twelve shoe flipped the switch down like lightning. There would be no alarm and no filming now for a while.

"I didn't hear anything. Sometimes the air conditioner compressor will make noise. I'd better check it out anyway." Lonnie unsnapped his holster and slid out the revolver.

Gil looked at Lonnie and smiled. "Don't worry about it. I might have been testing your reflexes, for all you know." Lonnie grinned and eased his pistol back into the holster. He slammed and locked the heavy double doors. They were back punching "L" and descending to the security desk downstairs. Roman heard the elevator as he stood in the hollow stairs. The noise faded as they went down.

Roman entered the hall from his stairway position. He was even more anxious to get in because of the time factor. The wait had seemed like two hours instead of less than fifteen minutes. He used his key to unlock the disarmed doors.

He moved past the empty offices until he reached Gardner Lowe's tower. It was locked tight as usual. He shook the door again to no avail. He wasn't sure where Marilyn Chandler worked. He checked the names and departments as he hurried down the hallways, turning at each corner and re-tracking. At last, he spotted her name on a door along with another name. She shared the small office near the back. The door was unlocked. He breathed a sigh of relief. Not as much privacy needed in these positions, he assumed. He turned the handle and moved inside quickly, easing the door to behind him. Her desk was not cluttered. The top right drawer was locked tight. Her Rolodex stared him in the face. He flipped through it, over and over. No trace of his number at home or office. He slid her file cabinet open and thumbed through file after file, labeled with other employee names.

He found his name and other information for insurance purposes. However, his phone number was listed as the Sherman Oaks number and nothing more. No Indian Bayou numbers in his file. Damn! That can't be right. She had to have something here.

He looked in every square inch, but turned up nothing. He could not even find her home phone or address. He glanced at his watch, Time was running out. He hurried from the office, dejected that he had gone to all this trouble and risked his job for nothing. He felt slightly embarrassed for having done this whole thing. He shook his head. No, he did what he had to do, considering the time he had out here. He needed some answers now.

Roman glanced at the other large office, as he made his way to leave. Elton Sanders would have his locked for sure. Wrong. Roman turned the knob and to his surprise the door cracked open. He nudged the door completely open and closed it behind him. The most conservative, detail-man in the company had forgotten to lock his door, or maybe the cleaning crew had done it. If so, they would pay later. He was grateful for the opportunity while he was here.

Then it hit him. Sanders personally poured over every expense account, every phone bill within the company, even though there were accountants within the company who did the same. He had always done that and nixed many being approved without documented proof.

Roman could not open any of the top drawers. The filing cabinets were inaccessible also. He was batting zero. He started back for the door when his eyes caught the wire basket on top of the cabinet to the right of the desk, labeled "Pending". He grabbed the papers and shuffled through them. There was phone bill after phone bill which revealed the separate numbers within Worldwide executive offices. He was in luck! They were coded with the name of each department head on the top right.

After hurrying through six or seven, he saw "Chandler-Insurance". He scanned each number. Nothing on the first page. His eyes rolled down the second page calls. Then his eyes stopped on two numbers with red circles around them on different dates, October 7 and 8. It was the area code and number of his office in Indian Bayou. No other numbers were circled on any other bills. He looked back at other department head's bills. Only one had a check mark by it. No circles. He noticed the circles had been gone over two or three times, as if to emphasize importance. He started to pull his pocket calendar, but could see without it that those calls were the hang ups only a couple of weeks ago. The short time billed for them solidified it. These had to be calls Marilyn had made before the most recent one he had recorded on Caller ID. She had probably called from her home phone, as Mrs. Hendrix, that first late night when he and Diana were together; the call that tipped him off about Zach Stiles and the New Orleans rendezvous with the unscrupulous looking group.

Roman flipped the switch, locked the door, and hit the stairs running. He made it before the big guard returned, slipped behind the camera to the side door, and was back at the car in no time. Gil followed in a matter of seconds as soon as he saw Roman was clear. Roman rubbed his forehead and frowned as they pulled away. Why did Elton Sanders have those calls to his office in Indian Bayou circled over and over? Why were they not just checked like any other questionable one?

CHAPTER *27*

The plush offices on Wilshire were humming at 8:00 a.m.. Roman stepped off the elevator and exchanged greetings with clerks, young executives, and secretaries as he headed for Gardner Lowe's office, where he met Julie Bradford, Lowe's administrative assistant, a title Gardner used instead of secretary. She was a gorgeous, petite blonde in her late twenties. Roman knew very little about her, having seen her only a few times since she replaced Marilyn Chandler. Her shapely, tanned legs were exposed considerably above the knee. The clingy, short dress left no doubt about her anatomy. Red-rimmed glasses framed her face, however, and exhibited a look of intelligence. A small copy of her diploma from UCLA rested on her desk. She looked and acted very ambitious. "Mr. Beckley, it's good to see you back. How long are you here for?"

"Couple of days or so. Call me Roman, if you will."

"I know you suggested that before, but it's better to be safe than sorry with names and titles."

"Is Gardner in?"

"Not yet, but he should be coming through the door very soon."

"I'll go by accounting for a while and come back."

"I'll tell him you're in. I think he was expecting you yesterday." Roman frowned slightly about the yesterday part and headed down the hall.

"Elton. Good Morning." Elton Sanders looked up from the coffee pot and gave his imitation of a smile. He was the only one at this point, beside Roman, with his jacket still on. The rest of the place was buzzing in shirt

227

sleeves only.

"Hello, Roman. Come on in the office." He looked preoccupied, but always did. Roman entered the same office he had been in only hours ago, but it looked different in the daylight. Roman slid back the lone chair across from Sanders's desk. They sat down and exchanged polite smiles. Roman wanted to ask about the phone bill, but knew he couldn't initiate the subject.

"I hope you approve of the salary for the secretary I hired in Mississippi, Elton. It's a little more than the going rate around there, but I wanted someone competent and dependable."

"Oh, yes indeed. It's all right. I gave my approval right off." He still looked unusually preoccupied. His eyes wandered. He shuffled a stack of papers, then set them down, only to pick them up again. Just then, the phone rang, causing Sanders to flinch. He replied "no" twice and was more emphatic on the third no. He hung up and Roman noticed his hand shake slightly. To his recollection, he had never seen Elton this way.

"Are you all right, Elton?" Roman asked, leaning forward in his chair.

"Yes. Yes," Elton smiled nervously. "I didn't sleep well last night. Sinus trouble. Too much caffeine this morning, I guess. No problem." He changed the subject at once. "You let me know anything you need, as far as my approval down there, and you've got it. You're doing an excellent job, as always." He pushed his chair away from the desk to signal the end of the conversation. They shook hands and Roman left his office. He brushed off Elton's behavior to overwork and headed down the hall for administrative payroll to personally submit his latest expense report. After a few casual conversations up and down the halls, he knew Lowe had to be in. It was now well after 9:00.

The beige suit with red silk handkerchief and paisley tie were perfect. Not to mention his hair and the even tan. Gardner Lowe stood and pumped Roman's hand, flashing his ever-ready smile. "Have a good trip?"

"It was fine."

"You must have had a delay," Lowe said, rounding the desk to take a seat in his plush leather chair. "I thought you were coming in yesterday morning." Their eyes met and Lowe's moved away, twitching uncharacteristically. He cleared his throat and moved a file on his desk.

Roman tried to hide his own expression. He had not told him what time the flight was, never mentioned yesterday morning, and Gardner Lowe was not one to confuse the facts very often. He fumbled for the words.

"I originally booked a morning flight out of Jackson, then changed my mind and left on a later one out of Memphis. Didn't arrive until mid afternoon. I had lots to do at the house, so I went straight there. You know how it is. Wanted to be sure it was still standing after being gone." His mind darted back to the question about arriving yesterday morning. Where did he get that? Lowe said nothing.

Hysterical crying rang out from down the hall. The two secretaries were almost uncontrollable. A middle-aged, thin lady who shared the office with Marilyn screamed, "Oh, God. Marilyn's been murdered. Shot to death." The hall filled up with concerned co-workers. Gardner Lowe and Roman quickened their pace until they came face to face with the two.

"Tell me exactly what you heard." Lowe put his arm around the skinny lady and patted her back.

She continued to sob. "All I know is — the lady she car pools with—called to say they just found her. When she came by for her this morning and Marilyn didn't come out, she got concerned. She rang the doorbell again several times, then went to the manager of the town houses where she lived, and he found her body. I believe Marilyn lived in Van Nuys. I can't even remember what her name was, only that she worked in a law firm. I know only the two of them car-pooled. I think she lives in North Hollywood and works in this building. I can't believe it. I just cannot believe it. Who would want to hurt that lovely lady?"

"What did the police say?" Gardner asked. Roman, shocked and saddened, observed Gardner Lowe's ice coolness.

"The lady said they thought it was a robbery. But she said the police were puzzled, because whoever did it had overlooked most of the valuables. Only her purse was taken."

Several onlookers shook their heads and stood in shock, in disbelief that this type tragedy could strike so close to them. Others made their way back slowly to their separate work areas. There was a lull. A strange quiet came over the entire floor. Lowe and Roman silently moved back to his office. Lowe shook his head. Then, as if he had turned off a faucet, he began opening the pile of mail before him. Roman sat motionless.

"Oh, I guess we'd better get back to business." He was stunned at the transformation made by Lowe. "If you remember, I asked that the road leading to the site in Mississippi be paved. How's that coming?"

Roman shook his head, collected his thoughts and spoke just above a whisper, "Well, it's being addressed. They're paving, probably as we speak. They've done some major patching and are grading off and paving other parts. Best they can for now."

"That will probably do for now. I'll know when I get back down there. If you think it is, I trust your judgment. Be sure and tell them, no power lines. I don't want any poles along that road. Be sure they run any power lines under ground."

"I'll check into it to be sure. I don't think they intended to anyway." He concealed his shock over Lowe's behavior.

They went over various aspects of the project for over an hour. Marilyn Chandler's name was never mentioned, and he could stand it no longer. "Gardner, Marilyn worked as your assistant for years. Aren't you going to call about this?" Lowe was looking at a file and never acknowledged the question. "She must have family. Don't you need to check with the police?"

Lowe looked up from his paperwork for the first time since the questions were asked. "Roman, I guess this is my way of dealing with this kind of horrible tragedy."

Roman studied Lowe's face. It seemed to feign the sadness. His voice trembled. "She was a fine lady and a dedicated employee. I will truly miss her. You are right." He punched in the intercom button.

Julie Bradford looked ashen as she opened the door and eased in.

"Julie, call the best florist and get an arrangement sent to whatever funeral home her body is brought. I'm leaving all the details up to you. I can't deal with it right now. Keep me posted on what the police have to say about the case." She barely nodded and appeared numb as she moved toward the door. She glanced back at Roman with a lingering look of concern, or was it fear, and eased the door shut.

Lowe and Sanders went their separate ways, and Roman sensed he was not invited. He was complimented on his progress on the site and asked when he was heading back to Mississippi.

He left Sherman Oaks early enough to go by the LAPD/Van Nuys Division, and find that they were too early into the investigation to divulge anything. He assured them he was only a concerned co-worker. He left his name and headed for the LA International Airport for a 11:45 a.m. flight back to Memphis via Dallas.

He could only stand so many nights without much sleep. Last night was no exception. His head was filled with questions and no answers.

He looked behind him as he boarded. This was a habit now, watching and observing everyone more closely. He couldn't get Lowe off his mind, nor Sanders, and certainly not Marilyn Chandler. He might never know how she had information on Stiles, or why the other calls came from her office and home, but he wouldn't give up the hunt.

The Delta Air Lines Boeing 767 banked out over the Pacific to turn and head back west to Dallas and on to Memphis. When the pilot announced it was clear, he tilted his seat back and closed his eyes to sleep, out of necessity.

CHAPTER 28

Clifton filled his plate with runny eggs, crisp bacon, and decent toast; probably better food than some inmates were used to on the outside. He slid in next to Alonzo and spoke, but the noise level was deafening from chairs sliding, plates clanging, and the droning voices. Clifton leaned over, his shoulder touching Alonzo's rib cage. Elicio sat across from them, steadily scooping up his eggs with his fork and hand, as if another inmate might snag them.

"You given any more thought to gettin' me set up with you-know-who?"

Alonzo looked straight ahead and chomped on the toast and jelly. He did not respond.

"No problem," Cliff mumbled. "But I hope it's soon, because I need the bread, and I don't mean the kind on this table."

Alonzo leaned toward him until his shoulders were touching Cliff's. Still staring straight ahead, he spoke so quietly that Cliff had to strain to hear. "Can't talk here. Too many ears. I'll be at the printing shop at 11:00."

"I'll be there."

Whirring and slamming noises reverberated throughout the large building housing the printing shop. Five black inmates and three whites stacked paper and attended the heavy, methodical machines. Clifton was busy rolling his cart from machine to machine to move the stacks of paper. Another "trusty" followed close behind, lending a hand to get the moving accomplished. Cliff looked at his watch. 11:15. He wrinkled his forehead and looked at both entrances. No one entered. He pulled the cart to the side and felt the urge for a bathroom stop. Coming out of the bathroom, he checked his watch again only minutes later. Still no Alonzo. He started out the door when he heard a voice from one of the three stalls. It was Alonzo. Cliff looked under the other two to make sure they had no company, then sat down on the one next to Alonzo.

"All right, Cliff. I talked to a guy who is tight with Panther. He said for you to come by the shipping department tonight after we eat. That's the shipping place I showed you the other day, way out back, close to the open fields. I don't know how you gonna get out of the unit, but that's up to you to think of somethin'. Panther has his connections and can go and come when he damn well pleases, I think."

"I'll be there. Leave that up to me."

"You be careful with him, little man. Remember you the one wantin' to make money and you the one gotta take the risk."

Cliff barely touched the evening meal before hustling over to the Chaplin's office. Father Nelson Allman was at his desk, on the phone, and signalled for him to be seated. He was a young, stocky, clean-cut priest, with short black hair and a gentle smile. He didn't appear to be over thirty. He hung up the phone and gripped Cliff's hand firmly. They shook like old friends.

Cliff sat on the edge of his chair, his eyes widened as he asked, "Father, can you talk right now?"

The young priest got up and closed the door. His small office was in a building adjacent to the chapel. It was an older, brick building, used for several denominational services that were rotated to accomodate different faiths. "I can now for sure." He leaned toward Cliff and spoke in a soft, barely audible voice.

"Well, I make contact tonight," Cliff confided to him.

"Tonight. What time?"

"Right after I leave here."

"Good, Cliff. Very good. I'll call Harold Lloyd to let him know. I'll be there behind you, out of sight."

"No. No! Don't do that. This guy is obviously sharp as a tack and probably has someone else watching out for him. You could blow it before I get started good."

"I don't know. I need to be around."

233

"Trust me. I can handle it." Cliff wiped the perspiration from his top lip with his hand. "I know you FBI guys are good, but I'm capable of takin' care of myself. If I need you later, I'll make contact. I told y'all I would keep you posted."

"Better still. I won't tell Harold Lloyd until after you see whoever it is. What's the name?"

"Panther."

"Panther? That fits with what was written on John Sessions's note pad. Now it's up to you to find out what the rest of it's all about."

"I'm on my way to start findin' out. I'm glad to get a little break. It's been tough gettin' any information right off the bat. These guys don't trust anybody. Especially a new inmate." Cliff shook Nelson Allman's hand as he stood to leave. "By the way. I appreciate the way you've visited me only once. I'm not the best Catholic, and if you overdid it, then somebody might wonder. But, I appreciate it anyway. Thank you, 'Father'. They both smiled.

As Cliff left the Chaplain's office, darkness surrounded the prison grounds. Only one other priest was in the far end of the old building, and he really was a man of the cloth.

The large warehouse at the far back of the prison was dimly lit. Two pickup trucks were parked near the dock, and the shed was filled with machinery and implements of various kinds. Cliff picked up his pace as he strained to see the building, some 100 yards in the distance. No stars shined to help his overworked eyes size up the large, dark structure. He was winded, stopping long enough to spit out one of the Delta bugs he had inhaled. Perspiration rolled off his forehead, his mouth dried, and the shirt stuck to his back, despite the mild, fall weather. He stopped again to get his breath, then approached the large metal door to the wooden structure, knocked twice, and waited. No response. He knocked three more times. As the door slowly opened, his eyes focused on a wiry, jet-black man sitting in the only chair near the entrance. The whites of his eyes glowed in the dark room. His cheekbones looked sculpted and his jaw protruded, displaying a set of teeth that matched the white eyeballs. His grin looked permanently fixed. The eyes seemed to sear a hole in Cliff. The slight smell of baled cotton and cotton poison were foreign to Cliff. He had never even been to a cotton plantation.

Cliff waited for a word from Panther. The stare continued. Cliff nervously attempted to maintain his composure. "I'm Clifton Arceneaux. I'm over in...."

"I know who you are." The voice was high and shrill as it rang out suddenly, echoing around the cavernous building. "You got a Cajun accent. What you doin' in a Mississippi prison?"

"I did the crime down in Harrison County on the Gulf Coast. I got relatives down around Biloxi."

"I just wanted to see if you told me what I wanted to hear. I already had ways of checkin' that out." Cliff wondered if he were telling the truth or bluffing. "I don't tolerate lyin' or squealin' to the warden or head of security. Those two are dedicated to their job and will ruin my butt. If I let you in to make a little money, you better not speak a word to anybody. I mean anybody, or you won't live to get out of here. You may not live through the night of the day you let it slip. I been able to move around anywhere I want as a 'trusty', but I can use another man to do some loadin'."

"Loading?"

"That's what I said. There you go, wonderin' about what you gonna be loadin'."

"No. I didn't mean anything by it. Just a comment."

Panther pushed the switch on a beam and sprayed a huge area with dim lights. Cliff's eyes widened. "You see all those bales of cotton. You'll be doin' lots of loadin' them. And don't ask onto what or where it's bound for. Get it?"

"I do." Cliff tried to be casual, as his eyes wandered over the big white bales stacked up to the sixty foot ceiling. Rows and rows of them were exposed by dim lights hanging from the beams every few feet.

"That's all for tonight."

Cliff was stunned. He wanted to ask more questions, but knew better. He was in the door. "You must have checked me out then, huh? I'm ready. I need the money and will do whatever it takes."

"I'll be in touch, Cajun." Cliff nodded and offered his hand to shake.

Panther only nodded. "No friendship in this deal. You do right or die. I don't make friends with someone in this. Never know when they might disappear."

Cliff walked toward the door, threw his hand up halfway to his chest and left. He was in, but for how long? He sensed an evil exuded by this man.

Meanwhile, Panther made his way to the figure who remained hidden behind the bales. "Well, had you seen him before?"

"Yes, unfortunately." The shadowy figure answered.

Cliff was allowed back into his unit by the hand-picked guard. He had his orders in advance from Nelson Allman to let Cliff go discreetly, in and out, at will. The next three hours, Cliff did what he could to occupy his mind. He paced and tried to read a murder mystery. It didn't seem appropriate under the circumstances. He had avoided contact with Alonzo, who was occupied at the other end of the unit, talking with two other inmates. Finally, time came to try to sleep. He dozed off about 11:00.

But just a half hour later, he jumped straight up in the bed, feeling someone's hot breath next to his ear. "Panther wants to see you. Now! Back at the same place." The messenger disappeared as quickly as he came. Cliff jumped up and rubbed his eyes, but couldn't identify the inmate who disappeared within the dark rows of bunk beds.

He jumped into his clothes, slipped on his shoes, and tiptoed toward the front. The sound of snores and few mumblings echoed in the night. No one seemed to notice him leave, or care either.

He stumbled over an old wooden box outside the unit and cursed. He wished for an automobile. It was a haul back out to the old warehouse. He started to run, then realized he wasn't in that kind of shape. He slowed to a jog, then a fast walk. It was almost midnight before he saw the outline of the building on the horizon. He wiped the perspiration from his face with his sleeve, brushed back his hair, and tried to compose himself.

The building was almost completely without lights — darker than it had been at the beginning of the night. He knocked three times and waited. This time he heard the door creak and slowly open. A spider web latched on to the side of his face as he moved in at a snail's pace. He wiped it away and kept walking. Somehow, he expected Panther to be seated in his same place, but he wasn't. Just then, someone tapped his shoulder. He jumped, but managed to keep his composure.

"Glad you could make it." It was Panther emerging from behind the first row of cotton bales. "Or, should I say, we're glad you could make it." He pointed to four bales that were now stacked in the middle of the building, away from the other bales. A dim light hanging down near the bales had apparently been pulled down from the beams. Cliff quickly searched the bales for company and saw none. "I'll explain later, since you're a new recruit," Panther said, authoritatively. Cliff exhaled, trying to relax. His eyes moved over the cavernous warehouse, finding no one. A whisper would resonate in the silence.

"Who are the other people you mentioned?" Cliff asked, trying to sound upbeat.

"You'll find out in time. I know you're wonderin' what goes on here. Not the legitimate part, but what you want to get involved in, the money part. Yeah, there's lots of money connected to this building. You'd never think that by just lookin', would you?"

Cliff shook his head. "No. You never would."

Panther circled around him, sizing him up. The silence lasted for a least a minute, while Cliff wiped the perspiration from his forehead and face.

"What I am about to tell you will blow your mind, Cajun. What we have here is a money-making operation — a well-coordinated operation that's beginning to hit its stride. We're gonna make so much money that I may not want to leave prison at all, except the Governor's office has promised me early release. At least someone with connections tells me that, and he better not be lyin'."

Cliff couldn't resist. "Exactly what have you got here?"

"Don't get impatient. Are all Cajuns like that?" He frowned and glared at Cliff. "I don't give a damn if they are. You can wait until I'm good and ready to tell you."

"I didn't mean anything by it. Sounds very interesting. That's all."

Panther, emulating his animal namesake, surveyed his prey, the whites of his eyes glowing. Cliff glanced toward the bales stacked in the middle of the building. Panther stopped near a beam, and Cliff moved closer to the four bales in the middle.

"What I'm gonna tell you will further blow your mind," Panther exclaimed, taking his time speaking. "Look at all those bales of cotton. There are tons and tons of that white cotton." A corrupt grin came across his face. His eyes were glazed, maniacal looking. "Well, we've got lots of white cocaine we put in them."

"Cocaine?"

"Yeah, Man. Cocaine! The purest you can get from Bogota, Columbia." Clifton's heart beat faster. His palms were soaking wet. His eyes pictured cocaine-filled cotton bales, naturally disguised, white on white, and his imagination ran wild. "You see, Cajun, what we've got here is an unusual distribution network."

"It sounds like it, so far."

"The number one man around here has a connection with the big boys in Bogota. They fly it in to New Orleans. The main man flies out of Greenville to New Orleans. He's got a black Rallye airplane. I believe that's what he calls it. Anyway, it's customized for this hauling. Good for short take-offs and landings. It'll hold more pounds than you would believe. He picks up the white stuff in New Orleans and follows the Mississippi River up to Greenville — always at night — and no lights."

"Back to Greenville?"

"Yeah, like I said, he follows the river up to Greenville and only flies ten feet above the water to keep radar off his butt. Of course, he adjusts when he comes to the two or three bridges along the way. I think he flies under 'em." Panther let go with shrill laugh. "This man is a pilot! I mean good! You got me?"

"Yeah. I do. Go on."

"When he gets to Greenville, he lands at an abandoned air strip he's got real close to the Mississippi River. Keeps the plane under wraps. Camouflaged. You dig?" Cliff nodded, hanging on every word. "The stuff is transferred to another kind of plane that flies all over the Delta, and nobody would suspect. A crop dustin' service plane. A double wing job. I think it's called a Steerman."

"Wow." Cliff tried to contain himself. "Where does the Steerman go, from Greenville?"

"Here. Parchman Penitentiary. Yeah. He flies to here and knows everybody around these parts. Peterson is his name. He has 'CB Crop Dusting'. You've probably seen some of his planes around. Green with a white cotton boll on 'em. Never raises any suspicion when one of his planes lands in the far back part of this prison at night. You can see there's miles of open land back here. Got a natural flat landing strip back here. Hell, there's even an old highway he uses sometime."

"But, what do you do with it then. There's no place to sell it here, except a little, I guess, to inmates."

"That's just nickel and dime and ain't in the plan. It's what happens to it when we meet the crop duster. That's even slicker than how it gets here. Shouldn't say that. It's all part of the master plan."

"Man, tell me the rest. I'm dyin' to know."

Panther walked away from the cotton bales to stand face to face with Cliff. He spread his arms apart and gestured. "The cocaine is put in the cotton bales and shipped out to some places in...well, that's not important right now."

"What a plan!"

"Ain't no plan. It works. Has worked several times in the last few months. Let's just say, we've been testin' the water, compared to what may be coming up, I hear."

"Who does it go to, and where does it go?"

Panther hesitated, looking toward the isolated four bales in the middle of the huge structure. Suddenly, the lights went completely off throughout the building, except for one light encased in a wide tin shade, dimly glowing over the isolated bales. A tall, hooded figure stood atop the bales. The long black robe covered him from head to toe.

Cliff's heart jumped into his throat. It must be an initiation he told himself. No need to panic. He started to back away, but he felt a sharp object thrust into his lower back. He tried to ignore the pain and keep his faculties. He was punched again and moved forward until he was no more than four feet from the foreboding figure. He saw Panther and another hooded man move behind the tall figure.

"Hey, guys, if this is a club to join, I'll do it. I don't need the pain, though." He forced a laugh.

The tall figure slid the robe aside and pulled at his belt slowly, brandishing a razor-sharp blade that shined in the dim light. He raised the blade to his own hooded face and with an almost rhythmical movement, nicked the bottom of his hood and flung it off, exposing his identity. Cliff's heart sank. He felt weak and faint. It was the unmistakable face of Zach Stiles. Fear gripped his very soul. He sensed there was no way out. Stiles stared, crazed, as if he were anticipating the conquest. He pointed to his own face in slow motion.

"There must be a mistake! Don't do anything foolish," Cliff begged, his voice trailing off. He knew there was little hope as two revolvers were pointed to each side of his head.

"I wanted you to see who was sacrificing you tonight", Stiles boomed. "I think you know what for. We only told you about the operation, because I was merciful enough, not let you go to your grave, without hearing all about what you were searching for."

"Please don't. I have a family," Cliff cried, making the sign of the cross across his chest. Then, with one vicious swing, the deadly blade sliced his throat and he crumbled. Blood gushed freely from his neck down his chest. Stiles mumbled something about Satan and Panther and Wiggins's eyes widened slightly. Even these two appeared shocked, keeping their distance from his bloody body.

"Take his body to the front of his unit. Quietly! That's why I used the blade instead of a firearm. For quiet. Take him and deposit him outside the wire fence. He'll be dead in a matter of minutes. Be gone and let anyone beware of the consequences of plotting the demise of our brotherhood." Panther and Wiggins raised their fists toward the sky, smiling.

Nelson Allman couldn't sleep. It was almost 1:00 a.m. It had not helped that he had not heard from Cliff as expected. His crash course in the priesthood and the Catholic religion had so far served to hide his identity. Allman threw his clothes back on, donned his collar, and was out the door in a matter of minutes. He walked the several hundred feet from his quarters toward the building Cliff was supposed to be locked in for the night. He crossed the street and passed the first of the lockups. It was dark, except for the silhouette of the armed guard he could see through the window. He rounded the corner to the unit. The sound of a dog barking startled him. A son of one of the guards had come to exchange vehicles after getting off a midnight shift at a nearby factory. His beagle had leaped from the back of the pickup and was jumping and barking wildly near a clump of bushes. The young man remained in the pickup with the radio playing and called the dog again and again. He was obviously not concerned enough to get out and look, or maybe he was a little afraid. Allman stopped suddenly near the outside guarded entrance. The dog did not let up. Allman eased toward the bush and saw the feet. He called for the dog's owner to get him back, then leaned over the body as the young man pulled the jumping, yelping, beagle back. The light from the outside of the building showed the bloody upper body of Clifton Arceneaux. He felt frantically for a pulse on Cliff's bloody neck and yelled for help. More lights flashed on, and two armed guards were on the scene in seconds flat.

"Get him into your truck," Allman yelled. We don't have any time to waste. Get him over to the infirmary, now!" The three loaded Cliff into the back of the truck and Allman placed his coat over him. The blood still oozed slightly. Allman ripped off his T shirt, pressing it to Cliff's neck, trying to help. He thought he felt a pulse as they rounded the corner to the infirmary, which was less than three hundred yards away.

They burst into the small emergency entrance and summoned the two nurses and one doctor that were standing by. They immediately took charge and got Cliff's vital signs. There was a pulse. His blood pressure was dangerously low and he was in shock, but there was a chance They rushed to get his blood type; B positive. An IV was started in one arm and blood transfusion in the other. Working furiously, his wound was attended to, and the bleeding stopped.

Allman waited close by and paced. He had become attached to Cliff, acting as his "priest". Harold Lloyd had to be notified. Allman called Lloyd's home in Memphis and woke him from a sound sleep.

"Mr. Lloyd, this is Agent Allman calling from a pay phone in the infirmary."

Lloyd sat upright and looked at the clock. It was 1:40 a.m. He put on his glasses in case he needed to write. His wife rolled over, pulling a pillow over her head. "Yes, Allman. Don't tell me something's happened to Arceneaux."

"Exactly. We found him lying outside his unit with his throat cut from ear to ear. I'm not sure we got to him in time. The doctor and nurses are giving intravenous fluids and blood. They're hoping. His blood pressure dropped out of sight. I just don't know if he'll make it."

"O.K., here's what you do. As soon as you can get an opinion from the doctor, do it. If he can stand it at all, we need to move him."

"Move him? But Sir...."

"I said if he can stand to be moved, I want him taken to the Greenville hospital. What I'm going to do is have a hearse come in and appear to pick him up. The hearse will be a decoy. About fifteen minutes after it leaves, then transport him with the medical team out the back route, in the emergency vehicle to Greenville. They'll know that particular route, I'm sure. I'm sure you know what I'm trying to accomplish here. I'll take care of the details to get him transferred to the Greenville Hospital. We have to have it appear that he died. You get that doctor and take charge. Tell him to keep this under wraps, at all costs. Let me know if there are any problems. Of course if Arceneaux doesn't make it, a hearse will come anyway and really take the body." Silence. "I want to hear from you tonight, the minute you find out the prognosis, whatever it is."

Allman hung up and hurried back to the emergency room area. He paced and waited. Finally, after another half hour, the young doctor emerged. Allman summoned him. "Doctor, I need to talk with you." He led the doctor to a small area, next to the soft drink machine, where they could sit alone. Allman dragged his chair around to face the doctor. "What can you tell me about his condition? Do you think he'll make it ?"

"Father, he is not out of the woods, by any means. I feel like the next two hours will tell the tale. He's lost a hell of a lot of blood. That was a huge cut. Luckily, they didn't get the carotid artery. I don't know how, but they didn't. Do you know what happened?"

"First of all, I'm not 'Father' Allman. I'm Agent Allman, FBI." The doctor smiled for a second. "No, this is no joke, Doctor." Allman wielded his badge for verification. "This is a very confidential undercover matter. We must insist on your utmost cooperation in what we have to do." They leaned toward each other and talked for another ten minutes about the situation. The doctor shook his head in agreement, slapped Allman's on his back, and went back to monitor Cliff.

At 3:55 a.m., Allman phoned Lloyd, who was on his third cup of coffee and anxious. At the dark hour of 5:05 a.m., a black hearse rolled to the front gate and was cleared immediately to proceed to the infirmary. Father Allman and the doctor rolled the gurney, bearing a body bag, out of the emergency room to the awaiting hearse. The hearse crept away, stopped at the main gate for clearance, then rolled south down Highway 49. Fifteen minutes later, an emergency vehicle left with no flashing lights. It routinely eased out the seldom traveled farm to market road # 32, which ran through several miles of the prison to the small town of Shelby. It then sped south to Greenville and the waiting staff at the well-equipped city hospital. The nurse and doctor from Parchman infirmary attended Cliff on the way and made the transition of the patient the Greenville staff would know as Brubec. Arnold Brubec. Nelson Allman arrived minutes later in a fresh shirt as Charlie Brubec, brother of the patient.

CHAPTER **29**

R oman had finished a long overdue run of four miles by 6:45
a.m. The night before was almost a blur. The plane had arrived
Memphis at 7:25 p.m., over two hours late, putting him back
in Indian Bayou after 9:30. He had slept half the night on the sofa, before
stumbling to bed.

This day would be different. He felt rested and ready for the first time
in several days. He had lost count. "The Today Show" was buzzing in the
background as he got out of the shower. He dressed in no time and was
sipping his first cup of coffee when the ringing phone abruptly ended the
tranquility.

"This is Delta Air Lines baggage department. Can you hold the line
while I get this other call?" He recognized Harold Lloyd and hung up. He
searched for his cellular phone and found it lying on top of his half unpacked suitcase. Lloyd picked up the phone after only one ring. "That was
quick, Roman. You've got a cellular one now, finally, I assume."

"Right. I should have done that when I first hit here. Let me give you
the number right now, so we don't have to play games anymore on the
phone." Harold jotted the number down.

"I'm glad you can talk on these without fear of being listened to.
That's worth the money right there. Never think about those things until it
hits close to home. What's up?"

"I'm afraid I've got some bad news, but some good news also."

"Let's have the bad first," Roman said with a tinge of sarcasm.

"It's Clifton Arceneaux..."

Roman interrupted immediately. "Damn it! I felt like something would happen to him. What is it?" His voice rang out in disgust.

"He's been cut pretty badly."

"Pretty badly? How bad?" Roman slammed down the partially filled cup, splashing coffee on his end table. He paced back and forth, trying to remain calm. "It's his throat. Now let me finish." Even Harold Lloyd's voice was shaky. "It seems he was onto someone that found him out. He told our contact that he was going to meet with this 'Panther'. Remember the name?"

"How could I forget it?"

"Our agent found him about one this morning, lying in his own blood, outside the fence of the unit he is housed in. He was taken to the infirmary and miraculously lived through it, and so far it looks like he will make it."

"Damn it, Harold, I had hoped my gut feeling was wrong when he went in. You promised me you would not let anything happen to him."

"I'm not making any excuses. We never thought it could happen. Especially this quick. My man was in close touch with him. In fact, he was checking on him since he hadn't heard from him in the designated time, when he found him.

"Where is he now?" Roman asked anxiously.

"Greenville. He's in good hands there. They think he'll pull through at this point. He was sent there just a couple of hours ago."

"You know if someone finds out he's in Greenville, they'll try to finish the job. I'm sure I know the bastard who would try, or have someone try. You know too, What does it take to convince you?"

"Let's not get into that right now. We're on top of everything. I had a decoy hearse go in and leave with a body bag, then he was actually put in an ambulance a half hour later, and brought out the back way through Shelby. No lights or sirens to attract attention, in case anyone was watching. The staff at the hospital thinks he's dead, except for the one nurse and doctor. We've taken care of all the details. No one knows he's in Greenville. I feel sure about that."

"Yeah. You felt sure nothing would happen to him inside there, either."

"I understand how you feel. There was a risk and we all went into this knowing. Cliff knew it also. According to the doctor, he was lucky his carotid artery wasn't severed. We're hoping he can respond to us — maybe even later today. We'll get with him as soon as possible."

"I want to go over there."

"Wait one minute. You sure don't need to show up there if you're being watched. Remember? It's like leading them right to him. I'm telling you no one knows Clifton Arceneaux is alive, other than you and me and the two medical people. You're going to have to be patient for now. I'll fill him in on why you can't come. Maybe he has some information we can use. We won't know until he comes around. Sit tight. I'll call you on your cellular. I know you don't have much faith in us at this point, but maybe that'll change."

"Maybe." Roman mumbled in a low tone and hung up. He sat motionless, reeling from the last two days' news, then took a deep breath to compose himself for the task ahead.

He saw Lucille Barnes coming through the hedges toward him as he began to back out the driveway. He smiled and hoped for a short conversation. He was wrong. This time the news wasn't trivial, either.

"Roman, it's good to see you back. We feel better knowing you're in the house next to us. I always told him we needed to be closer in to town, rather than out here on the edge of it. Could be worse, I guess. I could live in a city and not feel safe at all. That's not the reason I wanted to catch you before you left."

"What is it Mrs. Barnes?"

"Lucille, remember."

"Oh, yeah. What is it, Lucille?" She smiled with the correction and then stared seriously at Roman.

"You may not have noticed, but, since Willis's stroke, he spends most all his time gazing out that window. Not much gets past him. He has a hard time communicating since his speech was affected, so he doesn't even try to tell me much. Just stares. It kills me because he was such a strong outdoors type. You know?"

Roman nodded. "I do." He was getting slightly impatient, but would never offend her by cutting the conversation short. He cut off the engine and listened intently.

"Well, night before last when you were out of town...we always can tell when you're out." Roman smiled, and wondered who did most of the staring out the window. "Anyway, we saw this car pull up in the driveway and stop up toward the street. He didn't come on down to the back where most everybody does. We thought it was strange because it was Sheriff Stiles and he went into John's cottage. Had a key I guess. We just stayed put, and in a few minutes he came out. I guess he was looking for clues again. I don't know. Then, he proceeds to rattle your back door and open it. He walked around in there with a flashlight. Why on earth he didn't turn on the light, I don't know." She wrinkled her forehead and stared at Roman. "He stayed a few minutes and came out. I couldn't stand it, so I raised the window and yelled down at him. He wheeled around like I startled him a little. He said 'I'm only doing some more investigative work on that case. I wanted you folks to sleep better knowing I'm on the case constantly.' "That's exactly what he said."

Roman tried to smile, then re-started his engine. "Thanks so much for keeping an eye on the place when I'm gone. Keep me posted on anything you think I need to know."

"I will. I thought it was strange he was in your house. Doesn't he have to have a warrant?"

"I'll check into it. Thanks again, Lucille. See you tonight. I'll be in town. Tell Willis thanks too."

"That's not all." She hesitated and shook her finger. "Willis managed to scribble two words. He's still sharper than most people know."

"I'm sure he is. What were the words?"

'Same Car'. Then four more words. 'John Killer. Lights Top'. "He was trying to say that was the same car he saw parked near the street, during the storm. The one who killed John was in. And it had lights on top."

Roman gripped the steering wheel in rage and squeezed. He glanced as Lucille walked away through the hedges. He slammed the Blazer door and darted back into his house. He struck his fist down on the kitchen table, knocking the pepper shaker to the floor. He ran from room to room to see if any evidence of Stiles having been there was still there, but found nothing. He turned drawers inside out, slid the sofa back, slid his clothes back and forth on the rack. He wasn't even sure what he was looking for. Nothing was missing, and hopefully nothing planted.

What the hell was he doing making himself at home in his house? The .357 was still in his suitcase he hadn't yet unpacked from the trip back from LA. He grabbed the pistol and thought about confronting Stiles alone, to make him sweat. He thought about getting his bare hands on him. He locked the door and went back to his truck, his pistol in hand. He slid it under the seat, picked up his handy portable phone, and punched hard on area code 901 for Memphis. Then he stopped and changed his mind about calling Lloyd. This was another instance he would keep from him. If Lloyd wasn't convinced about the maniac by now, this information would not get any further action.

He pulled away from the house and made his way to the office. The pounding in his chest began to subside. He would win this battle with Stiles, no matter what it took and no matter if he were at a disadvantage.

"Good morning, Mr. Beckley." The soft southern drawl greeted him as he entered the front door.

He hesitated for a split second, forgetting he had a new secretary. "Good morning to you, Martha. I can't tell you how good it is to hear that from somebody." She stopped typing, glanced at him, then continued on the word processor.

"Oh, Mr. Beckley, coffee's on and I made some bran muffins. No cholesterol."

"Thanks, that was thoughtful. And, just call me Roman." She nodded and blushed and kept typing. He filled his cup and took a muffin. One bite and he picked up another. "These are excellent. They remind me of my mom's."

"You have a stack of phone calls to return. Not too bad. Maybe five or six. One was a personal call she said. Missy. She said you knew the number."

"Thanks. He felt guilty for not calling Missy more often since John's death. He dialed the local radio station, which was owned by her family, and recognized her voice. "Missy? Roman. How are you, Honey?"

"I'm doing fair. Trying to get back busy. Of course about to lose my mind."

"Say, can you have lunch today?"

"Well." She thought for a few seconds. "I think that would be nice. I do need to see you for a few minutes, anyway." It dawned on him, that he needed to keep the conversation to a minimum on this phone. "I'll pick you up at 11:45. Is that a good time?

"That'll be fine. I look forward to seeing you."

"Good, we'll beat the noon crowd."

Since the eating places were limited around Indian Bayou, Missy volunteered to use her membership at the Wildflower Country Club.

"I'm getting to be a regular out here." Roman said as he pulled out her chair.

"Chivalry is not dead." Missy tried to laugh. Roman tried not to stare, but the weight she had lost was evident. Her green cotton skirt and orange blouse hung very loosely on her. The eyes told the story. They were puffy and the make up couldn't hide the dark circles. They kept the conversation as light as possible, but she looked down much of the time they talked, staring blankly at the table. She was making as much effort as she could, but her heart was clearly not in it.

"Have you heard from any of John's family?" Roman asked softly, as the waiter brought the blue plate specials they had ordered.

"His Mom called and we both got so upset. I tried, but we had to cut it short."

"I know. Only time will heal some of the hurt. I know first hand. I don't know if I will ever get over Leah's death. Time is the healer of many wounds, though. Knowing John, I know he wouldn't want you to grieve forever. That's easy to say now, but there will come a time when it will get better."

"Thanks for your words. You were very special to him, you know."

Roman swallowed and cleared his throat. "The feeling was mutual, I can assure you. He was quite a guy." He sat back and sensed a time to shift the converation. "Every time I eat here, I can't get over how good it is. I can use a good, home-cooked meal and that's what this one looks like," he said, lifting a fork of mashed potatoes to his lips, glancing at the string beans and sliced tomatoes beside the sliced roast beef. She picked at a bite or two then set her fork down on her plate, and stared out toward the golf course. "Roman, you know the night of John's death, I recall you mentioned something about Zach Stiles, but we never finished. I was in such a state that I never thought to ask about it further. What was it about him?"

Roman searched for the words, caught slightly off guard. "I, uh, guess it was that John had told me to watch myself around him. That he was extra tough. Fanatical is the word he used. But now that you mention it, I wonder if John ever had any run-in with him."

A concerned look crossed her face as she shook her head. "It's probably nothing. I don't know why it hasn't come to me before now. Guess my mind hasn't been exactly clear though."

"I can imagine. Go on. Tell me what you remember."

"One night I recall now, we were sitting on my parents patio, and Dad brought up the increase in drugs in cities and even small towns. John looked particularly engrossed in that conversation and I remember him commenting about the billions of dollars of cocaine alone, that must be brought into the country. He even said that there was a resurgence of heroin on the scene lately." She leaned forward as she tried to recreate the conversation. "He did say something to the effect that he had mentioned drugs to Zach Stiles one day at either Parchman, or here. It could have been there, since I'm sure Stiles goes there often, being with law enforcement and Parchman being in the county. Anyway, I can't remember exactly what John said, but I remember he was shocked at the reaction of Stiles when he said drugs were becoming rampant, even down here. He said Stiles quizzed him about where he was talking about. One thing I remember was that John said Stiles told him he'd better be careful, that drug dealers might kill him if he said the wrong thing to the wrong person. It was something about the conversation that spooked John. Of course, he didn't like Zach Stiles anyway. Like I said, I don't know why this didn't dawn on me before now."

"I can understand. You've had no reason to be thinking about that." Roman leaned across and patted her on the shoulder. He tried to hide the rumblings inside as he thought of Stiles.

He put down his fork when he heard his portable phone ring. He knew it could only be Lloyd since no one else had the number. He expected the worst. Lloyd was talking in a louder voice than his usual. "Roman, I thought you'd want to hear. Arceneaux is coming around. He's still very weak and all, but is stabilizing nicely, according to his doctor."

Roman excused himself and took the phone with him toward the hallway to the men's room. He was not overly receptive, though he was overjoyed to hear the news.

"That's good news. He'll be all right in time, I hope."

"Yes, they seem to think so."

"Has there been any problem about him being there? I mean, no one knows anything except that he's supposed to be dead. Am I right?"

"You're right. No one ever will, until this is all solved and prosecuted. Maybe not even then, if he so desires." Lloyd hesitated. "I'm going to break a rule and let you see him. If you will come this afternoon to the Greenville Mall, on Highway One South, I'll pick you up there. Leave your car in the parking lot and go to the big department store that anchors the place. It's not a Penney's but starts with MC something. Big blue and white letters. I've gone blank, but just saw it."

"I know exactly which one you're talking about."

"Look for me at 2:00 in the men's' suit department and follow me out the door. I'll pull up to the alley that runs behind the building. I've already checked it out. You can't miss me. Of course, make sure no one follows you."

"I don't think you've got to worry about that, Harold." The sarcasm was evident. "By the way, things are happening so fast about this Stiles, it's like the flood gates have opened. It's not only he's guilty of John's murder or not, but something more. I'll explain today. Then again, you probably won't think it's enough to make a move on him yet."

"Timing is everything, Roman." Lloyd tried to be upbeat. "We'll discuss it when you get here. See you at 2:00."

"Oh, and do me one favor. Refer to him as Cliff, at least, not Arceneaux. You could at least sound like you're on a first name basis with him."

Roman hurried back to the table. Missy was again staring vacantly towards the golf course. "I'm sorry, Missy, I wish I'd never gotten one of these phones."

She smiled. "That's quite all right. I understand you've got lots to do with that project getting started. I hope it's all progressing."

"It is. A few headaches, but it's coming along."

Missy no longer tried to smile. She stared at him. She was adamant. "Roman, if you find anything out about John's death, I want to know, and I want them punished. He's not able to avenge his own life. Someone must make sure it's done. I want to know who did this and why. I guess the anger is beginning to set in, after the initial shock."

"You'll be the first to know. I'll never let this die. Sometimes, the law will, but you have my word, I will not."

After paying, Missy turned to Roman as they walked out, and grabbed his hand. "I can't believe I forgot to ask about you and Diana. I heard you two were apart now, but maybe not for much longer."

"I'm afraid it may be. I'll tell you all about it soon, when there's time." He kept walking.

"That's what I wanted to tell you. I hear she is coming home in a few days. I didn't get the exact dates, but Norris, Sr. told my dad the other day when he ran into him. Seems like they are cutting the trip a little short."

"Are you sure?" He looked surprised, stopping.

"That's what he said." Roman felt like smiling, but how could he? Not a word had been spoken between them since Diana left.

CHAPTER *30*

T he Greenville Mall was filled with shoppers taking advantage of Fall sales and promotions. Roman had checked the rearview mirror no less than twenty five times in the last 10 miles coming in, and no one followed that he could tell. Clerks were buzzing around the racks displaying discounts. A large, red-faced clerk, with a suit in one hand and a shirt in the other, bumped into him near the dressing room. His customer was stripped down in the room waiting for the next offering. Several ladies rummaged through piles of marked-down, name brand shirts, shopping for their men. What a meeting place! Finally, he spotted Lloyd examining the streams of ties cascading from revolving racks on top of the counter. He strolled by. Lloyd nodded and kept looking at the ties. Roman walked slowly past the male fragrances, and sampled a little Ralph Lauren cologne. He ambled out and caught Lloyd from the corner of his eye, heading down the wide corridor for the parking lot. Roman made his way outside, put on his Ray Bans, and walked toward the designated spot. Lloyd pulled up in a nondescript Chevy, and they were off to the hospital.

"Roman, you're going to see him as a family friend, if anyone asks. I'll think of some connection to him if I'm asked. Probably won't be necessary in the first place."

"I may not be any kind of a friend to him after what I've gotten him into."

Lloyd glanced over at Roman, who looked straight ahead. He knew Roman was upset with him, but tried to smile. "You said we would talk about some news you had about Stiles." His eyes moved to the road and back to Roman. "Can you give me a hint?"

"Don't try to be funny, Harold. I don't know what it takes to convince you of the man's guilt. I found, for one thing, he went into my house while I was out." He started to say while he was in L.A., but decided against it.

"How do you know that?"

"The elderly couple in the two-story house next to mine. The man is paralyzed from a bad stroke. She takes care of him and all they have to do, most of the time, is look out the upstairs window. God bless them, that's about all they can do. He can't talk, but wrote on a piece of paper, according to his wife, that the car he saw a couple of nights ago, was the same car that was there when John was killed. He said it was parked up the driveway, near the street. He could only scribble some words like, 'same car' and 'John's killer'." Roman turned to Lloyd, who was veering toward the hospital lot, trying to show some attention to him at the same time.

"That's not all. I just finished lunch with the girl John was about to marry. She told me she recalled John had an uneasy conversation with Stiles about drugs in this part of the state. She said Stiles was almost obsessed about where he got the information. He told John he could get killed by talking too much about this kind of thing. According to her, John said Stiles overreacted about it. I know damn well John hit a nerve with the guy. That may be what ultimately got him killed. Stiles suspected John had knowledge about something he was involved in. It's got to come out, eventually."

"First, Roman, it's not that I don't want to arrest the man if this all comes together, but do you think that a jury will believe an old invalid man, who said the car was similar? A man whose eyesight would probably be suspect, especially looking from a second floor. Wasn't it pouring down that night also?"

"Yes, but...."

"And as far as John's lady telling you this other, I know you feel he is guilty of the murder and other crimes, but we don't want to miss the other baggage that will come along with him. See what I'm saying?"

"Not exactly, but what can I do? Do you need a videotape of him killing someone, along with dozens of witnesses around, to arrest him?" Roman shook his head and slammed the door. He walked just ahead of Lloyd toward the hospital room.

Although the halls contained the usual crowd of nurses racing from room to room, interspersed with an occasional doctor, or an orderly, very few visitors were roaming around. An old lady helped her husband walk the hall. He was bent from age and recent gall bladder surgery. They made their way to the intensive care unit. Roman checked the faces in the waiting room. Two middle-aged ladies and one young man, whose grandfather was hanging on to life, were holding down the fort. The head nurse gave Roman and Lloyd permission to visit, but for no more than fifteen minutes.

Roman smiled broadly as they entered the room. He tried not to stare at Clifton, while Lloyd stayed in the background. A huge white bandage covered his neck from ear to ear. His face was swollen by all the fluids from the IV, flowing into one arm. The other was taking in blood. His nostrils were inserted with plastic oxygen tubes. Despite it all, Cliff managed to smile, and reached out slowly with the hand that was taped to the tube bringing the blood transfusion. Roman bit his lip, glanced away, then managed another smile. He took Cliff's hand in both his and gently squeezed it, avoiding the tubes. He brushed Cliff's thinning hair back from his forehead, as he glanced above him at the heart monitor that Cliff was hooked up to. He saw Cliff's resting heart rate on the digital machine: 125. High, but understandable for a man that had been through that kind of trauma and whose heart was compensating for the loss of blood.

"You're a tough Cajun, Cliff." Roman patted his head again. He felt guilt and pain for Cliff, and his face showed the concern. "Is there anything I can do. Anything at all. Don't try to talk. If you can whisper or feel like trying to write...."

Cliff tried to smile, reaching out for Roman's hand for help to shift weight from one hip to the other. He settled back into the bed and exhaled. "Paper," he whispered, in a strained, barely audible voice.

Roman reached out to Lloyd, who jerked out a black notebook and pen. Roman put it by Cliff's side. Cliff eased the tubes away from his hand enough so that he could write, gingerly. Roman and Lloyd both tried not to stare. Roman studied the machines hooked into Cliff. Lloyd stared out the window below, pretending interest there. It seemed like an hour, instead of few seconds for Cliff to write. Roman pushed the button and raised Cliff's head very slightly, as he seemed to be straining his neck to see the paper. He was too weak to write more and handed it to Roman. As Roman read, his heart pounded almost out of his chest. His face reddened — he could hardly control the rage. It read, COCAINE - BIG TIME -

PARCHMAN -SHERIFF CUT ME.

"Damn that bastard. If you don't arrest him. I may kill him myself. I'm telling you, Harold, he has to pay. Now, do your job and bring him in." He handed the note to Lloyd and gave Cliff a reassuring pat on the shoulder.

Lloyd kept a poker face as he read, but he shifted his weight back and forth and sounded short of breath, when he spoke. "Cliff, what you've done, took a brave man. You will be recognized for your courage. This man will be arrested and will pay for this, and whatever other despicable crimes he may very well have committed. You have my word on that." Roman stared at him as he spoke. "What you have said in this note tells me that this man, and others, are running a cocaine operation. You know how vital it is that we not only arrest this man and get him out of society for what he did to you, but also to break up this operation. Many lives are ruined by drugs, and crimes are committed, and on and on. I don't have to tell you that. I just want to get the others that are connected. Maybe if we can hold off for a while, we can get them all."

"Wait a minute, Harold. You're surely not going to stand by now and let the man roam the streets anymore, especially under the cloak of a law officer." He was face to face with Lloyd. "Hell, he cut this man's throat!"

Cliff grimaced with pain as he swallowed and whispered. "More." Cliff moved his hand again to write. Roman positioned the notebook again. "Miss. map?"

"Yes, I have one in the glove compartment. I'll be right back." The nurse entered and ordered them to leave. It was time for medication and rest.

"One minute and we'll be out of here." Roman promised. Cliff smiled at the nurse, and she agreed to a couple of minutes.

Lloyd returned with the map and spread it out on the bed. He gave Cliff a large felt-tipped pen to make it easier to write. The map showed all of Mississippi with the extreme southern portion of Louisiana to the south and Memphis above the northern part. The pen squeaked as he slid it from the bottom, up to near the northwest corner of the state, then back and forth at that point. He scribbled slowly again on the notebook: Cocaine-Bogota-New Orleans, up river Greenville, up to Parchman, Indian Bayou headquarters.

They looked at the note and the map. Roman commented as he stared, "It looks like a triangle in the Delta, from Greenville to Parchman, back down to Indian Bayou. That's unique in itself."

"Why is that?" Lloyd asked.

"I read some tourist information when I first got here. The symbol for Delta is a 'triangle'. It's the fourth letter of the Greek alphabet."

"Like fraternity and sorority symbols." Lloyd responded toward Cliff.

"I doubt if Cliff gives a damn about fraternities or sororities, especially right now."

Cliff managed a few more words on the notebook and slid them toward Lloyd.

"WAIT. DON'T ARREST. GET ALL THEM."

Roman touched the tips of Cliff's fingers on his right hand, which was taped with needles and tubes, and gave him a thumbs up. "Get some rest. You're going to be fine. Don't worry about anything. They will pay, one way or the other." Roman and Lloyd left the room as the nurse entered again.

Harold stooped by the water fountain and spoke in a low voice to the orderly standing nearby. "You and the other agent rotate and keep an eye on his room 24 hours a day. Understand? Check out everybody." Roman overheard and felt better about the security part, though he didn't acknowledge to Lloyd that he heard the conversation.

They rode back to the Greenville Mall in virtual silence. They turned near the south entrance and Roman reached for the door handle as they slowed to a crawl.

"Roman. You have to trust me about this. Understand, we have to get them all."

"I'll try, Harold, I'll try." He slammed the door, found his car, and sped off back toward Indian Bayou. No one had followed that they could tell.

Martha was still on the word processor when he returned after 4:00 p.m. He was glad to see her ever-present smile and smiled back. She got up from the computer, gave him his messages, then remembered the package. "Oh, by the way, you got a Federal Express package while you were out. I left it on your desk."

"I didn't happen to get a call from a lady, did I?" he asked, thinking it was a long shot that Diana might have called.

She thought for a second. "No, no lady called at all."

The Fed Ex package was on the corner of the desk. He returned phone calls to the construction engineer and then another sub contractor connected with the proposed sight.

Finally, he reached for the package, thinking it probably some directive from the company or some report being sent for his information. He opened the light package and pulled a lone sheet from it. It was typed in capitals. "PLEASE MEET ME AT DALLAS/FORT WORTH AIRPORT TOMORROW, 19TH. I'LL BE AT AMERICAN AIRLINES ADMIRAL'S CLUB AT 3E, OPPOSITE GATE 32 AT 1:00 P.M. SORRY FOR THE LATE NOTICE, BUT IT WAS MY ONLY CHOICE. THIS IS DEFINITELY A MATTER OF LIFE AND DEATH. I MUST SEE YOU. CANNOT SIGN THIS, BUT I KNOW YOU, AND YOU ME . COULD NOT PHONE BECAUSE FEAR OF WIRETAPPING. PLEASE BE THERE. TOMORROW, THE 19TH. IN CHECKING, THERE IS A FLIGHT OUT OF JACKSON YOU CAN TAKE AT 9:45, ARRIVE 11:55 A.M.

He sat stunned for a moment. Still reeling, he stood and walked past Martha, who was busy filing. He walked to his Blazer and opened the glove compartment to find his cellular phone. He dialed American and made a reservation for the 9:45 a.m. flight from Jackson, to arrive 11:50 a.m. at DFW airport. He sat motionless in his truck for a moment. Then, he shook his head and drove toward his home. Martha would have to lock up today.

CHAPTER *31*

The flight to Dallas arrived only ten minutes late, and Roman had almost an hour to kill before heading to the Admiral's Club. He weaved his way through the maze of people hustling to board flights, and the deplaning Dallas passengers, hurrying to get out of the terminal. The few that were killing time awaiting flights were either reading in the waiting areas and wandering around the gift shops and news stands, or deposited in the several lounges, restaurants and stand-up snack bars. DFW was always busy and today was no exception.

He was already in terminal 3E, so no change of building. He headed for Gate 33 and looked for the sign above the door to the Admiral's Club. As he entered, voices of varying kinds and volumes droned together. He took a table near the back and looked the place over. It was crowded with men and women, mostly in business attire, but he saw no one he knew. Then, to his right, where the courtesy telephones and fax machines were, he spotted her. He couldn't believe it! It was Julie Bradford headed in his direction. There was no mistaking that shapely, petite, blonde. She smiled nervously as she approached his table.

They both looked behind her as he pulled out a chair for her. "Julie, I assume you sent the note."

"Yes. I am so glad you showed up." Her voice trembled, and she began to cry. Roman leaned forward and offered his handkerchief. She touched her eyes with it.

"Take your time, Julie."

"I don't know where to start, so I'll jump right in. With everything that is holy in my life, I am about to tell you the absolute truth."

Roman felt a rush of anticipation. "Yes, go on, please. Nothing would shock me much after all the changes I've been through lately. Some big time revelations."

"This will. And hurt too." He motioned the waitress away for the moment. "Roman, do you have any idea what's going on around Worldwide? Primarily with Gardner Lowe, but also with Elton Sanders."

"I'm not sure I know what you're getting at."

"Gardner Lowe is a very complex man."

Roman interrupted, half smiling. "I know that very well, but what are you driving at? Get to the point."

"Gardner Lowe is a womanizing, corrupt, evil person and an alcoholic for starters. After I took over the job as sales administrator, or whatever he refers to me as, Marilyn Chandler was booted down the hall. She'd been tight with him for several years. More than tight. Lovers."

"I had an idea of that."

Tears streamed down her face as she hesitated. "Gardner Lowe had her killed."

"What? What are you saying? That's a strong accusation. You'd better have something to back it up."

"I do." She dried her eyes and sipped the water the waitress had brought. "She came to me a couple of months ago. I forget the exact time frame. She came to me because she was still very much in love with Gardner. She gave me this run down on his life and more details than you can ever imagine about him. Also, lots about their love life and the complications, like his wife, to mention one. She said his wife liked the house in Bel Air and the country club and her lifestyle. Since the children were grown, she had her way of life, and he had his, and she looked the other way, as long as he didn't embarrass her."

"Go on," Roman urged.

"According to Marilyn, he promised to marry her after she got divorced. Well, she did and he didn't. She became despondent after he took her out of his office and ignored her. The hurt was evident. She came to me one night after a company function. I think it was when we landed the contract on the facility in Arizona. I'm not sure. She thought he and I were having an affair and probably did until her death."

"Well, are you?"

"No. I'll admit he's pursued me and promised anything I want. That kind of thing, but the answer is no. She spilled her heart out to me about everything. I didn't believe most of it, because I didn't know him well enough at the time, so I dismissed most of it to her having 'sour grapes'. She proceeded to tell me that he was an alcoholic. That he had kept it hidden from the employees. You know the image he tries to portray. She said that on many occasions they would rendezvous in his office. That he even had a private deal rigged up to throw off the security cameras; so they wouldn't film that part of his little palace." She reached for the water to wet her dry lips.

"I detected a little sarcasm just then. Has he dumped you for someone else?"

"He can't do that, since we've never been together. We're not an item, I assure you. He has tried, like I said. He offered me a straight run up the ladder at Worldwide, but I will not be a part of that. Getting back to what Marilyn said, Gardner is a drunk. A carefully concealed one. If he has a drink or two, he goes over the edge and drinks so much that he doesn't remember a thing he says or does the night before."

"Julie, I'm not being rude, but let's get to the bottom of all this."

"O.K. In a drunken stupor, he told her he had this drug operation, cocaine smuggling, started in Mississippi. This was several weeks ago. He said the money would be laundered through Worldwide. That he had bank accounts in three or four foreign countries. She remembered that he mentioned an account in Switzerland."

Roman slid to the edge of his chair and grabbed her arm. "He what? Tell me again, slowly what you said."

"He told her that he was the key player in a big-time drug operation that would be moving cocaine from somewhere in Columbia to Mississippi through the prison system and shipped out to somewhere. I believe she said North Carolina. I didn't pay too much attention, again, because I thought she was after his hide."

"Go on and don't omit a detail that you know, please, Julie."

"She told me just the other day in the break room when we were alone, that she was going to call you to tip you off."

"About the drugs?"

"Yes. And about some sheriff that was part of the scheme down in Mississippi." Roman felt his insides shake as a wave of nausea came over him. His palms were wet. He was in a daze, hearing her, but trying not to believe it was true, even though he knew it had to be. She was laying it out all too well.

"Did she mention the sheriff's name?"

"Yes."

"What is it?" He made one last attempt to test her for accuracy and anticipating the answer.

"Stiles." He knew now she was telling the truth. He wanted it all out.

"Can I ask you why you're coming to me with this?"

"Yes, Roman. She was bitter, I guess, about him and wanted some revenge. She even told me he forced her to get an abortion a few years ago. She felt like as her beauty waned, so did his interest. She was obviously right. Getting back to him getting so drunk... he spilled it all to her about the drug set up and everything. I wish I had believed her to begin with. She told me she feared for her life. I still didn't believe her, because he had been so smooth about it all."

"I can imagine," Roman replied.

"He told me she was obsessed with getting older and losing her beauty and had always been infatuated with him. Naturally, he said, he had rejected her advances. You know, company man, married, happy. He said he had to move her down the hall to get her away from him. Then, he began to come on to me, and slowly I saw the light. Now, I fear for my life. He did the same thing to me. He got drunk one night when I was working late and really came on. We had a round about it and he stopped, but he was adamant about making me privy to the drug details. It's strange."

"To say the least. Go on."

"It's like some high feeling or excitement for him. I would have never believed it. He can be such a straight businessman most of the time. I guess he thinks I'll be intrigued by his position of power. It's like he wants to share that feeling with someone. I'm sure he can't with his wife. Anyhow, he told me that it came from Bogota to New Orleans and up the Mississippi River in a plane flown a few feet above the water to Greenville. That town is by the river, right?"

"Right." Roman ordered a glass of white wine and a Bud Lite to move the waitress.

"Then, it's unloaded off the one plane and put on a bi-plane plane that is usually used for crop dusting. Cotton, I guess. The plane lands at the back of the prison grounds and unloads cocaine, lots of it. Some black guy, maybe two, unload it and it's carried to a warehouse and put into the cotton bales. Can you believe, cotton bales? From there, he said, it was shipped to various places. He said heavy to the Carolinas."

"Does he not have any recollection that he told you that?"

An unmistakable look of fear came across her face. She swallowed slowly and the tears came. "Yes. He called me into his office the next morning. He made a couple of jokes about it, and said he had always wanted to be a writer in Hollywood. Something about liking practical jokes. He was fishing to see my response. I played dumb, like I had paid no attention. I think I said something about that was 'whiskey talk', trying to act like I brushed it off as comical. He stared at me and said he would hate for something unfortunate to happen to me if I mentioned it to anyone."

"He said that?"

"He said he hated to see two murders around here. I will never forget the look in his eyes. He had a crazed look. Then, he turned and walked back into his office without another word. And, he's made no particular efforts to cover up his phone calls. It's like he's so confident that I won't say anything, or go to the police, that he's not particularly secretive about his phone calls anymore. He has even installed a separate line for nothing but calling about the operation. I had answered once or twice when Stiles has called."

"What'd he say?"

"That — I haven't paid much attention to until now. Now that I know it's really going on. That there really is a drug smuggling operation." She stopped and glanced around the room. The noise level subsided as a wave of travelers left for their flights.

"Is that it, generally? Is there anything more specific you can tell me?"

Silence.

"What is it? Julie, Go on."

Her voice trembled and her hand shook as she lifted the wine glass. "Marilyn said that Gardner was responsible for..."

"Go on. It's all right."

"Your wife's death."

He heard the words, but sat frozen. Perspiration popped out on his forehead. The veins in his neck protruded from the building rage. He could no longer stay seated as a surge of nausea came over him. He rushed to the men's room, pushing chairs aside in his path as he went. He gagged, but couldn't throw up. His mind was like a runaway train. He had to compose himself. He shook his head and splashed two handfuls of water on his face. Then, he slowly walked back to the table and sat, staring numbly at his glass.

Julie grasped his hand, studying his face compassionately. "I'm so sorry. I couldn't keep that from you. Not now that it's all being laid out in the open."

He patted her hand then withdrew his. "No. You did the right thing. I'll be all right in a second. He wiped a tear from his eyes with the same handkerchief, slowly focusing them with piercing intensity. "Go on with what you know."

"Are you sure?"

"Yes."

"Marilyn said that your wife... Leah, that's her right name isn't it?"

"Yes. It was."

"This is some more of what Lowe told her when he was drunk. She said he even told her didn't have to happen the way it did. Leah had come by the office the day she was coming to pick you up at the L.A. International airport. Somehow, Leah overheard Lowe in a conversation about the drug operation in Mississippi. She was in the outer office, and he was shouting about something on a conference call to the sheriff and maybe the guy in Columbia. I'm not sure who, but that's close. She overheard much of the conversation, because she was waiting there to ask Gardner something about your trip to New York and future assignments. She wanted to coordinate her schedule the next few weeks after that with what your itinerary would be."

"Damn."

"Marilyn was out for the moment, but came in at the tail end of the conversation and saw Leah. She said Leah looked stunned and wide eyed, apparently over what she had heard. Then Gardner Lowe came out of his office and about fainted when he saw Leah. He always had Marilyn screen any visitors carefully, and send them away when he was on some calls. Well, she said this particular time, she was only gone to the ladies room for a few minutes and that's when Leah wandered in to see him. He talks so damn loud sometimes that... well, you can see what I'm saying."

"That's not all, is it?"

"No. According to Marilyn, Leah left the office in pretty much of a hurry and Lowe left shortly after her." Julie wiped the tears again.

"What is it?"

"Then he followed her, and, at the right point in Coldwater Canyon,... you know how curving and steep it is in places, he..."

"He what?" Roman asked.

"He ran her off the road, down that steep drop off. You know the rest."

Roman gritted his teeth and fought back the tears. He jammed his fist down on the small table, lifting the wine glass off the table, onto the floor. A nearby waitress asked if everything was all right. Julie covered and sent her away.

"Where is he — right this minute?"

"Now, Roman. I don't know."

"You do. I'll find out. It's over for him!"

"Wait. Wait. You'll have your opportunity right away, I'm sure with him." She grabbed his hand and held it again. "There's more. I have made a point since Marilyn's death to listen carefully to his calls. With his voice, it's not hard to do. I heard him tell Elton Sanders yesterday that they needed to make the move on the 'giant load' right away. That they needed to go to meet the North Carolina connection today. Today, as we speak. I know that's true, because he had me call the pilot and get the Lear ready. He always tells me the destination, except this time. I got the pilot's beeper. He called back, but Lowe was on another long distance call. He asked me to verify that Gatlinburg, Tennessee was to be the destination. I entered his office, and Gardner looked like I had shot him, when I asked about Gatlinburg. Unlike him, he stuttered, then said yes, he had to stop on the way to the East Coast. A relative was having surgery, is how he put it."

Roman remembered how his own tenacity, yet calmness, had always helped him prevail. This was the ultimate test. He would have to keep his faculties intact, and not do anything foolish. They all had to be brought down. He wasn't sure whether to tell Harold Lloyd, since he felt there'd been a lack of action on his part.

"Julie, listen to me. You seem so sharp that I may not even have to say anything. I know you're in fear for your own life, but I hope you'll help some more. If you can't, or don't want to, just say so about what I'm going to ask. Would you go back tomorrow, and act like you're not aware of anything going on at all? By the way, how did you get away with flying down here?"

"My home is in Tyler, not far from here. I told him I had some family business, that I needed to see about some family property, and come right back. Besides, he's on the way to Gatlinburg, remember? He'll never check on it. Back to your first question, I don't think he cares if I hear or not."

"O.K. Back to what I was saying. Listen out for the date of this big shipment he's talking about. Sounds like anytime now. I have to know it, and the location, anything you can give me." He handed her a piece of paper with his cellular number. "Memorize that and call me the second you know. Do whatever you have to, but find out when this is coming down. The more advance notice I can have the better, but let me know even if it's only an hour before. I'll keep this phone with me every second. I can't very well call you to check on this, as we both know. Hell, get the sorry bastard drunk if you have to, if it means getting the information."

"I can probably overhear everything you need to know. I won't leave the office for a second. I promise."

"Julie, I can't thank you enough for what you're doing. I'm shocked beyond belief at this, but justice will be served, one way or the other. Be careful."

"You do the same. I'm sorry I had to be the one to tell you about your wife. Oh, Roman, I can't believe I haven't told you another reason for my asking you to come." She wrinkled her forehead and her voice shook. "They plan to kill you when they can make it look accidental. First, Marilyn told me that she knew they were concerned about what you knew, and you might be killed. I still dismissed it, coming from her at the time. Then, I heard Gardner tell Stiles that he had his approval to kill you. His very words were, 'If you have to do away with Roman Beckley, then do it. Can't take him off the project — too suspicious looking — to him especially. If you think he knows too much, then do it when you can make it look accidental.' That's almost verbatim. That was the day before yesterday, late afternoon. That's when I could wait no longer, and sent you the message."

"I've thought that for a while. I believe everything you've told me, and I can take care of myself. I plan to take care of a few others also. This nightmare is going to end soon. As far as telling me about Leah, you can't imagine how I feel, but I always knew she couldn't have just run off Coldwater Canyon in broad daylight. I will get him, no matter what it takes."

He paid the bill, they embraced and said goodbye. She would depart in 35 minutes for L.A., and he had a flight in an hour for Mississippi.

CHAPTER 32

The Lear's high-pitched whine mixed with the skidding sound of tires on the landing strip at the small Gatlinburg airport. Sanders climbed out and shook the awaiting hand of Nick Bennotti. Lowe exited a few seconds later in his usual dramatic fashion and did likewise. Bennotti was a short, robust man in his early fifties. His hair was dyed jet-black, greased, combed straight back and curled up on the ends. He had not seen a barber in some time. His constant companion, a Camel cigarette, was locked between two fingers. He punctuated every other sentence with a cough. His expensive designer suit smelled as if it had been left all night at a singles bar. He sported a huge gaudy diamond on his right hand and a heavy gold bracelet on his left wrist. In stark contrast to Gardner Lowe, it appeared that no matter what he wore, or who dressed him, the results would still be lacking.

His appearance, however, had not prevented him from accumulating millions. He had inherited handsomely from his father's textile riches and multiplied it many times over, but textile mills were only part of his bulging portfolio. His greed was second to none in the Carolinas. With a flick of his finger, the Camel flew fifteen feet away from the plane.

"Everything fine in Asheville?" Gardner asked.

"You bet. Welcome again to Gatlinburg. Seems like you must like it here to come back so soon. I'm sort of partial to it too. It's close to my part of North Carolina, and yet far enough so no one much knows me. I'll have to bring you both in to my place outside Asheville. It's not that far. Maybe 80 miles. Sebastian has a showplace spread just below the state line in

Spartanburg, S.C., about another hour or so past my place. Must have paid three million at least for the acreage alone. He and I have a little friendly rivalry when it comes to making money and spending it." He snorted and coughed as he laughed.

"You know we love to come to this part of the country. The mountains are gorgeous and weather is fine. Plus, this is one of those situations that must be done face to face. I like eye contact when I want a man to bring over nine million dollars. Or, rather, eighteen. Nine from you and nine from Sebastian." They both laughed and walked toward the limo with hands still clasped. The pilot was instructed to be ready for takeoff again upon return, in two hours or thereabouts.

Lowe climbed into the back of the limo with Nick Bennotti, relegating Sanders to a front seat, allowing them more room. Bennotti signaled the driver and they were off to his place in the heart of the Great Smoky Mountains, just minutes away.

Bennotti commented on the kaleidoscope of colors of the tree-covered mountains. It was especially beautiful in the fall of the year. Lowe and Sanders looked for a moment, but their minds were preoccupied with the color green, as in millions.

"Nick, for a man about to spend nine million dollars soon, you look very relaxed. Maybe it is the scenery that does it." Lowe slapped him on the knee. "I guess you came prepared to get right down to business." Lowe said, glancing at Nick while they wound their way higher into the hazy mountains.

"Of course, I came to get right to business. We'll be at my cabin in another two minutes."

The cabin was secluded between two mountains, accessed only by a dirt and rock-filled road the last half mile. It was at least five-thousand-square-feet of expensive pine logs and furnishings that must have cost in the hundreds of thousands. In true keeping with its setting, a huge bear-skin rug spread over much of the floor in the main den under exposed beams. The rustic beauty and serenity would have moved most people to absorbing the surroundings. Not Lowe and Sanders, or even Bennotti today. There was too much at stake. Lowe refused the offer of spirits this time of day. Sanders did likewise. "We'll pick up some sandwiches before we leave for South Carolina to see Sebastian," Lowe said.

"No need to do that." Bennotti chimed in.

"Why is that? We've got to be in Spartanburg right after we leave here.

Sebastian is expecting us to finalize his part." He looked at Bennotti and lifted his eyebrow.

"I've taken the liberty of getting Sebastian to come here. We can all talk together that way. He should be here in a matter of minutes. He's never late for an appointment, unless he's counting his money." Bennotti laughed and Lowe and Sanders faked it.

"You afraid he might negotiate something you didn't, Nick?" Lowe tried another phony laugh.

"No, I thought I would make it easier for all four of us to have opportunity for equal input. If it's as important as you say, we had better be in accord, right?" Lowe nodded in agreement as Nick coughed a couple of more times.

Sebastian was right on time. No sooner had Bennotti finished his sentence, a silver Rolls Royce glided up the rocky driveway. Sebastian Mullins stepped out of the car, stretching his tall, skinny frame. He was past sixty, bald, with a pencil thin mustache and a spring in his walk resembling that of a thirty year old. He wore a long sleeve royal-blue silk shirt and loose, pleated, linen pants that blended in color with the shirt. He favored no socks with the expensive Italian loafers. His aviator-style sunglasses were pushed up stylishly on top of his small, round head.

Much of his initial start was from his wife's family who had huge local holdings in tobacco. His reputation as a shrewd, meticulous businessman was well known around the Carolinas. His association with Nick Bennotti came through owning several textile mills and related businesses. The textile mills were his love and expertise.

"Good to see you again, Sebastian," Gardner smiled, extending his hand. An ego equal to his own had appeared on the scene.

The four gathered around a thick, heavy table in the middle of the huge den. Lowe stood while the others slid their chairs in.

Lowe honed in on Nick and Sebastian. "I'll get right to the point. You're extremely wealthy men, with the desire to keep that wealth and accumulate much more with relative ease. These facts I am sure of. It's my job to insure that is done with a minimum of risk. Let me assure you that risk is almost nonexistent. We take steps constantly to make sure of that. You both know that the shipments of 'white stuff' have been as smooth as ice. You've received prime, top-grade Columbian cocaine in your cotton bale shipments. That ingenious method of concealing, I might add, was the brain child of our crop dusting pilot. Nothing like pure white in pure white. Wrapped and concealed deep inside the bales. But enough of that. We know what a working plan we have. Correct me if I'm wrong, but I believe you both have gotten four shipments each, over the last two months. I believe they've been moved through your network, and an average of two million dollars profit was made apiece on each shipment."

"I feel a cut being attempted in our arrangement," Bennotti quipped, frowning.

"Not at all. Quite to the contrary," Lowe shot back emphatically. "But, this meeting is urgent. We'll call the first shipments the smaller shipments since that is what they are compared to what you'll hear. You've moved them flawlessly through your connections in Charlotte and Charleston. There's only one change. The head man in Bogota is making demands. He holds the ultimate card and we know it. He is the supply. Without it, we have nothing to sell."

"What are you getting at?" Sebastian asked. He leaned back, crossed his legs, and glanced at Nick for his reaction. Nick nodded his approval of the question.

"The Columbian is suggesting strongly, that we take the ultimate shipment. I said he suggests, but it's more like demands. The big shipment we planned to take a few months down the road, we should take now — I mean in the next two days or so. He says it's a test of good faith. He wants to see if we can move this much now. If not, he'll move on to someone who can. He says this is a one-time giant load. Afterwards, we go back to our normal set-up, doing business as usual through the prison, trucking to you in the bales. First, we have to handle this shipment. We're talking nine million apiece, gentlemen. That much paid and that much made! It's your call." Lowe would wait out the silence.

Nick and Sebastian stared at Lowe, then exchanged glances with one another. "I'm not sure I can make contact and move that much." Nick said, hesitantly. He lit up a Camel and Sebastian fanned the cloud that moved near his head.

"Now, Nick. I know with your resources and contacts this can be accomplished — without much of a hitch. It's a lot of money, I admit, but that's also a lot of quick money for you both to make. Eighteen million on nine put out." Lowe was giving his best sales pitch, as if he were offering them a lifetime opportunity. He knew he wasn't with a couple of gullible hillbillies. They were razor sharp businessmen, but also he knew the big money lured and intrigued them. It would enhance their lifestyle even more. And his.

"Sebastian, I know with your connections, you won't want to miss the opportunity." Lowe continued smoothly, moving in to seal the proposition.

"Go easy on the sales pitch, Gardner, you don't have to convince me." Sebastian blurted back, as he took out his leather portfolio and made some notes, then closed it. Slowly he raised his head, lifted his eyebrow, and looked directly at Lowe. "I'm in. I'm in, provided it's air tight and the shipment is top grade like the others. If not, you have to answer for it, Gardner." Elton Sanders squirmed in his chair on that statement.

"Nick, you in?"

Nick was silent for a moment. Then he stood and pointed toward Sebastian. "I can't let him get ahead of me in this. I'm in — if my connection gives the go ahead."

"Great!" Gardner exclaimed, relieved. "Gentlemen, stress to your connections that this is a much larger than usual shipment. It's to show good faith. Whether or not you tell them the Columbian is adamant this deal comes down in two or three days, is up to you. We are at his mercy, so to speak. He's a worldwide supplier, so he gets what he demands. Either we move it or we lose it. It'll be over 800 pounds of the very best cocaine on the planet. And, if this goes well, we'll be able to start getting better deals and sizeable shipments of heroin as well. He's aware that we need heroin since it is enjoying a resurgence in America and all over. The heroin will open up even more avenues." Lowe spread his arms apart to gesture. "This shipment will be so big and so much money that we must forego our regular method of shipping. We need to act swiftly and fly it in. I mean fly it the rest of the leg, not just the first parts from Bogota to New Orleans to Mississippi."

"Why the big rush? I've been comfortable with the shipments coming from the penitentiary by the trucks in the cotton bales. Hell, we even legitimately use the cotton in the mills. What could be better? I don't know about flying it from Mississippi to over here. I don't want to take any more chances. This other way has been so smooth." Sebastian began to stroll around the room after his remarks, arms behind him, staring at the floor.

"Let me put it this way. Would you want 18 million dollars of pure cocaine at street value, lumbering in on the trucks we use for the penitentiary shipments, or would you rest better knowing it was zipped from Mississippi to North Carolina on your Citation jet in no time and no risk?"

Lowe alternated stares at Sebastian and Nick.

Nick managed a greedy smile and stepped toward the picture window, looking out into the magnificent fall day in the mountains. "Is this an even split between Sebastian and myself ? No one is getting an edge on the deal, are they? I mean, I don't ever want to hear that he got an something extra that I didn't."

"That works both ways, Nick." Sebastian grinned and shook his finger at Nick.

"As even as we can get it. You won't be able to tell an ounce of difference. Pardon the pun." Sanders even grunted out a laugh. "This will make two of the richest men in North and South Carolina even richer.

"The way my family spends it, I can always use several more million." Nick wheezed and coughed. The smoke covered his head.

"The way you smoke those damn things, your family is going to be the only one enjoying the tons of money. You won't be around." Sebastian pointed to the cigarettes laying on the table.

"I'll be here. If they don't kill me, something else will. I intend to enjoy and accumulate all I can along the way."

"And I thought I was greedy. Now tell us where is this safe point we can pick up this mega load." A hint of sarcasm surfaced in Sebastian's voice.

"You know that Worldwide is legitimately buying the 1,100 acre tract northeast of Indian Bayou. We also have an option on another 1,000 acres to the north, which belong to Norris Palmer. He's in a cash bind and has to go along with the deal on the land. I've mentioned him before too. He's in tight with Stiles on the whole operation. Good man to have on board. Real pillar of the community. Although we haven't paid him a dime yet on the land, he's given us rights to use it, like in *landing* our aircraft. This gives us 2,100 acres of flat ground to land and operate in. Not only is this a natural site for the waste facility, it's perfect for the drug operation. Worldwide will make money hand over fist there in the waste business. Our venture will flourish in the best of both worlds. And, Gentlemen, you don't know secluded until you see this. It's on an old farm-to-market road where no one lives and no other farmers are around. There's no problem landing there at night, especially. Stiles will bring the shipment in on the customized Steerman. He's moved the seats to make more room, along with some other adjustments. Don't worry about Stiles, if there's a way, he has found it. The cocaine will be there, ready to be loaded into your Citation and jetted back to each of your key mills. Or wherever you want to unload, it's entirely up to you. You make those plans. Just be there at the appointed time, ready to load, and get back to this part of the country."

"What about the exact location?" Sebastian asked.

"I'll fax you the coordinates to the landing site."

"Fax? I don't want to send something like that on a fax. I know the odds are slim, but why take a chance someone might accidentally see it?"

"Sebastian, like Emil in Bogota, our faxes are encrypted and impossible to trace. Like our phone set up. Likewise, the Rallye that Stiles flies the stuff up from New Orleans to Greenville, has a radar interceptor. You both know that already. I'm sure I told you of that precaution. Hell, Stiles even has the Rallye painted black to reduce the chances of being spotted, he says. The black plane even fits his sinister personality. It's more like a trademark. We never take unnecessary chances. This has been very carefully thought out, from one end to the other. The only departure from regular procedure is, that we will fly from New Orleans as usual on the Rallye up to Greenville, and load onto the Steerman. Peterson has the big crop dusting service near there. You know also that his planes are all over the Delta during the day and sometimes at night. So the Steerman won't arouse anyone's suspicion if seen. The Rallye might. Another precaution. Then, instead of the Steerman flying up to the penitentiary to unload, it will fly directly across to our site in Indian Bayou, unless Stiles decides he *has* to fly the Rallye. That's the perfect meeting place."

"Fax the coordinates the second you get them, because I need as much time as possible. You're already pushing us, time-wise."

"I'll do that. The wonders of computerized instruments never cease to amaze me. Your pilot will put it in your GPS, better described as Global Positioning System, which will zero you in on the exact spot. If he doesn't have a GPS, he will have a Lorans, which will do the same thing. He'll be able to put the Citation down precisely in the road. He can tell you more about what they do to locate landing spots in remote areas. They'll have just enough lights along the old road to light up the strip. I even had them resurface much of it with this in mind. I gave strict instructions for no power poles along the road. They were so anxious to accomodate Worldwide, they ran the power underground. I didn't want any obstructions to landing along that old road. We'll use either car lights facing one another on each side of the road, at a few intervals along the way, or some type of carrying lights. He can keep his lights on and be on the ground in no time, loaded, and you two will be on your way back, eighteen million richer. Each of you bring nine million and get back eighteen when you sell. Bring the money in attache' cases. You know the denominations. Palmer will count it quickly and bring the cases to the plane. We trust you both, but with that much money, better to be safe. He and the Deputy Wiggins will load your plane with the cocaine. You can examine and weigh it or whatever at that point." Lowe closed the presentation with a roar. "Quite a return on your money!" That brought sly grins from all three. Even Sanders nervously attempted a smile.

"I never thought I'd have my pilot land in an old Mississippi cotton field." Sebastian slapped Gardner Lowe on the back.

"For those millions that quick and easy, I'd have him land in a crocodile farm."

They all laughed, ending the meeting with greedy smiles and high expectations.

CHAPTER 33

Julie Bradford entered Gardner Lowe's office at 8:45 a.m. and managed a flirtatious morning smile. She had a handful of documents for his approval. He obliged and seemed preoccupied, but managed to notice the smile. She purposely left the door ajar a couple of inches on her way out, then sat quietly at her desk. He had made no calls that she could hear. She prayed that he wasn't suspicious of her and worked quietly through the stack of papers on her desk, to sort out and pass on to Lowe. Her eyes darted back and forth at the clear plastic button on the separate phone line. It had no action so far. The morning moved slowly. She even passed up her morning coffee break and ran only once for a quick rest room visit.

She jumped as the intercom buzzed, summoning her to his office. She braced herself. "Julie, how was your trip to Texas?" He never looked up as he made notes on a document before him.

"Fine. My Mom was glad to see me for a change. I don't get down there that often." No more volunteering information. Let him speak, she thought.

"How about going down to the deli and pick me up a sandwich? I'll buy yours, if you will."

She scrambled, offering an excuse. "I would, but Mom's attorney is supposed to call me before noon, his time. I didn't have some information with me on the property. You know how lawyers are. He may call any minute or two hours from now." She put on her most convincing look. "I need to get this property matter finalized. I hope I don't have to deal with another lawyer for a while. I'll ask one of the ladies from the next office though."

Lowe hesitated and stared out his window on Wilshire Boulevard. "On second thought, I'll hold off for now. Need to watch the waistline."

She smiled and faked the words. "Oh, Gardner, you always look so trim and fit. You can afford to eat a sandwich."

"Thanks for the compliment. I'm not in bad shape for a man my age, I guess."

"You're certainly not." She tried not to gag.

"That'll be all for now." She turned for the door. "By the way, I trust you took to heart my little advice to you about keeping totally quiet, as to what you've been privileged to know." His eyes were piercing and cold.

She smiled as seductively as possible. Her hair hung strategically over one eye, and her full breasts were exposed just enough. "I am always intrigued by power, Gardner. There's no danger of my saying anything. You should know that." By the enamored look on his face, he bought it. She hoped.

She left the door open again, just enough so he could see her pull her clingy little dress considerably above the knees, exposing her tanned, muscular thighs. Just then, a call came over the separate line she had been watching. It blinked only once, and he answered it at the same time as she did. She and Lowe hesitated.

"I've got this one, Julie. Close that door, if you will." He tried to sound nonchalant. She eased the door almost to and stared at the line. Time was crucial. Her hands trembled as she looked behind her and slipped her left hand over the receiver button. She lifted the receiver up with her right hand and placed it to her ear. Then, slowly, she eased the receiver button up and prayed there was no noise. She kept glancing over her shoulder. The rolling chair was slid as far to the left as possible, so only her legs would be exposed.

She listened as the voice with a foreign accent on the other end gave the orders: "I am ready to hear your answer, Gardner. Either you are ready to commence with this tomorrow or not. I have no room for extensions."

"This is even sooner than I expected. I just got back from meeting with the Carolina men yesterday. Can you wait one more day?" Lowe was asking, but didn't sound pressed. More like a game to him.

"I told you this was a test of your allegiance to our future business dealings. You must either do it my way or we sever our arrangement. You know I want this out of my warehouse at once. Is it tomorrow or not?" The voice was cold and demanding.

Lowe sighed and leaned back in the chair. "We will be ready tomorrow. Full scale. We'll be in New Orleans for the pick up at 9:00 p.m. at the regular transfer place. I will, in all likelihood, be with Stiles on this trip. We need to cement our working relationship even more. I promised when we started this venture that I'd fulfill my end of the deal. I've not been remiss thus far, and never intend to be. There's no need to say that they expect top grade cocaine all throughout this large shipment. I know it'll be done, since you are personally taking care of the arrangements."

"Never doubt my intentions. This is an honorable arrangement that will make us millions for years to come. I would never skimp on any shipment, especially since I now own the controlling interest in your company. I wouldn't want my president's name to be tarnished, now would I?"

"No. I'm sure you wouldn't, Emil. We'll see you and the 'white gold' tomorrow evening at 9:00." Julie heard the click on the other end without a goodbye. She held the phone until she heard Lowe rattle the receiver down. Then he said only one word, emphatically. "Yes!"

She shook some papers, pretending to be neck deep in work. She felt his breath over her right shoulder. "Gardner, you scared me!"

"Sorry, I thought you might have changed your mind about going to get us a sandwich at the deli." He touched her shoulder and let his hand linger longer than he should. She smiled and moved forward like she was retrieving some paper from the front of the desk. The hand slid off slowly.

"What are you trying to do? Make me lose my figure. I've got to keep up with you, Gardner." He sucked in his stomach slightly and slid his hand inside his double breasted coat, straightened it and adjusted the knot on his red silk tie. "Thanks anyway, but I need to stay in and work. Look at that stack calling me." She pointed to the six-inch-high pile of papers before her.

Without a glance, he moved back into his office. Clearly, his mind was not on those papers or a sandwich for lunch. Minutes later, the intercom buzzed. "Julie, can you come in?" She hurried in, trying to look nonchalant. "Would you run down to the fax machines and get this off for me? Use the one on the far end of the three. Thanks."

"You don't want to use the one in my office?"

He stammered. "I...the one on the end sends the very best copies. Sanders even likes it. It must be good." Another uncomfortable laugh from him.

"Whatever you say. I need to hurry back and get through with this."
She continued to look detached, interested only in her work. She tipped
through the office and down the hall. As she rounded the hall, she peeped
at the document. The words and numbers on it jumped out. It gave mileage
and numbers about latitude and longitude. It read at the bottom: GENTLE-
MEN, BE AT THE SITE AT MIDNIGHT TOMORROW NIGHT WITH-
OUT FAIL. ANY PROBLEMS, CALL ME TODAY WITHIN THE HOUR.
SEE YOU MIDNIGHT. SEVEN MILES OUTSIDE INDIAN BAYOU,
MS.. ALL SYSTEMS GO. EVERYTHING AIR TIGHT. YOUR PILOT
SHOULD HAVE NO PROBLEMS WITH THESE COORDINATES.
THEY WILL PUT YOU DOWN ON TARGET. ROAD WILL BE
LIGHTED PER OUR CONVERSATION. CAN'T MISS. HAVE A PROS-
PEROUS FLIGHT, GARDNER.

Her heart pounded and her pace quickened. She felt a headache coming on. Then she stopped suddenly and headed back to Lowe's office.
"Gardner, I do feel like that sandwich. I'll hand this to one of the girls to
fax and go get us one."

"No." He almost shouted. "I mean, you fax it. There are two numbers
at two different area codes. Send them both the same fax. I don't like just
any of those girls looking at what I send. You are different. I think you
know what I mean."

He winked and she winked back and headed out the door. She breathed
in an out in fast spurts, trying to catch her breath. Her leather heels pounded
the marble floor, sounding like a racehorse. She rounded the corner and
jammed the fax into the machine. She had it in crooked. She fumbled with
the paper before hearing the short humming sound of the paper now engaged. It seemed forever. She dialed the area codes, 704 and 803, for North
and South Carolina, then the numbers. She looked over her shoulder, expecting Gardner to come up behind her at any second. Finally the buzzing,
popping sound of the fax machine ended. Her hands shook as she slid the
document into the nearby copying machine. The white copy rolled out and
she grabbed it, turned her back to the hallway and crammed it into her bra.
She hurried back to his office, laid the fax back on his desk and smiled.
"Thought you might want this back. You want your usual tuna on rye?"

He grinned seductively. "Yes. You are observant, as well as gorgeous."

"Oh, thanks for the compliment. I'll be back in a jiffy."

"Here. At least I can pay for it." He flipped a ten out on the desk and began looking in his desk drawer.

She casually picked up her purse and strolled to the elevator. She punched the lobby button and watched anxiously as it descended. She hit Wilshire Boulevard, checked behind her, and began trotting. After one block, she entered the tall, black, reflective building, catching her breath. She knew there were pay phones on the wall down the hall from the lobby. She squeezed as much of herself as she could between the two partitions where the phone was mounted on the wall, looked over her shoulder, and saw no one. Her hand shook again as she deposited the quarter and dialed Roman's cellular number in Mississippi. He answered after one ring.

"Can you talk?"

"Yes, I'm in the office. Let me close this door." He was back in a heartbeat. "Julie, I'm surprised to hear from you this soon, but glad. Fill me in on what you've found out."

"I'm going to fax you what he just had me fax to numbers in North and South Carolina. He thinks I'm too afraid to talk, I'm sure. At this point, a fax to your number won't matter. I'll find a place to send it. It mentions longitude and latitude and a message to meet him outside Indian Bayou tomorrow at midnight. Ever hear of coordinates?"

"You bet I have. Tomorrow at midnight, huh? Good. The sooner the better. Julie, you've been a tremendous help. It took guts to do what you're doing. Thank you. Be careful and I'll see you soon, I hope."

"It's been my pleasure to help and hopefully get that monster his dues. Sanders too. Another wolf in sheep's clothing. Be careful. I hope you have the authorities ready to pounce on these guys."

Roman paused. "Oh, yes. I've been dealing with them. I'll be by the fax."

The fax number buzzed and the paper creeped out in two sheets. Roman ripped them off and studied the note carefully. "I'll be damn. He must be coming into the waste building site. Just need to check a GPS to confirm," Roman mumbled pilot lingo to himself. "That's fine with me. I'll be ready." He grabbed his sunglasses, rounded the desk and headed for the Greenville airport. This time, not to fly.

The small airport was typically uncrowded on the ground and the air space above it. Roman entered the small terminal building and approached a short older lady, behind the information counter. "Is there an instructor around that could give me some assistance?"

"Yes, Sir." She responded in a soft Southern drawl. "Go down the hall and take the second door on the right. There will be two qualified instructors in there."

"Thanks"

Roman found one young instructor doing some paper work as his radio blared. He turned down the volume as Roman attempted to speak. "Hello. I'm going to be doing some flying around here soon. I don't need instructions, but do you have a GPS or a Lorans I could look at in one of your planes?"

The young pilot never questioned why. "Sure, you can look at one in that Cessna 337." He pointed out the plane, Roman thanked him and walked over, less than fifty feet away, crawled in and found the GPS. He unfolded the fax and punched in the coordinates. Bingo! The waste site. The old road running next to the site was the designated landing strip. He waved his thanks again and headed back towards Indian Bayou. He did have one more stop. At the gun shop on Highway One South.

The Blazer ran a little smoother on the old road since the patching and some resurfacing had been done. Roman scanned the remote area, but saw no one within a mile or so. The adjoining fields had been picked for the cotton, with remaining bits and pieces of white clinging here and there, dotting the rows. He suddenly realized what a perfect place this was for a rendezvous. It could be one similar to the recent night when the Steerman used the end of the site. Only this time, he knew the stakes had to be higher and more complex.

He drove the Blazer into the huge open field, flat as far as the eye could see, and on to the point where the plane had been parked that night. He knew he was trespassing; he had ignored the signs nailed to three or four trees he passed. He stopped his vehicle and looked in every direction. No sign of anyone or anything. As he started to pull away and head back to town, he had the urge to look past the property line, into the surrounding sprawling stretch of land. He still saw nothing. As he made a 180-degree turn to point the Blazer toward the front gate, he caught a flash out of the corner of his eye. He stopped and eased back. There in a clump of bushes, he saw the small shiny flash. He drove to it, got out of the Blazer, and trudged through the brush. Then, he saw the large camouflaged tarpaulin draped over a large object. It was clearly a plane. Its wings were clearly defined, along with the fuselage. He felt the rush of adrenalin. He jerked and wrestled the heavy tarpaulin, noticing the hole in it where the windshield had reflected sunlight — the flash that had caught his eye. It was a black plane. He recognized it as a Rallye. He remembered reading in an aviation magazine that this single engine plane was particularly useful for short takeoffs and landings. He glanced at the road and observed how far it ran in a long flat direction. Most any plane could land in that space, almost a mile and a half. He cupped his hands over his eyes to see inside the aircraft. He couldn't tell much, except that there was plenty of cargo room. He covered the plane back carefully, then drove away slowly, noticing the surroundings, the lack of inhabitants. Suddenly, an explosion in the distance caused him to flinch, stopping his vehicle. Far ahead, his contractor and two of his crew, were excavating and blowing up stumps from the area. Roman breathed a huge sigh of relief, and continued to sort the pieces into the right places for tomorrow night. Before leaving, he waved the contractor over, huddled with him, and received detailed information about the dynamiting.

CHAPTER **34**

R oman awakened at 6:00 a.m., after three hours sleep. He checked the Remington 7400 semi automatic 308 he'd bought in Greenville. He had familiarized himself with it and other details, late into the night. His .357 Magnum lay beside it on the bed.

He debated whether to call Rex McCall. He picked the phone but put it down. He left Martha a message that he would be coming in later this morning. He hoped there would be another morning to come in to, after midnight tonight. Then, his better sense prevailed and he dialed Rex. Joan informed him that Rex was enroute to Jackson at that very moment, probably rolling down I-55 close to Grenada by now. She volunteered the car phone number. He dialed and Rex yelled back in the receiver. There was a touch of static. Two cellular phones in action.

"Rex, I know you've backed off this whole thing because you put me with Harold Lloyd and the FBI. However, I've had problem after problem, I feel, convincing him to take action when it should be taken. Know what I mean?"

Rex yelled again through the crackling. "I know it can look like that. He's called me a couple of times and said he didn't think he had endeared himself to you."

"You can say that again. I won't mince words now. I know a big shipment of drugs is coming down. Tonight, at midnight, here. If you tell Lloyd, our friendship will be rocky at best."

"I won't if you say so, but don't you think he ought to know? You're not thinking about doing something crazy. You could get yourself hurt or killed."

"Rex, too much has happened to explain on the phone. I might could use another man with me to watch my back side."

"What? These guys don't mind killing. You can't do this alone. You're right. I'll be there. What time?"

"Get here before 10:30 tonight. It's supposed to come down at midnight, at the site I came down here to establish for the hazardous waste facility. I've uncovered lots more. If you want, come anytime after dark. I'll give you my cellular number so you can reach me on the way, if need be. In fact, call me when you get close to town. I'll give you the directions. I live on the out skirts. Might have told you that. But get here by 10:30, so we can get in position out there. It's only a few minutes drive from my place. Rex, if you're not here by 10:30 at the latest, I'm gone. See you tonight. I'm sure you're armed as usual?"

"Naturally."

"Oh, and Rex, this is the most important thing I've ever done in my life. There will be somebody there, who I can't afford to let escape. Again, don't call Lloyd. He's failed to act on everything I've given him. He even let Cliff damn near get killed in Parchman. I won't take any chances with him again."

"I think you're wrong, but you sure can't call the local sheriff for help, can you? I'll probably be there by 10:00 in fact."

Roman hesitated. "Rex,... the real reason I don't want Lloyd notified is that I'm not so sure he might not be involved some way. I don't trust him totally. He's been too hesitant to move too many times. I mean, no one would've thought that the sheriff of Wildflower county would be a key player in a big time drug operation, either. Think about it."

At 9:30 P.M. Roman's phone rang. Rex was on the line. He was leaving the city limits of Greenwood, some 25 miles away to the east. "I'll be there in 20 more minutes if you're on the east side of town."

"That's exactly where the house is." He gave the directions and cut the front porch light on for the first time in a while. He reconsidered and cut it off. He paced and checked his rifle for the fifth time. His pistol was now in its holster with a belt run through it. He had plenty of ammunition for both, if necessary.

Soon, he heard Rex's Lincoln pull into the front driveway. This was the first comforting feeling Roman had experienced in a while. He met

Rex at the door with a hearty handshake, then cut off the outside light instinctively.

"I need my head examined for coming over here without contacting some back up," Rex said, shaking his head as he readjusted his shoulder holster. "You're no law officer. I know you're either brave as hell or crazy, but we may be getting into something we can't get out of alive. How many of them are there? Do you even have any idea?"

"Seven or eight, depending on how many the guys from the Carolinas bring with them. I'm counting on no more than eight."

"Eight! And just two of us. You know what those odds are?"

"Rex, if you want out, there's the door. No hard feelings. I know Stiles killed my friend John and tried to kill Cliff, the Cajun that went undercover to Parchman. Remember him?"

"Yeah, I do. You just mentioned him earlier on the phone."

"I also know that Gardner Lowe, the president of the company I work for, or change that, used to work for, is responsible for Leah's death. He also killed the lady who tipped me off about Stiles. She worked for the company in L.A. and was having an affair with Lowe. After he booted her, she turned on him. She saw him for what he was. I was in L.A. when her murder happened. No doubt he did it. He's even threatened the young lady who works for him now. She's the one who gave me the information about this deal coming down tonight at midnight."

Rex looked shocked, even though he'd spent years investigating heinous crimes and killing his share of criminals. "Roman, I can't say that I wouldn't do the same thing, under the circumstances." He had gotten Rex's undivided attention. "What we have to do tonight is try to position ourselves to take advantage of their vulnerable points, if they have any. I feel like they may not be expecting any firepower to show up. You don't think they suspect that anyone is on to them, do you?"

"Well, they know the local law, as we said, won't be around. I'm sure Stiles has scouted that out and made sure of that, don't you? You know he'll have any clean cops on his force, assigned off somewhere else. If there are any clean ones."

The sleek Citation jet slipped through the dark sky near the eastern Tennessee and western North Carolina line. The pilot checked the coordinates again with his GPS and headed west, zeroing in on the dark old road in rural Wildflower County, Mississippi. A bottle of Dom Perignon sat unopened, chilling in the bucket, awaiting the return home celebration. Nick puffed on a huge Dutch Master, and Sebastian tried to relax with headphones and a classical tape. They would be loaded with $18 million worth of pure white Columbian cocaine, that would soon be turned into $36 million in cold cash. Thirty-six million to be split between the greedy pair, who had been reeled in by the lure of easy money.

The black, single-engine Rallye landed on the isolated strip near LaPlace, some twenty miles west of New Orleans, right on the Mississippi River. It was quickly loaded with the multi-million-dollar cargo, and was soon cruising through the dark night only ten feet above the mighty river, between Baton Rouge and Natchez. Despite having the radar interceptor, Stiles favored flying black, just over the water, as extra precaution. It was really more for the thrill than the precautionary factor. Their destination was also the old deserted farm-to-market road outside Indian Bayou. The adjoining spread of acreage added to the intrigue for him.

At 10:45 p.m., Roman and Rex creeped down the site road with their lights off, staying between the ditches, aided by the little light the night afforded. Rex got out, closed the door, and took his position in the weeds bordering the road. Roman pulled off immediately to the right, drove another 500 yards and hid his vehicle away from the road, opposite the site. He moved away from Rex, nearer the anticipated spot of the deal and crouched behind two small bushes. Perspiration rolled down his face as he waited.

At 11:45 a pair of headlights flicked on, facing another pair from across the road, illuminating the road parallel to the site. Approximately one quarter mile down from them, one light faced another single light on the other side of the road, creating a crude runway pattern. Another quarter to half mile, was the final single light, crossing another. They were ready for the landings.

At 12:05, the Citation's lights penetrated the darkness and flooded the tiny road below. The lights came closer to the ground, as the plane roared in and touched down on the site road, between the makeshift lighted runway. The aircraft came to a halt approximately a mile from the point of touchdown, then turned and taxied toward the edge of the site property, very close to where Roman was waiting. The lights on the plane were turned off immediately. The temporary runway lights remained on.

Roman strained to see his watch. Despite the midnight coolness, he continued to wipe beads of perspiration from his forehead. He could hear voices near the parked plane. He searched the sky and saw more lights appearing from the same direction. This aircraft moved in slower. The lights beamed in clearly on the road, and the single engine plane came to rest in a much shorter distance than the jet had needed. He taxied for a short distance, turned toward the other plane in the field, and stopped 100 feet or so away. His lights were left on, lighting the space between them. The engine continued to run, though idled down. Roman spotted Stiles and Gardner Lowe. Barely able to contain himself, he knew he had to stay down and still. He shook his head. He hadn't expected Lowe to be in the aircraft with Stiles. They waved across at the other plane's passengers. Then, appearing out of the darkness, Norris Palmer, Sr. came from behind the black Rallye and ran through the lights to the passengers and pilot in the jet. Roman strained his eyes, but he couldn't make out all the figures. In less than one minute, Palmer ran toward the Rallye and rounded the plane away from the pilot's side, disappearing for a moment in the darkness. The doors to the black plane swung open and large tightly-bound packages began falling to the ground. At least twelve to fifteen of them, wrapped and filled with prime grade cocaine, fell into a pile.

Suddenly, like lightning, a barrage of lights converged from everywhere, flooding the scene. Roman jumped and almost dropped his rifle. "FBI! FBI! Get your hands up!" Six or seven agents tore out of the darkness.

"Damn, Rex told him." Roman mumbled to himself. He moved closer to the planes.

Then, like a crazed mercenary, Stiles abruptly opened fire with the assault weapon. The deafening sound of gunfire filled the quiet night. Roman spotted Stiles, jump off the aircraft and spray more rounds toward the agents. Two went down, either injured or possibly dead. Others returned fire defensively and moved backward. It was evident they wanted someone alive. Roman couldn't find Rex in the mixture of light and darkness. He saw the armed agents move in swiftly and grab the others at the jet and force them into the dark shadows away from the plane. Stiles jumped back into the cockpit; behind him was Gardner Lowe, scrambling to get in.

"Gardner, you murdering bastard! I know what you did to Leah." Roman screamed, aiming the semi-automatic on Lowe. Lowe crouched and suddenly swung around in a blur, firing his assault weapon in a burst of bullets toward Roman. Roman felt the searing thud, as one tore into the flesh of his upper left arm. He fell and grabbed the wound. His adrenalin was pumping wildly and the pain was secondary. Lowe stood to get back into plane, then turned and fired another round at random, spraying bullets in all directions, as Stiles raced the engine furiously.

Roman glanced to his right and saw Harold Lloyd grab his leg and go down in pain. Lowe took aim at Lloyd again. The plane roared, its wings shook in anticipation of take off. Roman rolled over, raised the semi-automatic weapon, aimed and fired. Lowe crumpled over, falling toward the seat. Roman's adrenalin was now maxed. Stiles pulled Lowe's limp form inside, as he roared forward. Then, Roman couldn't believe his eyes. He saw Norris Palmer Sr. run to the aid of Lloyd. Roman raised his rifle and pointed toward Palmer.

"Don't fire! Don't, he's with us." Shocked, Roman reluctantly lowered his rifle. He turned his eyes back to Stiles's plane that was blasting down the road, taxiing for take off. Lloyd limped away toward one of the downed agents, leaving Roman and Palmer standing and watching the black plane and its devious pilot lift off in another barrage of bullets.

"Damn it! He's getting away. I can't believe he's going to make it out of here." Norris shook his head in disgust and kicked the dirt causing a cloud of dust to arise. "After all this, he's getting away." He stared at the blinking red lights from the plane that were becoming smaller, fading away.

"No. He isn't." Roman said, calmly.

He ran to his truck, jerked open the door, and grabbed the apparatus on the front seat. He turned, as if in slow motion, pointed the black box, and squeezed violently. Suddenly, the entire skyline lighted up with fire and explosion. Trails of amber trickled through the sky, falling into the fields on all sides. The deafening explosion echoed in their ears as they watched the last flaming pieces spiral down through the black sky to the earth below.

As the others stood in shock, Roman moved his eyes away from the spot of the blazing spectacle to Palmer, and shook his head. "I don't understand about you, Mr. Palmer."

Palmer pointed toward the sky momentarily and lowered his hand. "This will be between you and me. Let's just say we both got who we wanted. In your case, both of who you wanted."

Roman stared back into sky as the last pieces careened downward. "I hated for all that money to go up in smoke, but ...."

"It didn't." Palmer pointed near where the plane had taken off from. It's lying out there in two suitcases, all eighteen million." They both laughed and bear hugged.

"Back to you and why you were in this, or rather pretending to be." Roman looked at Palmer, who looked away again at the point in the sky of the explosion.

"The whole thing is a long story. I'll try to give you the gist of it, though."

"I want to hear it, please." Roman looked at him anxiously.

"First, the explosion. How'd you....?"

"Let's just say, I had an interesting conversation with the contractor who was blowing up the stumps on this site. He was very informative." They both smiled again and leaned against the hood of the pickup, while Palmer gathered his thoughts.

"When Norris Jr. became a paraplegic in Vietnam, it never seemed to fit to me. He was a good soldier — patriotic and dedicated. For some reason, he was driven to try to please me with his military career. I told you the first time we met, that my wife should have left my medals in the cedar chest. That night he was injured, he was only a few miles out of Saigon. Supposedly, his Jeep was overturned by enemy mortar fire, causing his paralysis. No need to give you every detail, but I have ways of finding out information in the military. I've done it before. I know, after some digging, that he had gotten a call earlier from Zach Stiles."

"Stiles?"

"Yes. He was an enlisted man. A non-commissioned officer during Vietnam. He got word from around here that Norris was a lieutenant in the 1st Battalion, 4th Brigade of the 6th Infantry Division, stationed at Nha Be, south of Saigon. He made friendly contact with Norris to meet him in Saigon in a bar. They were practically raised together on my plantation. Unfortunately, Zach's father was killed in a tractor accident when he was fairly young. Ten or eleven — I think — and I guess he hated us ever since. Anyway, they met and had a drink. Note, I said one drink! Norris has never been a drinker. According to my source I uncovered months ago, Norris never finished the drink but *felt* drunk and left the bar. When he was outside Saigon a few miles, headed back to Nha Be, he passed out, lost control, and the jeep overturned, causing his paralysis. That devil had drugged him with secobarbital sodium. Stiles, obviously had in mind another plan, but while following and seeing the wreck and Norris's condition, he capitalized on it."

"How's that?"

"He knew of Norris's dedication as a soldier, which was partly to please me. He knew Norris couldn't stand to be known as a drunk who wrecked a jeep, coming from a bar in Saigon. So that's where Stiles came in. Norris, to this day, doesn't know that he was drugged by Stiles. He really thought he had gotten drunk. Anyway, he told Norris, who thought he was doing him a huge favor incidentally, that he would confirm the fact to the proper military personnel, that *enemy mortar* fire had caused the jeep to overturn. Therefore, he would be sent home a hero with a "Purple Heart", which would help soothe his condition. So Zach told Norris he could repay him one day when Zach needed it. That the secret was forever between the two of them.

I accepted the fuzzy details of his paralysis until about six months ago, when I finally knew it didn't add up after all these years of pain for him, his mother and me. The last time Zach ran for re-election, Norris was adamant that I use all my resources and connections to help get him back in office. Well, six months ago, he was even more fanatical that I let Zach lease a big stretch of land next to the site you've been working on for a nominal price. I also found some sizeable checks Norris had written to Zach for his campaign. Well, hell, his next time up for re-election isn't for two years or more. It didn't add up. I knew Zach had to have been putting the squeeze on Norris. It wasn't enough what he did to him." Norris Sr.'s veins protruded in his neck and his anger was still evident, despite what had just happened. He shook his head and stared into the blackness. "That's when I did some deep searching with the military and came up with the one person who was at the table with them that night in Saigon. Randolph Wohner. The last name made it a little easier to track him down. I did just that, in Tucson. He reluctantly revealed, after all these years, what Zach had done. He said he had threatened him with his life, if he ever told anyone. That got me to feeling around Zach about the land he was interested in and all. I hinted that I had a cash flow problem with such a large farming operation. I knew he had to be up to nothing good. I was right, but never dreamed it would be to this extent. He took me into the plan, and I went along to work toward the day I could destroy that devil. I can say that honestly, since he was an avid devil worshiper. I played along with that too, in order to stay in this. That's another unbelievable part we can discuss later, but you get the picture. Excuse me a minute, Roman." He walked away toward his truck.

Rex appeared with Harold Lloyd limping right behind him. He called Roman to the side. "I didn't tell Harold or anyone that I was coming to meet you and what was coming down. Palmer came to the FBI only days ago, when he thought he had enough information for them to go on. He was the one, of course, who knew about tonight."

"I know. I just talked to Mr. Palmer and I'm glad he did."

"Good." I'll be on my way back to Coahoma county. I may have to call you if my wife thinks I've been out cavorting around until the wee hours of the morning. I forget, I've got to ride back with you when you're ready. Oh, hell, I didn't see that wound." Rex looked at Roman's upper arm. "Better get you to a hospital too. They've got two agents that the ambulance is on the way for. Harold's leg wound isn't too bad."

"No. I can drive. I'll take care of it when I get to town. The bleeding is about stopped." Roman pointed to the torn off part of his shirt, wrapped around his arm.

Harold Lloyd thrust his hand forward and Roman shook it firmly. "Thanks for saving me with that shot. Luckily, we didn't lose any agents. Wounded ones will be okay."

"I've got to admit, I was very glad to see you and your men tonight. I was going on blind instinct before then."

"Roman, you and I may have been on different circuits for a while, but I hope you know I was working toward the same ultimate goal. I wouldn't recommend doing what you did. You took a hell of a chance. You know I had to have it all in place to make a move. It took a while, but thanks to you, it was accomplished."

"Not just me. Other people gave the effort. Some gave their *lives*." Roman's voice was shaky with emotion.

"You are right." Lloyd motioned four agents on with the prisoners, Nick and Sebastian and their pilot. " Greed will do it every time. They want more and more. It ultimately gets them one way or the other. Peterson, the crop dusting pilot, is being picked up as we speak. And, you saw the deputy in custody. Sanders is being picked up in Los Angeles. We have the honorable Mayor in custody. Neither he nor Peterson, were even informed of this load by Stiles. Nevertheless, they are as guilty as can be, from being in the conspiracy all along. The Panther lost more than his 'trusty' status and is headed for maximum security. The DEA picked up the head kingpin in New Orleans right after they left their loading at LaPlace, along with his local connection in New Orleans, Ardavino. You know Emil Cortez called the shots for Worldwide Safe Waste Industries. Worldwide was laundering their money and growing by leaps and bounds. Mississippi was another notch in their belt. Or, so they thought. They sent the wrong man down here to get established, I guess."

Roman looked almost embarrassed. "Harold, I admit, I suspected everyone along the way, including you. I even noticed that the Lt. Governor and Gardner Lowe looked alike. I thought there might have even been some conspiracy there at one point. I'm glad there wasn't. I may even stay in Mississippi now that I'm back."

" I assume the plane went down because of *gunfire* that must have struck the gas line." Lloyd added, almost smiling. "But I'm sure of one thing."

"What's that?"

"There won't be any further investigation." Lloyd winked and Roman smiled. "By the way, Cliff will get his wishes. He'll be transported back to New Orleans in the next few days, when he's well enough. He sends his regards and wants to see you as soon as possible. He'll definitely get his wish and go home in a different light to his family. I'm going to make sure of that. Stay in touch."

"You do the same, Harold."

"Rex, you can ride back with me to pick up your car. I think I see someone coming to see Roman." Harold pointed toward the car that just arrived in the field.

Roman turned around to see the figure emerge from the headlights that appeared behind him. He could never mistake that form. It was Diana.

Norris motioned to Roman. "I took the liberty of calling someone on my cellular phone a few minutes ago, who I thought you might want to see."

They walked toward each other, and she reached out for Roman's extended arms. "Roman, we've got a lot of talking to do. I owe you an apology for not listening to you. Are you okay?" She wiped a tear from her eye, then leaned back to look at his wound.

"I'm fine. No apology necessary." They kissed tenderly. He held her and pulled her shoulders into his chest. The soft fall breeze blew her hair up, across his face. He brushed it back and kissed her again. They turned and smiled back at her father.

"Honey, I guess you don't have a job anymore." She studied his face compassionately.

He hesitated and smiled back. "Well, I always wanted to have a crop dusting service. A legitimate one. And there's no better place than back home in Mississippi."

"Want a partner?"

"I was thinking...."

"Thinking what?"

"About a permanent one."

She eased back from their embrace and smiled. "Offer taken, 'Cowboy'."